About the author

Edinburgh-born Marianne Wheelaghan travelled extensively before moving back to Edinburgh with her family. Her first novel, The Blue Suitcase, was published in 2010. Partly based on her mother's life it tells the remarkable account of a teenage girl growing up in Nazi Germany. The interest in The Blue Suitcase has been remarkable. Food of Ghosts is Marianne's debut crime novel and the first in a series of exotic thrillers set in the Pacific and featuring feisty Detective Sergeant Louisa Townsend.

www.mariannewheelaghan.co.uk

Food of Ghosts

Marianne Wheelaghan

Pilrig Press

Published 2012 by Pilrig Press, Edinburgh, Scotland

A CIP catalogue record for this book is available on request from the British Library.

ISBN 978-0-9566144-3-8

www.pilrigpress.co.uk

Printed in Great Britain by Imprint Digital

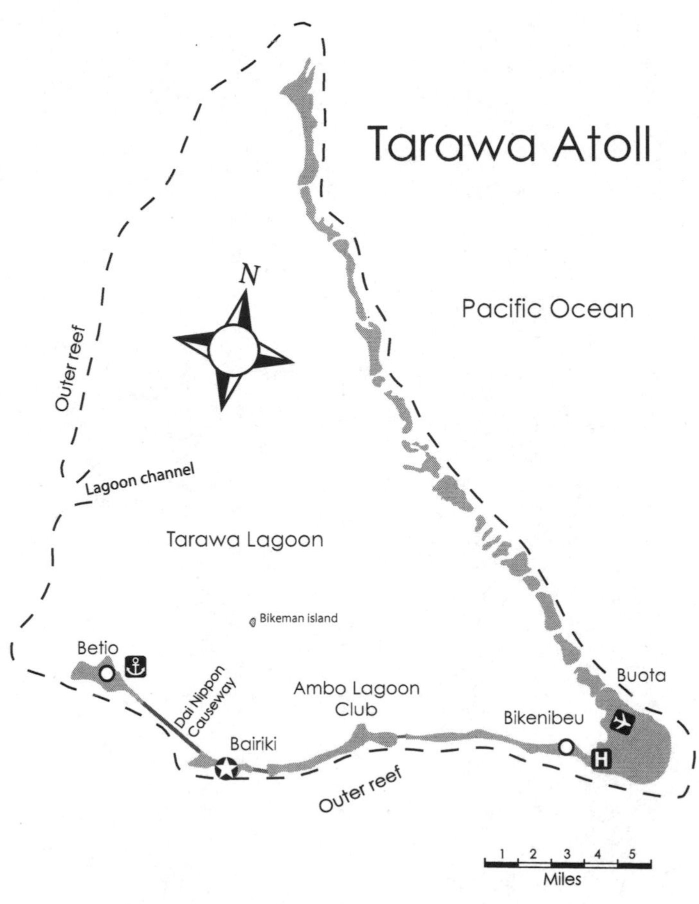
Tarawa Atoll
N
Pacific Ocean
Outer reef
Lagoon channel
Tarawa Lagoon
Bikeman island
Betio
Dai Nippon Causeway
Ambo Lagoon Club
Bairiki
Buota
Bikenibeu
Outer reef
1 2 3 4 5
Miles

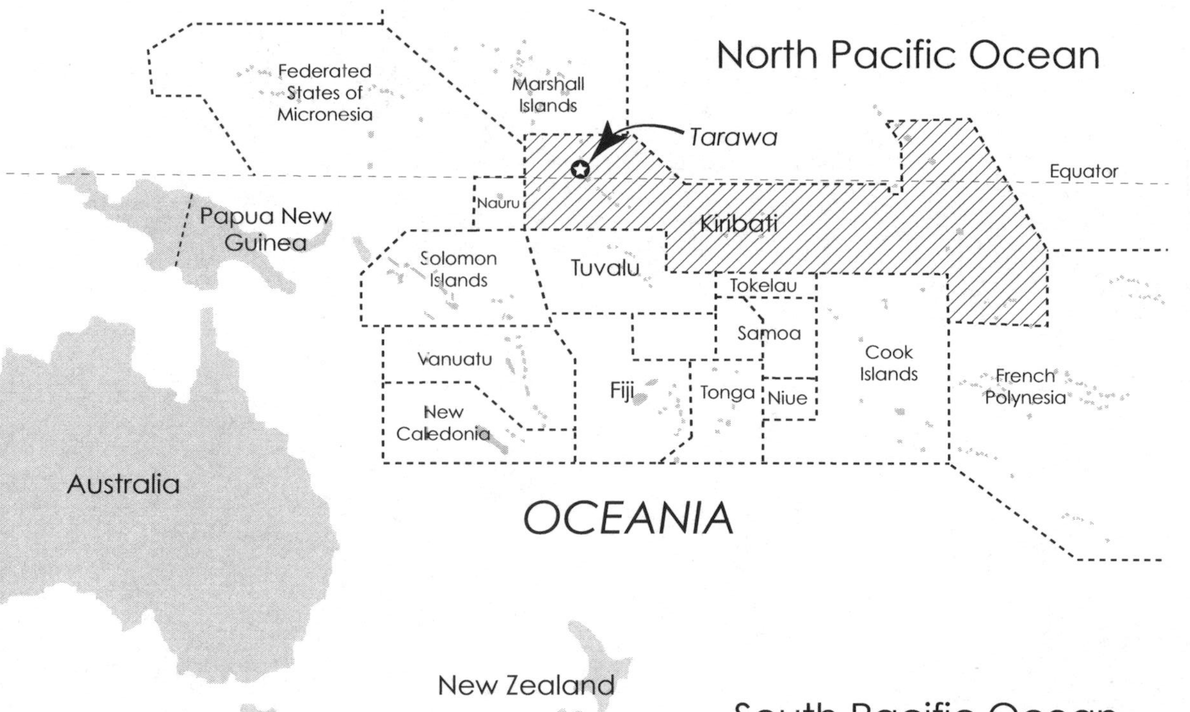
North Pacific Ocean
Federated States of Micronesia
Marshall Islands
Tarawa
Equator
Nauru
Kiribati
Papua New Guinea
Solomon Islands
Tuvalu
Tokelau
Samoa
Vanuatu
Cook Islands
French Polynesia
Fiji
Tonga
Niue
New Caledonia
Australia
OCEANIA
New Zealand
South Pacific Ocean

1

It took Louisa twenty minutes to clean up the sick, throw her bed sheets in the washing machine, swallow a cocktail of multivitamins, paracetamol and Imodium, shower, brush her teeth and put on her lemon blouse and baggy linen trousers. Throwing up had actually helped Louisa feel better. Hopefully, whatever she had was a twenty-four hour bug and not typhoid or dysentery. She daubed on a splash of lippy and swept a brush through her hair, which was already dry. Just because she was in the back end of the Pacific, it didn't mean she didn't have to make an effort.

Daisy was a male dog, despite his name, and all white except for two brown circular patches, like balloons, in the middle of his emaciated body. He had the biggest ears on any dog that Louisa had ever seen and was by far the ugliest. He snoozed outside the back door and blocked her way. Louisa didn't like dogs but Daisy belonged to Reteta. Reteta cleaned for Louisa a couple of times a week. Louisa hadn't wanted a cleaner but when Reteta had turned up offering her services, she'd said yes. Reteta was her cousin. It had sounded like a good way to get to know her again. That was before Reteta set up what Louisa called 'the squatters' camp' in her back garden.

Louisa shouted at Daisy to shift. Daisy heaved himself up, hobbled wearily into the scrubby garden and flopped down next to the pig. The pig, which Louisa thought had tripled in size since arriving with Reteta (was that only six weeks ago?), snuffled beneath a giant pandanus tree in the middle of the back garden. A length of rope attached to its front trotter tethered the animal to the trunk of the tree. As far as Louisa could tell, the pig spent all its time searching for the orange nugget-shaped pandanus fruit that never seemed to drop from the branches above. The sour stench from the make-shift pen made Louisa want to retch.

A cabbage-shaped man in a blue, short-sleeved shirt and brown shorts stood at the back of the garden where the spindly grass stopped and the sandy beach began. He faced away from Louisa and looked out over the ocean. His feet were bare and his hair was a tussled mess of squashed charcoal fuzz. She'd had a phone call earlier – it had woken her up – to say a man was coming with a letter for her. Presumably, he was that man.

Louisa shouted but the noise from the waves hurling against the shore beyond the garden drowned out her words. The tide was in and this meant the local fishermen would be out in their boats. She looked around. No Reteta. It was unusual for her not to be out the back.

As she approached the round man, he turned. Louisa cursed under her breath. It was Sergeant Tebano. He was the station sergeant at Betio nick. Shortly after arriving on Tarawa Louisa had arranged a workshop for the constables at his station. She'd waited all day for the officers to turn up, with only Tebano for company, or rather lack of company. It was clear from his behaviour that he'd not wanted to talk to her and that he thought the development of an Initial Crime Investigators

Programme, her reason for being on Tarawa, a waste of time. She suspected Tebano was behind the officers' no-show but couldn't prove it.

Without saying a word Tebano handed her the letter, which wasn't in an envelope. Louisa refused to let herself think about the number of people who had touched the letter before her. Instead, she took the folded piece of paper in her left hand then passed it to her right. She always did this. It was one of her things.

A man had been stabbed at the Ambo Lagoon Club. The entire detective division of the Kiribati Police Service (all sixteen of them) were unavailable: six were at a funeral on the outer island of Beru, and the soonest ferry back was next Friday, the remaining ten were at an internet security conference in Auckland, New Zealand, and not able to return until Wednesday. Louisa had a quiet chuckle. What internet? It was 2004 and while there were a dozen or so surprisingly up-to-date PCs in the Ministry of Justice, there was no broadband, never mind WiFi. On a good day, and if you were lucky, there was dial-up access to the internet for an hour, but no one was allowed to use it. Emails could remain unopened—or unsent—for weeks. There wasn't even a mobile phone network. Louisa read on. Until the detectives could get back to South Tarawa, Assistant Police Commissioner Nakibae requested that Detective Townsend would do him the favour of being the SIO, the Senior Investigation Officer, in charge of the case. Sergeant Tebano would assist her.

Louisa resisted punching the air with her fist. The phone call earlier had said the Kiribati Police Service needed help investigating a killing. It had never occurred to her that she, a mere detective sergeant, and a visitor, would be made the SIO of the case. It was a fantastic opportunity and the way her life was at the moment, she needed it. She put the letter in her pocket and nodded to Tebano to lead the way. He sauntered off down the side of the house and to the road. She followed, determined to ignore her cousin Reteta's things, which were spread across the garden and included various pink, plastic washing-up basins; half a dozen straw sleeping mats covered with pillows airing in the sun; five bundles of white mosquito nets; four plywood tea chests packed with cooking utensils and rusty biscuit tins; a couple of battered metal buckets full of miscellaneous items wrapped in old newspaper; bulging blue and white and red stripy nylon bags of all shapes and sizes, including super large—Reteta's wardrobes, Louisa supposed—and a giant tin kettle, a big, shiny, black motorbike and a wheelbarrow with a flat tyre. It seemed giving Reteta a few hours' work a week also meant agreeing to let Reteta and her family camp in her back garden. Her scowling husband, their four giggling daughters, a twenty-something nephew, all smiles and muscles and the owner of the motorbike, and an elderly, anxious, skinny mother-in-law were usually there. Louisa had no idea where they had got to that morning and she didn't care. Not even Reteta and her family, or the chaotic mess they made of her garden, could dampen her thrill at being in charge of her first murder case.

2

The road at the front of the house was deserted. Louisa was surprised. She'd expected to see a patrol car. 'Where's the transport?'

Tebano raised his thick eyebrows in a fleeting arc. 'No car.'

Louisa frowned. She knew the Ambo Lagoon Club was at least fifteen kilometres away. 'How are we going to get there?'

Tebano lifted his eyebrows again, mimicking the same gesture as before.

'And?' she said, trying not to sound impatient. Louisa knew from her mother, who was originally from Tarawa, that the gesture of swiftly lifting your eyebrows in this way was a bit like shrugging your shoulders, it could mean 'no' or 'yes', and wasn't very helpful.

The sergeant nodded to behind Louisa. She turned. A fifteen-seat mini bus hurtled towards them. Tebano stuck out his arm and the vehicle screeched to a halt, covering them in billowing clouds of coral dust. The side bus door flew open and flopped downwards. One rusty hinge stopped it from bouncing off the ground.

'You need fifty cents for the fare?' said Tebano.

She was to take a bus to go to a murder scene? He had to be taking the piss! 'No thank you.'

'We have to hurry now,' said Tebano, inviting her to go first.

A bucketful of upturned yellowfin tuna sat on the step of the bus. Avoiding touching the silvery, forked tails of the fish, Louisa climbed on. The bus was packed. Louisa squeezed her way down the narrow aisle towards a small space in the corner at the back. Just before she reached it the bus thrust into life. Louisa was hurtled into the lap of two large women. After repeated apologies, giggles from the ladies, and much shifting and shoving, Louisa found herself wedged between the window and the women. Louisa looked out the open window and found herself staring directly at Tebano, who was still outside.

'You're going to get left behind,' she hissed.

He shook his head 'No room for me. I take the next bus.'

'But I've only been to the Ambo Lagoon Club once before. I'm not sure where I'm going.'

'You look out for the House of Parliament, when you

pass it the trees go very thick you will see the twin trunk coconut tree. It looks like a "V" for victory sign. You get off there.'

'You were to assist me!'

He shouted after the moving vehicle. 'Follow the arrow! Bye bye!'

The driver zoomed through the chaotic, overpopulated, shanty town of Betio, ignoring the various people trying to wave him down from the side of the road. Louisa fumed silently. Going to a murder scene by bus was unheard of! And who the hell did Tebano think he was, telling her what to do? She was the detective and he was the plod! The letter specifically said he would assist her. She looked out the window. They were crossing the long causeway that linked sprawling Betio with the smaller, tidier town of Bairiki with its government buildings. Louisa sucked in air through her nose and quietly blew it out through her half-open mouth. In. Out. In. Out. She could not let Sergeant Tebano or the island of Tarawa get to her. Yes, the torn plastic of the padded bus seat was digging into her, and, yes, she was being squashed by a woman the size of a small hippo, and, yes, she was taking a bus to go to a crime scene—she wouldn't think about the germs—but it would be worth it when she found the murderer. Assistant Police Commissioner Nakibae would be so impressed he'd order all the officers in the Kiribati Police Service to support her development of the Initial Crime Investigators programme. Her bosses in the Office of the European Commission in Suva would give her a glowing reference and, if there was any justice in the world at all, Tom at the British Aid Office, her European Commission representative on Tarawa, would be sacked for not supporting her and being such a useless waste of space. Lazy bastard!

The bus zipped on and on, passing heavy headed coconut trees, their green-brown fronds swirling and flapping in the wind. Behind the trees to the left, the lap, lap, lapping turquoise lagoon twinkled. To the right the vast Pacific roared. The ocean was what Louisa remembered most about Tarawa, and most liked, from when she'd lived there as a child. It didn't matter where you were, you were never far from its pulsating pull. Wild and furious on the ocean side and calm and placid on the protected, inner lagoon side, the Pacific surrounded the elongated 'L' shaped, narrow strip of land that was Tarawa, and separated the atoll from the rest of the islands that made up the Republic of Kiribati, and the rest of the world.

Louisa gripped her stomach. Violent pain. Again and again. This was the worst gut bug she could remember having. Hallelujah for Imodium, she couldn't be a metre away from a toilet without it. What had she been thinking of letting the waiter put those ice cubes in her drink the night before? Such a rookie mistake. She of all people should know the water on Tarawa wasn't safe to drink. Only boiling and filtering killed the microscopic pathogens, and what was ice but frozen water?

Louisa had had some notion of coming home when she'd applied for the Pacific island post. The family had left Tarawa when she was eight. She was the first to return after twenty-six years. She'd thought it would be fun. Mum had warned her against the move, saying the I-Kiribati men wouldn't respect her authority. Louisa dismissed her mum's warnings as exaggeration. The Republic of Kiribati had a democratically elected government. Things had changed since her mum had lived there. Besides, Louisa had wanted to get as far away from Edinburgh as possible, and Tarawa was probably as far away as you could get from Scotland.

3

Louisa spied the white, triangular parliament building on the lagoon side and watched the trees grow dense. Tebano's twin-trunked coconut palm looked more like a giant two-fingered gesture than a victory sign. Very fitting. She shouted, 'Ikai!' Before she'd even peeled herself out of the sticky plastic seat, the driver had jerked the vehicle to a halt. She nodded to the two fat ladies, who beamed back at her, and hurried to the front. A skinny girl wearing black cycle shorts under a shabby faded cotton dress sat in the corner of the top step—the bucket of tuna fish had gone. The girl collected the fares in a battered, square biscuit tin. Her long black hair fell all the way down her back. Louisa threw a fifty-cent coin into the tin, put on her Ray-Bans and stepped off the bus.

The heat always surprised Louisa. It was only eight forty-five in the morning yet the sky was a blistering white-blue and the air was already oven hot. There was nothing at the Ambo Lagoon Club bus stop, just a thicket of palm trees on one side of the shimmering tarred road, and opposite, metres from the kerb and behind a sea wall, the spewing purple ocean splattering against the shore. Louisa quickly saw what she was looking for—a slab of wood tacked to the weathered trunk of a coconut palm. The wood had a faded white arrow scratched on its worn surface. The arrow pointed inland, into the thicket of palms. Luckily, she had been to the Ambo Lagoon Club once before. Tom had taken her there the day she'd arrived on the island.

Tom was Louisa's first point of contact for the European Commission, which had no office on Tarawa. He worked for the Department for International Development, or DFID, in the UK. His office was in the bottom half of the old British High Commission building. He had one secretary and a cleaner. It was rumoured DFID were pulling out of the Pacific, but Tom was still there, looking after the few remaining DFID aid workers on Tarawa. He was a short, soft-looking man in his late thirties. When he walked his body appeared to wobble. His longish hair, which he combed backwards away from his pink face in long sweeps, always seemed greasy, or as if he'd just taken a shower. His ruddy cheeks made her think of 'jowls'. He'd referred to the Lagoon Club as 'a small oasis' for expatriates and had brought her straight there after picking her up at the airport in his Toyota Celica. He'd had the car imported from Britain. Louisa had been unimpressed. Who imports a Toyota Celica to a coral atoll? The first thing he'd told her was that he had a first-class honours degree from Oxford. The second was that as the EC Office representative on Tarawa, his job was to help her liaise with the Kiribati Police Service.

Louisa followed a set of car tracks. They twisted between the palms and took her deeper into the thicket. For a while she thought maybe she'd managed to get herself lost and cursed Tebano for not being with her. On that first visit with Tom she'd arrived from the opposite direction. Seeing the mwaneaba hall building for the first time, she'd been impressed. It sat in a sandy clearing on the edge of the lapping lagoon, fringed by a ring of magnificent spidery pandanus trees. The hall's huge thatch roof was supported on either side by a row of six sturdy posts. The open front looked over the lagoon and the back was closed off by a breezeblock wall and a makeshift bar, complete with a purple Formica counter and three purple Formica bar stools. A large, grimy American-style larder fridge sat behind the bar next to a giant chest freezer. They were chained and padlocked when not in use. The chains looked like the kind you saw draped around Harley Davidson motorbikes. Tom had offered to buy her a glass of chardonnay from a soggy cardboard box in the fridge. It was the first and last time he'd bought her a drink. He'd said if she wanted anything to come to him. There was no problem he couldn't solve. It wasn't long before she discovered this was one big fat lie and the only problem she had was him.

Louisa heard the shouting just as she spotted the top of the traditional thatched mwaneaba hall roof. She walked faster. What was going on? The wood thinned and the hall came into view just as she remembered it. A handful of sturdy officers, bulging out of their short-sleeved blue shirts and police issue brown shorts corralled fifteen, maybe twenty, older villagers into the open-sided building. Some villagers had stones in their raised hands, others had sticks. Inside the hall a bundle of expat children—no more than four or five years old—ran around a circle of agitated I-Kiribati women. It reminded Louisa of a Sunday school picnic she'd been forced to go to not long after arriving in Edinburgh, only the streamers and balloons were missing and no one was doing the egg and spoon race. Where was the cadaver? Was she at the right place? She shouted for quiet. No one paid any attention. She took her police whistle from her bag and blew. Its piercing shrill hurtled through the air. Everyone looked, even the children.

'I am Detective Sergeant Louisa Townsend,' she said, displaying her warrant card in her raised hand and approaching the building. 'Assistant Police Commissioner Nakibae has sent me to investigate a killing that has taken place in the vicinity. Please, can everyone sit quietly until I can ascertain where the deceased is.'

The villagers scowled. A child began to giggle.

'In case you are in doubt,' she said calmly, 'this means I am in charge and you do what I say.'

Still no one moved. Louisa stared at the assembled people. Sweat trickled down the back of her knees, which were beginning ever-so-slightly to tremble. If she couldn't control a bunch of villagers and a handful of toddlers, what hope was there of her finding a murderer? 'Sit down!' she roared. 'Or I'll arrest every single one of you for obstructing a murder inquiry!'

Reluctantly, one by one, the villagers and children obeyed.

4

Louisa counted six uniforms. She didn't recognise any of the constables. They stood behind the villagers in an uncomfortable row. She addressed the officers. 'Can someone tell me where the crime scene is?'

The officers stared at her blank faced.

She tried again. 'A man has been murdered, yes?'

A young, angular constable stepped forward. He nodded then blushed.

'And where is he?'

The young man's red face glowed more fiercely. 'Over there.' He pointed to the back of the hall.

Louisa thanked him and momentarily stepped outside the building towards where he had pointed. She didn't know what she'd expected to see but it certainly hadn't been a garden shed, the kind you could buy in any DIY store back home. It sat in the middle of a pond of sand and somehow reminded her of the house in Hansel and Gretel. One towering bread fruit tree shaded it from the sun. Little blue blinds covered two small square windows flanking the door, which was slightly ajar. The blinds looked like they were made from tarpaulin. She imagined there was no glass in the windows behind the blinds, probably some security wire though.

'Constable?' said Louisa, turning back to face the young man, 'Are you saying the deceased is in that hut?'

He nodded.

'And these people here—' she waved her hand towards the seated villagers and children '— have any of them been in the hut?'

'Oh, yes,' said the young man. 'They've all been inside, except for the children and the house-girls. They arrived after we closed the door.'

That was not what she wanted to hear. Any scene of crime evidence would be contaminated. 'Does anyone know who the dead man is?'

The constable shook his head. 'No one.'

'Kill the evil spirit!' yelled one of the villagers.

'Stone the ghostly ancestor!' screamed another.

'Stop the devil woman!' A voice in the crowd shouted.

'Silence!' yelled Louisa in her best crowd control voice just as a stone the size of her fist landed with a thud next to her foot. Louisa took a sharp breath. She knew how excitable the I-Kiribati could be, she'd not known her mother for more than thirty years and learnt nothing. A riot was the last thing she needed.

'The next person to raise their voice, or to throw a stone or wave a stick will be arrested for disturbing the peace and attempting to cause bodily harm!'

The villagers muttered and mumbled but they calmed down. Two of the children giggled. Louisa glowered at them and their faces crumpled.

'What's your name?' she asked the constable.

'Michael, Miss.'

'Michael, who are the villagers shouting about and why are they so angry, and does it have anything to do with the killing?'

Constable Michael drew his long lanky body upright, 'The villagers heard a terrible screaming. They rushed here and found a woman at the entrance to the small hut and the dead man inside. The villagers wanted to hurt the woman. She ran away. They chased her—'

'Whoa!' said Louisa, 'Is she hurt?'

'No,' he said firmly. 'We were driving past and we stopped the villagers attacking her.'

'But why did the villagers want to attack her?'

Michael scowled towards the villagers. 'They are silly superstitious people. In the olden days our ancestors used to offer the severed head of their enemy in sacrifice to the ghostly spirits for them to eat. The most prized food of ghosts was the eye. And even though our victim's head in the hut has not been severed, the gouged eyes—'

'His eyes are gouged?' said Louisa. There was no mention of that in her letter.

Michael nodded. 'The villagers believe the woman is a ghostly ancestor and that she killed the man and ate his eyes and is now going to haunt them. That is why they chased her.'

Louisa looked over the elderly crowd sitting cross-legged on the concrete floor. When they weren't shouting and waving sticks they looked perfectly harmless. But she knew how quickly that could change. Her mother had told her enough stories. But she'd never heard one about ghosts eating eyeballs. Ugh! 'And what do you think?'

'Of course there are no evil spirits!' said Michael crossly. 'They are stupid, uneducated villagers who like to cause trouble for no reason.'

Louisa was surprised by the outburst. 'I mean, could the woman they chased be the murderer?'

The young man frowned. 'She said she did not kill him. I believe her. The body is stiff and the blood has stopped running, which means he has most likely been dead for some time.'

Louisa nodded. 'And where is the woman?'

'She is somewhere safe, where the bad villagers can't get her.'

'Right. I'll take a look at the body now. By the way, has the medic been?'

'Medic?'

'The doctor who declares the deceased is actually dead.'

'Miss, he's dead,' said Michael puzzled. 'There's no doctor coming.'

Louisa sighed. 'Okay. I believe the hospital mortuary is the only mortuary on the island. The coroner can do the necessary when the cadaver gets there. We'll have to wait for SOCO to come before moving him though. Have they been sent for?'

Constable Michael looked down.

Louisa had a sinking feeling in her guts. 'Scene of Crime Officers? SOCOs? They're on their way, yes?'

Michael continued to avoid her eyes.

'The officers who collect the forensic evidence?' insisted Louisa. 'You know who I mean?'

The young man lifted his face and looked at Louisa. 'I know what a SOCO is. We don't have money for SOCOs or forensics on Tarawa.'

Louisa cursed silently. It had never occurred to her there wasn't at least one scene of crime officer to gather forensic evidence or a lab to send the evidence to. Despite her repeated requests to do so, until that day, she'd only visited one police station on the island and met virtually no officers. In her ignorance, she'd assumed the usual policing stuff went on. It seemed it didn't.

5

Louisa stood outside the hut. She recognised the pungent whiff of dead flesh, like gone-off rabbit. Until this moment her being in charge of a murder investigation hadn't seemed real. It was as if she'd been in some weird hallucinatory dream, a bizarre side effect of the ice cube poisoning. When she'd worked on murder cases back home she'd been part of a team of trained professionals. All striving to lock up the bad guy. Being solely in charge with one missing sergeant and a handful of reluctant constables, except for maybe Constable Michael, suddenly felt very scary, especially without forensics. The skin on her arms began to tingle. A dead body meant lots of germs. More than lots. Billions. She'd need to wash her hands immediately afterwards and she could see nowhere to do that. She breathed in long and slow. She'd survived the ice-cube poisoning. She could survive this. It was imperative she stayed strong and not let thoughts of germs take a grip.

With her right hand over her mouth and using a paper tissue to protect her left hand, she carefully pulled open the shed door. A bearded man's almost naked body filled the concrete floor. A ceremonial shark tooth dagger jutted out of his left temple. Bloody gunk from the wound smeared his ear and neck and had pooled in a puddle of inky purple beneath his head and shoulders. Two ravaged, bloodied openings gaped where his eyes should have been. He reminded Louisa of a character in a Greek tragedy. She glanced around. The gouged eyeballs were not obviously anywhere in the hut. Surely the killer hadn't really eaten them?

She recognised the dagger type. Her mother had been given two similar ornamental knives as wedding presents. In place of a metal blade, shark teeth lined either side of a tapering coconut wood middle. Louisa couldn't see all the teeth on this knife because three quarters of it was buried in the man's head, but she knew as the spine of the knife tapered the teeth became smaller. She reckoned the blade to be about fifteen centimetres long. Trails of elongated, bloody splatters snaked across the floor, consistent with a violent stab to the side of the head and a savage attack to the eyes.

The knife handle was covered in tightly woven pandanus straw and mixed with flashes of bright purple nylon. It had remarkably little blood on it given the circumstances. Louisa had always thought the knives looked faintly ridiculous, almost benign, but she knew they were not. Even though they were ornamental copies of ceremonial swords, the shark teeth were razor sharp. They could shred the toughest skin and in the tropics surface wounds caused by such blades can quickly become infected and lead to septicaemia. If you were unlucky enough to be stabbed with one, there was little hope of survival as it was almost impossible to withdraw the dagger without the serrated teeth ripping your insides out. It seemed unlikely the dagger had been used to gouge the eyes. Louisa didn't understand how the wooden tip of the blade had penetrated the skull. Sharpened coconut wood was hard enough to pierce skin, yes, but through the bony skull? Never. She made a mental note to get the coroner to double check that. As for the missing eyes, had they been gouged out before or after death? Had removing them been part of a bizarre ritual or pure gross depravity?

A faded green piece of cloth sat crumpled on top of the dead man's groin as if placed there. It looked like a lava-lava, a sarong-type garment worn by local men and women instead of shorts or skirts. Still covering her mouth, and with the tissue still firmly in her left hand and protecting her fingers, Louisa picked up the edge of the lava-lava. Yep, the man was naked underneath. She dropped the cloth again. The man's brown skin was grey. Louisa pushed his foot with hers, making sure only the sole of her sandal touched him and not any part of her bare foot. He didn't budge. The stiffness suggested full rigor mortis had set in. Checking for algor mortis would be a waste of time. In the tropical heat the post mortem temperature could increase or decrease. It was a relief not to have to touch his skin with her bare fingers.

Flies crawled in the deceased's eye sockets, on his head, on the dagger, on his neck and his chest and all over the glue like mess on the floor. Louisa shivered. What if one of them flew from the body and landed on her? No. She would not think like that! She would focus on the victim. The man's tanned skin and dark hair suggested he was a local but Louisa wasn't convinced. First, his long black hair was swept back in a pony tail and this was not something a local man would do. Second, it was not custom for I-Kiribati men to wear beards. Third, he looked too tall for an islander from these parts. Louisa guessed him to be about twenty centimetres taller than her and she was one metre and sixty-five centimetres. Like the Scots, I-Kiribati were all short stops. Finally, his hands looked manicured and, rightly or wrongly, after her brief two months on the island she couldn't imagine a local man grooming himself in this way.

There were no obvious defensive wounds and no flesh or skin under his nails, at least not that Louisa could see. Had the victim known his killer? The arc of blood splatters suggested he'd fallen more or less where he'd been attacked and died soon after. He looked to be in his early forties, about ten years older than Louisa. She could not imagine why he had been in the small hut, which appeared to be a storage place for children's toys. To the left of the body a packed shelf held a row of Ladybird reading books in alphabetic order. Beneath the books were bundles of tied-up skipping ropes, small net nylon bags of colourful wooden building blocks, jigsaw puzzles, trays of chubby crayons and white plastic safety paint pots with brushes sticking out of them. At the back of the hut someone had stacked a dozen tiny wooden chairs—the kind of chair Louisa imagined Baby Bear to have had in the Goldilocks story. Behind the chairs was a small free-standing railing full of hangers of children's dressing up clothes. A bunch of bright yellow hula hoops dangled from a hook directly above the deceased. To the right spread across the floor, lay half a dozen white pieces of A4 paper with a childish drawing of a tree painted on each—the blood had miraculously missed them.

Louisa checked her watch. It was nine thirty on Friday morning. Full rigor usually took between nine and twelve hours to set in, which suggested he'd died late Thursday evening. She'd know more after the post mortem, which had to be done as soon as possible. In the tropical heat the corpse could be reduced to soup and bones in days. When she had an accurate time of death, she could start identifying the people who had the opportunity to kill him. As for a motive, she hoped one would become clear the more she discovered about the victim.

The gamey smell outside was a relief after the hut's ghastly stench. Louisa closed the door behind her. Finding and preserving evidence from the scene was not an option. Apart from the sandy location having been trampled over by the villagers and the officers, the hut's wooden door, walls and the concrete floor had uneven surfaces which would yield little when checked for prints—but no SOCO probably meant no means of checking for prints anyway. She wished she'd thought to bring her camera. Photos of the scene were always helpful and she was going to need all the help she could get, if she was going to solve this bizarre killing. What was this man doing in a children's toy cupboard? Who was he and why was he all but naked? Had he been having sex? She had only seen one case of eye gouging in her life. High on drink and drugs a lad had prised his girlfriend's eye out of her head with a Biro. There was evidence of frenzy here, too.

6

One of the older constables stretched blue and white crime scene tape between the ring of pandanus trees around the hut. Michael talked to the local women. The expat children sat beside them and ate bright orange cheesy Twisties from tiny foil packets. The other constables were taking statements from the last few villagers as she'd requested. Louisa called Michael over.

'If the childminders have given their statements, send them home with the children, this is no place for little ones.'

'The house-girls are waiting for the mothers of the children to pick them up.'

Louisa frowned. It was about the third time Michael had used the term 'house-girl'. It surprised Louisa it was still in use. Her mother had been her father's 'house-girl' before they'd become an item. Even way back then her mother had disliked the term. While she didn't mind being called a cleaner or even a housekeeper, she was never anyone's 'girl'. 'Show me where the lady witness is then go back to the childminders and tell them to wait in the shade over there by the police truck. I don't want any of the children looking inside that hut.'

Michael nodded seriously and Louisa followed him as he led her behind the bar. The smell of stale beer and rancid grease was nauseating. Louisa pointed to a rolled up mat and a bundled up mosquito net and pillow squashed beneath the bar counter, next to a box of cling film.

'Someone clearly sleeps here. I want to know who. He—or she—may have seen something.'

Michael nodded and stopped in front of a dingy door next to the fridge. He took a key from his pocket. 'We are here.'

Louisa's heart skipped a little beat. The stale pee stench was unmistakable. 'You left her in the loo?' Witness or suspect, a toilet wasn't a suitable place to keep anyone.

'There was nowhere else.' Michael unlocked the door and pulled it open.

A fair-haired, white woman sat slumped on the dirty floor, leaning against a pee-splattered toilet bowl.

'I'm Detective Sergeant Townsend,' said Louisa. She didn't know what shocked her more, the state of the disgusting toilet or the fact the witness was a white expatriate.

'Help me,' whimpered the woman. The woman's eyes were glazed. She was clearly in shock. She reached her hand up towards Louisa.

'You're safe,' said Louisa, taking the woman's hand and trying not to think about the dirt and germs that must be on her fingers.

'They chased me—' the dazed woman stumbled to her feet. Her voice became high-pitched and scared '— then I was locked up, like an animal!'

'Please don't worry,' said Louisa, leading the woman into the bar and gently freeing her hand from her grip. 'Let me get you a drink.' Louisa indicated to Michael with a nod that he find one. She hoped the woman wouldn't cry. She hated it when people cried. Louisa pointed to the bar stools. 'Why not sit down?'

The woman saw the last few villagers still in the hall giving their statement. 'It's them! Arrest them now!'

'Please don't worry. They've been told to behave. Are you sure you won't sit? I need to ask you a few questions.'

'I don't want to stay here. I want to leave,' said the woman, her voice quivering, 'I want to leave!'

'It must have been terrible for you,' said Louisa as Michael handed her a can of red cola. It was a make Louisa had never seen before. 'But you are safe now.' Louisa used her left hand to remove the ring pull and hand it to the woman. She'd have preferred to have got a tissue out and put that between her fingers and the lid of the can but there was no time. 'Here. You must be thirsty.'

The woman hesitated before grabbing the can and greedily gulping down the fizzy drink.

Louisa watched her and waited. She was short and plump, what her mother would have called 'solid', about sixty-five kilos. Close to Louisa's age, or a couple of years older. Her accent suggested she came from the south-east of England. Her pink face was streaked with tear stains. Her white cotton trousers were crumpled and dirty and her grey T-shirt was stained under the arms with dark spreading circles of sweat. Louisa wondered if her being a blonde, a white expatriate, had somehow helped incite the villagers. She knew from her mother that the ghostly ancestors were supposed to have been fair -skinned people from the land of shadows in Matang. That was why expatriates were called I-Matangs, people from Matang, and people from Kiribati were called I-Kiribati.

7

The woman placed her can of drink on the bar counter and sat on the stool next to Louisa. 'They threw stones at me,' she said.

'I know. I'm sorry. But you weren't hurt, were you?'

'I could have been.'

'Can I ask your name?'

'Is it still in there?' She nodded towards the hut.

'We'll be taking him away soon. Can you please tell me your name?'

'Jill Wilson,' she said, picking the can up again and taking a sip. 'My husband, Paul, works in the Ministry of Justice. Can you call him and ask him to come and get me?'

'Of course, we can.' Louisa was surprised. She knew

who Paul was. 'But first I have to ask you some questions.'

'I've lost a flip-flop,' Jill said, looking at her feet as if seeing them for the first time.

'We'll help you find it. I know you're upset, but I do need to ask you about the man in the hut.'

'I've never seen him before,' she said, her hands beginning to tremble.

'Can I ask what you were doing in the hut?'

Jill took another gulp of cola from the red can then put it back down on the counter. 'Nicole asked me to open up—'

'Nicole?'

'She's Australian. She set the playgroup up with Christine, Christine's not Australian though.'

'Go on,' said Louisa. If she let her talk, it would calm her down.

'It's a place for the expatriate kids to meet and play while their mums get some time out. At least that's how Nicole describes it. I've been helping for the last few months. Not every day, just when I feel like it.'

'And what happened today?'

'Nicole's children were sick or something. She said she'd be late and asked if I would open up—'

'What about the other woman, Christine?'

'It wasn't her turn. They take it day about, that way they get a break too.'

'You don't have children,' said Louisa, glancing back at the group of youngsters still seated on the concrete floor of the open hall. 'But you help out?'

'I don't mind kids and it's something to do. None of the other expatriate mums want to help. They complain they're bored but say they're too busy to help, even though it's their children who come.' She cleared her throat. 'At least Nicole does something.' She looked down. 'Do you think my other flip-flop is in the toilet?'

Louisa nodded to Michael to go and check. 'What time did you arrive this morning?'

'Before eight. I would have driven but Paul, my husband, he needed the car—' Jill's eyes glazed over again. She stopped talking and looked around blankly.

Louisa knew it was the shock. She tried another tack. 'What do you do, or at least what did you do before coming to Tarawa?'

'I'm a book restorer. I don't know why I imagined I'd get work on a coral atoll.' Jill looked down at her fingers.

'You gave up your job to come here with Paul?'

'It's a great career move for him.' She picked up her cola and took another sip.

'So, what happens at the nursery?' said Louisa.

Jill swallowed. 'The house-girls drop the children off and then wait under the trees in the shade. We play games then do a bit of art and craft, followed by some reading, some writing exercises and a page or two of sums. Christine's always trying to get the kids to do more of the school stuff. It drives Nicole mad. Christine says there's no point in having the school if it's not educational. Nicole says games are educational. I leave them to it. I'm just glad to get out of the house. It's all over by midday when the house-girls take the children home.'

'And when you arrived today? said Louisa, giving what she hoped was a reassuring smile. 'Did you notice anything unusual?'

'The smell around the hut. It was awful. But you can sometimes get a bad smell off the lagoon. I went to get the key for the door. Nicole keeps it hidden under a small stone. It wasn't there. I saw the hut door was open a bit. I assumed Nicole had forgotten to lock up. She's scatty like that. Christine is always having a go at her about it. Nicole says Christine's a control freak. But she only says that to me, of course.' Jill smiled suddenly. 'Christine's daughter is five and she can read and write better than Nicole's daughter who's seven. I thought Christine's kids just happened to be bright. Nicole said it was nothing to do with being bright. Apparently, when Christine's daughter was nine months old and in her high chair Christine had big posters made with the words YES and NO on them. At mealtimes Christine would offer her daughter certain foods. If she wanted to eat any of them, she had to point to the word YES when Christine asked. If she pointed to NO by mistake she didn't get whatever it was. Nicole reckons the girl could read before she could speak. She taught her son the same way. I was impressed but Nicole said it's because Christine's really competitive—' Jill's speech had grown more and more rapid. She paused to catch her breath. 'And controlling.'

'The hut door was slightly open?' said Louisa gently.

'Oh yes.' She put the can of cola back down on the counter but kept a hold of it, as if steadying herself. 'It opens outwards. He was in the middle of the floor. I couldn't miss him with that ugly dagger sticking out of the side of his head, and his eyes...' She cleared her throat. 'You saw?'

Louisa nodded.

Jill shivered. 'So much blood too. It was horrible. The smell was worse with the door open. I screamed. At least I think I did. I can't remember properly. One second I was alone, the next villagers were pushing to get past me to get into the hut...' She wiped her hands on her trousers. 'Someone shouted, "She's the killer!" Or something like that. I looked to see who they were talking about and saw everyone staring at me. I said, "No, no, I didn't kill him!" It was like a trigger. They all shouted. "Evil woman!" "Devil woman!" Something like that. Someone waved a stick. A stone flew past my cheek. It just missed me. I ran...' She fiddled with the can. 'I got stones thrown at me for doing nothing. Then I was chased and locked up. What sort of country is this?'

'I'm sorry,' said Louisa, 'It was a misunderstanding. But

you're fine now, aren't you? And you're not hurt, are you?'

Jill's shoulders slumped. It was as if her body was too heavy for her to hold up. She shook her head. 'If the police hadn't come—'

'But they did come,' said Louisa, trying not to think what the consequences could have been had they not. It was her mother's worst trait, react first and think later, but she'd never tried to take the law into her own hands. 'And you're sure you've never seen the victim before?'

She shook her head.

'What about the dagger?'

'They're all the same, aren't they?'

A tingle of excitement fluttered across Louisa's chest. 'No. Each one is individually made. The pattern on the handle is usually the signature of the maker. Please think. This is very important. Have you seen the dagger before?'

The noise of cars screeching to a halt made Louisa turn away. A bundle of distraught expat women in Capri pants and strappy tops scrambled out of three white Mitsubishi estate cars. Before Louisa was halfway across the hall the women were inside. For a couple of minutes it was chaos again as mothers, childminders, villagers, police officers and children all yelled at once.

8

Once more the shrill scream of Louisa's whistle sliced through the air. 'My name is Detective Sergeant Townsend. Everyone stop shouting!'

One of the expat women had a bandage round her ankle. She was the only woman not in Capri pants. She gripped the hands of a small boy and girl, faced Louisa and said, 'How dare you detain our children next to where someone's been murdered!'

'Your children have seen nothing, nor have they been detained. They have been waiting for you to collect them. Now, unless you know anything that you think may help me with my investigation, take your children and let the constables do their job.'

'Please!' Jill pushed in front of Louisa, 'Someone take me home!'

'Jill?' The elegant woman looked shocked. 'What are you doing to her?'

'Jill's helping me with my inquiries,' said Louisa.

'Not in that state, she's not!' The woman put the little girl's hand in the same hand as the boy's, put her arm around Jill's shoulders and began hustling her towards the parked white vehicles.

'Stop right there!' yelled Louisa.

The woman ignored her.

What did she think she was doing? Louisa was an officer of the law and Jill was her witness! Louisa ran forward and reached the cars before the little group. The keys were still in the ignition of the first car. Louisa leaned into the open driver's window and removed them. 'Jill is going nowhere until I say so.'

The woman thrust out her hand, palm up, her fingers rigid. 'Give me back my keys!'

'Can I have your name, please?"

There was a hush.

The woman straightened her shoulders. 'Christine Brown. My husband works for the Ministry of Trade and Commerce. He knows the President personally!'

'Christine, I appreciate you've had a shock,' said Louisa, briefly wondering if the woman was going to try to leap forward and wrestle the keys from her—well, bring it on! 'I also appreciate your concern for your friend. However, Jill is an important witness in a murder investigation and I have some more questions to ask her. Take your children and childminders and leave. My officers have your names and addresses from your childminders. If we need to ask you anything, we'll be in touch but Jill must stay—'

'No!' wailed Jill, flopping to the ground in a heap. She sobbed, 'Let me go home! Please!'

'What is happening here?' said an older man, appearing from the path, looking angry and confused. He was followed by four or five male villagers.

'Nothing is happening here!' said Louisa, recognising the local men from earlier.

'I won't stay here any longer!' screamed Jill. 'I won't!'

Louisa cursed silently. Short of dragging Jill kicking and screaming back to the bar, upsetting the children and inciting the villagers to riot all over again, she'd have to let Jill leave with the Christine woman. Louisa calmly placed the car keys on the bonnet of the car. 'Jill, you will need to come into Betio police station to make a written statement. Do you understand?'

Jill nodded between sobs.

'It is very important.'

Jill nodded again.

'What about at three this afternoon?'

9

Louisa walked into Betio police station's only toilet and took a small pack of tissues and a blue oval soap box from her handbag.

It was a habit of hers to always have four packets of tissues on her, and soap, at all times. She took a tissue from the packet and then set the packet on the sagging leather mouth of her bag where she'd already placed the soap box. Next, with the tissue protecting the tips of her fingers, she turned on the single tap in the sink then dropped the tissue in the open pedal bin below the sink. Now she opened the lid of the plastic soap box and took out a sliver of pink soap and began lathering her hands under the running cold water. Eventually, she slipped the soap back into its box, rinsed her fingers, shook off the excess water, picked up the soap once more and started all over again. She did this four times.

The rule of four wasn't something she liked to revert to because if she wasn't vigilant, the phobia could take over. That meant doing everything four times, not just washing her hands. At its worst the rule of four made any simple act a trial. There had been times when she'd not been able to walk through a door without going back in and out another three times, ditto locking a door, switching on or off a light, washing a cup, having a shower, cleaning the shower, changing the bin bag. She'd thought she'd defeated the voices because she'd not heard from them in months. But they'd started up again when she'd been driving back from the Ambo Lagoon Club in the police car she'd commandeered.

The voices were quiet at first. No more than a whisper. Then they'd got louder and louder. Like frenzied Daleks screaming 'Exterminate!' over and over again, except the voices screeched 'Contaminated!' 'Contaminated!' They said she was a killer. They said people would die because of her. Her mother would die. It was so stupid. Her mother was thousands of miles away in Edinburgh! It was impossible that Louisa, in Tarawa, could cause anyone's death anywhere, let alone her mother's, just because she'd not washed her hands. It embarrassed her even to think about it. But even though she knew it was the biggest load of crap, she'd made a deal with the voices and promised them that as soon as she got to a sink, she'd wash her hands four times. But she'd only do that if the voices promised not to come back. The voices agreed and then became quiet. She was ashamed she'd made the deal. It was never a good idea to give in to the voices, but, on the other hand, she'd been planning to thoroughly wash her hands as soon as she could anyway—after all, she had been next to a corpse. What harm was there in washing them a few extra times?

Louisa dried her hands four times, on four different tissues, using the fourth tissue to turn the tap off, before throwing it in the pedal bin. She snapped the soap box shut and dropped it, and the remaining clean tissues, back into her bag next to the other three packets. Job done! She was glad there wasn't a mirror above the sink, otherwise she could have been tempted to look at herself and touch up her lipstick and she didn't want to stay a second longer in the stinking, dank toilet. It was by far the worst thing about Betio station. It was even worse than the toilet in the Ambo where they'd locked Jill Wilson.

After the toilet, the next worst thing about Betio nick was its general state of disrepair and lack of facilities. Mildew covered the blue painted ceiling and the scuffed fibreboard walls looked as if someone had punched holes in them with a giant fist. The blue lino floor tiles were cracked and broken in the corners, revealing a crumbling black concrete floor. There was also a total lack of privacy. Stations back home were clearly divided into two areas, the public front reception and the private back area. This was where the offices, interview and incident rooms and cells were. Locked doors separated the two areas and there was no way of getting in without a police escort or police pass. Louisa thought Betio station was more like a doctor's waiting room with its simple reception counter slap bang in the middle of it.

There were two small single cells (and the toilet) to the left of the counter. To the right, and directly opposite the cells, were three small interview rooms. Only the two cells had locks. Jill was due in fifteen minutes. Louisa picked the interview room furthest from the front door for her interview. It was the brightest room, it was also the least dirty and the only one with furniture: an old-fashioned wooden desk, a metal filing cabinet and two scuffed, hard-backed black plastic chairs. The windows had no louvres but criss-cross heavy duty security wire made the room secure. One window looked on to the side of the station and the car park, where she'd parked the police car she'd commandeered from the Ambo and was keeping for her use from now on. The other window overlooked the back of the station and a scrubby parade ground-cum-football pitch, where a squabble of children kicked a ball around.

Louisa used two of her paper hankies to give the desk and chairs and the top of the filing cabinet a quick wipe. A quiet niggling voice told her to wipe them down another three times, but she ignored it. A glance in the cabinet revealed tired brown cardboard files with yellowing paper documents inside. Someone, somewhere, giggled. Louisa looked around. A small boy with curious brown eyes and a runny nose peeked over the edge of the rotted window frame. Then a skinny faced girl appeared. They grinned at her through the security wire. Louisa barked at them to go. They didn't move. She darted across to where they were and lifted her hand as if to give them a clip. Even though the wire meant she couldn't have touched them, the children scarpered. Louisa yelled after them to keep away and sat down at the desk.

10

Louisa took out her make-up mirror and lipstick from her bag. She groaned when she saw her red-rimmed eyes and flaky pastry skin. As for her hair? She licked her fingertips and tried to pat down some of the more unruly kinks. Coconut oil might do the trick but she didn't have any. Trust her to have inherited her dad's mad brown curls rather than her mum's raven straightness. She jabbed the rebellious wisps behind her ears, swiped a layer of pink across her lips and put the compact and lipstick back in her bag. She leaned back in the chair, closed her eyes and hoped the thumping in her head would soon cease. As soon as she'd arrived at the station Louisa had given the duty officer, an older, quiet man, and the only other person around, five dollars to find her a bottle of cola and some paracetamol. He'd sent one of the lads playing football out the back to a local store to get them for her. The boy had still not returned.

It had been a mistake to let Christine hijack Jill from the Ambo Lagoon Club. Louisa admitted that. It would have been better to have finished interviewing Jill there and then, while the incident was still fresh in her mind. However, what had followed after the women had left the Ambo had been out of Louisa's control. She liked to think she'd made the best of a bad job.

The first disaster was finding out the hospital mortuary van was out of action so there was no suitable vehicle to collect the corpse. But the inside of the hut was getting hotter and hotter. If the body wasn't moved, it would cook. The police lorry had been the obvious choice. To help preserve evidence on the body for the coroner, she'd ordered the officers to wrap it in the cling film she'd spotted on the fridge earlier. Much to Constable Michael's embarrassment, his colleagues had balked at the idea of touching the cadaver. Louisa was taken aback. She knew they'd handled corpses before. She'd read reports to say as much when doing her background research. When she pressed them further, Michael said the villager's talk of evil spirits had spooked them. Louisa gave the men short shrift. She had no time for such nonsense. Eventually, with Michael's help, they persuaded the constables to wrap the deceased in the plastic film. Getting the body on to the lorry was the next problem. While the officers discussed how to best lift it in, Louisa had carried out a quick search of the surrounding area. She'd found nothing, not even a cigarette stub. She returned to find the corpse face down in the sand by the wheel of the lorry, conspicuous in its rigid nakedness—and not a shred of cling film in sight. That was the second disaster. A red-faced Constable Michael explained that Sergeant Tebano had turned up and ordered them to leave the cadaver on the ground. The mortuary refrigeration unit at the hospital had broken down and it was Tebano's opinion there was no longer any reason to take the corpse to the hospital. He had also ordered them to take the cling film off the body because he said it was making it too hot. Tebano had then disappeared. Louisa had lost her temper big time.

'When I give you an order, you follow it. I don't care what Tebano says! I am in charge of this case. You obey me. Not him. Got that?'

None of the men would look at her.

'That body is our main evidence,' she'd said, pointing to the dead man, 'and by leaving it exposed in the sand like that, apart from showing it appalling disrespect, you have hastened its decomposition and destroyed whatever trace of evidence we could have got from it!'

The men had still refused to look at her.

'And for Christ's sake cover the poor man up. Where is his sarong?' She glanced around, she couldn't see it anywhere. 'The lava-lava that was on the body in the hut? Where is it? It is also evidence!'

It had been an out and out balls-up. But she'd been determined not to let the mortuary freezer breaking down stop her getting a post mortem. She'd ordered Michael to take a rock from the beach and break the padlock on the chest freezer with it. The freezer was full of frosted packets of small, bright red sausages called Wee Willy Winkies. She ordered the men to dump the packets on the floor and put the freezer in the back of the lorry. After a lot of moaning and heaving and groaning and sweating and mumbling, but no actual outright complaining, the men managed to get the freezer in the back of the open lorry as ordered. The officers then placed the body in the freezer. Louisa hoped the freezer would stop it decomposing further, at least until the post mortem could be carried out.

Like a bad smell Tebano had turned up after all the heavy work was over. He'd had laughed out loud when he saw the freezer in the back of the lorry. Louisa had wanted to slap him but she'd refused to lose her temper. He was an anachronism, a sexist throwback to the days when her mum had lived on Tarawa and was clearly out to undermine her. She was surprised such men were still around on Tarawa in 2004. However, he was the most senior officer on the island at the moment and she needed him. She'd ordered him to take the lorry, and five of the other constables, including Michael, to the hospital. They were not to leave until the coroner had taken charge of the freezer—and the body inside it.

She'd been left with the green lava-lava and the pandanus handle of the murder weapon—somehow, in the chaos of moving the body, the handle had become dislodged from its shark tooth blade and trampled on. Louisa had wrapped the small item carefully in four pieces of cling film, and then in a tissue, and put it in her bag. The grubby lava-lava she left with the older constable, who was to stay and guard the crime scene.

Louisa opened her eyes. Her head ached. She hoped the boy would return soon with the cola and paracetamol. Evidence had been tampered with; the corpse manhandled; the crime scene trampled over, and her key witness had left before being fully questioned. She'd have lost her stripes for less back home. No wonder the voices in her head had come back! The only good news had been meeting Sammy.

Sammy was a wiry, twisty, elderly man, with a mouthful of missing teeth and shiny gnarled mahogany joints. He was the manager of the Ambo Lagoon Club. He wore the smallest of lava-lavas Louisa had ever seen, more a loin cloth than sarong, over a pair of tattered black shorts. He'd appeared as the men were loading the freezer into the back of the lorry. He was dismayed when he saw what the freezer was being used for. He could never store food in it again. But then Louisa got her first break: Sammy knew the dead man. His name was Joe. He was an I-Matang businessman from Singapore, who'd lived in Betio and sometimes came to the Ambo. Sammy had not seen him for weeks and certainly not the night before, when it had been so quiet he'd shut early and gone home.

11

It was almost three. Louisa looked at the can of Coke on her desk. Unable to find any bottles of soft drink, the young lad sent shopping had returned with a can. A small cardboard packet of paracetamol lay next to the can. Two blue and white capsules sat on a foil sleeve on top of the packet. Louisa hated drinking from a can. Years ago she'd watched a schools science programme, which revealed all fizzy drink cans had traces of rats' pee and faeces on the ring pulls. It was something to do with the way the cans were stored in warehouses. She'd not been able to drink from a can since. But the raw thirst at the back of her throat was making her desperate. A glass or a cup would have made drinking the fizzy liquid easier, but there was nothing like that in the station. Louisa licked her parched lips. Jill was due any minute and Louisa needed to focus. She couldn't afford to be distracted, she wanted no more mistakes.

Holding the can in her right hand and using a tissue in her left, she carefully opened the can and tipped it slightly sideways. Without letting the cola pour back inside, she allowed a small amount to swish over the metal top. Next, she soaked up the excess juice and any germs with the tissue and threw it in the bin by her desk. She did it once, and then before she could stop herself, twice, three, four times. She promised herself it would be the last time she'd carry out the rule of four ritual. Keeping minimum contact between her lips and the cool metal surface, she washed down the two paracetamol capsules. At least the sugar in the cola would give her an energy boost. She assessed what she'd found out about Joe in the brief time she'd been in the station.

The Departments of Trade and Immigration had told her Joe's full name was José Rivada Garcia. He was thirty-eight and had been on Tarawa two years. Before that, he'd lived in Singapore for ten years. He was, apparently, Spanish by birth, though everyone knew him as Joe and not by his Spanish name of José. There was no evidence of what he'd done in Singapore but on Tarawa he'd exported sea cucumbers, also known as bêche-de-mer, to Japan. His export licences were in order. He was not married and didn't have any children. He had a house in Betio, which the duty constable said was ten minutes by car from the station.

Louisa went outside and checked her watch again. It was three ten. If Jill had not arrived by the time she'd finished her drink, which was almost empty, that was it. Louisa would go and check out Joe's house and leave Jill to give her statement to the duty constable. Across the road a clothes market was in full swing. To be this busy, Louisa supposed it was a Pay-Friday. On Tarawa everyone got paid every fortnight, on a Friday. The scrappy ground was covered in colourful, higgledy-piggledy mounds of imported second-hand clothes. The bales had probably come off the recently docked ship from Australia. One woman in a tent-like shiny purple dress with short puffy sleeves was shouting 'Na second hand? Na good bargains!' She waved black bicycle shorts in the air. The shoppers ignored her. They sat, cross-legged, around the edges of the mounds of clothes. Their hands sifted and sorted mechanically. Nothing seemed to distract them from their task. Even their thick, long hair, which was usually worn down their backs, was tied up and out the way in double-decker buns on top of their heads. While they sifted, the bundles of hair wobbled precariously. Louisa saw an expat in the crowd. It was Jill, hurrying through the market.

Louisa waited for her at the entrance to the station. But instead of coming towards the building, Jill did a right turn and darted off in the opposite direction. Louisa frowned. Jill couldn't have failed to have seen the concrete police building. It stuck out like a sore thumb next to the colourful trade stores with their cheerful displays of bolts of Chinese cottons and plastic toys. Louisa hurried into the station to put her drink can in the bin. When she came back out, Jill was so far down the road she was almost out of sight.

After a couple of months Betio should have been reasonably familiar to Louisa, but it wasn't. She had a poor sense of direction and preferred never to stray from a familiar path. As a consequence Louisa had no idea where Jill was headed. She followed her down a scrubby lane towards a row of dilapidated E graded government houses. It had been explained to Louisa on her arrival that E houses were for the lowest paid civil servants. Expatriates, or I-Matangs, lived in A or B houses, as did senior civil servants. Louisa considered herself lucky to have been given a B house—she was sure if it had been up to Tom, she'd have found herself here in one of the E houses, which weren't really houses, more like large cardboard boxes, swimming in patchy yards of badly drained soil. But her contract came with certain clauses and a B house was one of them.

Jill went deeper and deeper into the muddling mess of downtown Betio. The yards of the small E houses were crammed to bursting with what Louisa would have called 'scrap': rusty washing machines, scratched sideboards, damp plywood crates, car tyres, upturned bicycles, plastic basins and cardboard boxes—there was even the metal frame of a hospital bed in front of one house. The further she went from the main road, the quieter it became. Road traffic all but ceased. A blast of heavy rock music startled Louisa. Chickens pecking for scraps scattered. Ahead of her Jill stopped at last. She appeared to be looking at something. Louisa held back. She'd been intent on catching up with Jill but now she wanted to see where she was going. And then she saw him: Paul, Jill's husband. Louisa knew that blond crew cut and smooth confident chin instantly. She'd been in and out of the Ministry of Justice often enough to know who Paul, the magistrate trainer, was.

Paul stood in the rear doorway of a small E house. A local girl stood next to him. Her long, thick black hair swung down beyond her slender waist, almost to the back of her knees. She looked younger than Paul's thirty-something, about ten years younger. Her eyes were red. Had she been crying? Paul wiped something out of her eye with the back of his thumb. The girl smiled then leaned her head against his shoulder. He put his arms around her and enveloped her fragile body in his embrace. Louisa couldn't see Jill's face but she could imagine what she was thinking. She waited for Jill to confront Paul and readied herself to jump in if things got nasty. But nothing happened. Before Paul had a chance to see Jill, she'd turned away. Louisa darted behind a giant, round concrete water tank wedged between two houses, careful not to touch its crumbling wall. She watched Jill disappear up a side street. Louisa frowned. Did the fact that Jill's husband was having an affair have any bearing on her murder case? She thought not. And he was having an affair. She knew enough Kiribati to know that the gossip at the Ministry of Justice was Paul's extramarital relationship. She sighed, why was it, married or not, expatriate men couldn't keep their cocks in their pants?

12

Joe's house sat in a row of neat little C houses in a quiet, respectable part of Betio. An elderly woman appeared to be waiting for Louisa. The woman introduced herself as Joe's house-girl. She'd heard about his death—the news was all over the island. She asked Louisa if she could have the full length mirror in Joe's bedroom. When Louisa said it wasn't up to her, the woman shrugged, gave Louisa the key to the house and disappeared.

Louisa found Joe's passport in a drawer next to various bank statements. He had 20,000 Australian dollars in his personal savings account and no obvious outstanding loans—people had been killed for far less. The house was sparsely furnished with no personal mementos apart from a photo stuck to his fridge door, which showed a serious Joe holding up a sail fish. The body of the fish was almost as long as Joe's. He reminded Louisa of a thin Captain Haddock from the Tintin books. There was a weight bench and weights in his bedroom next to a single bed. His clothes were all good quality. Designer stuff. His T-shirts, she noted, were arranged by colour in the drawers of his cupboard, as were his boxer shorts and socks. There wasn't one sarong, or any other article of clothing that resembled the tatty lava-lava found with his body. Louisa placed the photo, the bank statements and the passport in the clear plastic evidence bags she'd brought from the station, and locked up behind her. The coroner would have to pass on the news of Joe's death to someone—and that person would inherit his savings and the business. She made a note to phone the Department of Immigration again to ask if they could find out who and where Joe's next of kin were.

It was five. All government offices closed at four thirty. Louisa had still not heard back from Tebano. Whenever she tried to call the hospital, there was no answer. She hoped they'd been able to keep the body cold, at least until the post mortem could be done. Jill hadn't appeared. It had surprised Louisa—having an unfaithful husband, while unpleasant, wasn't an excuse for not coming to the station and making her statement. Louisa still wanted to know what, if anything, Jill knew about that dagger. She'd get one of the constables to question her the next day.

In the absence of a desk with a lock and key, Louisa stashed the bank statements, the passport and the photo of Joe with the sail fish, and all the witness statements taken from the Ambo earlier, in a folder in her bag. She left the door of her little office open—it didn't lock anyway—and gave the duty constable her landline phone number. She wanted an update as soon as Tebano appeared. Having no mobile network on Tarawa was a right pain, as was the limited internet. However, far worse, as far as the police service was concerned, was the fact the officers had no personal police radios. It made communicating with them when they were out of the station virtually impossible.

Louisa switched on all the lights in the house. She didn't like the dark and especially not on Tarawa when dusk brought with it the raucous chorus of whining cicadas and seething crickets. A glance out the back window told her Reteta and her family were still not around. It was odd. They were usually out the back all the time. Louisa went into the kitchen. On the way home she'd stopped at the local supermarket. The ship from Australia had brought fresh food supplies. According to the rumours, the supermarket was now stocked with all sorts of goodies. That turned out to be a lie. The big shop she'd been waiting weeks for was on the counter in the kitchen where she'd left it: eight packets of frozen macaroni cheese. She'd passed on a battered cauliflower, bruised apples, misshapen tomatoes, soft onions, and a packet of weeping Coon cheese. But she had grabbed a packet of frozen sliced white bread, which she'd had to fight half the expatriate population on the island to get and had cost six dollars. She didn't even like toast, it made such a mess and she hated mess.

Louisa sat on a mat by a smouldering camp fire out the back. Reteta had set up the first fire at the edge of the veranda a few days after she'd moved in. It was the first of many. Someone must have been around during the day and lit this fire or it wouldn't still be alive. Softly hissing embers created a cosy glow. The garden had also been tidied. All the stuff that had been scattered across the lawn that morning, the basins and the pots and bags and mats, had been stacked under the veranda. The smoke smell reminded Louisa of crisp winter mornings and burnt barbecue sausages. It wasn't a bad smell.

A faint star winked. There was no moon. The ocean side of the house was her favourite side. One late afternoon, not long after she'd arrived, but before Reteta and her family had swooped in, she'd been sitting at that same spot, looking out to sea. A school of silver dolphins had burst out of the water. There had been dozens of them, twirling and sparkling beneath the glistening orange sun in front of her eyes. Now all she could see was an expanse of grey-black nothingness. It was there though, the ocean, she could hear it even though the tide was out. You could always hear it, no matter where you were on Tarawa, crunching and crashing mercilessly inwards, battering closer and closer, ravaging anything and everything that got in its way. At some very high tides the waves actually came up to a few metres from the veranda.

Louisa thought about Joe. She needed to find out what he had been doing at the club. Could he have been having an affair with one of the mothers? The red embers sizzled suddenly. And why had someone cut out his eyes? Did it mean the killer was a local? A dog barked and Daisy, who'd been snoozing in the scrub next to the tethered pig, lifted his head briefly. Louisa peered in the direction of the noise. A Gilbertese family lived further down the beach, beyond the graveyard. They had at least three dogs that Louisa knew of. She could just see the smudgy shadowy outline of their house. At that moment, as if by magic, the house pinged into yellowy being. From where Louisa sat, it looked like the shopfront of a department store on a winter's night. The traditional house had no walls, just four heavy corner posts, which supported a raised wooden floor area and a thatched roof. The cause of the illumination, a long fluorescent strip, dangled above various groups of bodies sleeping on the floor. Each group was separated from the other by a domed screen of flowing white mosquito netting. A cluster of toddlers lay beside two round-hipped women under one net; three skinny teenage girls snuggled together under a second; an elderly man and woman dozed beneath the third, and a bunch of broad-chested men lay stretched out under the last. One of the toddlers started crying. A woman stirred. Not for the first time since arriving on the island, Louisa wondered how, with so little privacy, did I-Kiribati men and women manage to make love. Daisy barked. Louisa started and dropped her mug.

Reteta's nephew stood at the back door.

'Shit!' she said, 'Where did you come from?'

'Sorry, I didn't mean to give you a fright.'

'Is there something wrong?' Even though he camped out in her garden, she didn't know Reteta's nephew well. Subconsciously, her body tensed.

'Reteta sent me.' Daisy nudged his wet nose into his hands. 'My cousin died early yesterday morning. His funeral is being held in his village. We went late last night and we'll be there until Sunday morning. '

'I'm sorry.' She had wondered where Reteta and the family had got to. Now she knew. She began picking up the shattered pieces of mug with her left hand. 'Was your cousin very old?'

'Only in his thirties. It was a tragic accident. Don't worry about the pig and Daisy, I'll be back and forward to feed them, and to keep an eye on our things.' He paused. 'You're investigating the killing at the Ambo, aren't you?'

She looked up. 'Yes.'

'Everyone is talking about it. They say the man was an I-Matang and that his eyes were eaten, is that true?'

'I can't discuss the case, sorry.'

He shrugged. 'Reteta thinks you should come back to the village and stay with us there. She says a woman shouldn't be by herself.'

Louisa blushed despite herself. She'd forgotten what her mum used to call women who lived alone. 'I'm fine.'

He nodded. 'Okay. No worries. Oh, and this is for you—' He handed her two freshly husked young coconuts. 'Reteta said you were sick. I thought you might appreciate some fresh coconut juice. It's good for you when you're sick.'

'Oh?' said Louisa, looking at the nuts but not taking them. She did like coconut milk. It was by far the most sterile drink you could get. Opening them to get at the milk, however, always seemed to involve a rusty knife.

'Can I open them for you?' The young man picked up a machete sitting against the wall of the house.

'Wait!'—she'd not even noticed the knife there. 'It's not clean. Let me wash it.'

The young man looked puzzled. 'Okay.' He handed it to her.

Louisa put down the broken crockery still in her hands. There was an outside tap by the back door. She turned it on until the water flowed freely and placed the knife blade under it.

'It'll get rusty,' he said, looking puzzled.

'I used it earlier. Germs.' She let the water wash over the blade for as long as she could, without becoming embarrassed, and handed the man back the knife. With one swipe, and then a second, he sliced the top of the young fruits to reveal the clear fresh liquid inside. 'Thanks.' She took the coconuts from him. 'It's silly, but I don't know what to call you.' Reteta seemed to refer to him as 'The Curate'.

He smiled. 'Everyone calls me TC.'

She laughed. 'Top Cat?'

'No, The Curate.'

'Oh, I see,' she said, not really seeing. The names on Tarawa were bizarre. 'And are you really a curate?'

He nodded.

'Well, TC, thanks for the drinks.'

As he walked away she wondered what exactly a curate did. She made a mental note to ask him the next time she saw him. A dog barked way off. Daisy growled. Louisa shivered.

13

Clink! Clink! It was the sound of glass bottle against glass bottle. At first Louisa thought it was Reteta knocking on her window again, but glass on glass like that meant only one thing: toddy cutting. Clink! Clank! Reteta's husband cut toddy at dawn and dusk. Nothing stopped for it, not even funerals apparently. His toddy bottles were two old wine bottles tied together at the neck by a piece of string. They clunked noisily as they dangled by his side. The sound reminded her of when she was small in Edinburgh and the milkman still delivered bottles of milk to the house. That had been a friendly sound. She wasn't sure about this one. She didn't like Reteta's husband much. While Reteta ran around cooking and cleaning, he sat and scowled. The only thing she ever saw him do was cut toddy, although he did also go fishing.

He collected the toddy from two coconut palms in Louisa's garden. He chose the trees the day after he'd arrived and sliced wedge-shaped chunks out of their trunks. The gouges created foot holes, like steps, right to the top of the tree. It made it easier for him to shimmy up. At the top he'd sliced off a frond sapling and dangled one of the empty wine bottles beneath the sapling stump. When he returned twelve hours later, the bottle was full of the sap that had dripped into it. This was the toddy. He replaced the full bottle with an empty one. Every now and then he'd pick a new young frond and start again.

Louisa's mother had said toddy was the Gilbertese equivalent of milk, or rather used to be. Unfortunately, in her mum's opinion, it was gradually being replaced by sweet tea, her mum's least favourite drink. According to her mum, subsidised sugar—and subsidised flour and rice—was the scourge of Kiribati, and had turned attractive lithe people into tubs of lard. Louisa thought that was a bit like the pot calling the kettle black, given that Mum was a bit of a roly-poly, but Louisa was never foolish enough to say that to her face. Worse still, according to Mum, was sour toddy, a lethal alcoholic drink made from the fermented toddy. Sour toddy had been her dad's favourite brew. Her mum had banned it from the house, but of course that hadn't stopped him drinking it elsewhere. It had been the cause of lots of arguments between her parents. Ironically, he'd become teetotal shortly before walking out on them on Louisa's tenth birthday.

Only men cut toddy and so they couldn't be accused of spying on anyone, especially not on women, they sang songs as soon as they were in the top of the trees. And as if on cue, Reteta's husband burst into song. Louisa could understand Gilbertese reasonably well, but the singing was so garbled it was impossible to make out the words. Had Reteta not been at the funeral, his singing would have been Reteta's cue to light the fire and get the kettle on. As soon as the fire took, the children would shuffle out from under their mosquito net and huddle around the galloping yellow flames. Together, in the early morning chill, they'd cuddle into their mum and silently wait for the sweet milky tea to get hot.

Louisa felt much better today. The stomach cramps had gone and a good night's sleep had left her refreshed. It was six thirty. Time to get up. She'd find Joe's friends and employees and interview them. Today a motive for the killings and a suspect would emerge. She was sure of it. In the kitchen she popped a couple of slices of bread in the toaster—crumbs or not, she was hungry. She thought she could even have a fried egg but that immediately made her feel squeamish. No, jam would be fine. She opened the fridge to get some cold water.

The first bottle she pulled out was empty. So was the next one, and the next. They were all empty! No matter how many times she asked Reteta to fill the empty bottles with water from the filter and then put them back in the fridge, Reteta always managed to put the empty bottles back in the fridge. As a consequence there was never any cold filtered water to drink. She checked the giant clay filter—it reminded Louisa of a giant sideways standing, old fashioned, stone water bottle, like the one her great-granny used to have. The filter was half full. At least she had water to drink, even if it wasn't cold. Someone knocked on the kitchen door. It was Reteta.

'I thought you were at the funeral?' said Louisa looking out the kitchen window.

Reteta shook her head impatiently and clucked, 'I asked The Curate to bring you to the village. You didn't come. Men think girls who stay alone are nikira-n-roros.'

Louisa knew what a nikira-n-roro was. 'For the record, just because a woman lives alone, doesn't mean she sleeps around.'

'Men are stupid. They only think about one thing.'

'Well I'm fine, you've had a wasted trip.'

'No. I want you to pay me my wages. It was Pay Friday yesterday and you didn't pay me. I need money to buy food for the funeral.'

Louisa groaned. 'I completely forgot. Sorry. Give me a second and I'll unlock the door.'

Louisa paid Reteta sixty dollars a fortnight for doing a few hours of cleaning a week. Reteta had tried to refuse any sort of payment, saying it was tradition for those who didn't work in a family to support those who did by doing their housework. But Louisa was having none of it. Her mum had talked often enough about family obligation and Louisa knew there was a price to pay for everything, eventually. Louisa preferred giving Reteta cash, that way her dues were paid upfront.

Louisa wrapped a lava-lava around the bottom half of her body and unlocked the kitchen door. She tried not to grimace as she watched Reteta rub the soles of her bare feet on her shins and walk through the small galley kitchen and into the living room. Louisa wished Reteta would wear shoes. At least then she could take them off when she came in. Who knew what germs she brought into the house on the soles of her feet? Louisa always changed from her outdoor shoes into her house slippers when she got in. Well, they were more flip-flops than slippers. She kept a pair at the front door, the back door and the side kitchen door. She'd bought Reteta numerous sets of flip-flops to wear for when she was in the house, but they kept disappearing, given away, no doubt, to the various cousins who'd asked.

Usually, Louisa's spare cash was in the top drawer of her chest of drawers, the one and only piece of furniture in her bedroom. There should have been at least fifty dollars there, if not more. It was empty. She rummaged around in the drawer some more. Not even a ten cent coin. Louisa looked in all the other drawers. Nothing. She glanced below the bed, checked under her pillows, the sheets, everywhere: no, there was no money.

14

Someone in Reteta's family had taken her money. They were the only people who had access to her bedroom. It wasn't a lot but fifty bucks was fifty bucks, and they belonged to her. She couldn't imagine Reteta taking it, or TC, but what did she know? The kids were too young and the granny was scared of her own shadow. It had to be Reteta's chunk of a husband. But she couldn't accuse him with no proof. Her mother used to say that even with solid proof, and even on Tarawa, which she always referred to as a confused island, you had to be very careful before calling someone a thief. The Gilbertese custom of bubuti meant if someone in your family liked something of yours, you had to give it to them. It was a very egalitarian custom. It meant that assets, which were very few on a coral atoll, remained evenly distributed. In theory no one needed to thieve, at least, that's what her mother had told her. It was, therefore, all the greater an insult if you accused someone of stealing because the accusation suggested the thief had disregard of a custom that was enshrined in the Gilbertese way of life. Louisa decided to say nothing but she'd be careful and she'd be watching.

'I've not been to the bank. Can I pay you later?'

Reteta's face crumpled into a scowl. 'You have no money at all?'

Louisa took her purse from her bag. Inside was a twenty dollar note and some change. She emptied the note and the change on to the coffee table. 'I'll give you the rest on Monday.'

Reteta took the note and scooped up the change. 'We have to buy all the food for the funeral today.'

'I'm sorry,' said Louisa. She wanted to add, 'but if your thieving bastard of a husband hadn't pinched my last fifty bucks I'd have been able to give it to you.'

Reteta raised her eyebrows in an arc, as if fleetingly surprised, then smiled. 'You do not have a television in the house?'

'You know I don't,' said Louisa cautiously and wondering what was coming next.

'I can borrow a television set and a video player for one night. I can bring it here and we can watch a film.'

What felt like a gust of wind fluttered across the back of Louisa's neck. What was Reteta up to? 'I don't think so.'

'Why not? You don't like watching films?'

'Yes, I do, but that's a lot of hassle for one night and I'm busy.'

Reteta shook her head. 'No. It will be fun. You don't

have to watch. The cousins can watch with me.'

So that was it. A party at Louisa's. She didn't think so. 'No, Reteta. No cousins. I'm in the middle of a murder investigation. I need peace and quiet to work—'

'We will make no noise. I have invited the cousins here tomorrow afternoon after the funeral is finished for talks. They do not have a TV in their village. It will be a surprise for them to see a video.'

'Wouldn't it make more sense to take the TV to the village?'

'They have been very busy in that village looking after everyone. It is my turn now. We will stay outside. We will use a long wire from the house for electricity. You won't know we are here.'

'I suppose,' said Louisa reluctantly. 'As long as everyone stays outside.'

'Yes! Yes!' said Reteta, a smile spreading across her face. 'Oh, and Lulu, you must come to the funeral.'

'I didn't even know the man!'

'You are a relative. Your mother would be very cross if you did not go.'

'I'm investigating a murder!'

'We will have the ceremony of "lifting the head" tomorrow morning, this makes sure the dead spirit is properly carried out on the tide and reaches the Land of Shadows with no problems. You must come then.'

'But—'

'You are the only relative that has not come. It is very bad in our culture to not attend a funeral of a family member.'

'Okay!' she said, anything to shut her up. 'Okay! I'll see what I can do, but I'm not promising anything.'

Reteta nodded in approval. 'I have to leave now. Ko raba,' she said and tucked the twenty dollar note into her bra under her T-shirt.

Louisa walked Reteta to the door. 'Assuming I can make it, should I bring anything?'

'One lava-lava.'

Louisa took a cloth and the pine disinfectant from the cupboard under the sink and went into the living room. First she wiped the wooden arms of the armchair where Reteta had been sitting and then she wiped the coffee table. She felt bad doing this because she knew Reteta's personal hygiene was impeccable and she was also an excellent cleaner—it was one of the reasons Louisa let her in the house. But Reteta had spent all night and the day before in her cousin's village. Louisa had been in the villages, she knew what they were like: chickens and pigs as well as mangy dogs and even the odd coconut rat roamed free. She was taking no chances but at least she'd not felt the need to revert to the rule of four. She was pleased about that.

Back in the kitchen Louisa put her cold toast on her plate. The problem now was deciding which cup for her tea. It was a silly habit but she liked to use the same knife and fork and plate and cup. Since she'd dropped her usual cup yesterday when The Curate had startled her—she found it difficult to refer to a grown man as TC—she needed a new one. She'd brought four bone china mugs with her from the UK. All identical except for the colour: yellow, pink, blue and green. She'd dropped the green one. After a long think she picked the pink one. She thought the dirt would show up on it more clearly. Even though it wasn't dirty, she washed it under the tap and dried it with a fresh towel from the drawer.

Louisa's fussiness, as her mum called it, had started when she was eight after the family had moved from Tarawa to Edinburgh. First she'd gone off certain foods, fish and bananas in particular. Then she'd started showering three, sometimes four times a day. This was followed by not being able to wear her clothes if they'd not been ironed and folded the right way—and if she'd tried something on and then decided not to wear it, she had to wash the item of clothing all over again. She was also fastidiously tidy. If her mum brought a cup of tea into the living room, she'd have to get up and check in the kitchen that the teabag had been thrown away in the bin and not left on the counter, making a mess. Didn't matter her mum had told her she'd put it in the bin. Then she'd started washing her hands four times. And then doing everything else four times. If she didn't, voices told her something terrible would happen to her mother and father, if it hadn't already happened to her father because she'd not seen him since he'd walked out on them when she was ten. She wouldn't eat in a restaurant unless she was able to check the state of the kitchen beforehand, which was, more often than not, impossible. She'd thought of herself as a bit fussy, nothing more. Then she'd overheard one of the coppers at work call her a screwball. It had infuriated her: she worked twice as hard as all of them, got better results and yet just because she liked to wash her hands a lot and maybe wear gloves more than others, they ridiculed her behind her back. It had shocked her. She made an appointment with her doctor. He'd recommended she see a cognitive therapist. She went. Not that she told anyone, not even her mum.

The therapist said she had issues to do with self-esteem and insecurity and her obsessive behaviour was her way of trying to control her environment and so feel less insecure. She thought it was all crap, but she didn't want anyone else to think she was crazy, especially not anyone at work. Besides, she hated the voices. They never let up. The therapist said she could take Prozac or do therapy exercises. She did the exercises. Her behaviour got better. When she'd applied for the job on Tarawa it never occurred to her that hygiene would be an issue—her memories of her childhood were blissful and 'bliss' to her equalled 'germ-free'. But on Tarawa nothing could have been further from the truth.

15

Sergeant Tebano lay stretched out flat on his back across the counter of the inquiry desk, snoring. His police shirt flapped down either side of his heaving bare chest. Louisa marched up to him and gave him a sharp, short prod on his sleeve with a pen from her bag. He half-jumped, half-fell off the desk.

'Do you think it is appropriate to sleep while on duty?' she said coldly. Tebano staggered to his feet. 'In case you are in doubt, it is not! And button up your shirt. Your uniform has to be respected at all times. If you don't respect it, civilians will not respect it, neither will your fellow officers!'

Very slowly, one by one, Tebano buttoned up his shirt. His eyes were bloodshot and his thick chin was covered in stubble. He refused to look at her.

Louisa took a deep breath. She knew from her mother that in Kiribati culture it was considered bad manners to look someone directly in the eye, but nevertheless it was difficult for her not to get angry when he kept refusing to look at her. She forced herself to stay calm. 'This is a murder investigation. Everyone needs to be focused. What happened yesterday at the hospital?'

'Nothing.'

'Did you leave the body with the coroner or not?'

'Of course we leave it,' he said, squeezing his police shirt over his big stomach and tucking it into brown shorts.

'And what did the coroner say?'

'He say the freezer very dirty.'

'And?'

'He send you his report when it done. I go home now.'

'You will not go home!' He was the only sergeant she had and she needed him. 'We're in the middle of a murder inquiry.' She hated the tone she was using with him, it reminded her of her mother but he seemed to bring out the absolute worst in her.

He finally faced her. 'I'm sleepy.'

'You'll just have to wake up.'

He scowled and looked away again.

'The deceased has been identified. His name is Joe—'

'I know his name,' he said sullenly, still not looking at her.

'Good! Then you'll know he exported sea cucumbers. I want you to find out everything you can about him and his business. I want to know who worked for him. Did he have rivals, associates, friends? Where is the business based? I want to know if he was a fair person to work for, or a mean person. I want you to find out anything and everything that might help us know better who he was. The more we know about him, the closer we'll get to understanding why someone wanted to kill him.'

Tebano sniggered. 'This is not CSI.'

'What did you say?' said Louisa quietly.

He yawned. 'Michael,' he nodded towards Constable Michael, who was sheepishly coming out of the toilet. 'He will help you. I too tired.'

'You're a policeman. Tired is what you do,' said Louisa, only just managing to stop her voice from shaking. 'Let me remind you that I have a letter of authority from Assistant Commissioner Nakibae ordering you to do what I ask!'

Tebano threw her a filthy look, turned and began walking out of the station. 'You only a sergeant like me and you a woman. I don't need to take orders from you.'

Louisa pulled her shoulders back. 'You will follow orders,' she shouted, 'and be back at midday for a debriefing or I'll go straight to Assistant Commissioner Nakibae and have you kicked off the force!'

Tebano continued to slowly saunter out the building.

Constable Michael gave a small cough.

Louisa turned to him. 'You do not sleep while you are in uniform, on duty or off. And, you never, ever, sleep on the front desk! I could have his stripes right now for being on that counter alone.'

'It was Pay Friday yesterday. There were many drunks and disorderly people.' He nodded to the cells.

For the first time Louisa noticed one of the little cell doors was closed. A dull snorting-cum-wheezing noise came from behind it.

'There's someone in the cells?'

'Eng. A naughty man got drunk and had a fight. When I arrived an hour ago Tebano has been on duty all night. It is not easy dealing with drunk people all on your own.'

Louisa instructed him to open the cell door. Inside a heavy, middle-aged man, wearing only shorts, lay flat out on the floor. His face was swollen and covered in bloody welts. One eye was so puffed up Louisa couldn't see the eye socket. 'What happened?'

'Tebano had to defend himself.'

'Tebano beat him up?' Louisa groaned

'The man was drunk and hurting people.'

'Hasn't Tebano heard of reasonable force, the emphasis being on reasonable?'

'It is not easy when you are the only policeman in charge.'

At some point Louisa was going to have to have a word with someone about Tebano. But not yet. She needed all the help she could get. Even Tebano. She took a deep breath. 'You'd better get a nurse from the Betio clinic to check him over.'

Michael nodded.

'Do you think he's going to do what I asked?'

Michael tentatively lifted up his bowed head. 'He's old fashioned, that's all. He doesn't like a woman telling him what to do, but he's also a policeman. He'll do it.'

'He'd better,' said Louisa.

Michael took a piece of paper from his top pocket. 'There's a message for you. It came late last night. From Jill Wilson. She wants to tell you something. Can you call her? This is her number.'

16

Jill lived in an orange painted B breezeblock bungalow with a corrugated iron roof, off the main road on the lagoon side of Bairiki, just along from the government buildings and on the same side of town as the President of Kiribati. It was not unlike Louisa's house. After unsuccessfully trying to phone Jill, a quick call to the Ministry of Justice had got Louisa her address. She parked the police car halfway up a long narrow drive. The curtains were all drawn. Both the screen door and front door behind it were closed. Louisa knocked on the outer screen door. Nothing. She knocked again. 'Jill? Are you there?'

A shuffling sound. From behind the main door.

'It's Detective Sergeant Townsend.'

The door in front of her opened a crack. Jill peered round the side of it. 'I expected you to phone me.'

'I tried. There was no answer,' she said, pulling open the screen door. 'Can you let me in, please?'

Jill opened the solid door halfway. 'I'm busy.'

'You left a message to say you had something to tell me.' What on earth was the woman wearing? Louisa was no fashionista but a clinging yellow vest top over sagging purple jogging bottoms was not a good look.

'I'm not in the mood now.' Jill began to close the door.

Louisa stuck out her foot and prevented Jill closing the door. Enough mucking about. 'Either you let me in—or you come down to the station. You decide.'

Jill's cheeks glowed pink. A lump of white brain coral the size of a large cooking pot sat on the floor just inside the house. She dragged it across the floor, propped the door open with it, turned and disappeared inside.

Inside, it was ridiculously warm, even for Tarawa, and the clammy air was thick with the smell of sweat and fried eggs. The only light seemed to come from the open door behind Louisa. It took a second or two for her eyes to adjust. All the windows were draped with heavy brown blankets. Jill stood by the nearest window and pinched the edge of one of the blanket-cum-curtains to the window frame with a clothes peg. The blankets completely blocked out the daylight. It was like a cave. What on earth was going on?

Jill said in a defensive tone, 'I'm not mad.'

'I didn't say you were,' said Louisa, wondering if she was.

'I saw you look.' Jill nipped the curtain with a second peg. 'When the louvres are shut tight it's virtually impossible for anyone on the outside to muck about and open them. But even if they do, they'll still have to get through the curtains and they'll not find that easy.' She stepped back and smiled. 'A lack of natural daylight is a small price to pay for privacy.'

'And no air,' said Louisa, feeling blisters of sweat forming across her forehead. 'Can you at least switch the fan on, and the light?'

Jill nodded. 'Sure.' She walked to the fan and light switches on the wall.

'Who exactly are you wanting to be private from?'

'You mean apart from those nutters at the Ambo Lagoon Club, and a murderer?'

'You're in no danger from the villagers. It was

unfortunate—'

Jill mock-laughed. 'Unfortunate? Let them try and stone you and see how you feel!'

Louisa shook her head. 'The villagers have been warned not to try to take the law into their hands ever again. Their bark is worse than their bite.'

'You're not the one who was attacked!' Jill turned the chunky fan switch.

The overhead blades swirled into motion and Louisa let the air whoosh over her. It felt good, even if it was warm. 'I appreciate it must have been unpleasant.'

'In one way what happened yesterday was a good thing, because it's made me think about what I'm doing here.' She flicked the light switch. The white strip light blinked on and off a couple of times and then stayed on

'And what are you doing here?'

'Nothing! Absolutely nothing. That's the point. It was a mistake for me to come.' She shook her head and her hair swung into her eyes. She swept it behind her ears. 'I'm not like the other women. I can't hang about and do nothing. When Paul's contract comes to an end we'll not renew.' Jill headed to the kitchen. 'Fancy a drink of water?'

'No,' said Louisa, wondering if Paul knew about Jill's decision for him not to renew his contract. She looked around the room. It was not unlike her own living room: a square with one set of windows overlooking the front and one set overlooking the back of the house, except, of course, Louisa didn't have a set of blankets pegged across her windows. The furniture was pretty much the same too: a round coffee table stood in the middle of the floor, surrounded by four utilitarian armchairs, with identical square, tan covered, foam cushions, back and bottom. A wooden dining table with six dining chairs took up one corner of the room and a sideboard the other. It seemed surprisingly empty. It was as if Jill and hubby Paul hadn't bothered to unpack.

Jill returned with a tumbler of water in each hand, put them on the coffee table, then flopped in the chair nearest her. 'You can sit down.'

'I'm fine. You wanted to tell me something?' It was hard to believe this relaxed woman was the same anxious woman as yesterday. But she had been in shock the day before and shock made people behave out of character.

Jill crumpled her nose. 'I've been thinking about it. I think I may have seen that dagger before somewhere.'

A tingle of excitement fluttered in the pit of Louisa's stomach. She took the grubby handle, still wrapped in the cling film, out of her bag and placed it on the coffee table, ignoring the glasses of water. 'This is the handle.'

Jill leaned forward and peered at it. 'It's those bits of purple nylon woven together with the pandanus. They're so tacky.'

Louisa smiled in what she hoped was a reassuring manner. 'Was it part of a display in someone's house, or in a tourist shop?'

Jill suddenly leaned back. 'It gives me the willies. That's another reason I want to leave, I don't feel safe any more.'

Louisa put the handle back in her bag and picked up the water again. 'When you least expect it, you'll remember where you've seen it, and when you do, get in touch immediately. What about Paul, could he have seen it before?'

'You'd have to ask him. He's out running just now. There's a crowd of them.' She sneered. 'They call themselves the Hash Harriers. After the run is over they pig out on booze and food. They're meeting at Nicole's today.'

'Nicole who runs the nursery?'

She nodded.

'I need to talk to her.'

'Her house is half a mile down the road. You can't miss

it, it's the biggest house in the row. Someone lays a paper trail and the others follow. In this heat! They're bonkers. Christine says—'

'She's there too?'

'They're all there.' Jill grinned. 'She was furious that you took the keys out of her car yesterday. She knew him, you know, the dead man. They all did.'

Louisa frowned. 'Really?'

'He was one of the runners. Apparently, he was here on Thursday evening.'

'The deceased, whom you say you'd never met before, was here in your house, very probably on the very night he died?' said Louisa, trying not to bristle.

'I didn't see him, if that's what you're trying to say. It was Paul's turn to have everyone round. Joe, that's the dead man's name—'

'I know.' Jill was beginning to get on her nerves. 'Was he or was he not in your house?'

'He was in the garden. It was Paul's turn to hold the barbecue after the hash. It was packed.'

'And you didn't go out into the garden once or look out the window. Isn't that a little odd?'

Jill waved her arms in a gesture of despair. 'I don't mind Nicole and Christine, even though they go on about their kids all the time, especially Christine. But the other women? All they talk about is the food they can't get, or how awful it is not to have biological soap powder. They're on a coral atoll. Duh!' She made a face. 'Laying paper trails and making small talk while playing silly drinking games isn't for me. I'd rather stay in and read my book, which is what I did.'

'And you're absolutely certain you didn't see Joe?'

'How many times do I have to tell you? No.'

'Thanks for your time. If you remember where you saw the dagger, don't forget to let me know.'

She snorted. 'Paul used to hate running, and joggers even more so. Now he can't keep away from them. It's this place, it changes people. And not for the better.'

17

Jill puzzled Louisa. Having had time to recover from the trauma of seeing a brutally murdered man and being chased by an angry mob, Jill seemed perfectly confident and capable, if not rather outspoken. Not the kind of person who would see her husband embracing a much younger woman without saying something. Yet, that's what happened yesterday. Maybe they had an open relationship? Or maybe she'd still been in shock from the events of the morning? Not that it was any of Louisa's business. Paul having an affair, or not, had nothing to do with the case. Her only concern was whether Jill had seen the dagger before, and if so, where and when.

Louisa parked on the road beneath two rambling purple bougainvillea and a sweet smelling frangipani tree. It was as close as she could get to Nicole's house. Judging from the number of 4x4s already parked in front of her, the hash was busy. At the end of the drive a woman stood under the front veranda of a sprawling house. Beside her two trellis tables groaned with bowls of crispy salads, quiches, cold meats and what looked like home-made breads. The woman looked exquisitely cool in a three-quarter length, sleeveless, pale blue, silk wrap-over dress, which set off her perfect alabaster skin. Louisa recognised her immediately. It was Christine.

'You're late. They left half an hour ago!' she yelled brightly. Her bobbed blonde hair was swept off her face by a navy blue ribbon. Her face fell. 'It's you.'

'I'd like to ask you a few questions.'

Christine's eyes narrowed to a slit. 'I hope you're here to tell us the murderer has been caught. It's very unsettling thinking there's a madman running around stabbing people in the eyes.'

'You'll understand that I can't discuss an ongoing investigation. When I saw you yesterday at the Ambo Lagoon Club, why didn't you tell me you knew the deceased?'

She looked puzzled. 'You didn't ask.'

'Not true. I specifically asked if you had information to tell me.'

Christine raised her shoulders in a dismissive shrug. 'It never occurred to me that you wouldn't know who he was.'

'But how did you know it was Joe? I didn't even know who he was at that point.'

'What are you trying to say?'

'You can answer my question here or at Betio Police Station.'

Christine glared at Louisa for a second or two then a smile shot across her face. 'I feel we've got off to a bad start. Are you a mother?'

Louisa took out her notebook and shook her head.

'You'd know what I meant if you were. When I heard Joe had been found dead in the play hut I couldn't believe it. My children were there. What if they'd seen him? What if the killer had still been around? By the time I got to the club I was beside myself. Look, why not stay and eat with us? It's Nicole's turn to hold the hash, she always makes too much. Food's a bit of a thing with her, she has to outdo everyone else. Given how little the locals have, it can be embarrassing.'

'I'll pass on the food, delicious as it looks. Thank you, though.' Louisa noted that the woman had performed an about turn in front of her. 'Joe? How exactly did you know he was in the play hut?'

'It's very simple. My house-girl's husband is the cousin of the Ambo manager. When Sammy saw Joe he immediately phoned his brother-in-law, who came round to tell me. I told the other mothers and that was it.'

'And what can you tell me about Joe?'

Christine flicked at something on her bare arm. Her nails were lilac and immaculately shaped. 'I didn't really know him. He tended to stick with the men. When did you arrive on Tarawa?'

'Sorry?' said Louisa.

'Have you been here long? I've not seen you around.'

Louisa didn't think it was any of Christine's business but despite herself she said, 'A couple of months.'

'No way?' Christine looked genuinely shocked. 'But where have you been? Apart from the hash, we have yacht racing, bridge nights, tennis and there's the mahjong, the film nights and the cocktail parties. You've not been to any of them.'

Louisa smiled coldly, 'I've been working.'

'What about after work? What does your husband do?'

'I don't have one. If we could just get back to the questions—'

'I mean your partner, then.'

'You misunderstand, I'm single.'

Christine raised her eyebrows in surprise then said, 'How about a Buck's Fizz?'

'This early?' She shook her head. 'Plain orange juice would be nice though. And I still have some questions.'

'Sure,' said Christine, pouring juice from an ornate cut-glass jug into a high-ball glass and handing it to Louisa. 'But I'll have to sit,' she nodded to her ankle. 'I stumbled at the beginning of Thursday's run and twisted my ankle. I had to go to the hospital and get it bandaged. It's beginning to ache now.' Louisa followed Christine to a vast Moroccan style tent set up in the garden at the side of the house and overlooking the ocean.

Plastic chairs had been placed under it in a half circle. They were the only people in the garden. The chairs were gleaming, they were so clean. Louisa sat down.

'I believe the Thursday hash meeting was at Jill's house?'

Christine nodded. 'I helped Paul with the food. Jill had refused. I don't know why Paul puts up with her.' Christine frowned, then smiled. 'Sorry, I shouldn't have said that, but Jill can be really annoying.'

'Even so, you gave her a lift from the Ambo Club yesterday?'

'She was distraught. How could I not give her a lift?'

'Did you see her on Thursday evening?'

'You mean at the hash meeting?' Christine laughed. 'Paul said she'd wanted him to cancel. When he wouldn't she got in a mood and refused to come out the house. So no, I didn't see her. What was the big deal? Even if she didn't want to run she could have helped with the food. They're supposed to be a couple.'

'And what about Joe?' Louisa sipped her juice—it was freshly squeezed. 'When did you last see him?'

Christine cupped her Buck's Fizz in both hands and leaned forward. 'We've all been talking about that. It was at the Thursday hash. He was one of the last to set off at five forty. Paul and I were the only two runners remaining after he'd gone, and Jill, of course, but she was inside.'

'You don't remember seeing him again at all?'

'I twisted my ankle just after he left. Paul took me to the hospital. It was chaos there. I didn't get seen to for ages. Dr Andrus, he's one of the UN volunteer doctors, he fixed my foot and brought me home around ten.'

'And do you know of any reason why Joe would be in the play hut?'

She shook her head. 'As far as I know he's never been in it.'

'And how many people were at the hash on Thursday evening?'

'Probably about the same as are here today, twenty-five, possibly more? They'll be arriving soon. It'll be best to give them a few seconds to recover before you ask your questions.'

There was a shout. They both looked. A chubby boy of about four appeared from the side of the house. He was in his bare feet and wore blue shorts and a white T-shirt, which had a drawing of stick boy on it. He was being chased by a scowling girl, slightly older than him. She wore a floating, yellow cheese cloth dress and her long fair hair was held off her face by a Hello Kitty alice band.

'Hey, little man, where are your shoes?' said Christine, getting out of her chair. The boy stopped running and caught his breath. The girl, who Louisa assumed to be his sister, caught up with him, grabbed his shoulders and threw him to the ground. The boy started to bawl.

'Stop that right now!' said Christine.

'I hate him!' screamed the girl.

'Sorry,' said Christine to Louisa, 'I have to deal with this.' She walked towards the children. 'Right you two, what's this about?'

'She started it,' said the boy in a squeaky voice, pointing a podgy finger at his sister.

'No, I didn't!' said the girl, stomping her feet.

Christine looked back at Louisa. 'If you need to ask me anything else, you can catch me later. Kids, eh?'

18

'Honk honk!' A middle-aged expatriate man brandishing an

old fashioned horn half-jogged, half-staggered around the side of the house and towards the tent where Louisa sat. His hair was plastered to his forehead with sweat. She thought he looked like he might pass out. His gaunt face was red and his legs and arms, all string and bones, flailed about awkwardly. He waved to her as he pushed past towards a barbecue area set up between the tent and the ocean. Louisa nodded from where she sat sipping her fresh orange juice. A handful of cheeky Gilbertese children, in bare feet, ran alongside him. They were followed by a handful of young Gilbertese women, all long legs, long hair, and cool, oh so cool. Louisa reckoned the most running they'd done was from the front of the house to the back.

The man honked the horn again before collapsing on to the sand. One of the pretty young women brought him a cold can of Foster's she'd taken from one of two giant open white cool boxes by the barbecue. One held cans of Foster's, the other soft drink cans, all bedded in baths of ice.

More and more expatriate men and women staggered into the back garden. Hot and bothered, with their T-shirts stuck to their backs and chests and their shorts flapping hopelessly around their trembling thighs, they hobbled towards the BBQ. The adults were followed by a smattering of expatriate children in gleaming white trainers. Louisa had no idea there were so many foreigners on Tarawa who liked to run. As they reached the BBQ, they either threw themselves onto the ground, or collapsed into a chair. People laughed and shouted, chatted and drank. The noise grew louder and louder. More and more arrived. Then in the middle of all the chaos there was an enormous cheer. Louisa turned and saw a very tanned expatriate woman being carried towards the back veranda by three burly expatriate men.

'What's this all about?' she asked a woman.

'Nicole was last to arrive,' shouted the woman. 'She has to do a down-down.'

'A what?'

The lady yelled. 'She'll have to down a yard of lager in one go!'

'And what if she doesn't want to?'

The woman gave Louisa a funny look. Above a sea of heads Louisa watched as Tom waddled on to the veranda. She cursed him under her breath. She should have known that pile of shit would be here. He wore giant red and yellow checkered cotton shorts, a red short-sleeved T-shirt, with spreading sweat stains under his arms and a yellow hand towel-cum-scarf round his neck. He carried a long slender glass full of lager raised above his head and handed it to the woman Louisa now knew to be Nicole. Bundles of loose black curls had been swept in a straggly bun on top of her head. Despite being covered in sweat, unlike almost everyone else, she still managed to look attractive.

'Down! Down! Down!' chanted the crowd.

At first Nicole drank the yellow liquid very slowly, but as the chanting grew quicker and louder, she drank faster and faster. 'Down! Down! Down!' They were almost hysterical. Unable to gulp any more, Nicole thrust the glass upside down above her head and what was left of the drink splashed all over her body. A roar ripped through the throng. Nicole made a mock bow and walked off, lager dripping from her face.

A tall skinny man with a goatee beard joined Tom, who'd remained standing on the back veranda. The skinny man raised his hands for everyone to stop. 'G'day gents, ladies. Just want to say we've only one of our special limited edition hash T-shirts left.' Someone booed. Louisa couldn't see who it was. The man smirked. 'And the bloody lucky man who gets it is our most enthusiastic hasher, Paul Wilson. Here, Paul, mate, come and get your T-shirt!'

Paul appeared from another side of the garden and climbed up the steps of the veranda to take his T-shirt. Most people cheered, some booed again but they were drowned out.

'Speech!' yelled someone.

Paul grinned, 'Nicole tells me the food is ready. Let's eat.'

'Well, g'day!' said Nicole, appearing from nowhere and putting her arm round Louisa's shoulder. 'You're the new detective. You caught the bastard who did it yet?'

Louisa carefully unwrapped herself from Nicole's hearty, lager smelling, embrace. She had an Aussie drawl but Louisa didn't know enough about accents to know where exactly in Australia she was from. She suspected the east coast. 'It's early days. If you don't mind, can I ask you a few questions about Joe?'

'No worries. On you go.'

'You know Joe was found in the nursery hut?'

'No one's talking about anything else, that and the eyes. Were they really gouged?'

She ignored the question. 'Do you know any reason why he would have been there?'

'You're kidding me, right?' said Nicole seriously, 'He hated ankle-biters. What do you reckon, Paul?'

'It's Louisa, isn't it?' said Paul, arriving from the veranda. He gave her his hand to shake. 'I've seen you around the Ministry of Justice, haven't I?'

Louisa didn't want to take his hand, but she had no choice. He had a firm grip. She was sure his hands were clean. She wouldn't think about it. 'I'm working from out of Betio police station at the moment.'

'She wants to know about Joe,' said Nicole. 'I was just saying how much he hated nippers.'

Paul laughed. He was definitely not child-friendly.' He became serious. 'It's a shocking thing to have happened.'

Nicole nodded. 'The worst.'

'They gave you the T-shirt?' said Christine, arriving

from the food table with a plate of green tagliatelle. 'Ian had hoped he'd get it.'

Paul held it out to her. 'He can have it.'

'Ian wouldn't want to get it that way.'

'What wouldn't I want?' said a tall man in his thirties with fair, almost white hair, cut very short to minimise his baldness.

'The T-shirt,' said Christine, 'I was saying how much you wanted it.'

'No I didn't,' Ian said flatly.

'Oh,' said Christine, looking slightly puzzled. 'Well, I must have misunderstood. Want some food?' She gave him the plate, which he took.

Ian turned to Louisa. 'You're the one looking into Joe's death?'

Louisa nodded. 'That's right.' No handshake from Ian, she noted, relieved.

'You'll have your work cut out. The locals aren't in the habit of telling the truth.'

'Hey, mate, you can't judge a whole nation based on your negative experiences,' said Nicole.

'It's a fact. They put family above the law.'

'It's a cultural thing!' said Nicole, raising her voice, then lowering it, 'which you've never really understood.'

'You're all assuming Joe was killed by a local person?' said Louisa interrupting.

'Wasn't he?' said Ian.

She smiled at the small group. 'It's odd. You all knew him but no one seems upset by his death. Didn't you like him?'

There was a brief uncomfortable silence before Nicole said, 'He was a mate we ran with, that's it.'

The others nodded.

'He never socialised with anyone?' said Louisa.

'He was a loner,' said Nicole, swiping a string of

tagliatelle from Ian's plate, to Ian—and Christine's—obvious disgust.

'There was that one time when he got the men pissed at the Royal Saloon,' said Paul.

'Shit! Forgot about that,' said Nicole grinning, 'Their wives were so hacked off.'

'But usually he kept to himself,' said Paul.

'What's the Royal Saloon?' said Louisa.

'The Royal Saloon is a bar-cum-den-of-iniquity in Betio,' said Paul, stealing the string of pasta from out of Nicole's hand and eating it before she could stop him.

'The hash girls are never away from the place,' said Christine, frowning at Paul and Nicole.

'The "hash girls"?' Her mother had certainly never told Louisa about them.

'The I-Kiribati girls,' said Nicole, nodding in the direction of the pretty girls Louisa had spotted earlier.

'He was investigated for bribing customs officials,' said Ian.

'Was he?' Was this a lead?

'Nothing came of it, but I wouldn't have trusted him.'

Louisa made a mental note to look up the investigation. 'Can I show you this? It's the handle from the ceremonial dagger that killed Joe. Do any of you recognise it?'

Christine pulled a face. 'That's gross!'

'Could it have been left in the nursery hut?'

'Not a chance,' said Nicole.

'Ceremonial daggers are lethal, you can't have them anywhere near little ones,' said Christine.

'So none of you have never seen it before?'

They all shook their heads.

'You sure?'

They nodded a second time.

'I'm shooting through for a shower,' said Nicole, tearing

away the band that was holding her dark curls in place and letting her hair fall onto her shoulders in a chaotic tumble. 'Then I'm going to grab a bite.'

19

Louisa was more than a little disappointed. Of all the people she'd talked to so far at Nicole's house, all twenty-six of them had been at the Thursday evening run, and no one, local or expatriate, had recognised the dagger handle. On the plus side, she had learnt quite a bit more about Joe. Not only had he been obsessed with running, so much so that he'd never missed a hash run, he'd also been a bit of a loner. Possibly a drinker too. But that wasn't conclusive—while some people said he liked a drink, others said he was teetotal. What was not in doubt was that Joe was last seen alive on Thursday evening at five forty leaving Paul and Jill's garden, heading towards Bairiki centre (which is in the opposite direction from the Ambo). He'd been dressed in white jogging shorts and matching white vest, cream ankle socks and expensive white Nike running shoes.

What was also not in dispute was that Joe was vain. He liked his designer labels and would have never worn a local lava-lava or anything remotely like a sarong. When last seen he was carrying a small black canvas rucksack, which contained his water bottle and a hand towel, which he took on every run. This canvas bag had vanished along with his running clothes and shoes. Louisa closed her notebook. Somewhere between Thursday evening and Friday morning Joe had lost his clothes, his shoes, his running bag, and his life. The lava-lava they'd found on the body appeared not to have belonged to him. So where had it come from?

As for everyone's whereabouts, only three people seemed not to have been with the hash group for the whole evening: Christine, who was at the hospital getting her foot seen to (which still needed to be corroborated); Jill, who'd been inside and wasn't strictly a hasher, and seemed genuinely not to have known Joe; and Jill's husband, Paul, who had taken Christine to the hospital and returned directly to the hash. The Ambo Club was on the way to the hospital. Paul would have passed it there and back. He could have stopped on the return trip. It didn't take long to kill someone. But what motive would he have had? Motive was everything. Her tummy rumbled. She was hungry. In fact, she was more than hungry, she was starving. It was way past noon. She had just one person left to interview and then she could leave.

Tom reminded her of one of the Three Little Pigs, the smug, sanctimonious one, who'd built his house with bricks. She found him drinking by the big cool box.

'I need to ask you a few questions about Thursday night.'

Tom took a swig of beer from the blue can in his hand. He sneered. 'No thanks, then?'

'Pardon?'

'Nakibae was shitting himself. All his detectives are in New Zealand and Beru and an I-Matang is murdered on his patch. He asked me if I thought you were a capable detective. I said yes. I could have said no. So, you see, if it wasn't for me, you'd still be lounging in the bowels of the ministry writing up workshops that no one wants to attend. You owe me.'

'Sure,' said Louisa sarcastically. As her European Commission Office representative on Tarawa, Tom was the closest thing she had to a boss on the island. 'Joe?'

He wiped his sweaty mouth with the back of his pudgy hand. 'You know nothing about how things are done here. You perceived my help as an obstruction.'

She almost laughed out loud at the idea of Tom being helpful. She'd gone to him various times almost in tears with frustration at the lack of support she was getting from the local police. He'd promised to help but did nothing. 'Thursday evening? Did you see Joe?'

He lifted his drink can and slowly drained it.

Louisa waited. The very last time she'd gone to see him, he'd made a pass at her. What had he been thinking of? The creep! She'd been furious and told him so. That had cemented their hatred of each other.

'I left for my run before Joe, at five twenty.' Tom chucked his empty beer can in the direction of a round plastic bin next to the cool box. The can missed the target and landed on the scrubby grass. 'I never saw him again after that.'

'And how did you get on with him?'

'I didn't.' Tom helped himself to another can from the box.

'You had nothing to do with him at all?'

'I didn't like him and he didn't like me. And now, if that's everything, you will have to excuse me, there are people waiting for me.'

Louisa watched him waddle in the direction of a group of young I-Kiribati girls. One of them waved to him. The others giggled. Louisa dropped her notebook into her bag. It was time to get back to the station. The hash horn suddenly honked. A ruddy-faced woman stood on a chair in the middle of the garden.

'Everyone!' she barked. 'Attention!'

People began to gather around. Louisa became wedged in the middle of the group. Two women in front of her whispered furtively in each other's ears. Louisa could just about hear what they were saying:

'You know, she was seen again?' the first hushed voice said.

'Where?'

'The Betio Causeway, of course.'

'When?'

'Skinny-dipping time,' hissed the first voice.

'Was she alone?' said the other voice.

The first voice shook her head.

'Not that man, again?' said the second voice.

Someone pushed into Louisa. It was Nicole. The women in front shuffled out of earshot.

'What's she doing standing on one of my chairs?' said Nicole, clearly furious.

'I'm sure you all know about the tragedy?' said the woman on the chair, pausing to blow her nose. A murmur rippled through the crowd. 'Joe was a man of dynamic energy,' she said between sniffs. 'I know I speak for us all when I say we will miss him. Let's hope the murderer will be found and swiftly brought to justice.'

'Hear! Hear!' a man yelled.

'Bitch! She should have talked to me if she wanted to make a speech in my garden!'

'I ask now, in memory of dear Joe, for everyone to show our respects by stopping what we are doing for one minute. When I toot the horn, we will be silent. Then I'll toot it again after the minute is up.' The woman tooted the horn, and the garden fell silent. A Gilbertese girl started to giggle. Someone tutted. The horn honked to signal the end of the minute and the crowd immediately began to disperse.

'She didn't even like Joe!' said Nicole to no one.

'I thought it was rather touching,' said Christine, who was now next to Nicole.

'Christine, love,' said Ian, appearing behind her, 'you're getting burnt. Time to cover up.'

'I have sun cream on.'

'Yes, but you know how sensitive your skin is.'

Christine smiled tightly. 'That's why I have cream on.'

'Your shoulders are already turning.'

'It's okay,' she said, her voice tensing.

'Love, it is not okay,' said Ian calmly but firmly.

'How many times do I have to tell you,' said Christine, her smile straining to stay in place, 'I've got cream on.'

'Cream is not enough. Look what happened the last time.'

A flush of pink flashed across Christine's cheeks. 'Excuse me, I think I'll check on the little ones.' She turned away from her husband and walked towards a group of children haring about the shore. Ian frowned and hurried after her.

'Bloody oath!' said Nicole, 'Christine stood up to Ian. It's a first!'

'Really?' said Louisa.

Nicole smirked. 'The worm has turned and about time!'

'That's a bit mean.' Paul had a fork in one hand and a plate in the other, smothered in green salad, quiche and steaming, buttered new potatoes.

'No it's not. The biggest shocker about Joe being killed is that it wasn't Ian.'

'Nicole!' said Paul, stabbing one of the potatoes with the fork. 'You can't say things like that!'

'Yes, I can,' said Nicole.

'Why would anyone want to kill Ian?' Louisa was a great believer in gossip, it was how you found out what was really going on—as long as you read between the lines.

'Ian works for the Department of Trade and Commerce. He has final say over who gets granted export licences. He's always knocking applications back, especially if the applicant doesn't brown tongue him! Look at Joe! He applied for a licence to export shark fins at least three times that I know of. Each time Ian turned him down. No reason given. He did it because he's a bastard.'

'I am sure Ian would have had his reasons,' said Paul, 'You shouldn't speculate.'

Nicole shrugged. 'I'm hungry. I'm going to grab a bite.'

Louisa watched Nicole disappear.

'I knew she didn't like Ian,' said Paul, wiping his fingers on the T-shirt still under his arm, 'but I didn't know she hated him.'

'Louisa nodded at the T-shirt under Paul's arm. 'Why did they give it to you?'

He licked some crumbs of quiche pastry from his lips. 'Who knows? Maybe because I'm a single guy?'

Louisa frowned. 'You're married.'

Paul blushed. He'd not shaved and had a layer of stubble. 'What I mean is I don't have children. Some of the blokes are sick of the mums bringing their kids to the hash. The special edition T-shirt is part of their "keep the hash a kid-free zone" campaign. None of the family men got one.'

'Giving the T-shirt to a woman wasn't an option?'

'None of them would have wanted it,' said Paul.

'Why?' said Louisa.

'Take a look,' said Paul, chucking it over to her.

Louisa threw open the black top. There was a square white box on the front. One long squashed up sentence in black lettering dominated the white square. At first Louisa couldn't work out what it said. The words were all bunched up together like an advert she'd seen once for Coke, or Pepsi. She read as far as 'Lipsmackingfannylovingtitgrabbing—' Louisa was shocked. 'You're not embarrassed to wear this sexist rubbish?'

Paul smiled. 'It's just a bit of harmless fun.'

'It's offensive!'

'That's what Nicole said. You're taking the women's side now!'

'Yep,' said Louisa, walking away. 'Got that in one.' Being on Tarawa was like stepping back in time. It was as if the men reverted to type—Neanderthal type.

20

It was late afternoon. Constable Michael sat opposite Louisa in the little interview room she now called her office. Whenever he shifted his body, which he did often, his long legs bumped into the small desk in front of him. Louisa wanted to discuss the case with him. Sergeant Tebano should have been there too, but he was, yet again, conspicuous by his absence. If she'd been back home she'd have tracked Tebano down by his police radio or mobile and ordered him to come to the station. But this was Tarawa and so she'd have to make do with Michael.

'Okay,' said Louisa, 'this is what we know about Joe: he was an expatriate businessman from Singapore. If his manicured nails and wardrobe were anything to go by, he took care of his appearance. He was in his early forties and lived alone. He did not appear to be in a relationship with anyone. He was not in debt, in fact he was relatively well off—by the way, have you asked the people in Immigration to try to track down next of kin?'

Michael looked away.

Louisa assumed that was a negative. 'Get on to it after this. Joe ran regularly in the hash, a mainly expat group. He appeared to have had no close friends and more than once this morning when I asked about him, he was referred to as arrogant. His papers were in order and he didn't have a police record we know of. Between five forty on Thursday evening and shortly before eight on Friday morning the victim was stabbed with a ceremonial shark tooth dagger.' She'd written a description of Joe's clothes and bag and handed it to Michael along with the dagger stump. 'I want you to ask the villagers around the Ambo about these items. Also ask them again about Thursday evening. Joe got to the club somehow and he had to be there for a reason. Someone, somewhere, must have seen something.'

Michael shifted in his chair again, his angular knees bumped into the desk.

'Yes?'

'Only a handful of women can make these daggers and the Catholic Women's Gift Shop is the main outlet registered to sell them. If the dagger used in the killing was bought from there, they should have a record of who made it.'

'Excellent thinking!'

Michael beamed.

'Get on to it as soon as we're done here. The shop may even remember who bought it. It could lead us to the killer. What do you make of the eye gouging?'

Michael shook his head. 'It could be a tactic to scare the local villagers.'

'They are genuinely frightened?'

'The death worries them less than the removal of the man's eyes. They think a ghost has eaten them.' He frowned. 'There was one very bad case a long time ago. A mad man, drunk on sour toddy and consumed with jealousy, strangled his wife and then ate her thumbs, big toes and breasts. The eating of her flesh was his way of humiliating his wife after death.'

Louisa pursed her lips. 'You think someone wanted to humiliate Joe even in death?'

'It is possible.'

'Let's leave that for now. Over three quarters of murders are committed by someone who knows the victim well. Who did Joe know well?'

'A friend?' said Michael earnestly.

'According to his fellow hashers he had no friends.'

'Brothers or sisters?'

'No evidence of any family on Tarawa, if anywhere.'

'Those hash runners you talked to?'

Louisa nodded. 'They appear to be the only people he knows, but everyone seems to have an alibi for Thursday evening. Ironically, the only person no one can remember seeing that night was Jill, the woman who discovered the body. But she appears to have no motive for killing Joe and either she's an incredible actress or very stupid to return to the scene of her crime the very next day.' Louisa frowned. 'Another thing, why take his running shoes and shorts and vest and leave him with only a dirty old lava-lava?'

Michael cleared his throat, 'Could he have returned home after running and changed into the lava-lava?'

She shook her head. 'His jogging clothes and bag weren't in the house when I checked. And the people who knew him said he would never wear a lava-lava. Oh, I want you to also find out what you can about Joe being refused a licence to export sharks' fins by an expatriate called Ian Brown. Sergeant Tebano was supposed to be checking on Joe's employees. Any idea where he is?'

'He's here,' said a surly voice. Tebano leaned against the wooden frame of the open doorway and addressed Michael. 'You're a detective now? Too clever to be at the front desk?'

Michael blushed and quickly got up out of the chair.

'Where have you been?' demanded Louisa.

Tebano sauntered into the small room and eased himself into the chair Michael had so quickly vacated. He stretched his legs out in front of him and looked around. 'So this is your office now?'

'Did you find out anything?' said Louisa, realising for the first time that Tebano had an orange pandanus fruit in his hand.

'Joe had a lock-up on the beach by the Marine College. His boat is moored in the lagoon not far from it. His divers all say he was a good man to work for. He provided the equipment and paid them one dollar for each sea cucumber they found…' He stuck the orange fruit into his mouth and sucked on it.

'And these men, where were they on Thursday evening, early Friday morning?' If he'd not stopped chewing by the time she'd counted to ten, Louisa would ram the knobbly fruit down his throat. At eight seconds he took the fruit out of his mouth and wiped his lips with the back of his hand.

'They were at a funeral,' he said.

'All of them? All the time?'

Tebano looked away. 'Yes,'

'That's it? No enemies?' She suspected she'd need to talk to these men herself.

He raised his eyebrows in a fleeting arc and said nothing.

This local gesture infuriated Louisa. It was the western equivalent of shrugging. 'Well?'

'They said Joe had borrowed money from a man. The man wanted his money back. Joe wouldn't give it to him. They argued.'

'When was this?'

'One week, maybe two weeks ago.'

'His name?' Maybe Tebano wasn't quite so useless after all?

'Dave the Fish—'

'His real name!' Why, oh why, did everyone use silly nicknames on Tarawa?

Tebano sighed impatiently. 'His real name is on file. Everyone knows him as Dave the Fish.'

'Could he have killed Joe?'

'He drinks too much all the time and starts fights. He has attacked many people with a knife. He is a very bad man.'

'Tebano,' said Louisa, standing up and slipping the strap of her bag over her shoulder and trying not to feel too smug. It was day two of the investigation and she already had a suspect. 'You come with me. I want to ask this Dave the Fish a few questions.'

Tebano crossed his legs at the ankles. 'I have already been to see him. He was not there. He was on his boat. Fishing. He will not be back until tomorrow morning.'

Louisa didn't know whether to be angry or pleased at Tebano's show of initiative. Pleased, she supposed. 'Are you sure he can't be reached until tomorrow?'

Tebano shook his head.

Could she trust Tebano? She had no choice. 'Okay. First thing tomorrow we bring in Dave the Fish for questioning.'

21

Louisa spotted the envelope as soon as she put the living room light on. It had been wedged under the front door. Inside a pristine white card with gold filigree edging cordially invited Louisa to attend a cocktail reception at the Otintaai Hotel to welcome the Japanese Ambassador to Fiji, who was on a visit to Tarawa. It was being hosted by the Minister of Foreign Affairs. It was for that evening. In the two months Louisa had been on Tarawa she'd been invited to a couple of after work parties run by the local staff at the Ministry of Justice. They had been low key, humble affairs, with local food. Not knowing where the food had been prepared, she'd struggled to enjoy the meals, but they'd been good occasions for picking up office gossip. This was her first invitation to a diplomatic cocktail party, though she knew all about them—the parties were one of the topics of office gossip, that and how all expatriates wanted to be invited to them. Paul Wilson having an affair with a young local girl was the other popular topic. Louisa chucked the card on the coffee table, cocktail parties were not her thing. The lights went out. Darkness. Everywhere. A power cut. She sighed. That was all she needed.

Louisa sat by the fire, even though it was out and completely cold. It seemed as if no one in Reteta's family had been around that day, not even to feed Daisy or the pig. She reckoned both animals would survive, the pig could do with going on a diet anyway, and they had water—there was plenty in a blue basin under the tree, she'd already checked. All around her crickets clicked and cicadas whined. Louisa shivered. Being in the half dark made her uncomfortable. She liked to be able to see when someone approached. But it had simply been too hot to stay inside without the fan on.

She sipped the coconut juice which she'd kept cool in the fridge and poured into her pink cup. The almost clear liquid tasted slightly perfumed and sweet without being sickly. It reminded her of her days of being small and happy. She tried not to get too excited about the news of Dave the Fish, but a violent temper, too much alcohol and a knife was a killer combination. He was her prime suspect and if he'd murdered Joe, she'd get it out of him. Far away waves rumbled over the reef edge. The tide was out. Ping! Ping! Ping! The garden was flooded in orange and yellow shadows. The power was back on. Louisa checked her watch. It was just after seven. She went back inside. As she passed the coffee table, the cocktail invitation seemed to wink at her. She checked her watch for a second time. It wasn't that late. Why not go?

Her black dress was creased but a quick iron sorted that. She showered, blow-dried her hair, regretting for the umpteenth time that she'd not brought her straighteners. She did her nails and dragged her best sandals from out of the bottom of the cupboard. Next she did her eyes, just enough to accentuate them without being tarty, and popped in her gold dangly earrings. Finally, she put on her posh red lipstick and checked herself in the small mirror in the toilet: not bad, even if she said so herself.

From a distance the Otintaai hotel looked like a giant wooden Swiss chalet, with two double storey wings like outstretched arms, jutting out from either side of the square reception block. The only street lights in Bikenibeu shone above a three metre high perimeter fence which surrounded the entire building and its grounds. A drive took you from the road to the entrance, which was marked by a boom barrier.

She drove and stopped at the gate. A security guard appeared from out of a small hut by the barrier. He grunted at her and the barrier swung upwards. Behind the guard's box, the drive took you up a small slope to the entrance of the hotel. Cars lined the drive. Louisa pulled in at the first free space. The cars were mainly white estates with green 'diplomatic' number plates: she'd be mixing with the great and good tonight.

Frangipani trees lined either side of the path from the drive towards the reception. A warm breeze filled the air with the sweet scent of their delicate blossoms. It reminded Louisa of when she was small on Tarawa but then she had a different memory, of a late summer evening in the garden in Edinburgh, of night scented stock and honeysuckle and sweet peas. Louisa smoothed her dress. She was glad that at the last minute she'd splashed on some Coco Chanel. Hopefully, the evening wouldn't be too boring.

Reception was a rectangular box with a wooden counter in the middle of it. Three of its four walls were made of sliding glass doors. The sound of disco music thudded from beyond the solid wooden wall behind the counter. A round-faced I-Kiribati girl with a flaming red hibiscus flower tucked behind her ear took her invitation and directed her to the lounge bar.

The lounge bar was a larger version of the reception box and it was heaving. The music was so loud everyone had to shout to be heard. A back wall of massive open sliding glass doors overlooked the lapping black lagoon. Round coffee tables dotted the area. Uncomfortable armchairs, with blue cushions like the ones in her own house, circled the tables, which were completely covered in half empty wine and fluted champagne glasses.

People of all nationalities stood or sat squashed side by side, holding drinks in one hand and pristine handbags or briefcases in the other. It was as if she'd walked into a scene from a James Bond film, where all the heads of state had gathered to talk about saving the world. The scent of expensive perfumes was almost overwhelming. Louisa recognised no one. She immediately regretted coming. She hated small talk. What had she been thinking of? A pretty waitress in a Hawaii style blouse and red lava-lava offered Louisa a choice of either champagne or fresh orange juice from a tray of fluted glasses. Like the receptionist, the girl wore a red hibiscus flower tucked behind her ear. Louisa refused.

'You've no glass, let me.' Paul Wilson appeared from behind the waitress and handed Louisa a glass of sparkling champagne.

'Thanks,' said Louisa, taking it despite herself.

'What are you doing here all by yourself?'

'I was invited. Where's Jill?'

'Oh, she doesn't like these things. She's a bit of a recluse, which is a pity for her. I sometimes think she's not suited to Tarawa but she says she likes it here. So that shows you what I know.'

'Oh?' said Louisa. It seemed Paul didn't know about Jill's plan to leave. 'Who are all these people?'

'Diplomats. Ministers. Representatives from the big aid agencies—'

'Detective Sergeant Louisa Townsend, don't you scrub up well!' said Nicole, appearing out of the crowd and draping a bare, tanned arm around Paul's shoulder. 'You missed the dancing. It was shit hot, wasn't it, Paul?'

Paul smiled and nodded.

'It's what they do here, traditional dancing with big grass skirts. They sing too. It's nothing like that Hawaiian hula hula tourist bollocks.'

Louisa knew all about the traditional dancing. She remembered the still tiny, bird-like movements that were made with the slight twisting of the arms, and the swelling swish of the grass skirts on the hips. She fanned her face with her hand. 'If I'd realised it was going to be so hot, I'd have worn something less figure hugging.'

'But you look so sexy,' said Nicole, her lips curling slightly.

'Hardly!' said Louisa, wondering if she should write bitch next to Nicole's name when she next made a note of it.

Nicole made a face. 'Oh, no! I'm so not up for those two.'

'Be nice now,' said Paul.

Louisa looked round. Ian and Christine pushed their way through the crowd towards them.

'I'm out of here!' said Nicole, turning and leaving.

'I thought Nicole and Christine were friends?' said Louisa.

Paul laughed. 'They are. I think it's Ian she doesn't get on with. Especially recently.'

Wham! A heavy weight, like a sack of coal fell against Louisa's side. She was almost sent flying. It was Tom.

Louisa pushed him away. 'Get off! 'He smelled of turnips and musk aftershave.

'Joe was with a woman…' Tom licked his red, puffy lips. '… night he was killed.'

'Say that again?' Had she heard correctly?

'Ignore Tom, he's pissed,' said Paul.

'He hated women …' said Tom, swaying.

'Joe was gay?' said Louisa.

'He wasn't gay. Tom's drunk,' said Paul. 'You can't take anything he says seriously in this state.'

'Joe was a wanker!' Tom staggered away into the throng of bodies, 'A bleeding wanker! Wasn't with a woman when he died. How could he have been? He hated white women.'

'Have you seen Nicole? I thought I saw her with you?' It was Christine.

'She went upstairs.' Louisa looked around for Tom but he'd disappeared.

'How's the investigation going?'

'I have to find Tom,' said Louisa, scanning the crowd.

'You're wasting your time,' said Paul.

'There has to be a reason why he said what he did!'

'Said what?' said Christine, not looking quite as cool as she had earlier in the day, despite wearing a designer purple, silk number.

'I still need to talk to him!' said Louisa, ignoring Christine.

'Fine,' said Paul, shouting above the music, which had suddenly got louder. 'But I think he went to the men's toilet and you really don't want to go in there. I'll get him for you. I'd better make sure he's okay anyway. He's had way too much, as usual.'

'What do you want Tom for?' yelled Christine

'I want to ask him about something he said. Where's Ian?'

'He's gone back, got a lift. Has an early start tomorrow. Where did you say Nicole was?'

Louisa pointed upwards to where the booming music was coming from. It sounded like Dancing Queen.

Christine nodded. 'She can't stay still for a minute. She gave up a really good job back home to come here and gets bored very easily.'

'What did she do?' said Louisa, watching Christine place her empty glass on the round coffee table beside her and take another full one from a passing waitress.

'Something to do with events management. She says she doesn't miss it, but that's a lie.'

'And did you give up a good job too?' said Louisa.

'The children are my job now.'

'And are the children not Nicole's job?' said Louisa.

Christine laughed out loud. 'You don't know Nicole very well, do you? Her daughters see more of their house girl than they do of Nicole.'

22

Paul should have been back with Tom by now. Where the hell were they? They'd been gone at least ten minutes. How long did it take for a man to have a pee? She should have gone to look for Tom herself. It was a mistake to have trusted Paul. And then Tom was at the bar. Beside her. Swaying slightly from side to side.

'Someone wants—' he said, his words slushing around in his mouth, '— to talk to you.'

Louisa struggled to hear him above the music. She shouted, 'What did you say earlier about Joe being with a woman on Thursday night?'

Tom pulled himself upright. His eyes were bloodshot and he seemed to have difficulty focusing on her.

'You said he was with a woman?' she yelled again.

'Someone,' he said, pointing a pink, flabby finger behind her. 'Wants to talk to you.'

'What?'

'To talk to you,' said Tom, still pointing.

Louisa turned. The hissing charcoal eyes of Assistant Police Commissioner Nakibae looked directly at her.

'Sir!' Tom licked his wet lips. 'Detective Sergeant Louisa Townsend.'

'Pleased to meet you at last,' said Louisa, immediately regretting wearing her clinging black dress. Why had she picked this one? Not only too tight, too short. She wiped her sweaty palms on the side of her dress and thrust her hand out for a handshake. 'Sir!'

Assistant Commissioner Nakibae ignored her outstretched fingers and looked at Tom. 'I was led to believe Detective Townsend held the rank of inspector?'

Louisa quickly pulled back her hand.

'If there's been any confusion, forgive me,' said Tom very deliberately and slowly, as if concentrating on every word. 'The Office of the European Commission says she has very good credentials.' For a second he looked as if he didn't know where he was or who he was talking to, then he became focused again. 'You asked for our help.'

'And she's a woman,' he said dryly.

'She's all there is.' He hiccuped. 'If you are not satisfied, maybe Fiji will give assistance?'

'Are you suggesting the Kiribati Police Service can't look after its own affairs?'

'No. Not at all. Sir!' Tom pushed his body upright, as if trying to stand to attention.

Assistant Commissioner Nakibae turned his gaze on Louisa. In sharp contrast to herself, he looked remarkably cool in his neat grey slacks and a colourful frangipani patterned short-sleeved shirt, open at the neck. Smart but casual. Louisa felt the size of a pea and her legs were trembling, actually trembling! It was so stupid.

'The killer is under lock and key, yes?' said Nakibae.

'It's only been 36 hours—' she stammered, furious with herself for letting him make her feel so pathetic.

'Yet, here you are, drinking champagne?'

'It's not like that!' she said, immediately regretting it. Why had she said that?

'Are you at least making progress?'

She nodded. 'Sir!'

'You have a suspect then?'

'New information has come to my attention and I am hopeful—'

'Hopeful?' he said dryly. 'In other words, you do not have a suspect. What about the post mortem?'

Louisa breathed in through her nose and out through her mouth. She would remain calm. 'I'm waiting for the coroner to get back to me. There have been delays. The refrigeration unit at the hospital mortuary is broken.'

'If it is not working, how are you storing the body?'

'We took the freezer from the Ambo club. We had no choice.'

He frowned. 'Sergeant Tebano is assisting you?'

'Absolutely, sir!' As if she would tell him that he wasn't.

The big man opened his mouth, frowned for a couple of seconds and said finally, 'Monday, first thing, I want a written update, on my desk.'

'Thank you for putting your trust in me.' She thought he would have been handsome except for his bad teeth.

'Trust? All my detectives are in New Zealand or Beru. They'll be back on Wednesday. If the killer's not under arrest by then the Office of the European Commission will hear what I think about your credentials.'

'Sir,' she said, trying not to let the people pushing past

her knock her over. 'You'll not regret it.'

'I'd better not. No one gets away with murder, not on my watch.'

The hotel forecourt was deserted. Louisa leaned on one of the white diplomatic cars and took in a few deep breaths of fresh air. She felt lousy. The result of too much champagne, devoured too quickly and on an empty stomach. Fortunately common sense had prevailed and she'd stopped drinking after five, or was it six, glasses? But champagne wasn't that alcoholic, was it? Who was she kidding? She was pissed. She pushed herself up and off the car. Assistant Police Commissioner Nakibae could screw himself! How dare he talk to her as if she were a nothing! So, he didn't like the fact she was a sergeant or a woman? Bastard! She took a few steps before promptly falling on to the bonnet of the next car. Her body felt heavy. She thought she'd stay there for a bit. Catch her breath.

She'd only seen Nakibae once before at the police recruits' passing out parade, or whatever they called the ceremony. It was her first week on the island, she'd still been jet-lagged and overwhelmed by the heat. He'd oozed authority. The chief police commissioner had also been there, and the other assistant commissioner, whose name escaped her for the moment. The other one had a much softer, more approachable face than Nakibae. She'd thought it lucky he was her point of contact in the Kiribati Police Service. He'd seemed so helpful that first week, arranging familiarisation trips for her and offering his total support for the development of the programme, even agreeing with a lot of her ideas. Then he was gone. In New Zealand on a six-month course and no one seemed willing to stand in for him with regards to her work while he was away. It was as if she had become invisible. That's when she'd turned to Tom. What a mistake that had been! Louisa pushed herself up off the car. Her legs wobbled. Why had she drunk so much? She hated being out of control! Was she fit enough to drive? A rustling ahead made her freeze. A shape. In the shadows. Someone was mucking about by the police car she'd commandeered from the Ambo and which she now considered to be hers. 'Hey?' yelled Louisa. 'What are you doing there?'

The shadow started to run.

'Stop!' yelled Louisa, running after it. A small, round Gilbertese woman, with thick black hair tied up in a double bun on top of her head darted into the bushes. 'I said stop!'

'What you shouting for?' It was the guard from the gate.

Louisa looked to where she thought she'd seen the woman. 'Did you see her? A middle-aged woman. She ran into the bushes. Just there.'

The guard shook his head. 'You had too much to drink. I help you.'

Louisa cringed. 'I'm fine! I don't need your help. Thank you.' She turned and walked back up the drive in as dignified a manner as she could muster. Then she saw her car. The front left tyre was slashed. Shit!

'Are you okay?' Paul Wilson stood behind her.

'No. Look!'

Paul bent down to look at the tyre. 'Vandals. Even here. The guard's a lazy bastard. I keep telling them to get rid of him. There are hundreds of good decent, local men who would do a better job than him. Let's get the spare, I'll help you change it.'

Louisa opened the boot. She groaned. 'There's no spare!'

Paul tutted. 'You really need a decent spare at all times. These roads are murder on the treads. Look, I'm leaving now. If you like, I can drop you off on the way—you live in Betio, don't you? One of your constables can sort out a tyre and come and get the car for you tomorrow.'

23

A shower of icy water powered over Louisa and she gradually gathered her thoughts. The good news was she'd slept well again and did not have a hangover. The bad news was the night before had not been a dream. Her meeting with Assistant Police Commissioner Nakibae had happened and someone had slashed the tyre of the patrol car she was using and she had no transport. The cold water made her shiver. Her situation was simple, whether she liked it or not, and car or no car, she had till Wednesday, when the Kiribati Police Service's finest detectives would be back, to find Joe's murderer. If she didn't, there was no chance of getting any help with developing her programme and there was every chance of Nakibae rubbishing her to the EC office people in Suva and getting sent back to Edinburgh in disgrace.

She dried herself and thought about the car: why would anyone, let alone a woman she'd never met, slash her tyre? Or was it a coincidence the mysterious woman had been in the car park? But if she'd not been guilty, why had she run away? Either way, it was going to have to remain a mystery. Just as Paul's relationship with his wife would have to remain a mystery. She simply couldn't fathom Paul. The trip in his car was bit of a blur—had she dozed off on the way home? But she did remember Paul talking of Jill with affection. Yet, after he dropped her off at her house, he'd definitely headed onwards in the direction of downtown Betio and was most definitely not going in the direction of his house. There was no doubt in her mind that he was going to see the pretty little girl she'd seen him with the other day. But who was Louisa to judge? Her history in the relationship department was far from perfect. In Edinburgh she'd committed the cardinal sin and slept with her boss. What a mistake that had been! If her mother knew that was her real reason for leaving her job, she'd be even more angry with Louisa.

Yes, Paul was probably cheating on his wife, but he had given her a lift when she'd needed it and had not once commented on the fact that she'd been pissed, which she had been—how she hated being such a lightweight drinker! Nor had he made a single, stupid, sexist remark about women being scared of the dark when she'd asked him to chum her into the house because she'd forgotten to leave the outside lights on. In her books he was a reasonably good bloke, although he did have very poor taste in T-shirts.

Louisa thought of the day ahead: while she fetched Dave the Fish with Tebano, she'd have an officer bring Tom in for questioning. He needed to explain what he meant by his remarks the night before. Perhaps Joe had met a woman at the Ambo. She could have witnessed something, if she existed. Her money was still on Dave the Fish as the killer though. He had a history of violence and he'd not liked Joe. She'd find out soon enough. She decided to wear her navy trousers and white shirt. It was a more serious look. Suddenly she remembered the funeral. Bloody, bloody hell! Why hadn't she tried harder to get out of going? Louisa checked her watch. It was still early. If she was quick, she could pop along to the funeral, offer her sympathies and be at Betio nick by eight.

It was going to be another stifling hot day. Louisa wished she'd worn her hat. Sounds of distant hymn singing suggested that even this early, there were people in church—though which church was anyone's guess. Louisa had never seen so many religions represented in such a small place: Mormons, Jesuits, Baha'is, Jehovah's Witnesses, Quakers, Protestants, Catholics, Evangelical Baptists and churches with names she'd never heard of. A rustling sound made her jump. It was silly. She'd been on raids in drug-riddled tower blocks in Edinburgh's

Craigentinny and had never once flinched, no matter what came. But deserted, country roads were out of her comfort zone.

A mangy dog snoozed flat out by the side of a concrete toilet block. Reteta had told her more than once the path to her village was behind the dingy building. The dog lifted its head and growled low and deep. Louisa quickly opened her bag and took out a small stone. She lifted her hand and aimed. The dog was on its feet and gone in seconds. Louisa kept the stone in her grip, just in case. She knew how to deal with dogs on Tarawa. It was one thing she did remember from living here when she was wee.

The dank toilet block was covered in graffiti as rude as any she had ever seen. Louisa was surprised the toilet was so far from the village. She'd not like to come all the way out here at night to have a pee. The building's stark lines were in sharp contrast to the soft contours of the coconut palms that surrounded it. The toilet 'gift' had been part of a campaign funded by the British to encourage villagers to stop using the beach as their toilet. Louisa hated to think about this local habit, something she'd forgotten about until returning to the island. The only time she'd talked to her mother on the phone since being on Tarawa had been about this. Her mother had called her a snob, insisting that the beach, which was washed clean twice a day by the ocean, wasn't such a bad place to do the toilet, especially on a coral atoll where the fresh water table was only a metre below the ground.

The campaign to change the Kiribati toilet habits had failed dramatically: western plumbing hadn't coped with traditional toilet paper—leaves and sticks—and very quickly the villagers, who were exceptionally clean people, refused to use the stinking, enclosed boxes and went back to using the beach. Louisa didn't doubt the beach being washed clean was probably more hygienic than the monstrous cubicles, but nevertheless, she was glad all the government houses came with Western plumbing, especially her one.

Within minutes of leaving the stinking toilet block Louisa heard mournful singing. It came from a group of around thirty men and women. They stood beneath a spreading breadfruit tree in the middle of a huddle of traditional huts. The largest hut was draped in swathes of colourful material, making it stand out from the rest. Villagers wandered quietly between the various huts or sat on pandanus mats scattered everywhere. Children quietly clung to their parents as chickens and skinny dogs scavenged for scraps. Smoke wafted from two campfires, one to the east of the main hut and one to the west. No one paid Louisa any attention. She spied Reteta immediately.

'You are just in time,' said Reteta, a huge smile across her face. 'We are starting the last bomaki ceremony very soon.'

'I can't stay,' said Louisa backing away.

Reteta shook her head. 'You must stay! It is the custom for people from Butaritari to sing songs and walk around the village three times to make sure the spirit of our dead relative travels safely on the tide to the Land of Shades. All dying souls are carried out on the tide and all new souls arrive on the incoming tide.' She pointed to the two campfires. 'We let the fires go out and if our magic is good the spirit of our cousin, Tion, will take the shape of a happy cricket and come and sing to us to let us know he has reached his ghostly home safely. But if our magic is bad, our poor cousin will not be carried safely to his spirit home in the shadows. His spirit will be lost at sea and he will return in the shape of an angry cricket and sing bad songs late at night. He will eat our children and make evil dreams. But you are here and you will help us make good magic, which will help make sure Tion will have a safe passing.'

Louisa shivered. She knew she'd disliked cicadas and crickets for a reason. 'I have to go to work. You know I do.'

Reteta's smile vanished. 'Five minutes is too much time

for your family?'

'No, it's just that—'

'You are happy for bad magic to happen to us?'

'Don't be so silly!' said Louisa, trying to keep her voice low.

'You think we are rubbish!' hissed Reteta. 'Stupid I-Kiribati who do stupid things?'

'Not at all!' She didn't have time for this.

'Then why are you leaving?'

Louisa sighed. 'Five minutes. That's all. But then I really have to go.'

Reteta beamed.

Louisa handed Reteta the carrier with the lava-lava in it. Reteta took the cloth from the carrier and thrust it back into Louisa's hand. 'In the olden day we wrapped the body of our dead relative in mats of straw but that is very expensive, now we use lava-lavas. Come.' Reteta grabbed Louisa's arm and dragged her through the front curtain of the main hut.

24

It was dim inside the hut. It took Louisa a few seconds for her eyes to adjust. The ground was covered in cream vinyl, with a brown swirl design. Reteta slipped off her flip-flops inside the entrance, bent over almost double and crept into the room. Reluctantly, Louisa kicked off her shoes and, bowing low in a similar manner to Reteta, followed her inside.

A group of men, three deep, sat cross-legged in a circle. Reteta led Louisa to the front of the circle. She whispered, 'You are a special guest, you sit here by the men.'

Louisa quickly hunkered down and tried not to gasp as

she found herself staring at the upright waxy toes of the departed Tion. His torso was wrapped in a red lava-lava and lay on the floor in the middle of the circle. A fatty, gamey smell, like lightly seared pork, oozed from his long, lean body. Some green leafy plant and what looked like part of a coconut palm had been placed next to his head.

'You stay,' said Reteta. 'I will come back with the food. After you eat you can swap the old lava-lava on the body with your new one.'

'Food?' Louisa tried not to retch. 'No way!'

'It is our custom. You must!' said Reteta and was gone.

Louisa had seen dead bodies before in her job, of course she had, but two in forty-eight hours was a record, and to be so close to them. The idea of wrapping a lava-lava around the corpse filled her with revulsion. Reteta was back. She stuck a white plastic disposable plate on to Louisa's lap.

'Na food,' said Reteta.

A mound of sticky rice sat in a swirl of gelatinous green gravy on the thin plate. Four small bright red sausages, a handful of deep fried breadfruit chips and a square of sponge cake, covered in pink butter icing, sat on top of the rice. A white plastic fork stuck out of the rice. Louisa fought back the bile rising in her throat.

'I am coming back,' said Reteta, straightening up and spraying the corpse in swirling mists of oily insect repellant from a giant can of Mortien. Louisa spluttered and coughed. The plate on her lap slipped sideways. An I-Kiribati man sitting next to her caught the plate and handed it back to her.

'Thank you,' whispered Louisa, not wanting to take the plate back but feeling she had to. The man burst out sobbing. Louisa started. His crying became louder. Reteta and an older man shuffled towards him and quickly helped him to his feet. Between them they half-carried, half-dragged him outside. Louisa followed them.

The brilliant blue glare of the morning light outside made it hard for Louisa to see. When her eyes had adjusted TC was next to her.

'He was with my uncle Tion when he died.' He nodded to where Reteta and the older man were still trying to pacify the distressed man. 'It was an accident at sea. He couldn't save him. He feels responsible. He's not left his side since it happened.'

'I'm sorry. I truly am but I have to go. Can I give you this?' She handed him the lava-lava, 'I know it's custom for a special guest to cover the deceased with the lava-lava but I'm in such a hurry.'

'It's not custom. It's just Reteta wanting you to stay. It's kudos having an expatriate at the funeral, even a half-expatriate like you, especially now you're being talked about on the radio.'

Reteta caught up with Louisa just as she reached the toilets at the edge of the village.

'You said you would stay!' Her face flushed.

'I have work to do,' said Louisa.

'You will miss the ceremony of the straightening of the head, you will miss swapping the lava-lava and you will miss the final bomaki!'

'I'm sorry but—'

'You cannot do this small thing after all I have done for you?'

'Done for me?' said Louisa. What was she talking about? 'I gave you a job, Reteta, not the other way around.' She wanted to add, and you live in my garden rent free, but didn't.

'Your mummy sent me a letter telling me you were coming to Tarawa. She asked me to look after you. I am looking after you and this is how you repay my kindness?'

'My mother wrote to you about me?' Louisa felt as if she'd been thumped in her chest.

'She said you are all alone with no husband. She begged

me to help you. So I helped. I came to your house and stayed with you. We all stayed! And now you will not do this one thing at your own family's funeral?'

'I didn't ask you to camp out in my garden. In fact, I don't want you to. And I pay you good money to clean for me. If you don't want to do it, fine, leave!'

'Of course I won't leave,' said Reteta, immediately calming down, 'but your mummy asked me to look after you and I am doing so.'

Louisa could hardly get the words out, she was so mad. 'Watch my lips, Reteta, I don't need you or anyone else to look after me!'

Special Constable John, a volunteer officer the size of a barn, manned the police station alone. All the other officers were out. The police patrol boat, a gift from Australia, had seized a Korean vessel illegally fishing in Kiribati's waters. The officers had been called upon to escort the Korean boat crew from Betio port, where the boat was now anchored, to a disused hangar at the airport. The Korean fishermen would be kept there, under house arrest, until the Korean government paid the fine they now owed the Kiribati Government. John didn't know when Michael and Tebano would be back. This bad news was followed by more: according to Tom's secretary, Tom had left on the dawn ferry to the outer island of Maiana and would not be back for a week.

Louisa stared at the description of Joe's missing clothes still on her desk. She'd asked Michael to distribute it yesterday, yet there it was. She tried not get too angry. It wasn't Tebano and Michael's fault they'd been called away. But now she had to find Dave the Fish's house by herself and didn't know where to begin. As for Tom buggering off to Maiana? Had she not bothered with the funeral, she might have caught him before he'd left. To have to wait a week to question him was one week too many. Her Sunday had gone from positive to downright shitty in a matter of a few hours. Was it always going to be like this on Tarawa? But then Constable John surprised her. Not only did he come up with the address and directions for Dave the Fish's house—and know that his real name was David Trout—he'd also managed to contact Maiana by satellite phone. The satellite phone system connected the main island of Tarawa with the outer islands. Constable John had asked the local officer on Maiana to arrange for Tom to come to the phone at a suitable time to answer Louisa's questions. John even said he would have the descriptions of the missing items and dagger distributed to stores and businesses in the three main centres of Betio, Bairiki and Bikenibeu, as well as the villages near the Ambo Club. Things were looking up.

In sharp contrast to the bus Louisa had taken to the Ambo on Friday, the bus she was now on was very slow. At the rate it trundled along, it was going to take her half the morning to get to Dave the Fish's place at Buota. She didn't care. With or without Tebano or Michael or a patrol car, she was going to question David Trout. She looked out the bus window. David Trout was her best lead. He'd not admit to the crime, she knew that. She'd need to think of a strategy to outwit him. She closed her eyes. It was impossible. Try as she might, she could not stop thinking about her mother writing to Reteta behind her back.

Until Reteta had moved into her back garden, Louisa had forgotten that Reteta had used to child mind Louisa when she was small, even though Reteta was only a year older than Louisa. On one occasion Reteta had thumped Louisa—Louisa couldn't remember why, no doubt Louisa had been cheeky and not done what she'd been told. Louisa had thumped Reteta right back. They'd fought. In the scrap, Louisa's shorts had torn. Her mum had believed Reteta when she'd said Louisa had started the fight. Louisa felt her chest tighten. She took a deep breath. It stressed her when she thought about her mum. She seemed to spend her life seeking her approval, and never getting it. She suspected she reminded Mum too much of Dad, she was his double, albeit a female version. Louisa could hunt down Jack the Ripper single-handed and her mum would still find something to criticise her about. Not like Euin, her brother and number one son. He'd got himself a first-class degree in actuarial science from Heriot-Watt University and a brilliant job with BP. At thirty he had a big house and big car, a trophy BP wife (she did charity work, whatever that was), and the piece de résistance, he'd made Mum a grandmother twice over (at least, the BP trophy wife had). Louisa paused to look outside and wipe some sweat from her forehead with a hanky. Why oh why did she keep forgetting to bring a bottle of water with her?

25

The road came to an end at a deserted beach of golden sand and a stretch of turquoise water about two hundred metres wide. Louisa half-expected Robinson Crusoe to pop out from behind a tree. This was Buota, where South Tarawa ended and across the water North Tarawa began. The minibus parked under the shade of a handful of coconut palms and the last two passengers, including Louisa, got off.

A one person outrigger canoe floated at the edge of the water. On the only other occasion she'd been as far as Buota, during her orientation week, she'd been told the canoe was the ferry to North Tarawa. For a dollar the ferryman would row you across the stretch of water and for another dollar he'd bring you back. She'd watched three oversized people squeeze into the precarious, narrow canoe. When the ferryman, a skinny wriggly man, also hopped on, the boat sank so low into the water that Louisa had thought it would caspsize. She presumed in an emergency the passengers would simply get wet and walk or swim to the other side. It wasn't that far, after all. But her guide at the time, a young woman from the police commissioner's office, said that most locals couldn't swim. Apparently, a bridge was being planned, funded by some aid organisation or other.

From where Louisa stood, the north of the island and the south of the island looked like two sandy outstretched arms holding a giant basket of water. The gap in front of Louisa was one of many, which allowed the water from the Pacific to channel in and out of the giant lagoon. One of the first things Louisa remembered her dad telling her was that Tarawa atoll was formed from coral and that coral was among the most ancient of life forms that still thrived on Earth. Time and time again he'd tell her how thousands and thousands of years ago tiny free swimming coral larvae had attached themselves to submerged rocks along the edge of a lonely volcanic island. After more thousands of years the volcanic island had eventually subsided but the coral fringing the island had continued to grow and expand upwards. Eventually, the coral expanded and grew so much that it emerged from the water as lots of little islands which now made up the semi circular Tarawa atoll with its massive central lagoon.

That such tiny creatures as coral larvae could eventually create something as big as an island seemed incredible to Louisa and for a while she'd wanted to be a marine biologist, like Jacques Cousteau, her dad's hero. Then two of the men from the airport hangar where her dad had worked as an aircraft engineer had gone out fishing one day and not come back. They didn't come back the next day, or the next. Everyone feared for their lives: once away from the relative shelter of the Tarawa lagoon and the reef edge of the atoll, there was no shallow place to anchor for thousands of miles. If the men's engine had failed, the ocean currents could have carried them for miles in any direction, drifting helplessly forever, a tiny speck on a gigantic moving mass.

The men's disappearance had upset Louisa. She'd thought of them as her friends. Whenever she'd visited the hangar with her dad, they'd given her Jammie Dodger biscuits and slipped her a dollar. She'd been seven when it had happened. It was the first time she'd realised people could die. Her dad had found her sobbing under her bed. He'd told her not to give up on the lads. Kiribati men were the best seamen in the world. He'd been right. Thirty days after they'd disappeared, the men had turned up miles away in the Marshall Islands, hungry and weak but alive. They'd survived by using a cardboard box to shade them from the sun and by drinking tuna fish blood to quench their thirst. She clearly remembered her dad asking them what the worst moment was. The younger of the two had said the howling winds had been terrible and the mountainous waves very bad, and when a shark nudged the boat and almost toppled them, they'd been petrified. They'd also been driven to distraction by a gnawing hunger and a terrible thirst. But all of those things were nothing compared with the thought they wouldn't survive. Giving in to their fear was by far the worst thing.

Dave the Fish's house was a hundred metres along the water's edge, heading towards the lagoon. Louisa spotted it immediately. It was a local style hut on giraffe-leg stilts with coconut thatch walls and roof. It towered above a couple of aluminium fishing boats anchored in the water. A narrow, long, wobbly looking gangplank took you from the scrubby ground up to the house. Battered dive tanks, dirty cool boxes and reams of plastic fishing netting littered the ground at the base of the gangplank. A water hose snaked between the debris. Louisa looked around for a tap and saw four smaller local huts nestled in the trees behind her. Flattened blue Foster's cans littered the sandy ground between the huts, along with empty crisp packets, discarded blue Winston cigarette packets, upturned pink plastic wash basins and scattered white plastic knives and forks—she couldn't see any plates. Louisa approached the gangplank. It was another hot morning. Sand had got in her shoes and the blazing sun made her squint even with her sunglasses on.

She heard voices from the house and called up. A thin, tight faced I-Kiribati woman appeared from one of the small huts. Louisa introduced herself and explained she was looking for David. The woman looked her up and down once and then nodded towards the gang plank. 'Up there,' she said, not smiling. Before Louisa had turned round the woman had disappeared back into the shadows of the small hut.

Louisa didn't like the look of the gangway, it was made up of two black tree trunks worn smooth. Louisa knew enough to know the wood was not coconut palm, but she couldn't tell what it was. There was no railing to hold on to and it was steep—very steep. She walked up very carefully, stepping sideways nearer the top to better keep her balance. When she reached the platform landing she felt much better. She called out to let David know she was there and walked through the open doorway leading into the hut.

26

Four weather-beaten expatriate men lounged across a floor of straw mats. Despite a delicate breeze from windows on three sides of the room, the air stank of unwashed men and the sour yeasty smell of dope. The oldest man was slim and more neatly dressed than the others. His short-sleeved shirt was tucked into belted shorts and he sat upright, with his legs crossed. He wore white knee-length socks. Louisa assumed the pair of Jesus sandals at the entrance to the room belonged to him. He had to be at least seventy years old and looked shrivelled and tired. The other three men were unshaven, in unbuttoned washed-out, short-sleeved shirts and shorts. They looked like what Louisa would call 'right bastards'. Their gangly, sun-ravaged bodies took up three-quarters of the floor space. Two were broader and dark haired. The third was blond and wiry. All three were in their bare feet. Louisa couldn't see any signs of their footwear. They each had a can of Foster's in one hand and a cigarette in the other. They shared two overflowing round pub ashtrays and from the number of squashed cardboard roaches in them, joints were more popular than cigarettes. The pensioner, by sharp contrast, had a plate of cheesy Cheetos beside him. It was a given, if she wanted to get any information, she was going to have to ignore the dope smoking.

'David?' she asked.

The blond man looked up at her. His head was round and sharp, his short fair hair brittle. His skin was so weathered it was hard to tell his age, he could be anywhere between thirty-five and forty-five.

'That's me. Who wants to know?' He spoke with an Australian accent, which was much stronger than Nicole's.

'I'm Detective Sergeant Townsend. I have a few questions for you about your relationship with Joe Revada, the expatriate man who was killed recently. But first can I ask who you other men are?'

The older man was already on his feet. He called himself Pete the Pilot—did no one use a proper name on Tarawa? He said his wife was waiting for him and he had to leave. From his accent, he was clearly a Brit. He insisted he didn't know Joe personally or anything about his death. He lived this side of Bikenibeu with his wife and her family, a local family. Louisa made a note of his details, just in case she'd need to talk to him later.

'And you are?' she said to the other two men after Pete the Pilot left.

Dave the Fish nodded to the larger of the two dark haired men. 'This is my mate, Bob—'

Bob nodded.

'And that's Stevo.' He nodded to the thinner man next to him.

'G'day,' said Stevo, clearly another Australian.

'Why don't you join us?' said Dave.

Louisa stayed standing, she knew things were done differently on Tarawa, but getting comfy with these reprobates was never going to happen.

'If you could just tell me about your relationships with the deceased?' she said, addressing them all.

'Who said we knew him?' said the man called Bob. Unlike the other two, Bob sounded British, probably from the south-west.

'Didn't you?'

'He was a jerk,' said Dave, flicking the ash off his fag at the ashtray and just missing Louisa's foot.

'Sick poofter got what he deserved,' said Stevo, crossing his outstretched legs and plucking a cheesy snack from the plate left by the older man.

'What do you mean by that?' said Louisa.

'We don't have to talk to you,' said Dave, his mouth slipping across his face into a smile.

Louisa had met his type before. He was a bully. She looked directly into Dave's button eyes. 'I believe you export sea cucumbers and shark fins. Obstructing a murder inquiry could lead to the loss of your export licence.'

Dave laughed. 'Don't get your knickers in a knot, Sarge, just teasing.'

'Let me ask again, what was your relationship with the deceased?' She couldn't help noticing the spittle on Dave's mouth had formed a yeasty crust over his lips.

Stevo, the other Aussie, said, 'He was a dickhead.'

'Bastard thought he could come and take over my business,' said Dave. 'Used money I loaned him to buy a boat and dive tanks. I'd never have loaned the bastard the money if I'd known that's what he was going to do with it!' Dave paused to take a draw of his fag. 'So, he's dead? Good. I'll keep my customers and my lawyer says the boat will be mine in lieu of his debt.'

'Sounds like you were pretty angry with him?'

'Too right I was.'

'Angry enough to kill him?' said Louisa, disliking Dave the longer she had to stay in his company.

Dave shook his head slowly. 'You're not pinning his death on me. I had words with him, that's all. Told him I export all the sea cucumbers and shark fins on this island and no one else.'

'And what did he do?' said Louisa.

'He carked it, didn't he!' said Dave, sneering.

'I heard someone swiped his mud pies,' said Stevo, 'that true?'

'Killer must have been hungry,' said Bob.

Louisa tried not to show her revulsion. 'I want to know where you all were Thursday from six in the evening until the following morning?'

'We were here, together. Never left, did we?' said Dave lazily, lighting a fresh cigarette.

'For sure,' said Stevo.

'All night until the morning,' said Bob, smirking. 'Ask the women.'

Louisa marched to the bus stop. The men were lousy bastards

and all her instincts told her they were lying. As soon as she could get some muscle she was hauling the three of them to the station—she'd think of a charge later. If she could separate them, she reckoned she'd have a chance of getting to the truth. And her money was still on Dave the Fish being the killer. He'd even admitted to hating Joe. They must have argued. It got physical. Dave pulled the knife, though what he was doing with a ceremonial dagger was anyone's guess. Until there was new evidence to suggest otherwise, Dave was her number one suspect. She cursed the Korean fishermen. Had their boat not been in Kiribati waters illegally, she'd have had a couple of officers with her for back-up and she would have brought them in there and then.

The minibus revved up ominously. Louisa began to run. She did not want to get stuck in Buota, Dave the Fish country! There was one space in the passenger seat at the front of the minibus, next to the driver and a local woman. With her hanky in her hand, she pulled open the side passenger door, hopped in and sat down just as the minibus started to move. She nodded a hello to the driver and to the woman passenger. Louisa did a double take. The passenger was the woman in the hotel car park the night before. At least it looked very much like her. Was the woman following her? Surely not. It was too ridiculous. The woman stared straight ahead, apparently oblivious to Louisa's existence. Louisa was sure it was her. She had the same barrel body and her long black hair was wrapped up on top of her head in a double bun.

'Excuse me, didn't I see you last night in the car park of the Otintaai Hotel?' said Louisa.

The round woman said nothing.

'It was you, wasn't it?' insisted Louisa.

The woman's eyes didn't so much as flicker.

'Someone slashed the tyre on my car,' said Louisa. 'You didn't happen to see anyone in the car park area while you were there?'

'I saw no one,' she said, still staring directly in front of her.

'But you were there, weren't you?'

'I can be where I want,' she yelled. 'It's not a crime. Ikai!'

The driver screeched to a halt and Louisa watched in disbelief as the woman got off the minibus.

'Do you know that woman?' Louisa asked the driver. He seemed not to hear her. Louisa asked again. He gazed ahead and said nothing. His eyes were bloodshot. His heavy body sank into his plastic seat, which spilled foam cushion from its side. It was as if he was sitting on an omelette. Louisa looked back to see if she could see the woman. She'd disappeared.

27

The hospital was just before Bikenibeu town, on the ocean side of the island. It was a modern sprawl of low, green, rectangular hospital buildings in a massive clearing. It had been built by the Japanese. Louisa had been born in the old hospital. Her birth had been sudden and painful, something which her mother never let her forget. Louisa got off the bus. With the police tied up with the Korean fishermen, there was nothing for her to rush back to the station for. It made sense to track down the coroner's report while she was at this end of the island.

A scrubby path brought Louisa from the road to an exposed car park. A dozen meandering narrower paths twisted outwards, spider leg like, from the body of the almost empty car park. Louisa followed the middle path. It brought her to a covered courtyard dotted with four concrete benches. Heavily pregnant women lay sideways on the benches and snoozed.

More women, with lava-lavas draped over their heads to protect themselves from the sun, sat on the ground outside the yard. Children sat or lay scattered beside their mothers. The bulging women made Louisa feel exhausted. The first building beyond the courtyard was Outpatients. There was no one to ask for information. She carried on.

Beneath the glaring sun all the green buildings looked the same. She found a dispensary, a gravel basketball court and a couple of medical wards, but no mortuary or coroner's office. At one point two local girls in their late teens approached her and shyly asked if she needed help. But they didn't know where the mortuary was either. As they wandered away a third girl joined them. Louise recognised her. She was the same girl Louisa had seen with Paul. The same girl, she presumed, he'd gone to visit in Betio after he'd dropped Louisa off at her house the night before.

Louisa spied a man and a woman in white doctors' coats. As she got closer to them she realised they were arguing. The man, who was very tall, and exceptionally blond with blue eyes, stood as if to attention. His pale face was tight with tension. The woman, whose dark skin suggested she was local, appeared to be pleading with him.

Louisa showed them her warrant card and explained what she was after. The tall man took Louisa's hand and shook it firmly. His name was Dr Andrus. He was a UN volunteer surgeon from Estonia. His English was impeccable. The woman doctor introduced herself as Dr Jennifer, she was I-Kiribati. Her English was also impeccable. As senior surgeon Dr Andrus was also the coroner. He had all but finished the post mortem on Joe and invited Louisa to follow him to the mortuary.

Dr Andrus unlocked a double metal door in a square concrete building at the back of hospital. Inside, he flicked a light switch and a long fluorescent striplight in the ceiling blinked on to reveal a windowless, rectangular office dominated by a large old fashioned wooden desk. Apart from two chunky medical textbooks, a coffee mug and a bunch of car keys, the desk was bare. Andrus took off his pristine white coat and placed it on a hook on the back of a metal door in the back wall.

He coughed. 'Was it your idea to use the freezer?'

'There was nothing else,' said Louisa.

'It was extremely unhygienic.' He washed his hands up to his elbows with a purple-red liquid from a dispenser above the sink. 'However, the technician has scrubbed it and made it work again, thus preventing the body decomposing further. This has allowed me to carry out a fair post mortem.' Holding his hands in the air, he pushed open the door next to the sink with his shoulder and went into the next room.

The sour smell of chemicals, sickness and dirty nappies was nauseating. Metal shelf after metal shelf held glinting, sharp, steel instruments. A sluice, about ten centimetres wide and three centimetres deep, sliced the concrete floor into two halves. One solitary metal gurney sat on top of the sluice and dominated the room. Joe's naked body lay on the metal bed. His skin was so pale it was almost translucent. His chest had been sliced open and gaped upwards like the open mouth of a giant parrot fish gulping for air. From where Louisa stood, she was grateful she couldn't see Joe's face clearly.

Andrus nodded to a heavy steel door in the back wall of the room. 'We are waiting for a part from New Zealand for the cooler unit.' He pulled some thin green plastic gloves from a cardboard box fixed to the wall by the door. 'Do you have details of the next of kin? As coroner it is my duty to inform them of the circumstances of the death of the deceased.'

Louisa shook her head. 'I'll pass them on as soon as I have them.'

Andrus wriggled his long hands into his gloves. A metal trolley stood to the head of the gurney. A tidy row of various sized pairs of bloodied scissors and a bloodied metal basin sat in a tray on top of the trolley. A tall, angled metal contraption, the kind of thing you might see next to a dentist's chair, but bigger, much bigger, stood behind the trolley. Three instruments dangled from the contraption: a silver hose with a heavy sprinkler rose at the end of it; a second silver hose with what looked like the head of scrubbing brush attached to it, and a tall post, which carried a round, spring weigh scale. It looked like something you'd expect to find in a slaughter-house or old-style butcher's. The humming larder freezer from the Ambo sat against the side wall. Back home the results from the post mortem went directly to the senior investigating officer, who gave them to the murder team during a briefing. As a consequence Louisa had hardly ever been in a mortuary and that had been fine with her. Seeing the body cut up and surrounded by medical instruments gave her the creeps. It was somehow worse than seeing the body for the first time at the crime scene. On the plus side, mortuaries were usually as sterile as operating theatres. At least she hoped they were.

'Shall we get started?' said Andrus, plucking a paper mask from a box next to the gloves and pulling it over his mouth.

28

Louisa breathed through her mouth to minimise smelling the mortuary stench. It wasn't working.

'The murderer, has he or she been found?' said Andrus approaching the body.

'No.'

'So you will want the results from my post mortem as

soon as possible,' he said. 'I would have had them done but Dr Jennifer called me away.' He took a heavy-looking yellow plastic hazardous waste sack, the size of a carrier bag, from the bottom shelf of the trolley by the gurney. 'If a second post mortem is required, the organs are all there.' He placed the plastic bag inside Joe's open chest cavity and began pushing the two halves of the rib cage down on top of the bag. 'A Russian fisherman from a factory ship has had an accident. He was flown here by the ship helicopter. It seems we are the nearest hospital. He can speak no English and she does not know exactly where he has pain. Dr Jennifer was of the belief that I would happily help interpret his words.' He turned to face Louisa for a second. 'You are remaining there, by the door, yes?'

Louisa nodded. She had no intention of getting any closer. In fact, she didn't know how much longer she'd be able to cope in the airless room. The rumble of the air conditioner suggested it was on, but it didn't feel—or smell—like it.

'Had Dr Jennifer not distracted me, I would have finished by now.'

'Did you find out what was wrong with the Russian?' said Louisa, not really interested but feeling as if she had to say something.

'Estonia and Russia have a bad history, very bad. I speak Russian fluently but I do not want to use it. It is the language of our oppressor. But I suppose I will talk to the Russian after I have finished here.' Andrus drew himself upright. 'With difficulty I removed the dagger from the head. The blade penetrated the pterion. Pterion takes its name from the Greek *pteron*, meaning wing. If you think of Hermes with wings attached to this part of his temple, you will understand.'

'Ah,' said Louisa, ignoring the bile rising in her stomach and trying to concentrate on what Andrus was saying.

'The pterion,' he nodded towards the deceased's head, 'is the junction of four separate skull bones, the frontal, parietal, temporal and sphenoid. Sometimes referred to by my colleagues as "God's little joke", because the bony pterion is not just a hazard zone because it is so thin, but also because the middle meningeal, which is a very big artery, runs immediately beneath it. In this case the dagger penetrated the thin temple bone and severed the artery behind it. As you know, blood from an artery is pumped very fast. Death would have not taken long. The attacker was lucky, if the blade had gone into any other part of the skull it would not have penetrated the bone.'

'I'd wondered about that,' said Louisa. 'And the eyes? Were they removed before or after death? Can you tell?'

'The lack of defensive wounds suggest probably after death. A blunt instrument was used, possibly a spoon or a knife, but even a pen or stick could have worked. It is not as difficult as people think to remove an eyeball but psychologically it is a repulsive act. Only a certain kind of person can do this.'

Louisa cleared her throat. 'Why remove them?'

'You are the detective.'

'And why take them away from the scene?'

'Again, you are the detective,' said Andrus curtly, 'However, they need not have been taken. It is far more likely that the eyes were eaten by a wild animal. A coconut rat, for example, would have devoured them in seconds.'

Louisa hadn't thought about the possibility of the eyes being eaten by animals. 'The body doesn't show any evidence of animal bites, does it?'

'No, but that does not mean rats were not present, smaller animals too could have eaten them.'

Louisa thought she was going to be sick. 'Would force have been needed for the blow to the skull?'

'Some force, yes.'

'A man then?' she said.

'No, not necessarily. Now. Even skilled as I am, it was not easy to tidy up the head. Do you want to see the wound area, or what is left of it?'

She shook her head.

'There is one thing. The wound area shows bruising, suggesting the victim received a blow to the side of the head with a blunt object before the knife attack. This could have stunned the victim, which could explain the absence of defensive wounds. I have seen three such knife wounds since being here. Each time the attack was as a result of an excess consumption of alcohol. I'm afraid the local men cannot tolerate alcohol very well, did you know that?'

'Not just locals,' said Louisa. 'Some expatriate men can't handle their drink either.' Look at her dad, after all, and not forgetting Tom.

'I am talking about an intolerance, not a weakness of character,' said Andrus curtly. 'The I-Kiribati man can especially not tolerate Western beer. I don't know why that is, it would be a good area to study, don't you think?' He leaned over the corpse and with two hands he gave the rib cage a final press down. 'When they start drinking they do not know how to stop. If they are married, they believe someone is looking at their wife in a suggestive way, or that their wife is looking at another man in such a way. They grab whatever is at hand and strike out. One imagined wrong look and someone loses an eye, a leg or sometimes a life. It is tragic and there is no evidence that they are developing a tolerance to it.'

'It sounds like Friday night after the clubs have closed,' said Louisa. She couldn't remember the number of fights she'd had to break up in Edinburgh, caused by similar imagined wrong looks. 'Are you saying this was an alcohol related attack by a local person?'

'Not at all,' said Andrus. 'But the attack is savage. Although there does not appear to have been a struggle. It is possible he did not fear his attacker.'

'So, the cause of death is the one stab wound to the side

of the head and that's all?'

Dr Andrus threw her a withering look. 'Are you questioning me?'

'Not at all. I meant, were there any extenuating causes? Could the deceased have been drugged or drunk at the time of his death? '

Dr Andrus frowned. 'There is no facility for me to test such things. However, looking at the conditions of his organs, which are very healthy, and based on the contents of his stomach, there is nothing to suggest death was not sudden and the cause was not the one fatal stab to the side of the head. If he had not been killed, all the indications are he would have lived a long and healthy life.'

Louisa nodded. 'Do you have a TOD?'

'A TOD?' said Dr Andrus, his voice ringing with disgust. 'We are a lazy American now, are we? Does it really take up too much energy to say the three small words "time of death"?'

Louisa didn't know what to make of Dr Andrus—efficient but mad? She smiled. 'It's a term in colloquial usage in Scotland.'

The doctor was unimpressed. 'Courtesy of the Ambo Lagoon Club freezer and yourself—' he bowed slightly towards her '—and, of course, I cannot be accurate, that is the stuff of fantasy and ridiculous American police programmes, but my best estimate under the circumstances is between six o'clock in the evening of Thursday and midnight of Thursday.'

'Thank you,' said Louisa. She had to get out of that place. 'One last thing, Dr Andrus, have you heard of the hash?'

'From time to time I run with the hash people. It is good to exercise. A healthy body is a healthy mind.'

'Did you treat Christine Brown on Thursday night for a twisted ankle?'

'Yes. I believe Paul Wilson dropped her off. She had to

wait. We had an emergency, a man had almost sawn his foot off with a chain saw. It was very messy.'

29

The umbrella leaves of the banana palms behind the chicken wire fence were coated in white coral dust. Ahead, the tarmac road and hazy sky met in a shimmering sandwich of blue. The road seemed to have got narrower. Where the hell was she? Louisa had been walking for at least ten minutes and had expected to have spotted the sign for the Otintaai Hotel by now. Had she gone the wrong way? Dr Andrus had said the hotel was within walking distance of the hospital, in the direction of the Ambo. She couldn't miss it, he'd said. Well she had missed it! The last house was ten minutes back and she was thirsty and getting a headache from having to squint so much to avoid the midday glaring sun.

The preliminary post mortem report had been a little disappointing. She'd learnt nothing new. Basically, Joe had been a healthy man before he was killed. Death had been instantaneous, or as near as. His eyes had been crudely removed after death, for what purpose Andrus had no idea. Anyone could have done it, although perhaps not someone who was under the influence of alcohol. She stopped to look around. Where the hell was she? It had seemed a good idea to call in at the hotel and check on the patrol car when she was at the hospital. Now she wasn't so sure. Why were there never any signs anywhere?

'Miss, where you going?'

Louisa jumped. It was one of the two girls who'd offered to help her earlier at the hospital. She looked older than Louisa remembered, more like twenty than eighteen. Her red lava-lava had seen better days, as had her shapeless, washed-out white T-shirt. She was in bare feet.

'Are you lost again?' said the girl, her face serious.

Louisa smiled. 'If this road doesn't take me to the Otintaai Hotel, then, yes I could be.'

'Oh no. This road takes you to Tarawa Teachers' College.'

'Bloody hell! I am lost!'

The girl blushed. Louisa wondered was it because she had said 'bloody'?

'Don't worry. There is a shortcut to the Otintaai Hotel through the college grounds. I will take you.'

'I can't ask you to do that. If you give me the directions, I'll be fine,' said Louisa.

'I don't think you will be fine,' said the girl earnestly. 'Let me help you. Come.' She turned and ducked through a hole in the sagging chicken wire fence and disappeared.

Louisa took a second to think about it then followed the girl and around a thicket of banana palms to a swamp of giant dirty green rhubarb-like leaves, shaded by a ring of breadfruit trees.

'That's babaia,' said the girl pointing to the leafy vegetables. 'We make stew with the leaves.' She walked around the side of the pit.

Louisa thought she could almost taste the damp, tangy soil on her tongue. It was a good smell immediately spoiled by a whiff of pigpen. She wanted to hold her nose but she resisted.

The girl pointed to a second bush path winding its way to the left of the babaia pit. 'That goes to the men's dorm, we don't go there because it stinks. We must go this way.' She nodded ahead. 'My name is Meere. What's yours?'

'Nice to meet you, Meere. I'm Louisa. Detective Sergeant Louisa Townsend.

Meere looked serious again. 'You are with the police?'

'Yes, I'm a police officer,' said Louisa. 'And what about you, what do you do?'

Meere suddenly looked uncomfortable. 'I am training to be a primary school teacher.'

'So you study here, at the college?'

Meere's face suddenly lit up. 'Look, there is my friend!'

They'd stopped at a second copse of banana palms. A girl approached them from the far side.

'That is Tiabei,' said Meere, beaming. 'She was with me earlier. You remember? She is very ugly, but she is a good friend.'

Louisa blushed. She felt embarrassed for the girls. Talk about saying it how it was.

'Hello again, Miss,' said Tiabei.

Tiabei may have been a bit lanky but she wasn't unattractive. By whose standards was she ugly? 'Hello, Tiabei.'

'This is Detective Louisa,' said Meere.

'Where are you from?'

'I'm from Scotland in the United Kingdom.'

'How exciting!' said Tiabei, beaming, 'Did you know Lady Di?'

Louisa couldn't help smiling. 'No, sorry, I didn't know Lady Diana. But can I ask you both a question?'

Both girls nodded vigorously.

'Who was the girl you were with at the hospital, the thin girl with the very long hair?'

'You mean Eretibete,' said Meere. 'She is my cousin. She is very pretty, isn't she?' Tiabei made a face when Meere said that. Louisa carried on. 'Was she ill, is that why you were at the hospital?'

Meere looked away.

Tiabei said. 'It is Meere who is ill.'

Louisa tried to ask more questions but both girls stopped talking after that. They walked the rest of the way in silence. Louisa wondered what it was she'd said that had upset them.

30

The main college building was a long timber-framed structure which had so many holes in the walls, it looked as if someone had attacked it with a demolition ball. Tiabei said the staffroom, the school office and the refectory were all housed in that building. An ugly, two-storey concrete building stood opposite it. The girls' dorm, Tiabei said. Brightly coloured lava-lavas and towels hung from twin rows of open windows.

'To get to the Otintaai Hotel, you go past the dorm, out the gate and turn left. It is at the end of the road,' said Tiabei, pointing to an open double gate made of chicken wire. 'We will come with you.'

'No, of course not. This is perfect. You've been really helpful. Good luck with your studies. And I'm sorry you've not been well. I hope you get better soon.'

Meere looked away. Tiabei frowned. 'Meere was not sick. She was stabbed.'

'What?' said Louisa.

Tiabei said, 'The man has been arrested and is in jail.'

'That's terrible!' Louisa turned to Meere. 'When did this happen? Are you sure you're okay?'

Meere continued to refuse to look at Louisa. Tiabei said, 'Last week Meere went to the medicine man for a treatment for her back. His house is very far away. He is very good except when she went last time he was not there. She did not want to come all the way back to college with the pain in her back. So she waited for him. She waited so long she fell asleep. When she woke up it was very dark. Something was wrong. She was very cold. Her lava-lava was not there. Her underwears were also missing. Isn't that true, Meere?'

Meere nodded sheepishly.

'As her eyes grew used to the light she saw him watching her. He was drunk. She asked for her clothes. He moved fast. There was a knife in his hand. He said that she was not to scream. But she did not want to get pregnant. She screamed. He cut her but she got free and ran. By now the villagers have heard her screams and they came and stopped him catching her and cutting her any more.'

'You're lucky the villagers were there,' said Louisa, genuinely shocked.

Meere lifted her T-shirt and pointed to a white dressing the size of her fist below her rib cage on her left side. 'The doctor said I was fortunate that the knife didn't cut anything serious.'

Tiabei said, 'The man wrote to Meere. He said he was very sorry, that he'd had too much to drink. He is in prison now. Meere's family say they will kill him if he ever comes out.'

'In Scotland you can talk to someone, a counsellor, when you have had a horrible experience like this. It can help. Do you have anyone like that here?'

'There's Tererei,' said Meere frowning. 'She's head of the girls. But she says she can't make an exception for my case.'

Louisa didn't understand. 'What do you mean an exception?'

Meere looked down. Louisa thought she saw tears in her eyes.

'Tererei says Meere disgraced the college and they are going to kick her out,' said Tiabei said.

'But it wasn't Meere's fault she was attacked.' Louisa was bewildered.

Tiabei grabbed Louisa's arm. 'That's what I've been saying but Tererei won't listen to me. Maybe you can talk to

Tererei on Meere's behalf? You are a policewoman. And an expatriate!'

'Wait a minute! I can't just—'

'Yes! Yes, you can!' said Tiabei, 'You can give Meere a chance! Her case is coming up very soon and she has no one to help her.'

'Please, Miss,' said Meere. There were definitely tears in the girl's eyes now. 'My family are on Beru. They spent all their money sending me here. If I have to leave before finishing my training, I'll not get a job and won't be able to help them. And they will be disgraced.'

'Meere, you take Louisa into the staffroom,' said Tiabei full of excitement. 'I'll get Tererei.'

Before Louisa could stop her Tiabei had gone and Meere was dragging Louisa into the timber-framed building. Louisa couldn't believe it. All she'd wanted to do was pop into the Otintaai and ask if there was a garage that could help with the flat tyre. Now she was caught up in a rape case and some college dispute.

The staffroom was long and rectangular and stuffy. Half-closed shutters blocked the light from a row of windows overlooking the front of the building. Desks of various shapes and sizes lined the walls. Some were covered in books and papers, others were bare.

Meere sat on a desk near the door. 'We can wait here. Tiabei will be back soon.'

None of the desks seemed as rickety or as old-fashioned as the one Louisa was being invited to sit on, or as abandoned. A layer of dust appeared to cover everything. Louisa decided to stay standing.

'I'm sure there must be a mistake. No one would expel you, you're the victim in this.'

Meere looked down. Louisa didn't know what to say.

She should be getting back, not hanging about some staffroom. 'What about your cousin Eretibete? Is she also studying here at Tarawa Teachers' College? Can she not help you?'

Meere tutted. 'She is not here at TTC. She lives with her brother in Betio.' Meere looked around as if checking they were alone and whispered. 'She has an expatriate boyfriend. She says she is going to live in England with him.'

'Does she?' said Louisa. 'And what's her boyfriend's name?'

Meere shook her head. 'It's a secret.'

'Maybe he doesn't exist,' said Louisa. 'Maybe she's having fun with you?'

'Oh, no,' said Meere, 'I saw him. He was at the hospital on Thursday evening when I was having my dressing checked. He gave Eretibete a lift home to Betio. I don't know his name but he looks like Prince Charles!' said Meere, laughing.

Louisa laughed too. She couldn't imagine anyone to look less like Prince Charles than Paul Wilson.

Tiabei burst in. 'Nei Tererei is coming! She's coming!'

Meere jumped off the desk where she'd been sitting just as a small fat woman, with a round face and barrel body, entered the room. Louisa started. It was the woman from the car park and the bus.

At the sight of Louisa, the woman shouted, 'You are not welcome! You go! You go now!'

The girls looked horrified. Louisa was stunned. 'I'm Detective Inspector Louisa Townsend. Meere here—'

'You leave now! I will not talk to you! I will never talk to you!' screamed Tererei.

31

An odd rustling noise woke Louisa with a start. Her lips were dry and she had a sick taste at the back of her throat. She glanced at her travel alarm clock on the floor by the bed. It was two o'clock. Louisa cursed. She'd only wanted a quick nap—the visit to the funeral, the trip to the far end of the island, the listening to Dave the Fish and his cronies talk bullshit, the visit to the mortuary and then the detour to the teachers' college had left her shattered. Louisa sat up. It was day three into the investigation and she had a report to write for Nakibae with very little to put in it: so far she had a possible suspect, but no evidence to link him to the killing, and no witnesses of any importance and no clues. She needed to interview Dave the Fish and his cronies again and soon, but Michael and Tebano were still guarding the Korean fishermen. It was maddening! Her one hope was that someone somewhere would recognise the dagger and know where Joe's missing clothes were—Constable John had assured her he'd distributed the details. If the items could be linked to Dave the Fish, she'd have him. Louisa suddenly thought about Meere. She felt sorry for her. Being forced to leave the college under such terrible circumstances was simply wrong. Louisa had felt obliged to promise the girls she'd return to the college and talk to the principal, though she had no idea when that would be. As for the woman called Tererei? She was clearly mad. There was no other explanation for her behaviour.

A scraping noise. Just like earlier. It came from outside. It was followed by the sound of children squealing and giggling. Louisa hurried into the living room. Reteta was out the front. She pushed a wobbly, long-handled cart up the path. A giant television set and state-of-the-art video recorder sat on top of the cart. Half a dozen children danced alongside her.

Louisa opened the front door. 'What are you doing?'

Red-faced, Reteta stopped pushing the trolley and carefully set it on the ground. 'The burial of Tion is over and I have been a very lucky person because I have been able to hire one video recorder and one television set for a very cheap price from my Catholic church group.'

Louisa wasn't sure what Reteta's priest would have said about the bomaki ceremonies earlier. 'Now?'

'You said I could show a video to the families before they go home.'

'I forgot.' So that's why Reteta was being so friendly. 'I suppose it's okay.' After their argument at the funeral Louisa had expected Reteta to blank her for at least a couple of days. She was glad she was speaking to her again. They'd never been close, but she hated it when they didn't get on. 'As long as you keep the noise down. I have a report to write up about the murder case.'

'Good! Good!' Reteta beamed. 'You find the killer yet?'

Louisa shook her head. 'It's not straightforward.'

Reteta tutted and took up the long handles of the unwieldy cart and began pushing it towards the front door. 'Of course not. How can you arrest a ghost?'

'There are no such things as ghosts.'

'The eyes of humans are the food of ghosts.' Reteta rested the cart at the bottom of the front step. 'That is why the eyes were taken. The Ambo Lagoon Club is not a good place now.'

'We don't know why the victim's eyes were gouged.' Louisa frowned. 'Where are you going?'

'I am bringing the television set and video recorder into the house.'

'Oh, no.' Louisa was having none of this. 'You said you were going to watch the video outside.'

'I was. I was. But everyone is coming sooner than I

thought and it is too light outside to see the screen properly. It is much better to watch the screen inside in the shade, with the curtains drawn.'

Louisa did not want a houseful of villagers and their germs in her house. 'I have work to do. Important work.' They'd touch everything. Poke everywhere.

Reteta's smile vanished. 'You agreed.'

'For you to show the film outside. You won't even be able to get that huge machine up these steps!'

'It is not a problem. We will all stay in the one room and you can work in your other room. And I will tidy after everyone goes away. You will not have to worry about the dirt. I will make the house clean. Very clean.'

Louisa blushed. Could Reteta hear inside her head? Surely not? But how did she know she'd been thinking about the germs? What if she could hear the voices? 'I need to work.'

Reteta scowled. 'You will make me look bad in front of my friends. I promised them they could come. You told me it was okay. I promise I will make everything clean afterwards.'

Louisa couldn't think straight. Surely Reteta couldn't see her thoughts? It was impossible, wasn't it? Despite herself Louisa said, 'Okay. You can have the film inside. But just this once.'

Reteta beamed. 'Tikiraoi! Just the one time only. You will not know we are here.'

32

The water from the giant tank at the side of the house trickled into Louisa's bucket. There was a power cut and the worst thing about having no electricity meant no power for the water pump, so no shower. But Louisa was desperate to be clean. A bucket wash was better than no wash. While she waited in the sticky heat for the water to collect, five voluminous women, all smiles, bustled into the back garden and sat down next to Reteta by the fire. Louisa assumed they were the first wave of people for the film show. She'd thought the film show would be cancelled because of the power cut, but Reteta was confident the power would come back on in time.

For a brief second Louisa thought to join the women, but there was no room. Besides, she'd want to bring her own mat to sit on. How would she explain that? She checked the water level in the bucket. It wasn't even an eighth full. Disgusted, she turned the tap off and went inside to write her report. Without the overhead fan to keep her cool, Louisa's fingers slipped across the keyboard of her laptop and she made silly typos. She was also worried she wouldn't get the report finished before the battery ran out. And then there was her unclean skin, it itched so much to be washed it felt on fire. And, worst of all, a tiny voice in her head, just loud enough for her to hear, muttered 'dirty' over and over again like a broken record. She knew she had to do something before it got louder. She saved her file, snapped the laptop shut, put on her baseball cap, a leaving present from Lothian and Borders Police, and told Reteta she'd be back soon. Exercise stifled the voices. She was going for a walk across the causeway.

The Betio causeway had been built by the Dai Nippon Construction Company. It was four kilometres long and connected Betio to Bairiki. When she was little her dad had told her that Nippon meant Japanese. He'd said the Japanese had built the causeway to keep in the Kiribati Government's good books because they wanted to be granted rights to fish in Kiribati's vast sea area. The Japanese had also built the new hospital (where she had not been born!) and more recently the new House of Parliament. Louisa imagined the Japanese and

Kiribati governments had to be best pals now.

The voices finally disappeared when Louisa was two thirds of the way across the causeway, which was just as well as she couldn't have stood the heat any longer, or the smell. It came from the thousands of tiny dead crustaceans trapped in the mud flats of the low tide, fricasseed alive in the searing sun. If there had been a breeze, maybe it would have wafted the smell away. But there was no breeze. As she turned to go back to Betio a jeep pulled up behind her. It was Christine and Nicole.

'Hello,' said Christine, sticking her head out of the passenger window of the 4x4. Her face was serious. 'Have you seen a medium sized terrier running around anywhere?'

Louisa shook her head. 'Sorry.'

'Oscar's a few kangaroos short in the top paddock,' said Nicole, peering over Christine's shoulder, 'but we love him. Can't find him anywhere.'

'I'm sure he'll turn up,' said Louisa. 'Most missing people do. Can't see why dogs would be any different.'

'Hope so,' said Nicole. 'By the way, what happened to you at the hotel last night? One minute we saw you talking to Nakibae, the next you were gone.'

'Needed my beauty sleep,' said Louisa, hoping she was so flushed by the heat they couldn't tell she was blushing.

'It's rather hot for a walk, isn't it?' said Christine.

Louisa smiled. 'I wanted some exercise but I underestimated how hot it would be.'

'Jump in, we'll give you a lift,' said Nicole. 'You live in Betio, yes?'

Louisa didn't think twice. She climbed in the back of the vehicle. 'Has your dog been missing for long?'

'Just since this morning.' said Nicole, pulling away. 'But he's never gone off for this long before. I roped Christine into helping me.' She smirked, 'She was in the middle of making a Sunday roast.'

'Occasionally,' said Christine, defensively, 'it's nice to have some good old British food.'

'But a roast?' said Nicole, laughing, 'In this heat? You know what? We should go for a dip.'

'Now?' Was the woman serious?

'Sure now!'

'I've got to get back for the little ones,' said Christine.

'Can't you trust Ian for half an hour longer?'

Christine looked out the passenger window and said nothing.

'What about you, Sarge?'

Louisa smiled politely. 'The tide is out.'

'The channel under the causeway bridge always has water.'

'I'd have to get my swimsuit—'

'I've got spare cossies in the back, enough for the three of us. Christine?'

Without looking at Nicole, Christine said, 'It's too public.'

'There's no one here! Look around.' Nicole screeched the jeep to a halt and turned and looked at Louisa. Her mirrored aviator sunglasses reflected Louisa's face right back at her. 'The water's fast moving, crystal clear and clean. A five minute dip, that's all?'

Louisa started to laugh despite herself. She didn't particularly want to spend time with either of these women but she wanted even less to go back to the house. And the idea of a refreshing dip and getting out of the appalling heat was enticing, never mind the chance to wash away the sweat and gunky grime of the day. 'Why not?'

'Yeh! said Nicole.

33

Nicole pulled up at the bridge. It wasn't a true bridge, rather an opening in the middle of the concrete kilometre long causeway, which allowed small boats to go between the lagoon and the ocean without having to travel all the way around the Betio islet.

Nicole jumped out of the car and opened the back door. She rummaged around and chucked a bundle of clothing at Louisa. 'You're about my size. Try these swimmers and use the shirts and T-shirt to cover up. It's not like at home.'

Louisa silently laughed. Nicole was telling her it wasn't like home!

'Christine?' Nicole chucked a swimsuit at her.

'Five minutes,' said Christine, catching the bathing suit, 'that's all.'

Nicole's costume was a tight fit, but it did the job. Louisa stood on the roadside with Christine while Nicole locked up the car. She could hardly wait to get in the water.

'Oh, no!' said Christine, looking over the embankment wall and down to the channel.

'What?' said Nicole.

'The boat!'

Louisa looked over the wall. In the middle of the deep, fast flowing channel water, two local men, naked apart from their board shorts, heaved their dripping bodies on to a bobbing aluminium boat. Two more men clung to the side of the boat and heaved a silver air tank out of the water and into the hands of the men now in the boat. A fifth man on the far shore dragged a second tank from a line of four into the water.

'That's that then,' said Christine, her voice gritty.

'Who are they?' said Louisa, shielding her eyes from the glare of the sun.

'Just some men,' said Nicole. She frowned.

'What are they doing?' said Louisa.

'I'm not swimming,' said Christine, ignoring Louisa's question, and taking the car key out of Nicole's hand, 'with an audience.'

'Wait! I've got a beaut idea, we leave the men to loading their boat and go for a snorkel!'

'No,' said Christine.

'Don't be such a wimp,' said Nicole.

'You go if you want. I'll take your car and check on the kids. I'll be back in half an hour.'

Nicole pulled a face behind Christine's back then turned to Louisa. 'Sarge? What about you? There's a magical snorkel spot straight ahead. A few minutes walking in a bit of shallow water and we're at the reef edge. Low tide is the best time to go. Totally safe. Should have thought of it sooner. You know how to snorkel, don't you?'

'Yes.' She'd done it once or twice, on holiday. 'But—'

'Bloody brilliant!

Louisa carried a pink mask and snorkel and a pair of clear plastic fins. Nicole gripped a similar yellow set under her arm. They'd been unearthed from the back of the car. Nicole told Christine to pick them up in forty minutes. By the time they'd scrambled over the embankment wall and jumped on to the sandy bank at the other side, Christine had driven off.

'Keep the fins under your arms,' said Nicole, striding down the embankment to the water's edge. 'It's easier to walk through the shallow water without them. We'll put them on when we're in the deeper water. I'll tell you when.'

Louisa nodded. Nicole was the sort of bossy person that would irritate Louisa after a while. Louisa liked only one person being in charge and that was herself. But when it came to snorkelling, Louisa would bow to Nicole's superior knowledge.

'Christine's such a bloody chicken,' said Nicole now at the water's edge.

'I didn't have Christine down for being timid,' said Louisa, standing next to her.

'Are all you Brits wimps?'

'No more than anyone else,' said Louisa, surprised at the vehemence in Nicole's voice.

'And she's a racist!' said Nicole. 'Too white to swim in the same water as the black men!'

'You think so?' said Louisa. 'I thought she didn't want to swim because it was so crowded. The boat in the middle of the channel took up all the room.'

Nicole shook her head. 'I know what I'm talking about when it comes to prejudices and she's a racist. Let's go!'

Louisa followed Nicole into the shallow lap, lapping water. She could have told Nicole a thing or two about racism. There had been surprisingly few children at her school in Edinburgh whose mums had dark skin. And she couldn't remember the number of times she'd been called a 'Paki'. Bad luck for the name caller, though, if her mum had been in earshot of the abuse. She'd nab the offender and go to great lengths to explain that Kiribati was nowhere near Pakistan. Louisa smiled. The threat of a geography lesson from Mrs Townsend had probably done more to stop racist name calling in the playground than any number of assemblies given by the headteacher.

'Tia-bo, Miss Nicole!'

Louisa looked to her right. The shout came from the channel.

'Tia-bo!' Another shout.

All the men were now in the boat and seated around the tanks in the middle.

Nicole shouted, 'Tia-bo!'

'They know you?' said Louisa as the man at the back of the boat revved the throttle and the boat lurched forwards towards the open ocean.

Nicole laughed. 'I see them here from time to time, that's all. Saying hello's being polite. And look, they're going now. Christine could have easily stayed.'

'They've forgotten something,' said Louisa. A solitary air tank sat on the sandy bank on the other side of the channel.

'It's an air tank.'

'I know what it is,' said Louisa. 'What do fishermen need with air tanks?'

'Fishermen?' Nicole laughed. 'Some detective you are. Do you see nets? Rods? Gaffs? They're divers. Didn't you see the rest of their gear at the bottom of the boat?'

Louisa's guts did a loop the loop. 'What do they dive for?'

'Sea cucumbers mostly.'

The boat was already a couple of hundred yards away. Louisa groaned. 'Did those men work for Joe?'

'Who else would they have worked for?' said Nicole.

34

Joe's employees had been twenty yards away from Louisa and she'd had no idea. She was so angry. It was a missed opportunity to talk to them about the argument between Dave the Fish and Joe. 'Why didn't you tell me who they were?'

'Don't throw a wobbly with me!' said Nicole, her mouth twitching in anger.

Louisa stood with the water lapping at her shins and watched the small boat grow even smaller. 'Who do they work for now?'

'How should I know?' snapped Nicole. 'Are we heading

for a snorkel, or what?'

'I am investigating a murder,' said Louisa, unimpressed by Nicole's attitude.

'Look, they'll be back in a few hours,' said Nicole, 'you can talk to them then.'

Nicole was right. The men would be back. 'I just wish you'd said sooner that the men had worked for Joe.'

'You didn't ask. Look, you're not going to let this spoil the snorkel, are you?' Nicole strode ahead. 'They say Dave the Fish owns the boat now. He's a sleaze who lives in Buota. Been on the island for years. Married a local girl. Always pissed.'

'I've met him,' said Louisa sloshing through the shallow water after Nicole. She supposed she could still have a snorkel.

'One thing about Joe, he took care of his men. There was an accident the other day. One of the divers died. Joe was very good to the family. Dave won't do that.'

'What kind of accident?'

'Not sure. On the boat. There's no decompression chamber here and diving's not regulated. The men take risks diving too deep for too long. It was only a matter of time before someone died of the bends. Tion was a nice man, though. It was tragic.'

'Tion?' Louisa hurried through the wavy water to catch up with Nicole. 'Are you sure the man's name was Tion? The woman who works for me, one of her relatives died a couple of days ago. He was called Tion. Couldn't be the same man, could it? I was at his funeral this morning.'

Nicole looked at Louisa and smirked. 'Tion is a very common name. It means John in English. People die here all the time. You'd be surprised. And it's always the same thing they die of too, sickness and diarrhoea or TB. You do know never to drink the water unless it's been boiled and filtered?' She didn't wait for Louisa to answer. 'Drinking untreated water is one of the most common causes of diarrhoea.'

'I know,' said Louisa.

'You wouldn't believe the amount of visitors who check their water is treated but don't question having ice cubes in their drink at one of the bars. Imagine being that stupid?'

'Imagine,' said Louisa. For the second time that day she had the creepy feeling that people could see into her mind. First Reteta and now Nicole. She dismissed the idea immediately. Didn't give it time to take a hold. The water pushed around Louisa's thighs, making it hard to keep up. The waves on the horizon suddenly looked big. Very big.

'More than twenty-five percent of the population have hepatitis B. Not a good statistic. Most likely due to all the sailors from the Marine College going away and sleeping around and bringing it back. They say there's AIDS on the island too.'

Why had she thought a snorkel with this woman was a good idea? 'Or,' said Louisa, 'all the aid workers coming in and spreading it around when they're here.'

Nicole seemed not to have heard Louisa. 'The average life expectancy for a man is fifty-five years. Did you know that?'

Louisa did, as it happened. Her mum never stopped talking about the tragedy of her cousins, too scared or intimidated, or too downright poor, to go to the I-Matang hospital until it was too late.

'The latest killer is diabetes. Too much imported processed food and feasting. It's a bad combination. And the cars and buses mean fewer and fewer people exercise. It's a vicious circle.'

Nicole was beginning to get right up Louisa's nose. 'You'd get on well with my mother.'

'What was that?'

Louisa decided to change the subject. 'Tion the diver?' she said, stepping up her pace, determined to keep up with Nicole. 'When did he die?'

'Wednesday night, early Thursday morning.'

'That's an incredible coincidence because the Tion whose funeral I attended this morning also died early Thursday morning.' She snatched at breaths while she walked. 'It seems a bit of a coincidence that diver Tion died one day and Joe, his employer, was killed the next.'

Nicole roared with laughter. 'Hope that's not the best you're going to come up with?'

The woman was infuriating. 'What was Tion like?'

'How should I know?'

Nicole seemed to be walking faster and faster. Louisa was no slouch but she struggled to keep up with her. 'Did Tion get on with Joe?'

'How should I know? What I don't understand about the gross Joe murder thing, apart from the grotesque removal of his eyes, is why leave him in the school hut?'

You and me both, thought Louisa. 'You're sure he never visited you there?'

'Never.' Nicole paused to catch her breath.

Louisa was secretly relieved. 'Did he know any of the mums or child minders?'

'No more than he knew me.' She pursed her lips. 'If I'd killed someone, I'd have done it on the ocean side and dragged the body to the shore and let the tide and the sharks do the rest. Then there'd be no evidence and nothing to investigate.'

Louisa shivered. 'Sharks?' The water swirled around her chest now. It almost toppled her off her feet. It felt cold. 'What sharks? I lived here until I was eight, the only sharks I ever heard anyone talking about were the tiger sharks in the deep heart of the lagoon.'

'You're Gilbertese!'

Louisa groaned when she'd realised what she'd just said. She'd not wanted anyone to know she'd lived on Tarawa as a child. Least of all someone with a big mouth like Nicole's.

A broad smirk emerged across Nicole's face. 'I thought

there was something about you that didn't fit.'

'Cheers,' said Louisa.

'You know what I mean. Do you still have family here?'

'My cousin, Reteta. She does my housekeeping and calls me Lulu, which drives me nuts.'

'Lulu?'

'It used to be my nickname when I was wee.'

'Wait till I tell everyone you're a native.'

'I'd appreciate it if you didn't.'

Nicole stopped. 'Are you ashamed?'

Louisa laughed. 'Of course not. I just don't want to broadcast it.' She panted for breath.

'I understand,' said Nicole, nodding her head and also gasping for breath, 'the custom of "bubuti". You don't want your rellies to ask you for things.'

This wasn't the reason. But she said, 'Exactly. That's it.' She cleared her throat. 'If there are sharks, Nicole, I'm not snorkelling.'

Nicole groaned. 'I've snorkelled here dozens of times and I've not seen a shark once. The ocean's too full of fish for any sharks to bother about us mucking about along the reef edge.'

In front of them the waves roared. Louisa found it increasingly difficult to stand in the swirling sea. 'You're sure?'

'Are you always this anxious? How do you do your job? It's best to swim from here on though. When we get nearer to the reef edge just wait for a calm wave. As soon as it's about to break, swim into it and kick for all you're worth. The back wash of the wave will help carry you over the edge of the reef and you'll be there.'

'What's a calm wave?' shouted Louisa but Nicole had already gone. Louisa took her fins and fixed them to her feet under the water. Next she checked her mask and snorkel. Finally, she ducked under the water after Nicole. The sea below was a mass of turbulent grey flecks. Louisa kicked forwards. The swell of the water lifted her up and up and then let her gently down. She pushed on. Tiny golden and white striped angelfish darted here and there. Then—wham! A massive wave from out of nowhere threw her up, slammed her down. Louisa was upside down then downside up. Water everywhere. In her mask. In her snorkel. Her nose. Her mouth. She blew hard. She sucked. Sea water. In her mouth. She coughed. She swam. Upwards. Was it upwards? She blew. She sucked. At last. Air flowed into her mouth. Her head pushed up out of the water. Her feet paddled on the spot under the water. She wrenched the snorkel and mask from her face. Mouth wide open, she gulped in the warm air.

'Told you it was easy!' yelled Nicole, appearing at Louisa's side, also treading water.

'I don't know about easy,' said Louisa, fiddling with her mask, 'but I've made it.'

35

It was like being in a massive aquarium but better: clown fish scurried between ferns of red coral; wave after wave of silver slithers did the loop the loop; a bunch of toothy, multi-coloured parrot fish dive-bombed an oblivious gliding ray. She didn't know how long she'd been snorkelling aimlessly for when she spied the turtle. It paddled on the sea floor before swimming further and further into the cavernous ocean. Curious, Louisa followed it. The water became cloudy. The outline of the turtle grew fuzzier. Louisa kicked faster. Then it was gone and she was alone in the grey-green vastness of the bottomless ocean. A buzzing filled her ears. She shivered. Something dark.

Zigzagging to the side of her. Louisa glanced about. Nothing. There it was again. A sleek shimmer. At the other side now. She swivelled in the water. Nothing. She looked down. Two grey sharks. Both at least one and a half metres long. Silently slip-sloping in the murky water below. Louisa thought she felt her heart stop. The animals cut through the fuzzy water and disappeared. Louisa couldn't move. But she had to. They could come back. She wanted to pee. But everyone knew sharks were attracted to pee. She turned, kicked her fins as hard as she could. She didn't stop until she saw the foaming waves crash on the jagged iron stone shore at the edge of the reef wall in front of her

No sign of Nicole. Nothing. Louisa ducked her head back beneath the water. No sharks. They could return at any minute. Where was Nicole. Had Nicole gone in? What to do? Stay? Go? Louisa frantically trod water. Her chest felt tight. What to do?

Nicole exploded out of the water right in front of her. 'Fantastic snorkelling! I don't know why more people don't come here!'

'I saw a shark!' said Louisa before she could stop herself. 'Two sharks!'

'It would have only been reef sharks.'

'They were at least as big as me!' she said, gasping for breath, 'and they could come back at any minute. I'm going in!'

'Christ! Calm down! Even nippers know reef sharks aren't dangerous. But if you really want to go in, we'll go.'

'Right then.' Louisa couldn't look at her. At that moment, she absolutely hated Nicole. 'Let's go.' A big wave came. Louisa kicked into it. The wave caught her. It carried her inwards. She kicked harder. Moved forward with it. She was almost over the coral edge. The wave broke. She waited to be washed forward. But something was wrong. She was sucked back. Into the throbbing ocean. She kicked against the pull. It was useless. She'd been dumped back in the deep water.

Another wave came. She swam into its curving swell. It carried her forward. She kicked and kicked. She was nearly over. The wave broke. She was tugged backwards. She struggled and struggled. It was useless.

Nicole was beside her. 'We have to—' she gasped, '—we have to keep trying and as the wave sucks you back grab on to something, anything!'

Louisa gasped for breath. 'There's a current. A bad current. It's like a rip tide or something.'

Nicole shouted above the noise of the crashing foam, 'Just push for all you're worth!'

'We need to go somewhere else—' But Nicole was gone. Louisa tried to stay calm. It was silly to think she wouldn't get back over. But what if she couldn't? What if the current caught her and took her away? How long could she survive? If they couldn't find drifting boats, how would they ever find her, a minute speck drifting in the ocean? What about the sharks? Her legs felt heavy. Her fingers and toes tingled, they were so cold. She felt scared. She would not give in to fear. Ignore it. Just like the voices. She took a deep breath. She ducked back under the sea. A wave rumbled up behind her. It lifted her up. She kicked her feet as hard as she could. She spied a round clump of coral ahead. Was it brain coral? Could she grip it? She propelled herself forward. The coral head was just in front of her. The tips of her fingers nearly touched it. Just a few centimetres further forward. Just one centimetre. Whoosh, the wave tugged her back. She kicked and kicked against its pull. It was useless. She was washed back in the deep ocean. But she had nearly made it. She felt energised. She would do it this time. She flicked forwards again. She kicked faster. Another wave came. It caught her. It drove her on. And on. Her hands stretched out. A spiky column of coral appeared ahead. She thrust forward. She grabbed a jagged corner. The wave broke. It sucked her back. Finger by finger she clung on to her hold. The tips of her fingers burned. Her eyes blurred. She lost the grip. She tumbled round. Water filled her snorkel. She choked. Then somehow Louisa was able to stand. The spewing foam of a spent wave surrounded her half-submerged body. Had she made it? She had! She had actually made it back across. Nicole stood fifty yards along the shore. Louisa shouted and waved. Nicole saw her and waded over.

Louisa tried to pull her fins off but her legs were shaking so much she couldn't lean over without falling back into the water. She spat out some salty water still lurking in her mouth. The tips of the fingers on her right hand were bleeding, but she didn't care. She was so glad to be over the reef edge, out of the deep water and safe.

'Are you okay?' Nicole was beside her.

'I think so,' she panted.

'You should have kept to the channel!'

'The channel?' Louisa burst out laughing and flopped backwards into the water, 'That was probably the most dangerous place to come in. The water was being compressed into that small area, and the force of it as it washed back was twice as strong as anywhere else!'

'Why are you getting your knickers in a knot? We made it!'

Louisa lifted herself up. The water slopped around her waist. She stared at Nicole. There was a red ring across her forehead where her mask had been and her eyes were black. 'But we nearly didn't, doesn't that bother you?'

'The waves were a little bigger than usual. No reason to panic.'

Louisa was incredulous. 'You got the wrong place, and the tide's still going out. You said it was coming in. We were so lucky!'

Nicole laughed. 'Detective Sergeant Lulu Townsend,

you're such a wimp!'

Louisa walked back from the causeway—she refused to take a lift when Christine, who'd been waiting for them to return with the car, had offered it. She didn't know who she was more angry with: Nicole for being so cavalier about the tide times and currents, and their lives, or herself for assuming Nicole was trustworthy. It was being on Tarawa that did it. Her bullshit detector simply didn't work here. In Edinburgh she'd have immediately spotted Nicole for a pushy risk taker, who'd do anything to outdo anyone else, regardless of cost. From now on she trusted no one about anything.

36

The noise came from her house. It sounded like the booming twing-twang of an electric guitar. Shouts and yells now. Louisa hurried up to the front door. A couple of men and women, but mostly children, lay sprawled across her living room floor. It was the bloody film show! She'd forgotten all about it. It was all she needed! Mesmerised, the audience stared at the TV on the floor in the corner of the room. A posse of cowboys galloped across a tumbleweed-swept prairie. It was an old-fashioned Western. Louisa hated Westerns. But at least if the power was back on she could have a shower. That was something. As for her visitors, Reteta had promised to clean up after them, and she'd hold her to that, children were notoriously grubby! All Louisa wanted to do now was wash her sweaty, dust besmeared, sea salted skin and put the shitty, awful snorkel trip behind her.

Excusing herself, she tip-toed between the small lolling

bodies, doing her best not to block anyone's view—this in her own house—or touch anyone. A curdling scream made her jump. What the hell? She looked around. No one had moved. Another scream. It came from the TV. She watched aghast as a cowboy dragged a struggling semi-naked Cherokee by his long hair into a clearing, drew a large knife and sliced off the lad's scalp. Fountains of cherry red blood spurted across the screen. As the Cherokee writhed in pain, the cowboy hacked at his skull, again and again, taking half his brains along with his hair.

'Off!' Louisa marched to the VCR. She didn't care whose hand she stood on now. 'Children should not be watching such disgusting, violent, degrading rubbish!' she yelled. 'Reteta?'

A quiet voice said, 'Na ocean side!'

Louisa stormed through the back door. Reteta was by the fire with the same women from earlier, it looked as if they'd not moved, or stopped talking. Reteta beamed when she saw Louisa. 'Teka teka!' she cried and patted the ground at her side. The others budged up to make room for her. Some had sewing things in their hands, others were rolling cigarettes. Clearly they'd not heard her shouting.

'What on earth do you think you are doing showing such a horrible film?' yelled Louisa, 'It's foul and sick and, bloody hell, there are children watching it!'

The women immediately looked away.

Reteta scowled. 'You said it was okay to show a video.'

'But not that gratuitous violence! It's vile! It's grotesque! It's, it's—'

'It is an expatriate film!'

'I know what it is! You should not be showing it! It's irresponsible and stupid!'

Reteta poked the fire viciously. She refused to look up at Louisa. A scratching noise made Louisa turn: a handful of children stared at her through the screen door.

'Not got anything better to do?' said Louisa, rushing up to the door. 'Get out of my house! All of you! Get out!' The youngsters still lounging on the floor scrambled to their feet and shuffled out of the opposite door.

Louisa wanted to throw a brick at the TV! She would never understand the first thing about the I-Kiribati! How could she have ever considered this country as home? She had nothing, absolutely nothing in common with any of the people. The biggest mistake in her whole life was to have fucking applied for the fucking European Commission post! She marched back into the house, went into the bathroom and slammed the door behind her.

37

It was eerily still when Louisa came out of the shower. The cold water had gone some way to calming her, and being clean and in fresh clothes had also helped, but she was still angry. Letting children, some of whom were younger than five, watch a slasher horror was simply not on. Louisa went outside. Everyone had gone. Only Daisy and the fat pig were left, snoozing in their usual spot in the scrubby pig pen area under the pandanus tree. Louisa spread a lava-lava on top of Reteta's mat—a clean sarong had to be just as effective at protecting her as a mat. She kicked off her outside flip-flops and sat down cross-legged by the fire.

It was possibly her worst day on Tarawa yet. She picked up some dried coconut husks with her left hand, passed them to her right hand and chucked them on to the dying embers—the voices in her head may be gone for now, but that was no reason to stop doing the left hand first ritual. The husks burst into yellow fiery flames then sizzled softly. She still had a report to write and still had nothing to put in it. Three days into the investigation and she was virtually no further forward than when she'd started. In fact, it was worse than when she'd started because now a mad woman appeared to be stalking her, and, oh, yes, and she'd made enemies of just about everyone she knew. It was as if the case, along with her life, was unravelling and she could do nothing to stop it. Louisa told herself to get a grip. She would not give in to self-pity. It was a bad day. That was all.

Louisa focused her thoughts. She would follow procedure. There was information out there to be had. Someone knew who made the dagger and someone knew where Joe's clothes and his bag were. She'd bring Dave the Fish in. He'd crack and confess. He'd be jailed. As for friends and acquaintances, who needed them? A noise. From the side of the house. Louisa looked for a stick or stone to defend herself with. Daisy lifted his head and his tail began wagging. It was TC.

'It's you,' said Louisa relieved. 'I don't know what I imagined.'

TC's face was serious.

'Ah,' said Louisa, getting to her feet and clearing her throat, 'Reteta's told you what happened?'

'Me and everyone in the village who would listen.'

'It was a slasher horror film. There was no way it was suitable for young people to watch.'

'I don't doubt it,' said TC, still not smiling.

'She wasn't even watching it with them. She was out here with her pals, having some kind of "sewing bee"! It was irresponsible!'

'She said you deliberately humiliated her.'

'Not true,' said Louisa, shaking her head adamantly.

'So,' said TC, his face revealing no emotion, 'Let me get this straight, just so there's no confusion: you didn't shout at her in front of all her family and friends—some of whom are your family?'

Louisa felt her cheeks burn with embarrassment. 'I admit I lost my temper, but you should have seen this film—'

'And you didn't call her stupid? That wasn't you?' said TC.

'Studies have shown pre-schoolers behave more aggressively than usual in their play after watching violent television. By the age of eight children are especially likely to show increased aggression from watching violent films. If they believe the violence reflects real life, they are more likely to become more tolerant of violence in the real world. Adolescents are particularly susceptible to imitating violence!'

'Are you finished?'

'I'm just saying—'

TC sighed. 'It is the worst possible offence in Kiribati custom to humiliate someone in front of their peers, but you know that, don't you?'

She blushed for the second time. 'Is that what's she's telling everyone, that I deliberately humiliated her?'

'No. She's telling everyone that you are a crazy expatriate and that even your own mother says you are mad—'

'What?' Louisa threw her arms in the air in disgust. 'In Scotland I'm the Paki foreigner and here I'm the crazy expatriate! Cheers, Reteta!'

'She says you are insensitive and bossy—'

'She's the bossy one!' said Louisa, marching towards the beach. 'This is the thanks I get for letting her show her film in my house! I won't be doing that again, you can count on it!'

TC followed her. 'Did you actually call her stupid?'

Louisa stopped walking. Where was she going? She looked around. TC was beside her. He smelled of Lux soap and coconut oil. His smooth face looked earnest. A warm breeze brushed her cheeks. It felt delicious. Why was she arguing with TC? He'd done nothing wrong. She took a deep breath. 'I may have been a bit over the top. I've had such a rubbish day. Last night wasn't much better. Assistant Police Commissioner Nakibae tore right into me. Ridiculed my efforts with the investigation. It was as if he hated me.'

'Why should he like you?'

'Why shouldn't he? He doesn't know anything about me, yet he more or less suggested I was incompetent.'

TC shrugged. 'You're a sergeant, yes? And he's the Assistant Commissioner? Yet you're probably earning twice as much as him on your European Commission Aid package, and you won't be paying tax. That's enough to put anyone off a person.'

She shifted uncomfortably. 'He should take it up with the EC, not me.'

TC's face softened. 'You know you'll have to apologise to Reteta?'

'Or what?' said Louisa, looking at his eyes and thinking for the first time they were a lovely oval shape. 'She won't come back?'

TC smiled. 'She'll be back. We'll all be back, unless you'd rather we stayed away?'

Louisa turned to face the ocean. The tide was almost in. The water licked Louisa's toes. 'It's just that I'm used to living by myself.'

'You have space in your garden and our village is very crowded. Reteta said you were happy to help out. It's what families do. At least it's what they do here on Tarawa. But if you'd rather be alone?'

'No. It's fine.' Louisa picked up a small pebble. 'By the way, your uncle Tion? Did he work for Joe, the murdered man?'

'Yes. Tion was one of his divers. Why?'

'Bloody hell! I don't believe it!' She chucked the pebble into the creeping waves. 'No one thought to tell me this?'

'What's there to tell?'

'Tion dies in an accident at work and Joe, his boss, is killed the very next day.' Louisa looked for another pebble to throw. 'It's a bit of a coincidence.'

'You think so?' said TC, following behind her as she scanned the ground.

'Yes and I don't believe in coincidences!' Sheets of oranges and pinks swept across the sky in vast vibrant swathes. It would soon be dark. TC wore a pair of washed out, dark board shorts and a white T-shirt. Louisa thought he had a particularly handsome body. He was muscular without looking like the Hulk. She also liked the way he wore his hair short. She stopped herself. Surely she wasn't getting the hots for him? No way. He had to be at least six years younger than her. What was wrong with her today?

'Maybe, but I don't see the connection,' said TC.

'It's unusual for two people who work together to die within twenty-four hours of each other, for whatever reason. It simply doesn't happen normally. How did Tion die again?'

'He was on a night dive. There was an accident and he drowned.'

'The men dive at night? Really?'

'Sometimes. If you really want to know what happened, ask Tion's friend, Nata. He was with him when it happened. He was very upset.'

Louisa groaned. 'I saw Joe's men earlier today but didn't know who they were.' She kicked some sand with her foot. 'I took my eye off the case and missed an opportunity to possibly acquire new information. It was a rookie mistake.'

'You're being too hard on yourself. Things take their own time on Tarawa. Besides, you can always talk to the divers tomorrow. They're not going anywhere.'

'I suppose.'

He stopped and smiled. 'If there is a connection, though, you'll find it.'

'I wish Assistant Police Commissioner Nakibae had your confidence.' She so liked his smile. He also had nice teeth and he didn't look away when she looked at him. She took a step towards him. Her foot squelched into something soft and wet. Louisa looked down. She thought she would convulse in disgust. 'No!' She hopped up and down on her left foot. 'No! No! No!'

'What is it?' said TC, his eyes flashing concern.

Through clenched teeth Louisa said. 'I've stepped in fucking shit!' She pointed to her raised right foot. Liquid faeces drip, dripped from her toes. She half ran, half hopped to the sea and thrust her foot into the water and thrashed it around. Behind her TC's stifled laughter sounded very loud.

38

The noxious shit smell in her nostrils refused to go. This despite the fact she'd washed her stinking foot in the sea twenty-four times and then again under the outside tap at the side of the house without stopping for twenty minutes—the bar of soap she'd used had completely dissolved. The one time she was in her bare feet and she had to step in shit! Why had she not put her shoes on? What was wrong with her? She'd lost it when TC wouldn't stop laughing. They'd argued about the hygiene, or the lack of it, on the island. TC had accused her of hypocrisy. He'd travelled all around the world as a seaman and had seen far worse things than the odd pat of human crap on the shoreline. He even cited the MV Gardyloo—a vessel in Edinburgh, her home town—which dumped tonnes of raw sludge sewage into the North Sea three times a week. She didn't care. As far as she was concerned nothing justified using the beach as a toilet. He'd said it was unfortunate. Unfortunate? He'd still been sniggering when he'd left. No doubt going straight back to the village to tell them the good news. Oh, how they'd laugh! Well, stuff them!

Louisa contemplated washing her foot one last time before going inside. What she'd really like to do was cut it off. From now on she'd struggle to touch that foot without washing it first. Daisy growled low and long. Pete The Pilot stood by the bushes. In the half light he looked a ghostly hundred years old and so thin a light wind could have snapped him in two.

'Why does everyone have to creep about on this island?' she said exasperated.

'I don't have long,' he hissed. 'I need to talk to you. It's about Joe. It's urgent.'

Louisa peered into the shadows. She was not in the mood for all this cloak and dagger stuff but if he had information that would help her discover who killed Joe, she wanted to hear it. 'What is it?'

'If I tell you what I know, you have to promise to help me with a problem I have.'

Louisa eyed the shrivelled old man. Could he really have something useful for her? It seemed unlikely. On the other hand, she still had that damn report to write. Any information at this stage was better than no information. She sat down on the lava-lava on the mat and nodded for Pete to join her. 'I'm promising nothing.'

Pete pressed his thin lips together, looked around furtively then hustled from out of the bushes and sat down, cross-legged next to Louisa.

Louisa would ignore her foot and concentrate on what he had to say. 'Well?'

Pete clasped his hands together on his lap. 'You didn't hear this from me,' he said.

'Will you get on with it?' She thought his hands looked as if they were holding a humming bird in them.

'On Thursday, the night Joe died, Dave had had some kind of meeting with him.'

'What?' she yelled. 'Why didn't you come forward with this information sooner?'

His thin lips began to tremble. 'If you're going to have a go at me, I'm leaving.'

Louisa forced herself to calm down. 'Where was the meeting and when?'

'I'm not saying he killed him or anything, but he was with him.'

'Where and when?' she demanded.

'They met at the Ambo. Around seven thirty. He came to my house afterwards. It was almost eight by then. He was with Bob and Stevo. They're attached at the hip those three.' Pete's mouth sloped downwards. 'He was like the cat that had got the cream. Him and Joe had come to some agreement about exporting shark fins.'

'I thought Joe only exported sea cucumbers?'

'Dave said something about Joe getting a licence to export sharks fins any day.'

'And why would Dave tell you all this?'

'My wife is Dave's wife's cousin. We go way back. If Dave is passing, he calls in and drinks all my drink, eats all my food and then leaves. Thursday evening, they wanted to party and when Dave wants to party that's it.'

'The deal was that good, was it?'

'Oh, yes.' He licked his pencil thin lips. 'They didn't leave till four in the morning.'

'Was there any blood on his clothes, or on the clothes of the others?'

Pete shook his head. 'He didn't look like a man who had just committed a violent crime to me, not that he wouldn't be capable of it because he would. But Joe owed him money for the new boat and he wanted Joe to pay it back and Joe's new export licence for shark fins made it look like he would be able to. Much as he hated him, I'd say Dave preferred Joe to be alive.'

'You'll have to come with me to the station and make a full statement,' said Louisa scrambling to her feet. Regardless of what Pete thought about Dave being a killer or not, his information placed Dave at the scene of the crime. It was the evidence she needed.'

'I'm making no statement. Dave is family. You don't tell on family.'

'He could be a killer!'

'You talk to Dave, you challenge him. If he clamps up, put pressure on those sidekicks of his. Especially Bob. He'll crack in minutes. He's soft as putty. They'll tell the truth eventually. I don't think he killed him, mind. He'd never have poked out the man's eyes. He's superstitious. It's too spooky for him. And now, you have to help me. My wife is planning to steal from me and I want you to stop her.'

'Your wife what?' said Louisa, momentarily forgetting Dave and his chums.

'My residency visa came up for renewal. The visa people wanted bank statements—'

'Slow down. You've lost me,' said Louisa.

'I've lived here for twenty years and my wife is I-Kiribati. We have four children and are happily married. Nevertheless, every few years, if I want to remain in the country, I need to renew my residency visa. It's a nuisance but usually a very straightforward procedure.' His fingers fluttered on his lap.

'And?' said Louisa, checking her watch. Could she go and arrest Dave now? Without back-up? No. Contrary to what Nicole thought, she wasn't a wimp but she wasn't a fool. She made it a policy never to put her life in danger if she could help it. If there was a chance Dave the Fish was the killer, she wanted some muscle with her when she arrested him. As soon as Pete left she'd call the station and see if the men were back. If not, tomorrow would have to do. But at least she had a real suspect and something to write in her report.

'Are you listening to me?' said Pete.

'Go on,' said Louisa, standing impatiently by the back door. 'But make it quick.'

'Last week, as usual, I arranged for the details of my various savings accounts in the UK to be sent to the visa office here.' He paused to make a little cough. 'I am reasonably wealthy and I am proud to say that my wife, who has equal access to my money, and my children want for nothing. However, unbeknown to me, my wife's cousin now works in the visa office. This cousin took it upon herself to disclose the full details of my UK income to my wife. Including, unfortunately, one account which I had been keeping a secret from her. Now my wife is very angry with me. She says if I don't let her have access to the money in the secret account she will cut me with a knife.'

'Is that it?' said Louisa, opening the back screen door to go inside, 'You said you trusted her, yes? So give her access to the money. What's the problem?'

'I have a daughter by my first marriage. Neither my I-Kiribati wife or I-Kiribati children know about her. The money in that special account is for her.'

'Again, what's the problem? Tell your wife the truth, that the money is for your daughter by your first marriage.'

'You don't understand,' said Pete, looking miserable. 'Knowing I have a daughter will make her even more angry with me. It's blackmail. You should be able to do something.'

'No,' said Louisa, 'it's not blackmail, it's a breakdown of trust. You need a marriage guidance counsellor, not the police.'

39

It was seven thirty in the morning. Betio station was deserted. There was no lorry outside in the car park and no sign of a patrol car. Even Special Constable John wasn't around. Louisa couldn't understand it. Had another boat been found fishing illegally in Kiribati waters? She searched for a note or a memo. Anything to explain where everyone was. Nothing. Outside the morning hustle and bustle of downtown Betio as people made their way to work carried on as normal. Louisa was desperate to arrest Dave the Fish and drag his sorry arse to Betio for questioning. She'd already waited all night to bring him in. When she'd phoned the station the evening before, Constable John had assured her all the officers would be available first thing that morning. She needed help! Where the hell was everyone?

After ten minutes of pacing the station floor and phoning everywhere she could think of and getting no answer, Louisa headed for the Ministry of Justice to see Nakibae. He would have her report by eight, as he'd demanded. She'd ask for a search warrant while she was there and hopefully he'd get her some back-up. She'd feel a lot better when Dave was in custody. If she were lucky, it would all be over with by the end of the day. She just had to be patient for a little while longer. She hoped Pete had told no one about his visit to her the night before. She should have arrested him for withholding evidence but she'd let him off with a warning. It sounded as if he was already in enough trouble with his wife.

A roar of a motorbike made her jump. TC pulled up beside her. She was surprised to see him away from the house. He yelled above the roar of the engine. 'You've not heard, have you?'

'Heard what?' said Louisa.

'Hop on. It's all over the radio. There's been another murder.'

Blue and white scene of crime tape cordoned off Jill's garden and house. Two constables struggled to keep a throng of expatriates and locals behind the tape. Louisa saw Nicole and Christine, along with some other faces from the hash, straining to see past the police and into the house.

TC dropped Louisa off at the side of the house. She pushed through the crowd, deliberately avoiding Nicole and Christine. A thin constable recognised her and lifted the crime tape to let her under. Jill's house looked exactly as it had when Louisa had called round on Saturday, except now Paul's 4x4 Hyundai was parked in the driveway. Who had been killed? Jill? Paul? Someone else? She hurried through the open door.

The gamey smell of sick and shit was revolting. Jill's bloated body lay face down on the living room in a puddle of muddy red slurry. Her vest and joggers were smeared with the same grubby blood and bodily fluid mixture as the slurry. From the state of decomposition, even Louisa could see she'd been dead a while. Probably as much as twenty-four hours in the heat. Who would want to kill Jill?

Paul sat on one of the hard backed dining chairs by the table. Louisa had been to enough violent scenes to know he was in shock. Assistant Police Commissioner Nakibae, Dr Andrus and Sergeant Tebano were huddled by the deceased's head, talking quietly. They wore thin, blue plastic disposable gloves.

Careful not to step in any of the bloody puddles on the floor, Louisa approached Nakibae. 'Sir, Paul Wilson shouldn't be here. We have to remove him from the scene as quickly as possible. Not only out of common decency but he could contaminate any evidence.'

'Detective Sergeant Townsend,' said Nakibae, his voice icy cold, 'you're not presuming to tell me what to do, are you?'

'Absolutely not, Sir. However, it's—'

'Good.' He turned round to Andrus. 'Turn her over now.'

Dr Andrus knelt down and with Tebano's help they turned Jill's stinking, fleshy, inflated body upwards.

Louisa winced. Jill's face was a soft, purple pulp. Her features were almost unrecognisable.

Dr Andrus said to Nakibae, 'You asked for a time of death. I can't possibly be accurate—the heat in here is only one variable which has affected the rate of decomposition. However, as you have insisted, I say the deceased has been dead for more than twenty-four hours. I estimate she died between Saturday midnight and Sunday midday.' He stood up. 'The cause of death appears to be blunt force trauma to the front of the face and head. Very savage. Very savage indeed. The survival time would have been very little. It is as if someone wanted to obliterate her.' He drew himself up and pointed to her arms. 'There appear to be no defensive wounds. I will make the arrangements to take her to the mortuary now.'

Nakibae and Tebano accompanied Andrus to the door of the house. Louisa's mind seemed to have short-fused. Jill's death had to be linked to the Ambo killing, but how? Had she recognised the dagger? Was that why she was killed? If Dave the Fish was Joe's killer, had he killed Jill to silence her? Louisa looked around the room. The murder weapon, or what looked to be the weapon, was on the floor next to Paul's chair. It was a white chunk of lumpy brain coral. Louisa had noticed it on her first visit when Jill had used it as a door stop. The top half of the white lump was smeared with traces of flesh and purple sinew. Elongated brown-red splatters fanned across the floor and decorated two of the lounge chairs nearest the body. Strings of ruby teardrops spotted the walls. The crime seemed opportunistic, savage and unpremeditated. Louisa suddenly wanted to throw up. She cleared her throat. 'Sir?'

Nakibae's face registered annoyance. 'Yes?'

'Do we know who did this?'

Nakibae nodded to where Paul sat with his head in his hands. 'Paul Wilson was arrested at seven forty-five this morning. He's been charged on two counts of murder. The first count for killing his wife, Jill Wilson, some time between Saturday midday and Sunday midday. The second count for killing Joe Revada on Thursday between the hours of 6.30pm and 7.30pm.'

It was all wrong. 'I don't understand—'

'If you'll excuse me,' said Nakibae. He nodded to Tebano. 'You can take him now.'

Tebano helped Paul to his feet and led him to the door. Paul's eyes were glazed. He sobbed. 'If I'd been here, she'd still be alive!'

Louisa couldn't believe it. 'Sir! There must be some mistake.'

'There is no mistake!' snapped Nakibae. 'Paul met a young woman called Eretibete late Saturday midnight at the Royal Saloon pub. They argued. Eretibete wanted him to leave his wife and he would not. She left and he returned home. He was drunk. Maybe he talked to his wife about divorce. She said no. He blamed her for ruining his relationship with his lover. They argued. It was one of those bitter, nasty arguments that went on and on, building in recriminations at every turn. He lost his temper and picked up the first thing to hand and killed her. Shocked at what he'd done and full of remorse, he fled to his friend's. He has motive and opportunity, and no alibi.'

'He admitted this?' said Louisa, astounded.

'No. Not at all. He says he has amnesia and conveniently can't remember anything from after he left the Royal Saloon on Saturday night until he woke up on Sunday midday at a friend's house. He claims he had a very bad hangover so he stayed at the friend's house until he felt better, which was this morning. He claims he stayed away because his wife did not like to see him drunk. He discovered his wife as we see her.'

Louisa struggled to process these latest developments. 'What about the friend he was staying with?'

'The friend is not on South Tarawa at the moment and cannot give him an alibi.'

Louisa tried to think. 'I don't know about Jill, but I've found someone who says a man called Dave the Fish was with Joe on Thursday evening at seven thirty. If that proves to be the case, Joe was alive when Paul was in Bairiki with scores of witnesses to prove it and Paul could not have killed Joe. It also means Dave the Fish was the last person to see Joe alive.'

'You have hard evidence of this?'

'I'm getting it!' said Louisa. No matter how likely it seemed, she couldn't believe Paul was a killer.

'I have a duty to the citizens of Kiribati to keep them safe. Until you can prove to me otherwise, Paul is our killer and will be tried for both deaths. And now you'll have to excuse me, I have to address Parliament within the hour. I want all the necessary statements taken and paperwork completed as soon as possible.'

40

Betio prison was separated from police HQ by a thicket of pandanus and banana palms which stretched for at least two hundred yards. It took less than five minutes to get there by foot from HQ. Louisa was not unfamiliar with the prison, even though she'd never been in it. The cleaner at headquarters was a prison inmate. He was collected at eight and escorted back to the jail at midday. Louisa liked the elderly man. It was almost impossible to believe such a gentle person could be a killer. But his story, which Louisa had heard time and time again, was a familiar one according to the other officers: drunk on sour toddy and beer, he'd got into a frenzied fight with his cousin and best friend and killed him. A toddy killing, they called it. He'd been in jail ten years and had the rest of his life to go. No doubt the man who attacked Meere was also in there somewhere.

The prison was a long rectangular concrete block in a clearing of scrub the size of a football pitch, surrounded by sagging chicken wire fence. Open doorways ran the length of the side of the building facing Louisa. It looked like a giant block of toilets. A handful of young men kicked a scrappy football around in a patch of sand just inside the fence. There was no shade anywhere. At midday the sun glared down. Louisa had already sent Michael and Tebano to bring Dave, Bob and Stevo in for questioning. She told the officers not to come back to the station without them.

She was sure the two killings were linked: both victims died from blows to the face, both killings took place indoors and on the lagoon side of the island. The lack of defensive wounds suggested both victims knew their killer. And, of course, Jill had discovered Joe's body. This was the biggest link between the deaths. Had Jill finally remembered where she'd seen the dagger? Was that why she'd been killed, to keep her quiet? It hadn't occurred to Louisa for one second that Jill had been at risk. If she found Joe's killer, she was sure she'd find Jill's. It was as simple as that. And she didn't believe Paul had it in him. If she could prove he was in Bairiki at the hash meeting when Joe was stabbed, she'd be able to rule him out and Dave the Fish in.

Louisa approached the main prison entrance. A padlock the size of a small shoebox held the heavy metal gate closed. She rang a little old fashioned bell, which was attached to a stiff wire dangling down from the side of the gate-frame, and waited. It was common knowledge at HQ that the gate only appeared to be locked. In fact, the padlock had seized up years ago. It never occurred to the inmates who knew the secret to escape—where could they go? They were inside as much for their own sake as for the safety of the public: the fence and gate kept victims' avenging relatives out and the prisoners in. Louisa was not about to give the secret away by lifting the bolt and walking in. She rang the bell again and waited.

To the right of the gate a large hardboard sign clung to the sagging fence. In flaking black paint, and in both English and Gilbertese, it said that it was absolutely forbidden to pass anything to the inmates through the fence. Next to the sign, in the middle of the fence, there was a hole the size of a large packing case. A clutch of people on Louisa's side of the fence passed bundles of food and clothes to half a dozen men on the inside. Louisa sighed. The inmates had to eat somehow. Very few of them were as lucky as the HQ cleaner with his paid work.

Beyond the fence and in front of the prison building two young lads swept the ground with what looked like witches' broomsticks, but without the handles. Their clothes were torn and faded. Louisa was suddenly overwhelmed by an awful sense of dread followed by panic: what if she was wrong? What if Paul was the killer? What if Nakibae was right? No. She had to trust her gut feeling. Everything was wrong about Paul being responsible for Jill and Joe's deaths.

A tall, angular man with short grey hair appeared from a room at the end of the main block and sauntered across to open the gate. After explaining why she was there, Louisa followed him along the side of the building to the last room in the block. It was tiny, with bare walls, one small glassless window, a concrete slab for a floor and no door attached to the doorway. It reminded Louisa of a mountain refuge in Scotland, where she'd once slept after getting lost. It had been the first and last time she'd been hillwalking. The guard indicated that she should go in.

'Mr Paul inside,' he said. 'You come to my office when you ready to take his statement.'

Louisa prodded the concrete floor with her toe before walking inside. A cockroach flapped in her face. Her heart thudded. 'Paul? It's DS Townsend.'

It was dark inside. At first glance the room appeared empty. Then her eyes grew used to the dimness and she saw him. He sat slumped on the floor in the corner of the little room. She had a deja vu of Jill on the toilet in the Ambo. Was that only four days ago?

'Louisa? Thank God!' He jumped up. His eyes danced with hope. 'I knew if anyone could get me out of here, you could!'

She shook her head. 'I'm sorry, I'm here to take your statement. That's all.'

'I can't leave?'

'You should have a solicitor present. I can arrange to get you one if you don't know any.'

'A solicitor? I don't even have a bed, never mind sheets or blankets. There's no food. Nothing to drink either. It's a slum—'

'Your friends will help you.'

'What friends?' he slumped back down on to the floor and leaned against the wall.

'I'll get a message to some of the hashers, I'm sure they'll bring you what you need. But I have to tell you, Paul, this is as serious as it gets. Charged with two murders—'

'I didn't kill anyone.' He put his head in his hands. 'Did you see Jill? It was awful! Who would have done that?'

Louisa hoped he wouldn't start crying. 'If I'm to help you, you need to tell me the truth.'

He suddenly became angry. 'Where's that bastard Tom? He should be here! He's the British Aid person, it's about time he came to my aid! I'm British, after all!' He shouted at the door. 'I'm bloody British!'

'You're going to have to calm down or I'll have to leave. You can apply for bail, which is another reason why you may want a solicitor.'

Paul looked up at her. 'I know we weren't getting on but I didn't hate Jill. In fact I still loved her. Her face was ...'

He seemed to have aged ten years since she'd been chatting to him on Saturday night. 'You are going to have to answer my questions and tell me about your affair with Eretibete.'

'What has that got to do with anything?'

'She was your lover, wasn't she?'

He ran his hands through his hair. 'It wasn't like that. You don't understand.'

'Maybe you'd better tell me how it was like?'

41

They sat in the prison office, either side of a small, old-fashioned wooden school desk. It reminded Louisa of a desk she'd had in her first primary school on Tarawa. The wood was scored with graffiti and there was even a small round hole for an ink well. If Louisa didn't keep her knees sideways, they bumped into Paul's. The dim prison office was not much bigger than Paul's cell. A rolled-up mat in the corner suggested the guard slept there. One solitary wooden shelf held two enamel tin cups, an open two pound bag of granulated sugar and a tin of evaporated Carnation milk, with two small triangular notches carved out of the lid at opposite ends from each other. The guard had reluctantly agreed to make Louisa two teas when she'd asked, though she was not optimistic they'd get them before she left. She took out her police notebook and placed it on the desk in readiness to take Paul's statement. Paul had declined to have a solicitor present, despite her advice.

'It's not what you think' Paul said when she asked him again about his relationship with Eretibete.

'And what do I think?' said Louisa.

'That I'm sleeping with her.'

'And aren't you?'

Paul also sat sideways. He crossed his arms. 'Eretibete used to come to the hash. One Thursday she had a giant purple and yellow bruise on her arm. I asked how she got it. She said she'd had a fall. Each week after that there was a different bruise—' He laughed suddenly. 'Everyone saw them but I seemed to be the only person it bothered. Then one day her arms were such a mess of bruises I couldn't keep quiet any longer. I insisted she tell me the truth. It was her brother. When he got drunk he hit her. Her parents are dead. She lives with him. I gave her my number and told her to contact me if she ever needed help, no matter what. The first time she called she was beside herself with fear. Her brother was on a drunken rampage and breaking everything in the house. I went there immediately. Sure enough the house had been turned upside down and she'd been beaten.'

'You met her brother then?'

He rubbed his chin with his hand. 'He was gone by the time I got there. I tried to get her to go to the police but she'd said it wasn't an option. Then a pattern sort of developed, whenever her brother got drunk and abusive, she'd call me. By the time I'd get to the house, the brother would be gone. She said if he knew I was coming round, it would be even worse for her—' He looked away.

'Are you okay?' she said.

He looked up. His eyes were full of tears. 'Who do you

think did that to Jill?'

'I'm going to find out.'

He nodded. 'Any chance of that cup of tea?' His voice was hoarse.

Louisa got up and popped her head round the office door. In the hazy blistering afternoon sun the yard looked deserted. 'The guard will be back when he's back, I suppose.'

Paul gave her a funny look.

She sat back down. 'Tell me about you and Eretibete and Thursday night. You did give her a lift from the hospital, didn't you?'

Paul licked his lips again. 'I bumped into her after I'd dropped off Christine at outpatients and offered her a lift home. We argued. Seeing her at the hospital gave me a fright, I thought her brother had really hurt her badly this time. I gave her an ultimatum: if she didn't report her brother's violence, I'd not speak to her again. She said I was as bad as her brother, that I'd been taking advantage of her—'

'Ah? So you did sleep with her?'

'That's got nothing to do with anything!'

'For the record were you, or were you not, having a sexual relationship with Eretibete?'

'Yes, but I'm not like those other men who're just with the girls for sex.'

'And what men would they be?' said Louisa. Silently ticking a little box in her head next to Paul's name. He was no different from the others, despite his protests.

'Some of the ones at the hash—'

'Was Joe one of these men?'

'Joe?' Paul sat upright in his chair. 'Not Joe. Hell, no. He was one of the good guys when it came to local women. He was the only other expatriate guy who agreed with me that Eretibete should go to the police.'

'So you never saw Joe with a woman?'

'No, not in a sexual way. But I only ever saw him at the hash.'

'Back to Eretibete. How old is she?'

'Nineteen, twenty maybe.'

'And how many years older than her are you?'

Paul scowled. 'What's this got to do with anything?'

'Answer the question, please, Paul.'

He shook his head wearily. 'I'm sixteen years older than her.'

Louisa continued writing. 'And what did she say to your ultimatum?'

He crossed his feet and then uncrossed them. 'She said she would only report her brother to the police if I married her and took her back to England with me. I told her I wasn't going to do that. She knew I was married!' he said full of sudden anger. 'I'd told her right from the start. She knew!'

'So what happened then?' said Louisa, finding it increasingly difficult not to judge Paul.

'She said she didn't want to see me again and got out of the car. I joined the hashers.'

'And what time was this?'

'By now it was nearly seven thirty.'

'She'll vouch she was with you the whole time, will she?'

'Yes.'

'And you never went into the Ambo Lagoon Club at any time on the way back from the hospital?'

'Of course not.'

'Now tell me what happened on Saturday night,' said Louisa.

Paul shifted in his chair. 'Eretibete called the Otintaai and got the girl on reception to find me. I don't know how she knew I was there. She said her brother had beaten her to within an inch of her life, taken all her clothes and left her tied to her bed naked. She'd only just wriggled free to get to the phone. She was petrified of him returning. She pleaded with me to help. I was appalled at what her brother had done but told her to call the police and put the phone down.'

'So,' said Louisa dryly, pausing from the note taking—even using shorthand it was proving hard to keep up. 'You thought that leaving her to get a second beating by a raving drunk was the right thing to do?'

'Don't you see?' protested Paul, 'As long as I helped her she would do nothing about her brother!'

'Why didn't you call the police yourself? It is an offence not to report a crime that you know to have taken place, or to be taking place, or that you have reason to believe is going to take place.' She didn't wait for his answer. 'But you did go in the end, didn't you? After you dropped me off, you went straight to her house, yes?'

Paul coughed. 'I could really do with that cuppa.'

'It'll be here when it's ready. What happened?'

'The door was locked. I had to break it down. She was naked but had partly managed to undo her binds. I helped her free herself and found her clothes and we went to the Royal Saloon—'

'Whoa!' said Louisa, thinking now she was going mad. 'Eretibete had been beaten to within an inch of her life and you took her to the pub?'

Paul's grubby face went deep red. 'He hadn't actually hit her yet. She'd just said that to get me to come—'

'So, you'd just left a swanky do to drive halfway across the island to help her and she'd lied. You weren't angry?'

'Of course I was angry but I was also glad, at least she'd not been beaten up.' He began fiddling with a tiny scrap of paper on the desk. 'It was a mistake. We argued again. She stormed off. I got blind drunk and found myself in Tom's house the next day with a raging hangover and no Tom. I stayed there until

Monday and, well, you know the rest.'

Louisa was beginning to find the tiny dank office stifling and oppressive. 'Did Jill know about your relationship with Eretibete?'

He looked away. 'I didn't tell her.'

'What about the other men who went to the Royal Saloon, could they have said something?'

'It's a sort of unspoken rule, what you see in the Royal Saloon stays in the Royal Saloon.'

'Oh, how very Fight Club,' said Louisa, hoping she sounded as unimpressed as she felt.

'Look,' said Paul, wiping sweat from his top lip with the back of his hand. 'I did not kill Jill because I wanted to be with Eretibete. The thing you have to know about Jill and I is that we had already sort of separated before coming to Tarawa.'

Louisa straightened her back. What bullshit was this now? 'What do you mean, sort of?'

'We had separated but we weren't divorced yet. It had been an amicable split and we'd simply not got round to doing anything about the legal situation. The thing is I'd applied for the job here ages before the break happened. When I was eventually offered the post, these jobs take ages to process, Jill and I were still in touch even though we weren't together any more. She asked to come overseas with me, she said she wanted some adventure. As my spouse her air travel would be paid, business class, and I'd get an extra married person's allowance. I agreed. After ten years together I thought I owed her that at least. We kept the fact we weren't a couple any more a secret in case people thought we were being mercenary.'

Louisa had heard everything now. 'And you think you weren't?'

Paul twisted in his chair. 'All I'm saying is that I had no reason whatsoever to murder Jill, which is why I have been stuck in here! I wished I hadn't agreed to her coming with me ...'

He paused to wipe his nose. 'If I had said no, she would still be alive. Poor Jill. She didn't even like it here. Almost as soon as she arrived she wanted to go home but there's a rule about needing to stay at least nine months at a placement or you have to repay all the airfare and allowances. It applies to spouses. Jill was waiting for the nine months to be up so we wouldn't have to pay back the fares.'

Louisa pursed her lips. 'Jill told me you were going to go back to the UK with her.'

'Did she?' said Paul, looking genuinely surprised.

'Was she lying?'

Paul squirmed. 'Our relationship was over but maybe Jill had hoped for a reconciliation.'

'Let me get this straight. Jill was due to leave Tarawa in a few months. In fact, at some point in the not too distant future you and Jill were going to get divorced?'

Paul nodded.

'If you wanted to, you could marry Eretibete?'

'Marriage is a big commitment. I'm not ready for something like that with Eretibete.'

'While you may have a witness who can corroborate your movements on Thursday evening, you have no one who can vouch for your whereabouts early Sunday morning when Jill was most likely killed.' Louisa put her pencil down and wiped some sweat from her forehead. 'Despite what you've told me about your relationship with Jill, I have to tell you, Paul, it's not looking good for you. Not good at all.'

42

Eretibete was missing. Louisa had sent a couple of young

constables, at her disposal since the second death that morning, to bring the girl in. They'd been unable to find her anywhere. Louisa sent them back out to look for her again. If what Paul had said was true about Eretibete's relationship with her brother, she could be in danger from him. The police had a duty to protect her. There was also the small detail of Eretibete corroborating Paul's statement for Thursday evening. Only when she had Eretibete's statement in writing could he possibly be released. Not that she doubted what Paul had said. She was sure he had not killed Joe and that made it very unlikely he'd killed Jill. Not that she had told him that. It was unkind of her not to have been more honest with Paul, especially after Jill had been so cruelly killed, but his ridiculous relationships had maddened her. It would do him no harm to stew in Betio prison a while longer. Meanwhile, she wanted to question David Trout. Regardless of what Nakibae thought, he was still Louisa's prime suspect. The frustrating thing was Michael and Tebano had still not brought him in. There was a garbled message from Tebano saying Trout had not been at home and they were searching the area for him. Louisa felt totally frustrated. She wanted that man in custody and to know where Eretibete was safe. The waiting was doing her head in. She had to do something. It occurred to her a girls' dormitory was an excellent hiding place for a young girl. And if Eretibete wasn't at Tarawa Teachers' College, maybe her cousin, Meere, would know where she was. By car—the tyre on the patrol vehicle at the Otintaai had miraculously been fixed and returned to her—the college was only twenty minutes away. Louisa could be there and back in no time.

The gravel parking area between the staffroom-cum-office block of Tarawa Teachers' College and the girls' dormitory was empty. Louisa parked her car in the first of two potholed parking spaces. A crowd of teenage boys and girls milled in front of the staffroom entrance. Louisa saw Tiabei but no Meere.

'I knew you wouldn't let us down!' said Tiabei, running to meet Louisa.

'Sorry?' said Louisa.

Tiabei grabbed Louisa's hand and pulled her towards the staffroom. 'They're discussing Meere's case now.' '

'Wait!' protested Louisa, 'I'm here to ask—'

'She's come to help Meere!' Tiabei yelled as she pushed Louisa into the crowd of young people.

'No!' said Louisa, as Tiabei propelled her towards the staffroom.

'Tell her good luck from us!' said a young man, patting Louisa's shoulder.

'I'm sending up a prayer for her!' said a girl.

'We won't abandon her!' yelled another.

'You don't understand,' said Louisa, but it was too late. She was inside the long room. It looked exactly as it had done the day before: dusty and dingy. At the far end of the room, beyond the desks, half a dozen people sat around a low, rectangular coffee table with a neat pile of unread Times Educational Supplements in the middle of it. Meere sat on a chair by herself. Separate from the group and with her head bowed.

Louisa gave her blouse a little tug to make sure it was straight. This was going to be awkward. 'Excuse me.'

Everyone turned to look at her. Including Meere, who beamed when she saw it was Louisa before blushing and quickly looking away again. Opposite Meere was Tererei, the woman who had been following Louisa, and the person Louisa believed had slashed her car tyre. She was the only other woman in the room. Tererei scowled when she saw Louisa and looked away.

Louisa smiled her most polite official smile. 'I am Detective Sergeant Louisa Townsend and I need to talk to Meere urgently in connection with a double murder investigation.'

Meere gasped. Some of the men muttered.

'May I ask who is in charge?' said Louisa, realising too late she should have got that information before she'd left the nick.

A big man with elephantine legs pushed himself up from out of the chair next to Tererei. 'I am Principal Tiribo.' He paused to dab his forehead with a small white towel draped around his neck, as if he'd just come from the gym. His salt and pepper hair stood up like the bristles of a shaving brush and his stomach bulged under a brightly coloured shirt tightly tucked into brown shorts. His bare feet looked like slabs of charcoaled meat and his legs were covered in glossy purple tropical ulcer scars. 'It said on the radio today that someone has been arrested for the murders,' said Tiribo.

Louisa nodded. 'That's very true, someone is helping us with our inquiries, but we still have a few loose ends to tie up, which is where Meere comes in. I won't be long. I just need to talk to her for a few minutes.'

'We are here to discuss the terrible case of Meere,' said Tiribo. 'It cannot be postponed. It would not be fair to Meere. However, if Meere has committed an offence that has brought the police to the college, you must tell us what it is immediately.'

'It's nothing like that!' said Louisa, taken aback. 'Meere is not in trouble with the police in any way. I repeat Meere is not in trouble. However, it is urgent I ask her some questions.'

Tiribo puckered his fat lips and his thick round face creased into a frown. 'This is a very serious development.' He dabbed his forehead again with the corner of his towel. 'Please sit.' He nodded to an empty armchair next to Tererei. 'We will be as quick as we can.'

Louisa sat down. What choice did she have? It was not ideal. She felt like an eavesdropper. Should she leave and come back? Too late. The man began addressing the group.

'We all know the circumstances concerning Meere's case. The gritties and the nitties are the father blames us for her situation. He asserts if Meere had been in her dorm, the attack would not have happened. I agree. But, I differ from Meere's father regards blame. We did not know Meere was not in the dorm. A bad friend forged her signature in the duty book. If students lie and do irresponsible things and conspire behind our backs and so bring shame to the college, they have to be made accountable for their actions. We, the college, are blameless. Meere lied and as a consequence of that lie, the college has found itself in trouble—'

Meere burst out sobbing.

'Don't you think she's suffered enough?' said Louisa before she could stop herself. Why were they being so cruel to her?

Principal Tiribo manoeuvred his big bumpy body around so he faced Louisa. His small eyes glistened.

'You do not seem to understand,' said Tiribo impatiently, 'Meere broke a college law. You, of all people, should understand the consequences of what happens when someone breaks a law. If we do not expel Meere, people will think we have no rules, that we have gone soft. We must not let the college get a bad name as a place for women to come to. If that happens no women will come to study at TTC and it will be like the old days.'

'It seems very harsh!' said Louisa, unable to stop herself.

'You think we are heartless? That we are like stones? We are upset for Meere, but we also have a duty to consider the reputation of the college, especially if the police are here because of her—'

'I didn't say—' said Louisa.

'Be quiet!' snapped Tererei.

Someone muttered, 'Crazy I-Matang!'

Louisa gripped her mouth shut. She didn't want to make Meere's case worse. What did she know? She was an expatriate. An I-Matang. This was local business.

Tiribo dabbed his forehead again. 'I think it would be beneficial for all concerned if we should call this meeting to a halt for the time being and let Sergeant Detective Louisa ask Meere her questions. We will meet again tomorrow afternoon when everyone has had time to consider her case. Meere, you can leave. Classes are cancelled for two days.' He nodded to everyone, then turned and left. Meere followed him, now sobbing uncontrollably.

Louisa felt terrible for the girl but she still needed to talk to her.

'Satisfied?' said Tererei.

Louisa stood up. 'I think you're being very unfair.'

'You make the mistake of believing anyone cares what you think.'

43

The students crowded round Meere. Louisa couldn't get close to her. Tiabei towered above the others. Louisa waved her over.

'I must talk to Meere.'

'Are they really going to expel her?' said Tiabei.

'They said she pretended she was in the dorm when she was not. She broke the rules and I'm afraid my presence hasn't helped her case.'

Tiabei blushed. 'We never thought anything was wrong when she was late back. We lied because we thought it would help her.'

'I don't want to interfere but Meere's been through a traumatic experience and the college needs to recognise that, whatever the rules are. You students could get together and talk to the principal and Tererei. Try to make them see reason.

Support for Meere in the form of counselling should be one of his first priorities. But look, the thing is, I need to talk to Meere about her cousin, Eretibete.'

'Tiabei made an ugly face. 'What about her?'

'Is she here?'

Tiabei scowled. 'It is forbidden to have visitors in the dorms at all times.'

'You didn't answer my question. Is Eretibete here, or has she been here recently?'

'Meere is in too much trouble already. If it was found out that Eretibete had stayed, it would be very bad for her, very very bad.'

'So Eretibete was here?' said Louisa. Yes! She'd been right to come. 'Look I'll do my best to help Meere as soon as this investigation is over.'

Tiabei shook her head. 'It will be too late then.'

'Is Eretibete still here?' demanded Louisa in a loud whisper. 'I need to find her, her life could depend on it.'

Tiabei sighed and moved out of earshot from the crowd. Louisa followed her.

'Eretibete always comes when there is a crisis.'

'What kind of a crisis?' said Louisa.

Tiabei snorted. 'One which only money can solve. Meere feels sorry for her because she has no parents and lives with her brother, who is very bad to her. Meere always gives Eretibete some money, even though Meere has very little herself.'

'What does Eretibete do with the money?'

'Eretibete spends the money on clothes or going to the mata mata.'

'The mata mata?'

'It means 'flickering light'—a nightclub.' Tiabei looked around to check no one was listening, the other students were still crowding round Meere making sympathetic noises.

'I share a room with Meere. I stayed with my parents over the weekend. When I returned this morning I could smell Eretibete's sickly perfume on my sleeping mat and I found make-up traces on my pillow cover. I asked Meere if Eretibete had been in my bed. Meere knows I don't like Eretibete so she lied and said no. That's what Eretibete does, she makes people tell lies for her.'

'I'll need to talk to Meere about this, I have to know if Eretibete was here late Saturday night, early Sunday morning, and what she said.'

'She'll not tell you.'

'If I have to take her to the station, I will!'

Tiabei clicked her tongue dismissively. 'Threats will make no difference. Eretibete is family. Meere will say nothing if she thinks it will cause trouble for Eretibete.'

'She will not be making trouble for her, she will be clearing her name and possibly saving her life! Two people have been killed. This is very, very serious!' Louisa was beginning to lose patience.

Tiabei untied and retied her lava-lava over her long shorts. 'Eretibete is not here now. She left early this morning to avoid getting caught. I will talk to Meere later. I will explain to her you are trying to help Eretibete. I will try to make her agree to talk to you.'

'Can't you do that now?'

Tiabei shook her head. 'She is too upset.'

Louisa took a piece of paper and pen from her bag, wrote the station phone number on it and handed it to Tiabei. 'Phone me as soon as she's ready to talk to me.'

The girl refused the note. 'We don't have access to a phone. You come back at teatime.'

44

The Catholic Gift Shop was five hundred metres from Betio station. It was more of an office with a picture window than a shop. In the window a metallic shelving unit displayed a threadbare assortment of handwoven traditional fans, various ceremonial daggers, similar to the one Joe had been killed with, and a selection of gleaming brown cowrie shells. The shop was in the middle of a corridor of modern shops and offices, referred to by the locals as the retail park. It sat between the Air Tungaru office and Molly Brown's ice cream shop.

Special Constable John had handed Louisa the message from the Catholic Gift Shop on her return from the teachers' college. It asked her to come to the shop at her earliest convenience. They had information on the dagger used in Joe's killing. It was the first positive in a day of negatives. Dave the Fish had still not been brought in and Eretibete was still missing. Louisa had a bad feeling about her disappearance. Had she done the right thing by not confronting Meere about Eretibete's whereabouts? Louisa frowned. Years of living with her mother had taught her one thing if nothing else. An I-Kiribati woman could not be made to talk about someone, especially not a family member, when she didn't want to. Louisa would call back on the girls later. In the meantime, hopefully, Eretibete was safe.

The gift shop smelled like the inside of a new car. The floor was carpeted with blue needle cord. A tall, tanned woman with an afro hairstyle jumped up from behind a gleaming desk and introduced herself as Suzy Tan, the manager. Before Louisa had a chance to explain why she was there, Suzy Tan had bundled her into a back room, where a dozen cumbersome, local women sat cross-legged on pandanus mats arranged in a horseshoe shape on the floor.

There was clearly some confusion. In a hushed voice Louisa quickly explained to Suzy who she was. Suzy blushed. She'd mistaken Louisa for their special guest, the New Zealand High Commissioner's wife, whom she had never met. At that moment an elderly expatriate man walked into the room and the women on the floor began clapping. The man waited for the applause to die down. Tufts of white hair sprung from his head like fresh sprouts of grass. He wore ridiculously short, baggy khaki shorts, a stripy short-sleeved shirt, grey knee length socks and sandals. Large square shaped glasses gave him an avuncular look. Suzy pleaded with Louisa to stay, promising to help her as soon as the brief talk was over. Louisa sighed. Of all the things she could be doing, this was not one of them. Reluctantly, she sat down on the floor in the middle of the horseshoe.

Suzy stood next to the man and welcomed everyone in the audience, including their special guest, Detective Louisa Townsend from the Kiribati Police Service. The women around Louisa beamed and clapped heartily once more. Louisa blushed. She was Suzy's token expatriate dignitary! When the clapping died down for a second time, Suzy introduced the invited speaker.

'We are particularly privileged today to have Mr Robert White, spokesperson from the Foundation of the Peoples of the South Pacific International. As you know, FSPI undertake programmes in key development sectors. Today Mr Robert has come all the way from Sydney to talk to us about the success our FSPI neighbours in Papua New Guinea and Tonga have had with their gardening for food programmes. I know he's going to give us some tips to help us make our very own gardening for food programme equally successful. So, let's put our hands together again and give Mr Robert a traditional I-Kiribati welcome.'

The women clapped again and both Mr Robert and Suzy sat down on the mat in front of the women and crossed their legs in the usual manner. Louisa glanced at her watch. Five minutes. That was all she would wait. No more. Someone giggled. Then someone else. Louisa looked up. Ahead of her and in clear view of all the women, a flaccid, white cock peeked out of the bottom of Mr Robert's shorts. Louisa stared in disbelief.

Mr Robert smiled benignly and said, 'Please, don't feel shy. I have come from Sydney to share my knowledge and skill with you all. Ask any questions. I have nothing to hide.'

The women erupted into half-stifled mirth. Someone near the front scuttled forward and whispered something in Suzy's ear. Suzy turned pale, quickly stood up and waved her hand at the group. The giggling stopped. She turned to Mr Robert.

'Please forgive us, Mr Robert,' she said, smiling, 'A grave error has been made. Our floor is far too uncomfortable for our special guest to sit on, we are bringing you a chair immediately.' She nodded to the lady who'd whispered to her, who was already dragging the one chair from the back of the room to the front. 'Please stand.'

Mr Robert shook his head and smiled. 'I am honoured but I know very well the importance of being equal in Kiribati tradition and would not offend anyone by placing myself higher than everyone else.'

'But I insist!' said Suzy looked bewildered.

'Unless there are chairs for everyone,' he said kindly, 'looking at the women on the floor, including Louisa, I refuse absolutely.'

Clearly, either Suzy had to tell him his knob was on show, or let him be. She opted to let him be.

Louisa spent the next fifteen minutes listening to Mr Robert give a reasonable introductory talk on the pitfalls of sustainable gardening on a coral atoll. However, at the mention of anything vaguely pointy, the women roared with laughter. When questions were invited not one woman missed a chance to ask about carrots, cassavas or tapioca root vegetables, sausages even got into one of the questions. At the end of the talk Suzy almost dragged Mr Robert White on to his feet. He left for his coffee, beaming from ear to ear, saying it was the first time he'd ever received a standing ovation before the start of a workshop.

'He's doing a workshop in thirty minutes,' said Suzy. 'We'll have to get chairs for everyone.' She cleared her throat. 'I hope I can rely on your discretion?'

Louisa had not had such a good laugh for months, if not years. 'My lips are sealed, although theoretically, I should arrest him for indecent exposure.'

Suzy gave her a furious look.

'Sorry,' said Louisa, trying to keep a straight face. 'In bad taste.'

'Why does a certain type of expatriate man not wear underwear?' She didn't seem to expect an answer. 'They've taken him to Molly Brown's ice cream shop for refreshments. They'll be back soon. She cleared her throat. 'You are here about the dagger, yes?'

Louisa immediately became serious. 'You know who made it?'

'We keep details of every item that comes into the shop. This includes the name of the maker of the item and the name of the person who buys it, if it gets bought. The records go back two years. It took time to trawl through them but the constable had stressed it was urgent.' She picked up an exercise jotter from her desk.

'Yes?' Louisa mentally awarded Special Constable John three gold stars and a smiley face for distributing the description of the dagger, after all.

'This is the closest match we can find.' Suzy opened the jotter and pointed to an entry halfway down the second page. 'It wasn't sold and so it went back to the maker. It was the purple nylon wool in the handle, I'm afraid it didn't stand a chance.'

Louisa recognised the name immediately.

45

Reteta was out the back of the house building up the fire with sticks of dry driftwood and a bundle of coconut husks. She was alone. Louisa had driven to the house directly from the gift shop.

'Reteta?' said Louisa.

Reteta stuck out her chin and deliberately looked away from Louisa.

Louisa joined her by the fire. 'I'm sorry I shouted at you yesterday. It was wrong.'

Reteta continued to ignore her.

Louisa bit her lip. 'I was very rude. I'd had a long day and I lost my temper and I shouldn't have.'

Still looking away, Reteta pulled out a pandanus straw mat from a pile by the wall of the house. With one sweep of the hands, she unfurled it and let it fall on to the ground in front of the fire.

Louisa persisted. 'I'm really, very sorry.'

Reteta sat down on the mat and slowly began to shake her head. 'No problem, Louisa. You I-Matangs cannot help being rude. We know you are all crazy.'

Louisa sat on the mat next to Reteta. 'Not all expatriates are the same.' She picked up a handful of coconut husks and chucked them on to the fire. 'Just as all I-Kiribati are not the same.'

'Maybe?' said Reteta. 'They say another expatriate has

been murdered and you have found the killer.'

'Who says?'

'Everyone. It was on the radio too.'

'It's not over yet. Look, I didn't mean to break up your film afternoon yesterday.'

'No problem. The film was almost over anyway, so I did not have to repay any monies.'

Had she heard correctly? 'You were charging people? I thought it was a family get-together?'

'It was. But I was also raising funds for our church group at the same time.'

Louisa shook her head in despair. 'What would your church group say if they thought you were raising funds by showing such an unchristian film?'

Reteta shrugged. 'They do not care how we raise the funds, as long as we raise them. We have already made four thousand dollars.'

Louisa was surprised. 'All from film nights?'

Reteta tutted. 'We play na bingo, we sell na pancakes, we make na fans and na sleeping mats.'

Louisa threw some more coconut husks on to the fire and yellow flames burst out of the embers and jiggled into life. 'And daggers, do you make daggers too?'

'Oh yes, I am very good at making daggers,' said Reteta, smiling.

Louisa took the dagger handle, still wrapped in cling film, from her bag and placed it on the ground between them. 'And what about this one?'

Reteta scowled. 'Where did you get that?'

'Did you make it?'

Reteta stood up and picked at a string above her head. It tied a bundled-up mosquito net to a hook under the roof. The net floated to the ground in a wave of white.

'Did you make this dagger?' said Louisa again.

'Mauri!' TC appeared from the beach, wearing only board shorts. He looked as if he'd been swimming. His half naked body glistened in the yellow afternoon sun. Beads of water drip-dropped from his shiny black hair. 'So you ladies are still not talking?'

Louisa smiled. 'No, we are talking, aren't we, Reteta? I made my apologies for my loss of temper yesterday, didn't I, Reteta?'

Reteta grumbled something and sat back down, leaving the net floating behind her.

'I've been asking Reteta about this dagger handle.' She pointed to the handle on the ground. 'I want to know if she made it.'

TC shook his head and water droplets trickled down his shoulders. 'You'd better tell her, Reteta.'

'Tell me what?' said Louisa, not wanting to raise her hopes that at last she was going to get some solid evidence.

Reteta prodded the fire with a long blackened stick. 'It looks like one I made last year. I gave it to the Catholic Gift Shop but it did not sell. They gave it back to me.'

'Is it yours, yes or no?'

TC picked up a towel hanging over a piece of string running from the pandanus tree in the middle of the garden to the corner of the veranda, like a washing line. 'Tell her.'

'Okay! Okay!' Reteta picked up the handle. 'It is mine. I made that special design with the pandanus straw and purple wool. I thought it looked very good. The woman said the nylon was too artificial, I-Matangs wouldn't like it. She said expatriates only like all natural looking things.' She scowled. 'Where's the rest of it and why is it wrapped in the plastic material?'

Louisa tried not to get too excited. 'The rest of the dagger is at the mortuary. The doctor picked it out of the Ambo murder victim's head.'

Reteta dropped the handle and tutted. 'You can't go

telling everyone that my dagger killed the Ambo man with no eyes!'

'Who did you give it to?'

'I didn't give it to anyone.' She glanced across to TC, who walked towards the washroom at the side of the house.

'It will come out eventually.'

'What will come out?' said Louisa.

Reteta threw her arms in the air in exasperation. 'Tion came to visit me a week ago or two weeks ago. I was tidying up. All my things were laid out on the ground. The dagger was with the things. After he left I couldn't find the dagger. It was gone.'

'He stole it?' Louisa scrambled to her feet.

Reteta looked to TC but he'd disappeared into the washroom. She scowled. 'I think so. I don't know why he didn't just bubuti it. I would have given it to him if he'd asked. He didn't need to take it.'

'Are you sure it was Tion?'

Reteta looked at the ground. Very quietly she said, 'He once stole money from me. But you must tell no one. It is very bad to call someone a thief. Even if he is dead.'

Louisa now knew who had taken her fifty dollars. 'But why would he take the dagger?'

'I don't know,' said Reteta. 'It is something we make for I-Matangs.'

'Could he have given it to Joe?'

Reteta laughed. 'Tion did not like Joe. Joe was always telling him off.'

'Let me get this straight. Joe was murdered with your knife, which Tion took from you. Tion couldn't have killed Joe with it because Tion was dead when Joe was killed. This means Tion must have given the dagger to someone and that someone killed Joe with the dagger.' She felt almost euphoric. 'Please try and think. Who could Tion have given the knife to?'

Reteta looked very unhappy. 'I don't know.'

'Maybe Nata will know?' said TC back from the washroom with a toothbrush in his hand and a tube of toothpaste in the other.

'Nata? Who's Nata again?' said Louisa.

'He worked with Tion.'

'And how exactly did Tion die again?'

'He drowned,' said Reteta leaning over and grabbing a couple of pillows from on top of a small crate by the wall.

'I thought it was the bends?' said TC. 'There's no decompression chamber here. Tion often complained Joe's dive equipment was in a poor state of repair.'

'But what does it say on his death certificate?'

'What death certificate?' said TC.

'From what you've told me Tion's death was sudden and unexpected. A coroner would have had to examine him to determine the cause of his death.'

Both TC and Reteta looked vague.

'There would have been a death certificate!' insisted Louisa.

'Maybe there was?' said TC.

Something didn't feel right. 'Where can I find this Nata person, I'd like to talk to him?'

Reteta scowled. 'I don't know.'

Louisa turned to TC, who was brushing his teeth. 'No idea.'

46

The big chicken wire entrance gate to the teachers' college was locked. Louisa reversed and pulled up at the side of the road. One overhead light hanging from the top of the middle gate post sent eerie orange shadows dancing against the silver trunks of the palm trees. There was no moon. Crickets whined. Cicadas hummed. Louisa squeezed through a gap between the gate and the gate post—it looked as if others had done the same thing before her. She hurried to the girls' dorm.

Before heading for the college, she'd gone to the station. She'd hoped to find Eretibete waiting for her in the one interview room and Dave the Fish in the other. She'd been disappointed: the station was deserted except for the duty constable, who didn't know where anyone was. Louisa added Nata's name to the list of people to be brought to the station as a matter of urgency and ordered the duty constable to track down Tion's death certificate. Was it possible Tion's death was not an accident? Either way, Tion was now connected to Joe's killing through Reteta's dagger. Had Tion known Dave the Fish? Had he given Dave the ceremonial weapon? She absolutely had to talk to Dave and Nata. It was madness that it was so difficult to find anyone on such a tiny island.

The girls' dorm was almost invisible it was so dark. When Louisa had been a child she'd dreamed about going to boarding school and living in a dorm. She was glad it had never happened. They had so little privacy. How did these young women have a relationship with a boy? TC's incredibly fit body flashed into her mind. She gave herself a mental ticking off, what was she thinking of him for? She'd been celibate for too long and was turning into an old letch. She pictured Mr Robert's flaccid cock dangling out of his shorts and all thoughts of sex evaporated.

Louisa knocked on the main door. Nothing. She hammered on it. She wasn't leaving until she'd talked to Meere about Eretibete. A rustle above her. Louisa looked up. A girl's head popped over the concrete balcony. It was Tiabei. 'You're late!' she hissed.

'Where's Meere?'

Tiabei pointed to the back of the building and disappeared. Louisa crept around the sleeping concrete block. The sweet scent of tropical lilies clung to the walls. She couldn't believe she was sneaking about in the dark in order to get the most basic of information. At the back of the block was a fire door. It slowly began to open. Tiabei peeked through. Meere hid behind her. Her eyes were wide with anxiety.

'Quick!' hissed Tiabei. 'We only have a few minutes before someone notices the fire exit is open. We are not allowed in or out after dark and definitely no visitors.'

'Was Eretibete with you over the weekend?'

Meere looked down.

Tiabei nudged her. 'Go on.'

Meere finally faced Louisa. 'Eretibete came to me very early on Sunday morning. She begged me to let her stay. Her brother was very drunk and she was scared he would hit her if she went home. She had nowhere else to go. I said she could sleep in Tiabei's bed because Tiabei was away. But she didn't sleep. All night she talked about her I-Matang boyfriend. She said he had asked her to marry him. They were going to go and live in England. She was very excited about it.'

'He had asked her to marry him, really?'

'Oh, yes. She talked about nothing else. She left early this morning before Tiabei came back.'

'Did she say where she was going?'

'To friends. But she did say she would be back at her brother's house this evening. She said he would have sobered up by now.'

'Are you sure?'

Meere shrugged. 'She has nowhere else.'

Louisa paused to gather her thoughts. 'How did she get here so early on Sunday morning?'

'An I-Matang friend gave her a lift.'

'Her boyfriend?'

'No,' she shook her head. 'It wasn't a man, it was a woman called Nicole.'

Louisa made Meere repeat the name to be sure she'd heard correctly. She did. It was true. Nicole had given Eretibete a lift to the college at two o'clock on Sunday morning. Meere didn't know where Eretibete had met Nicole. Louisa wanted to know what Nicole was doing driving around the island at the same time someone was staving Jill's head in.

Louisa squeezed back through the gate and hurried to her car. The right front tyre had been slashed and was flat as a pancake. Shit and bugger! Louisa glanced all around. The road seemed deserted. This was the work of her stalker. 'I know you're there!' she yelled. 'You're a coward to hide in the shadows! If you have something to say, why not say it to my face?'

Louisa checked the boot. Empty. No spare. 'Thank you very fucking much!' she said under her breath. Then shouted, 'Cheers! I have no means of getting back to Betio!' She slammed the boot shut. How could whoever had fixed the flat not have checked there was a spare in the boot? She took out her purse. Four dollars in change. It was a dollar to get to Betio. She checked her watch. It was nine thirty. Did buses run this late? A noise. Behind her. Louisa turned. Tererei stood in the middle of the road. She wore a white tibuta smock top, her mother called them Mother Hubbard blouses, a red lava-lava and cheap Chinese flip-flops on her feet.

'You did this, didn't you?' said Louisa, kicking the flat tyre with her foot.

'Ko uara?' said Tererei.

Louisa stared at her in disbelief. 'Pardon?'

Tererei smiled coldly. 'You speak Kiribati, yes?'

'Some,' said Louisa.

'Ko uara?' repeated Tererei.

'I mararung, ko raba.' said Louisa, 'I'm fine. Thank you.' She glanced around. They were completely alone. Should she be worried? 'Which is more than I can say for my car.'

Tererei nodded towards the vehicle. 'You have a problem?'

'You know I do!'

'No spare?'

'No. No spare. Thanks to you, I'll have to get a bus.'

Tererei took a step closer to Louisa. 'There are no buses this late.'

Louisa tensed. The woman wasn't thinking of attacking her, was she? 'You slashed the tyre, didn't you?' said Louisa, automatically balancing her weight on the balls of her feet and holding her body upright in readiness for a strike.

'I have a question for you,' said Tererei. 'About Joe. The Ambo Lagoon Club victim.'

Louisa frowned. What did this ridiculous round woman have to do with Joe? 'I can't discuss it.'

'They say a man has been arrested for his murder. Is that true?'

'Someone is helping us with our inquiries but the case is not closed. I repeat, however, I'm not at liberty to give you any information.'

'Joe was my nephew.'

'Rubbish!' said Louisa before she could stop herself, 'He was Spanish!'

Tererei shook her head. 'No. He was only half-Spanish. His other half was I-Kiribati. People do not care that he is dead. But I was very close to him. He was like a son to me, my only son.'

47

One striplight dangled down the side of Tererei's C house and cast a wavy glow over the building. T-shirts decorated the tops of bushes in the garden, trousers lay spreadeagled on straw mats and lava-lavas hung from the bowed trunk of a twisted coconut palm. The house was similar to Louisa's but one size smaller. Louisa followed Tererei inside.

A giant shiny black television and a sleek black video recorder dominated the main room. Mouldy whitewashed walls were plastered with photos and postcards and colourful pictures torn from magazines. Tererei sat cross-legged on a straw mat in the middle of the floor. She indicated for Louisa to sit down opposite her, which she did, albeit reluctantly. A skinny girl appeared with a heavy tray. Two chipped, enamel cups sat on a round tray next to an open packet of granulated sugar and a battered metal kettle. The bottom of the kettle was black from smoke. An open tin of Carnation condensed milk sat next to the kettle. Its jagged round lid gaped upwards. The can made Louisa think of Edinburgh and her Scottish granny. Every Saturday Louisa and her granny had made tablet together using condensed milk. The tinned milk was so thick and sweet it couldn't be poured. Her mother had never done anything like that with her.

Tererei poured milky tea directly from the kettle into both mugs and passed one to Louisa.

'Thank you,' said Louisa, avoiding looking at the chip in it. She would not think of germs. She would stay focused on the case. 'Can you please explain how you are related to Joe?'

'Joe's mother was Spanish and worked on South Tarawa in Mary's Motel when she met my brother. They fell in love and got married. The marriage was not good. They argued all the time. One day she left. Joe was two. My brother struggled to look after Joe and asked me to adopt him. My husband and I were so happy to be Joe's parents. The doctor said we could never have our own children. Then his mummy came back. My brother had died by this time. She had legal papers to say Joe was her son. Our adoption had been unofficial. We could do nothing. Joe was nine. She took him away. I never saw him again until last year. I didn't know he was on Tarawa. He came to see me. I was so happy. We met every week. He would tell me what he was up to and we'd talk about when he was small.'

Louisa thought it was so crazy it could be true. 'Do you have proof of this connection?'

Tererei pulled a piece of grubby white paper from under her blouse. It was a certificate from the hospital.

'Is that all?'

She handed the paper to Louisa.

Louisa carefully took it with her left hand. 'Maybe it can be checked against the hospital records?'

'Joe said he had a terrible time with his mummy. She never stayed in one place for very long. They lived in India, Afghanistan, Germany and then Singapore. In Singapore he planned to leave her but she become very ill and he had to look after her. You don't have children, do you?'

Louisa shook her head.

'I was so happy that my Joe was back. We had one long happy year. We told no one that we were relatives. He did not want any cousins asking for favours. My husband knew, of course. Then the awful news came that he'd been killed. I couldn't believe it. Everyone said an I-Matang woman had killed him and that you, the detective in charge of finding Joe's killer, had let the I-Matang woman go because she was your friend.'

'What rubbish!'

Tererei shushed Louisa with a wave of her hand. 'Everyone knows I-Matangs stick together. It made sense to me.

I felt so angry. My Joe was dead and it was as if you had killed him. Last Saturday night I was walking with my husband and I saw you drive into the Otintaai Hotel. I was filled with hate. I didn't tell my husband. After we finished our walk I went back to the hotel and slashed your tyres. I couldn't think of anything else to do that wouldn't make a noise.'

'It's wilful damage of police property,' said Louisa.

Tererei looked away. 'I hated you so much. Then this evening, once again, my husband and I were having our evening stroll. I recognised your police car. I picked up a stone to throw at the windscreen but my husband stopped me. We went home but then I came back and slashed your tyre. My husband had followed me. He was very angry with me when he saw what I had done. He said I was projecting my anger at Joe's death on to you. He said I had to wait here and apologise to you and hope you wouldn't arrest me. He thought that maybe if I talked to you it would help me stop blaming you. So, here I am. Talking to you.'

Louisa was stunned. It was the most backhanded apology she'd ever heard. If it was an apology. 'Fact one, the woman who found Joe was not my friend. Fact two, this woman did not murder Joe. She was killed—' a horrible thought struck Louisa. 'Where were you over the weekend?'

Tererei glowered furiously. 'I am a Christian woman. I do not kill people!'

Louisa left it for the moment. 'Fact three, you've withheld evidence from the police—'

'All I have withheld is that Joe was my nephew.' She paused then said quietly, 'I want to ask if I may have his body when the case is resolved so he can be buried properly?'

Louisa suddenly felt sorry for the little round woman. 'If you can prove you are his next of kin, yes.'

Tererei's face fell. 'His eyes were taken. Did it happen before or after he died?'

'I'm sorry, I am not allowed to say,' said Louisa.

'Please, you tell me—' she quickly wiped her eyes with the back of her palms. 'You tell me what you saw when you found his dead body. I need to know what it was like for the only son I ever had when he died.'

Louisa cleared her throat. 'There are rules about keeping the details of a crime scene confidential. When the case is closed I'll be only too happy to talk to you about it. Is that fair?' For all she knew Tererei could be a good actress and her story a complete fabrication. She could even be the killer.

'Please,' said Tererei, leaning forward and gripping Louisa's hand.

Louisa started. She wanted to pull her hand free but resisted. 'I wish I could.'

'When I close my eyes I see his body. Terrible things have been done to him. It makes me ill. Sometimes I think it would be better to be dead then I wouldn't have to see the terrible images in my head.'

It was against all the rules but she could not let her suffer such distress any longer. Despite herself, she gave the woman's hand a gentle squeeze. 'All I can say is that when I saw him he had already been dead for a long time. He lay flat out on the floor on his back. He wore a lava-lava, no shoes and no T-shirt, dressed very casually. The dagger penetrated his temple. His eyes had been removed after death. He didn't look angry, or sad, or frightened, you know, if anything he had a faintly amused look on his face.'

'Why take his eyes though—' Tererei sounded hoarse, '—I don't understand?'

'Neither do we. But I'll find out.'

'No fight? No other damage?'

Louisa shook her head.

'How long did it take for him to die?'

'We think death was instantaneous.'

Tererei fumbled for a hanky under her blouse, turned away, then blew her nose noisily.

'If we can prove you are his closest relative, I can arrange for you to see him. He's still to be officially identified by a family member.'

'I would like that.'

'It may be upsetting...'

Tererei smiled. 'He is with his God now and in a better place but I would still like to say goodbye.'

'As soon as we have the killer under lock and key, we'll release the body to you, assuming the paperwork can be sorted.'

'He was such a very nice boy. I don't understand who would want to kill him.'

'All I can say is that I am doing my utmost to track down the person who did this and when I do, I will make sure he or she is brought to justice.'

'You have helped, nei Louisa, ko raba.' She blew her nose for a second time, tucked her hanky in the sleeve of her blouse. 'Now, you say you want to go to Betio, yes?'

'Yes?' said Louisa puzzled.

'Then you take my key. You drive to Betio.'

'Are you sure?'

'Of course I am sure. Here.' She handed Louisa a small car key.

Louisa took the key from her. 'Thank you.'

'Come. I will take you to your transport.' Tererei stood up and led Louisa outside into the shadows.

48

A lonely Honda moped sat by the side of the C house. Louisa

did a double take. Was Tererei serious? 'I thought you had a car. I can't drive that thing.'

'Why not?' said Tererei indignantly.

'I don't know how to, that's why not.'

'But you can drive a car, yes?'

Louisa gulped. 'It's not the same.'

Tererei shook her head. 'If you can drive a car, you can drive this. It's easy. You are a clever person. Just get on.'

'But—'

'Tsk!' said Tererei. Ignoring her protests, she rolled the bike off its support and pushed the bike into the road. 'Try.'

Louisa straddled the small plastic seat of the bike and sat down, one foot firmly on the ground and the other hovering above it.

'Turn the key, rev the handle and move off,' said Tererei matter-of-factly.

Louisa put the small key into the ignition and turned. The engine purred into life. Louisa thought maybe it wouldn't be so bad, after all. She revved the handle. The engine roared. The bike flew forward. Louisa screamed, braked and skidded into some bushes at the side of the road.

Tererei threw her a filthy look. 'Get off!'

Louisa sheepishly dismounted the bike. 'I told you I didn't know what to do.'

'Akea te kanganga!' said Tererei, her nostrils quivering, 'I will take you myself! Wait!' Tererei disappeared into her house.

'Both of us on that wee thing?' shouted Louisa after her.

Tererei reappeared. Her hessian shopping bag dangled from her pudgy wrist. She slipped the bag over the handlebar of the bike and climbed on. 'Yes. Both of us. Do you want go to Betio tonight or not?'

'Meere's cousin, Eretibete, is in Betio somewhere. I really need to ask her some questions.'

'I know where she lives. I will take you there. Get on now before I change my mind!'

Louisa took half a second to think about it. 'Right,' she said, and quickly wedged herself between Tererei's enormous bottom and a small metal bar that stuck out at the back of the vehicle.

Tererei started the engine. 'Do not let go!' she yelled.

The bike jerked into life. Louisa gripped the back bar for all she was worth. The moped put, put, putted away and they were off. A cool breeze made Louisa shiver. She tried to look where they were going, but it was impossible to see past Tererei's furiously wobbling double-decker black bun.

For what seemed forever, Louisa sat behind Tererei. As they rattled past swaying black palm frond after swaying black palm frond, Louisa grew steadily colder. By the time they reached Betio Louisa was freezing, and although the grey outline of the tumbledown shacks was vaguely familiar to her, she'd no idea where she really was.

Halfway down a small track and in what seemed the middle of nowhere Tererei finally pulled up and dismounted. Her double bun had fallen to one side and some shorter strands of hair had worked themselves loose and stuck out in all directions.

'Eretibete's house,' she said, nodding towards a rectangular shape.

Louisa got off the bike. A smell of pig and rancid milk, mixed with just a hint of sweet frangipani, filled the air. She rubbed her arms in the warmth of the still night. A crescent moon gave off just enough light to see by. The lane was deserted. The houses looked boarded up.

Tererei gave Louisa a little push forward. 'She lives with her brother in there.'

The fibreboard door to Eretibete's house was old and

battered. Louisa vaguely recognised it from the time she saw Eretibete standing there with Paul. Louisa knocked. No answer. She knocked again. Silence.

Tererei rasped, 'Nei Eretibete?'

Still nothing. Louisa gave the door a small shove, to her surprise it swung open. She leaned into the shadowy room, 'Hello?'

Tererei touched her arm. 'There is no one home, we must not go in.'

'Okay—' said Louisa, pushing the door just a little bit further open.

'What you doing?' growled Tererei.

'Just a quick look—'

'But Eretibete is not here!'

'I won't be long.'

'No!'

Too late, she was inside. The narrow floor was covered in a long cut of dark red lino. There was a back door at the other end of the room, blocked by half a dozen rolled-up sleeping mats and a scatter of pillows. Two wooden shutters on either side of the wall were pulled tight shut. A new, widescreen TV and state-of-the-art DVD player stood below the near shutter. A tower of DVDs stood next to them. They looked brand new. The top DVD was the latest Jackie Chan movie. They certainly didn't look as if they'd come from the tatty local hire shop. Had Paul bought her them? Or did they belong to the brother? It was not how she imagined the house to be. Louisa glanced about. Nothing. What had she expected? A clue that linked Eretibete to the deaths? Or something that cleared her? There was no evidence of the bed that Eretibete had supposedly been tied to. Louisa went back outside.

'Tererei? Where are you?' she hissed. The woman seemed to have disappeared. A fluorescent light flashed ahead somewhere. It threw a rush of yellow on to a pack of dogs five metres in front of Louisa. They greedily tore at a patch of leathery material. Was that brown hair? Did dogs eat other dogs? The biggest dog, a white mongrel with a brown patch over its eye, looked up. Its eyes locked on to Louisa. It growled. Louisa looked away. Never stare at a dog. She'd read that somewhere. She grappled in her bag for her stone. It wasn't there. Shit! The other dogs looked up. One began to whine, low and long. Another barked. Louisa scoured the ground. She needed a stone. Anything to throw at it. Didn't matter how dirty it was. She'd rather die of a stomach bug than be torn to shreds by a pack of dogs. The big dog moved towards her. Louisa tried to shout. Her mouth wouldn't work. The animal drew back its lips. Slimy globules of spittle slithered down the side of his jaw. He snarled. A rock clipped the dog's ear. It yelped and bolted. The others darted after it.

'Nei Louisa!' snapped Tererei, appearing behind her and wiping some dust from her hands on her lava-lava. 'What are you doing with those dogs? I will leave you if you do not come now!'

'I was looking for you,' said Louisa.

Tererei marched towards the bike. 'I went to make pee-pee. I will leave here now. Do you want a lift to your house? It is very late.'

'Thank you.' Louisa climbed on the bike as Tererei started the engine. 'Do you know a place called the Royal Saloon?'

Tererei pulled away with a jolt. She cocked her head to one side. 'Tera?'

Louisa gripped the back bar. 'The Royal Saloon? I've heard that Eretibete goes there sometimes. It really is urgent I find her.'

'It is a bad place!'

'But is it far?'

Tererei revved the throttle and the bike pulled away.

Her bun wobbled violently. 'You are going to get me in trouble, nei Louisa!'

49

Above what looked like a reinforced door, a red neon sign flashed the words Royal Saloon. The building itself was a windowless box about the size of a large bungalow in the middle of an otherwise derelict patch of wasteground.

Tererei parked her moped on the opposite side of the road from the club. Fifty metres to the left of the building stood the dilapidated Betio bakery, fifty metres to the right the only two-pump petrol station on Tarawa—now closed for the night. The powerhouse, a conglomerate of grey turbines and rusted valves, throbbed just behind them at the other side of a barbed wire fence. The number of cars parked on the scrap of ground in front of the building suggested the Royal Saloon was busy.

Tererei dismounted and resolutely crossed her arms. 'I will wait here for you. Be quick.'

Louisa eased herself off the moped. 'It's just a nightclub. I'll be fine. You don't need to wait.'

'It is not safe. I will wait.'

'Have you ever been inside?'

Tererei puffed out her cheeks until they looked as if they would burst, 'Of course I have not been in there! What do you think?'

Just then the heavy door flew open and a drunken I-Kiribati man wearing baggy jeans and a loose T-shirt fell out of the building. The door slammed behind him. He stumbled towards the cars and threw up over the bonnet of the first one. Next, after missing his footing twice, he managed to climb into a double-cabbed truck and somehow start the engine. Louisa and Tererei watched to see what he would do next.

'About Meere,' said Louisa, eyeing the drunk trying to reverse his truck.

'What about her?' said Tererei, also watching the man.

'Is there really nothing you can do to help her?'

'Louisa, Louisa, Louisa,' said Tererei wearily. 'We are not heartless. Meere will go home and recover from her terrible ordeal. Then, next year, when everyone has forgotten what has happened, she'll come back and finish her course.'

'Watch out!' said Louisa. They both jumped back into the fence. The drunk driver roared towards them, narrowly missed crashing into Tererei's bike and made his way down the lane towards the bakery, finally disappearing in a cloud of blue smoke.

Tererei marched towards the door. 'I will come in with you.'

Louisa hurried after her. 'You don't need to.'

They both stopped outside the door to the building. The red-tinged door didn't seem to have a handle. Louisa looked for a bell, or a hatch, 'Do you think we have to knock?'

'I don't know!' said Tererei, breathing furiously.

Louisa thumped against the heavy door and waited. Nothing. She thumped again, but much more loudly. The door flew open and two young expatriate women charged out. Laughing loudly they nodded hellos to Louisa and Tererei and carried on. Louisa thought they were Australian volunteer teachers she'd met once.

Inside, on a tiny dance floor, a glittering disco ball bounced shards of silver light over a throng of writhing young people wriggling to the blaring sound of Tom Jones's Sex Bomb. I-Matang and I-Kiribati were equally represented. A bar ran along the left-hand side of the room and an enormous mirror covered the wall behind it. It made the cramped room seem quite large. The door slammed shut behind them. It was sweltering inside and there was no sign of Eretibete. Louisa pushed her way towards the bar.

Three young, big-eyed, tight-clothed I-Kiribati waitresses served drinks behind the heaving bar. The girl nearest to them had short spiky hair, wore three stud earrings in her eyebrow, one in the middle of her bottom lip, and what looked like a metal bar pierced through the top half of her left ear. Louisa tried to get her attention. Louisa leaned over and prodded her arm. 'I'm looking for Eretibete,' she shouted. 'Is she here?'

The girl snarled, 'Who do you think you are, touching me?'

'Detective Sergeant Townsend, that's who!' said Louisa. 'Is Eretibete here?'

The girl curled her full black lipsticked mouth into a sneer, 'Don't know who you're talking about!'

Tererei pushed in beside Louisa and began to bark at the girl in Kiribati. The girl's sullen mouth collapsed. She nodded towards the back of the room.

'A long time ago that girl was my best student,' said Tererei, barging through the throng ahead of Louisa.

The back door led to a dingy room full of empty crates and tall black tanks of carbon dioxide. It stank of pee and sweat and pungent aftershave. A forty watt bulb dangled on a frayed flex. It barely lit the cramped area. A small group of half a dozen women stood huddled in front of a tatty wooden door. Louisa assumed they'd found the queue for the toilet.

Eretibete stood in the far corner of the little room. She was all limbs in a skimpy mini skirt and a strapless boob tube. A tall I-Kiribati man towered beside her. His back was to them. They seemed to be arguing. The others were doing their best to ignore the dispute. The high pitched squeal of the Bee Gees singing Tragedy from the main room helped them.

'What are they quarrelling about?' whispered Louisa as loudly as she could without attracting attention to herself.

Tererei pouted. 'He wants to know what she's doing here. And so do I.'

'It's just a wee nightclub, Tererei. They're young people having fun—'

There was a shout. They looked across. The man with Eretibete had his hand raised as if to strike her.

'Oy!' Louisa darted across the small room to stop him. 'You can't do that!'

The man spun round, and then just a fraction of a second too late, Louisa realised what was going to happen. His knuckles powered into her face. Thump! Blood. In her mouth. Her knees crumpled. She was on the ground. The bastard had hit her.

50

It was chaos in the tiny back room of the Royal Saloon for a few seconds: girls screamed, doors slammed and Louisa didn't know what way was up. Then there was silence. Someone took Louisa's arm and helped her up.

'Tikiraoi?' said Tererei

'I'll have him!' said Louisa, wincing. It hurt when she spoke. She cradled her cheek. 'And when I do, I'll lock him up and throw away the key!'

Tererei looked at her blankly. 'You got in his way, what did you expect?'

'He assaulted me!' said Louisa, tasting blood on her tongue. 'And I'm going to find him and arrest him, you wait and see!'

Eretibete snorted.

Louisa threw her a furious look. 'He was about to hit you!'

'Nei Eretibete?' said Tererei, 'What are you doing here?'

Eretibete looked bored. 'Nothing.'

Tererei replied something in short sharp Kiribati, too fast for Louisa to follow. Eretibete looked down at the ground and blushed.

Louisa wiped some blood from the side of her mouth with the back of her hand. 'I need to ask you some questions about your relationship with Paul Wilson.' The small room was stifling—and it still stank of piss. Beautiful Noise by Neil Diamond thudded through the panelled walls.

'I don't have to tell you nothing!'

'Yes, you do,' said Tererei.

Eretibete looked down.

Louisa balanced on the edge of an upturned crate—for some reason her legs didn't seem to want to hold her up. 'I've been looking for you all day so don't bother pissing me about. I am not in the mood, especially not now your brother has fucking punched me in the face!'

'Tsk!' said Tererei angrily. 'You do not have to swear!'

Louisa felt herself blush. She didn't believe it. Tererei was making he feel guilty about using the 'f' word.

'What do you want to know?' said Eretibete sullenly.

Louisa took her hand away from her face, she was going to have a shiner in the morning. 'How long have you been having a relationship with Paul Wilson?'

'Six months, maybe seven. We met at the hash.'

'And, for the record, your relationship with Paul is a sexual one, yes?'

'What do you think?' she said, pursing her pretty little lips.

'And did you see Paul Wilson last Thursday evening?'

'I bumped into him at the hospital. He offered to give me a lift home. I took it.'

'You didn't ask him for the lift?'

She scowled. 'No.'

'And what time was this?'

'About six o'clock.'

'And what happened?'

She pouted. 'Nothing. He brought me to Bairiki.'

'You didn't stop on the way back, anywhere?'

'We talked outside his house. He wanted me to join him on the hash run but I didn't want to.'

'Why not?'

'I didn't feel like it. We argued.'

'What about?' said Louisa.

'It is always the same. He tells me he loves me and I tell him if he loves me he must leave his wife, but he doesn't. I said I didn't want to go out with him any more. He was very angry.'

'And what time did you leave him?'

'About seven thirty. You can ask the hash people. They saw us outside the house. Some of them are in here tonight,' she nodded towards the bar area, where the music was still thudding.

Louisa decided to leave that for the moment. 'What about Saturday night, you were seen in here with Paul. So even though you'd argued your relationship wasn't over at all?'

Eretibete sat down opposite on an upturned beer crate. 'He phoned me on Saturday night.'

'It wasn't the other way round?' Louisa suddenly felt tired. She looked at Tererei, who'd already placed a spare lava-lava from her bag on the floor and made herself comfortable, and then looked back at Eretibete scowling in the corner of the tiny room. How on earth had she ended up in this place with these two women? She said to Eretibete, 'You didn't phone Paul at the Otintaai and tell him you were in trouble, that your brother had tied you up?'

'No,' said Eretibete. 'He phoned me here in the bar. He asked me if I was with another man. I told him it wasn't his business who I was with.'

'If you're lying, we'll find out.'

'It's the truth. You can ask anyone in there,' she nodded to behind the door to where Sweet Caroline was blaring. 'He came to the bar from the hotel. He started shouting at me. He said I was his girlfriend and he didn't want me to go with anyone else. I told him I was not his possession and that we were finished and I left. I am a pretty girl. If Paul Wilson didn't want to leave his wife, I would find a new boyfriend. I went to the mata mata to see my friends.'

'Where's the mata mata?'

'By the docks. It's where the young people go. I was fed-up with the old men here.'

Louisa nursed her face. 'Did you see Paul after that, or his wife?'

'After the mata mata I went to the teachers' college to see my cousin Meere. I didn't see Paul or his wife. Ugh! She was so ugly.'

'The college is at the other end of South Tarawa. How did you get there?'

'The I-Matang from the hash, Nicole, she was at the mata mata. She is my friend. She gave me a lift to the teachers' college.'

'What was she doing there?' Louisa was surprised.

Eretibete smirked. 'She was with Nata.'

Tiny goosebumps nibbled up and down Louisa's arms. 'The diver?'

Eretibete pulled out a long toothed hair comb from somewhere behind the bun on top of her head. Her thick hair tumbled down her back. 'He is my brother's girlfriend's cousin. He dives for sea cucumbers and used to work for Joe.'

'Nicole was with him?' said Louisa.

Eretibete took a handful of her hair and slowly began to comb it. 'He and Nicole are lovers. It is clear her I-Matang husband can't satisfy her. I-Matang men are like Paul, they want to talk and talk and talk. It is so boring. Paul thinks that my brother doesn't like him but my brother wants me to have an I-Matang boyfriend. He knows I-Matang men earn lots of money. I heard that Paul has been arrested for killing Jill.'

Louisa ignored the question about Paul. 'Are you sure you saw Nicole with Nata?'

'Oh, yes. They had a big argument in the middle of the dance floor. Everyone saw her. She was the only I-Matang there. She is a very brave woman. Not even the I-Matang men go to the mata mata, they are too scared.'

'Then what?'

'Then nothing. She took me to Tarawa Teachers' College because she is my friend.' Eretibete stood up. 'Tomorrow I will visit Paul in Betio jail.'

'No, tomorrow you will come to Betio station and make a statement.'

'No problem,' she said as she sauntered out of the small room, her hair swinging behind her in swirls of black luxuriance. 'I'll see Paul later.'

51

Outside was deliciously cool and, apart from the chirping of some cheeky cicadas and the soft hum from the powerhouse, very quiet. It was a relief after the heat and noise of the Royal Saloon. An upturned wheelbarrow had been propped against the side of the building. Despite it being grotty, Louisa leaned on it and took long, slow, deep breaths. What a night. It was as if she'd been punched in the guts as well as the face.

'Well?' said Tererei waiting patiently next to her.

'It's all so confusing!' said Louisa finally. She touched her cheek and winced. Did it surprise her that Nicole was having an affair? If she were honest, no. Were all the expatriates at it? Probably. But it did surprise her to hear that Nicole's lover was Tion's friend, Nata. That was way too much of a coincidence to ignore. 'All I know for certain at the moment is Eretibete's brother is a shit.'

'Louisa,' said Tererei very calmly. 'You cannot believe a word Eretibete says. She was the naughtiest girl in her class at the teachers' college. Always lying. And very lazy. You have to watch out for lazy people, because they will do anything in order to do nothing.'

'Maybe, but she seemed to be telling the truth about her whereabouts. Of course, I will ask Nicole to corroborate Eretibete's statement, but if Nicole did drop Eretibete off on Sunday morning when she said, then Eretibete can be ruled out as a suspect.'

'Of course Eretibete is not a suspect! She is a silly little girl!'

Louisa ran her hands through her hair. 'It doesn't help that no one tells the truth on this island!'

Tererei took a second lava-lava from her hessian sack and began wrapping it on top of the one that was already around her body. 'So you are giving up?'

'If everyone had been honest from the start, I'd be a lot further forward!'

'You did not know the right questions to ask, that is all. The I-Matang Paul may have killed his wife, Jill, I don't care. You told me you were going to find my nephew's killer. You are not going to do that now?'

'Of course I am! It's just that I thought Jill's killer and

Joe's killer were one and the same person. I don't know now.' She threw her arms in the air. 'Maybe there are two killers? Maybe Paul killed Jill but not Joe? Maybe he should be in jail? Maybe I've got it completely wrong?'

'Feeling sorry for yourself will not help Joe.'

'And now I discover Nicole was with Nata on the night Jill died. Nicole was Jill's friend. Nata was Tion's friend. Both Jill and Tion are dead. That's too much of a coincidence not to be significant. There's something I am not seeing.'

'Who are Tion and Nata? Why are you talking about them?'

'They worked for Joe. Tion died while diving for sea cucumbers late Wednesday, early Thursday morning.'

'But this has nothing to do with Joe's death!'

Louisa pulled herself up off the wheelbarrow. 'What if Tion's death was a direct result of faulty dive equipment? Joe would have been in serious trouble. Not only would he have been under attack by grieving relatives, but presumably his export licence could have been revoked. What if Joe had bribed an official to not investigate Tion's death and to make the death certificate disappear? Joe has been accused of bribing officials in the past.'

'You are blackening my son's name now!' In one swoop Tererei swept the loose strands of hair together and stuffed them back into her wobbly bun. 'I am leaving.'

'Just listen!' The woman was infuriating. 'If there was some kind of cover-up over Tion's death, Nata would have had to have known about it. After all, he was with Tion when he died. I need to find Nata.'

'I will not hear any more bad things about my son!' Tererei marched towards the moped.

Louisa hurried after her. 'Don't you see, if Joe did try to cover up the death, that could have made Nata angry with him. Maybe even angry enough to kill him. Revenge is a powerful motive.'

Tererei clambered on to her moped. Without looking at Louisa she said, 'I am leaving now. I will drop you off on the way because it is not good for a woman to be alone walking at night.'

Louisa sighed. That was all she needed, someone else in a mood with her. She slipped on to the bike behind Tererei and looked up. The stars were like tiny silver stitches that had been sewn into a quilt of purple silk. It was beautiful. Tererei revved the throttle and putted away.

52

One look at the deserted blackness out the back window told Louisa Reteta was not out the back. Was she still in a huff with her? Maybe. She had not looked pleased when Louisa had said her dagger had been used to kill someone. Tererei hadn't even said goodbye after dropping Louisa off. Louisa should have cared, but she didn't. The events of the day, and especially the punch to her face, had left her exhausted and confused. She was too tired even to shower. She needed to sleep.

Louisa woke with a start. In her dream a naked Eretibete posed on the floor of the school hut in an extremely provocative manner. Paul, looking remarkably like a giant-headed chihuahua, ran around her in frantic circles. It was more of a nightmare than a dream. Was that what woke her?

Louisa threw off her sheet and sat up. She was wide awake. It was the case. She couldn't stop thinking about it, even in her sleep. Dave the Fish had been her number one suspect and then Jill had been killed and everything got confused. She had to go back to focusing on finding Joe's killer. That would lead her to Jill's murderer, whether the killer was the same person or not. Dave the Fish had to be found by the next day and when he was Louisa would at last discover what he was doing with Joe on Thursday night. Suspect number two had to be Nata. Nata was Tion's friend and Tion could have easily given him the dagger that was used to kill Joe. It was possible that Nata wanted to kill Joe to revenge Tion's death, which could have been due to negligence on Joe's part. Perhaps Joe bribed a government official to cover up the cause of death? Thinking about it was giving her a headache. Something wasn't right about Tion's accident and the sooner she talked to Nata about it the better.

As for Nicole? Louisa wanted to know what she'd been arguing about with Nata at the mata mata. It had to have been something serious to have brought her to downtown Betio in the middle of the night. Eretibete had cleared Paul, the only hash runner who could not account for all of his time on Thursday evening, assuming she was telling the truth. Louisa leaned back into her pillow. How could Eretibete's version of her relationship with Paul be so different from Paul's version of it? She sighed. Maybe they were both lying? Or maybe they were both telling the truth, just their own twisted version of it?

A noise. At first Louisa wasn't even sure if she'd heard it. The sound was very faint: a sort of quiet shuffling. It grew louder. Louisa slipped out of bed and tiptoed over to the window where it was coming from. The noise continued: a shuffle, scratch, shuffle. Louisa couldn't imagine what was making it. A mouse perhaps? A faint haze of silver moonlight soaked in through the thin cotton curtains she'd tacked up on the first day she'd moved in. The material fluttered. As if a gust of wind had lifted it. But there was no breeze. Louisa pressed her body against the wall next to the window. Her heart thumped. She kinked her index finger round the side of the curtain and pulled it about a centimetre away from the wall. Two thirds of the way down the louvres, a twig about a foot long pushed between the security wire and through the mosquito screen and the open louvred glass and lifted the curtain up. Some shit was trying to spy on her? In one movement she swept the curtain back and screamed, 'Bastard!' A terrified teenage boy stumbled backwards. 'Piss off!' she roared.

The boy scrambled to his feet and fled towards the beach. Next thing she knew TC was there, hair sticking out in all directions, eyes blurry, looking as if he'd just woken up.

'Where did you come from?' said Louisa.

'Reteta sent me to keep an eye on you. I must have fallen asleep. Are you okay?'

'Some shitty wee peeping Tom!' said Louisa, nodding after the boy, conscious suddenly she was in her underwear.

TC raised his arms in the air in a gesture of confusion. 'You took so long to get back last night, I thought you weren't coming. I went for a nap in the washroom'.

'I don't know how many times I have to say, I don't need a bodyguard.'

'Reteta insisted.' He frowned. 'What happened to your face?'

Louisa touched her swollen cheek. 'Nothing.'

'It doesn't look like nothing. You sure you're okay?'

'I'm fine. Really. That boy looked about thirteen. Think he got a bigger fright than me.'

TC frowned. 'Did someone hit you?'

Louisa sighed. 'It's a long story.'

He shrugged. 'I've got time.'

In the moonlight and through the security wire it looked as if she were talking to someone in a cell. There was no chance of her getting back to sleep now. 'You want to come in and have a cup of tea or something?'

He smiled. 'Wouldn't mind, thanks.'

Louisa slipped on a lava-lava and T-shirt and went to

the back door to let him in.

The phone woke Louisa at six thirty. It was Tebano. David Trout and his friends were in custody. Yes! At last! She quickly showered. TC had left earlier. Much earlier. It had been good chatting to him. He seemed so non-judgmental. As he was going, she'd had an overwhelming urge to ask him to stay. But she'd resisted. Why would he want to sleep with a thirty something grouch with a germ phobia? And what if Reteta had found out? She'd have dashed a letter off to her mum straight away, full of recriminations and talk of loose women. Louisa sighed. But, then again, if he'd said yes it could have been worth the risk.

53

Louisa gave Bob to Tebano to interview. Michael got Stevo. She kept Dave for herself. Her suspects had at last been tracked down in South Betio, in a drinking den, and brought into Betio nick. When she entered her office, he was rocking back and forwards on his chair. She sat down opposite him.

'How'd you get that shiner?' sneered Dave.

'I ask the questions,' said Louisa.

'I've done nothing wrong.'

'Either you tell me the truth about where you were on Thursday evening or you stay here, indefinitely.'

'I was at home. I already told you.' He continued to rock up and down. 'This is wrongful arrest.'

'No,' said Louisa,' You were not at home. I have a witness who saw you at the Ambo Club,' she lied. 'You've withheld vital evidence in a serious criminal investigation. That's called obstruction, that's seven years, and that's just for starters.'

'Bullshit!' he snarled, slamming the chair to the ground.

'Thing is,' said Louisa calmly, 'Stevo and Bob look a bit soft to me. Too much beer and dope and hanging around doing nothing probably. And while I'm positive Constable Michael will follow the law to the letter, Sergeant Tebano, on the other hand, is a right bastard. Wouldn't like to say what methods he might resort to, to get to the truth.'

Dave scowled. 'I've told you the truth.'

'No, you've not.' She stood up. 'I know you were at the Ambo on Thursday and I know you met Joe. It's just a matter of time before more witnesses come forward. When they do, I'm going to do you and your chums for either obstructing the police in a murder investigation, or for the murder itself. Either way you'll do time. Of course, that means you're export licence will be revoked and you'll be deported back to your home country—'

'You can't do that!'

'I can and I will. You have precisely one minute to think about it.'

'Bitch!'

She looked at her watch. 'Forty-five seconds.'

He began rocking the chair again. 'Okay. I was there.'

'Where?' said Louisa.

'The Ambo. It was a private business meeting between me and Joe. He was alive and well when I left.'

Louisa sat down and picked up her pen. She had the bastard now. 'What time was this exactly?'

His thin lips bunched up into a knot shape. 'Seven or as near as. The bastard was having a dip when I got there.'

'A what?' said Louisa.

He slammed his chair down for the second time. 'A dip. In the lagoon! Arsehole! I mean, who swims when they're about to have a business meeting? No one! He comes out of the water to meet me and he's bloody starkers!' Dave spat on the floor next to the chair. 'Fucking poofter!'

'Oy! No spitting and watch your language! Then what?'

'I told him to put his clothes on, that's what! I wasn't doing no talking with any faggot! He just laughed and said he'd been running and had got all sweaty so he'd gone in for a swim to cool down.'

'He'd ran from where?'

'He said he'd jogged from Bairiki. The twat had been to some meeting with that ponce running group. He'd not told anyone there he was coming cause he didn't want them to know he was doing business with me, especially not that fucking bastard Ian—'

'I'll not tell you again about your language,' she said quietly but firmly.

He threw her a filthy look.

'Joe didn't like Ian then?'

Dave curled his lip. 'Joe applied for a licence to export shark fins three times and Ian refused it three times.'

'Why?'

'Ian didn't need a reason.' David folded his arms and leaned back into the chair. 'Joe got on my tits, but that Ian's a creep. Back home he was Billy no-mates in some shit nothing job, then he lands his fat aid contract and thinks he's Mr Big. Bastard's so far up his own arse—'

'Okay!' Louisa sighed. 'I get it. You don't like Ian either. So, you talked to Joe, yes? And do you always do business with naked men?'

'I'm no poof! I told him to get his kit back on or I was out of there. He said he wanted to dry off some more and didn't want his running clothes to get damp. He was winding me up, that's what he was doing! He thought it was funny. I found a dirty old lava-lava behind the bar—who knows where Sammy had pissed off to? He's a bloody useless bludger, him. I chucked it at Joe. Told him straight, put on the lava-lava or there are no talks.'

'And then what?'

He lifted his shoulders in an indifferent shrug. 'Then what nothing. He put the lava-lava on. We did our business.'

'When did the argument start?' said Louisa.

'There was no argument!'

'So how did Joe end up dead?'

David slammed his fist against the desk. 'When I left him he was alive! Why would I kill him? He told me Ian was granting him the export licence for the shark fins. Exporting shark fins makes big bucks. That meant he'd soon be able to pay me back the money he owed me.'

Louisa ignored his outburst. 'I believe since his death you've been using his boat and divers?'

'It's my boat now and you must be really desperate if you think I killed him for a bloody tinny.'

'It's like this, David, you're the last person to have seen him alive and that makes you my prime suspect.'

'Bugger off! He was alive when I left him. You can ask that fat Sheila that was there!'

The skin on the back of Louisa's neck tingled. She cleared her throat. 'There was a woman at the club?'

Dave flopped back into the chair. 'As I was leaving she was hurrying along the path towards the club. She didn't see me but I saw her. I remember thinking she was in for a surprise.'

'Why?' Was this the expatriate woman Tom mentioned? She actually existed?

A wide grin slid across Dave's face. 'I swiped Joe's kit, that's why. His shorts, his jocks, his shoes, his ponce bag. They're still in the back of my cab. There was no way she could have missed him, not with him being bloody starkers.'

Louisa was furious. 'All the time we've been looking for Joe's clothes and they were in the back of your truck?' The man was an idiot! 'I'll be charging you for withholding evidence in a murder investigation!'

'Do what you want but I didn't kill him. Ask that Sheila. Last I saw of him he was alive and well and swimming in the lagoon starkers.'

'And what did the woman look like?'

'Typical I-Kiribati bird—'

'She was a local? You're sure?'

'I'm not a wombat. Mid forties, fat like I said, with her hair all wrapped up on her head in a lump. There was a moped parked further up, as if she'd not wanted anyone to see it—oh, yeah, and she had a shopping bag hanging from her arm. She carried it like she was royalty. Too old in the tooth and leathery for my liking.'

54

Louisa didn't want to believe Dave, but her instincts told her he was telling the truth. She was in no doubt Tererei was the woman he saw at the Ambo Club the night Joe died. It couldn't be anyone else. There was only one reason Louisa could think of why Tererei would keep quiet about being with Joe the night he died. She was the killer—or she knew who the killer was. As for motive? Joe had twenty thousand dollars in his bank account, which Tererei would probably inherit. Greed was one of the oldest motives in the book. Louisa didn't want to believe it. She had liked Tererei. Even thought they could be friends. What had she been thinking? The case was nothing like any investigation Louisa had been on before. As soon as she eliminated one suspect a new one popped up. It wasn't supposed to happen like that. She sent Michael and Tebano to bring in

Tererei. Meanwhile, she was going to talk to Nicole.

Even if it could be proved that Tererei was Joe's killer, what reason would Tererei have had for killing Jill—besides, Tererei had said she was with her husband at the time Jill was murdered, which could easily be checked. Louisa grabbed the keys to the police lorry—she was not using the bus again—and drove to Bairiki. She was angry with herself. Being on Tarawa was messing with her mind. She had been so convinced that Dave the Fish was her man, she'd forgotten to follow basic investigative procedure and missed the obvious: Nicole was linked to all the deaths. Nicole had been good friends with Jill and Jill was now dead. Nicole had also known Joe, and although she could not have killed him (her alibi for Thursday evening was solid), he was also dead, killed in her school hut. Nicole had known Tion and he was dead. In addition, Nicole had had an affair with Nata, Tion's apparent best friend, and now Nata couldn't be found. Nicole even knew Eretibete and Eretibete was missing. There was no doubt about it, Nicole had some questions to answer and the sooner Louisa talked to her, the better.

Courtesy of her cleaner Louisa found Nicole at the edge of the lagoon. She carried a rectangular white cool box towards a sleek, seven metre fibreglass twin hulled catamaran, which had been pulled onto the shore. A dangling rope clanked against a towering mast in the deck. There was a black outboard engine mounted at the back and a thin shiny railing ran around the edge of the deck. Nicole wore baggy shorts over a practical swimsuit, her aviator sunglasses and her bouncy curls were all bundled under a floppy fishing hat. Was it only twenty-four hours ago Louisa had been stuck at the reef edge with her?

'I need to ask you a few questions,' said Louisa.

Nicole glanced back at her before sliding the cool box on to the deck of the boat. 'The fearless copper!'

'Can you stop what you're doing, please?'

Nicole left the cool box, turned round, crossed her arms and leaned against the side of the hull. 'If you'd been doing your job right, Jill would still be alive.'

'I can't discuss an ongoing investigation with you.'

'How many more people have to die because of your incompetence? People are too scared to go outside. Who's going to be next?'

No way was Louisa going to let Nicole wind her up. 'I want to know about you and a local man called Nata?'

Nicole mock laughed. 'What old woman has been gossiping?'

'Can you confirm you are in a relationship with him?'

Nicole picked up a small green scourer off the deck next to the cool box and absentmindedly passed it between her hands. 'I was in a relationship with him, past tense. I am not now.'

'Why not?'

'It was a fling. It lasted as long as a fling does.'

'I need to talk to him. It's urgent. Do you know where he is?'

She shook her head. 'I've not copped eyes on him for days.'

'You are aware it's an offence to withhold information that could help in a murder inquiry?'

Nicole looked puzzled. 'What's Nata got to do with the murders?'

'I have a witness who saw you talking to Nata at the mata mata on Saturday night. Is she lying or are you?'

Nicole chucked the scourer back on to the deck behind her. She took her sunglasses off. Her eyes looked black. 'I did see him on Saturday. I forgot. So what?'

'What did you argue about? And don't say there wasn't an argument because you were overheard.'

Nicole put her glasses back on. 'What happened to your face? Looks like someone's punched it?'

'I thought you wanted to help find the killer?'

'Okay. You want to know about Saturday night? I'll tell you. I was bored shitless at that cocktail party at the Otintaai so I went into Betio to find Nata. He's usually good fun. He wasn't at the Royal Saloon, so I tried the mata mata. When I got there he was blotto and with a local girl. He didn't want to talk to me, in fact he didn't even recognise me. I didn't want to stay and make an even bigger fool of myself, so I left.'

Louisa didn't believe her. Something didn't fit, she didn't know what though. She let it pass for now. 'Was that when you gave Eretibete a lift to the teachers' college?'

Nicole laughed. 'I'm not allowed to give a mate a lift now?'

'I didn't know Eretibete was a mate?'

'She needed to go to the teachers' college. I was wide awake and bored. It's not a long drive. Why not help her out?'

'What did you talk about?'

'Eretibete has only one topic of conversation: Paul Wilson. She's convinced herself he's going to marry her.'

'And you know differently?'

'I suppose he might now that Jill's out of the way—' Her tanned cheeks turned pink. 'I didn't mean that to sound so callous. Poor Jill. Who would want to kill her? Is Paul still locked up for it?'

'He's going to be released.'

She laughed. 'Blind Freddy could have seen Paul wasn't a killer. They weren't suited. Jill and Paul. I think she still thought Paul would go back to her.'

'You knew about their living arrangement, about them sleeping in different rooms?'

Nicole looked down at her bare feet. 'She told me. He told me. It was never going to work. She followed him here, thinking he'd fall back in love with her, not that he knew that. I liked Jill, she helped me out with the play school but she was as gullible as mince when it came to men.'

'When you took Eretibete to the college you would have passed Jill's house. Did you see anything unusual?

She shook her head. 'I didn't give the place a second glance.'

'And you're sure you didn't stop at the house either on the way there or on the way back.'

'You beaut! You think I killed her now?'

'You were outside her house at or around the time she was killed, it's a perfectly reasonable question.'

'Bull!' she snapped.

'Can you answer the question?'

'I did not stop at Jill's house! I saw nothing suspicious and my house-girl and her husband were babysitting and wide awake when I got home. They'll confirm I wasn't covered in blood when I arrived.'

'And what about Nata?' Louisa felt like giving the woman a slap. What made her think she should be exempt from questions? 'You're sure you don't know where we can find him? It's very important.'

'No!' Nicole marched past Louisa and headed to the water's edge.

'I've not finished!' said Louisa.

Nicole stopped and looked back at Louisa. 'Nata is the least violent person I know. He couldn't kill a fly! So why are you asking about him?'

'Did Nata ever talk to you about last Wednesday, the night Tion died?'

'Here!' Nicole chucked Louisa her sunglasses and floppy hat.

Louisa caught the items without thinking. 'Well?'

'Some vandal's been mucking about in the water with

the buoy for the boat. It's disappeared. They wrap a chain around it to sink it. If I can't find it, I won't be able to moor the boat later. I'll be back in a jiffy.' In one swift movement she was in the water doing the front crawl and away.

55

Louisa stopped following Nicole when the water reached up to her shins. The sand oozed between her toes, smooth as silk. At least it was cool. Ten metres ahead or so Nicole bobbed beneath the turquoise water and disappeared. No doubt looking for her buoy. Well, she couldn't stay in the lagoon forever. Louisa would wait for as long as it took. She felt like locking the woman up but being a pushy cow was, unfortunately, not a good enough reason to jail someone. If she didn't know any better, Louisa would have said Nicole had deliberately avoided answering her question about Nata and the night of Tion's accident. She knew something. Louisa would have bet money on it and she intended to find out what.

Nicole exploded out of the water. 'Help!' She cradled something in her arms. 'Help me!'

Louisa threw herself into the sea and was beside Nicole in a dozen strokes.

'Oscar's tangled in the bloody chain.' Nicole's voice was tight. 'I can't get him free.'

Louisa could see it now. The body of a dog. In Nicole's arms. A rusty wire wrapped around the animal's bedraggled torso. Louisa ducked under the water. A sea of misty flecks danced in front of her eyes. A static hiss filled her ears. She followed the wire downwards. It twisted around a heavier chain that was connected to a concrete base. Louisa grappled with the thinner wire, tearing the skin on her finger tips as she did so. Somehow she untangled it from the thick chain. By the time she resurfaced she was gasping for air. 'That's it.'

Nicole waded to the shore with the animal in her arms, the wire trailing in the water behind her, and laid the small dead animal down on the sand. 'What bastard would do such a horrible thing?'

'I'm sorry,' said Louisa, gently touching her shoulder.

Nicole smeared tears from her face with the palm of her hand. 'What a horrible end. Poor, poor Oscar. He was deliberately left there for me to find, wasn't he? I know I can be a bit of a bitch but does someone really hate me so much they'd kill my dog?'

Voices behind them. Children's voices. Louisa and Nicole turned at the same time. Two mini Nicoles ran towards them, all giggles and squeals.

Nicole was on her feet in a second. 'They mustn't see him!' she hissed and ran towards her daughters.

Louisa grabbed a lava-lava hanging on the boat rail and threw it over the dog. Ahead Nicole lifted up the smallest girl and swirled her in the air.

'That's me off now!' shouted Nicole brightly, taking the girls' hands and leading them away from Louisa. 'See you!'

'What's going on?' It was Christine. 'I heard shouting! Not another killing?'

Louisa lifted the lava-lava and showed Christine the dog.

Christine's face fell. 'I warned her it would come to this.'

'What would?'

'Her relationship with that man Nata.'

'You think he did this?' Louisa was surprised.

'Of course he did. She told me she met up with him on Saturday night after the Otintaai party. She told him it was over.

He was furious and promised to hurt her if she stopped seeing him.'

'That's not what's she's just told me.'

Christine shook her head. 'The one thing you need to know about Nicole, if her lips are moving, she's lying.'

56

Tererei sat opposite Louisa, perched on the edge of the plastic chair. Her back was rigid. 'This is very bad,' she said. 'Everyone will think I have done something wrong.'

'You have done something wrong. It's an offence to withhold information that can help solve a crime.' Louisa had come to the station straight from the lagoon. Her clothes were still damp. 'You were with Joe the night he was killed and you didn't tell me.'

'It's not a crime to see one's nephew.'

'By not telling the police you were with him, you've withheld vital evidence, which could have helped us with our inquiry and could have prevented the death of Jill Wilson.'

'No,' Tererei said, flatly. 'No. That is not true. I saw Joe for a small while only. Nothing he said made me think he, or anyone else, would be killed.'

'Now it seems you were the last person to see him alive.'

'The killer was the last person,' said Tererei indignantly.

'And you stand to gain by his death by at least twenty thousand dollars. That's a lot of money.'

'Money is nothing. How can you think I would want him dead, after what I told you?'

Louisa sat back. She didn't want Tererei to be the killer, but she had both motive and opportunity. 'Please tell me what happened when you met Joe on Thursday evening. And if you want the killer found, and don't want to get into any more trouble, tell me the truth.'

Tererei found a hanky from under the short sleeve of her tibuta, wiped her nose with it and replaced it under her sleeve. She cleared her throat. 'He asked if I would meet him at the Ambo for a chat. Thursdays are usually very quiet there. It is a good place to meet. It was dark. At first I couldn't see Joe anywhere—'

'Wait, what time was this?'

'Eight o'clock.'

'Go on.' So Dave the Fish had been telling the truth.

'I heard my name. Joe was in the lagoon. The water was up to his waist. He explained he'd had been hot from running and gone for a swim. However, while he'd been in the water a naughty man called David had taken all his clothes. I had a lava-lava in my bag. I left it on the sand for him and turned away while he came out of the lagoon and wrapped it around his body. He was very very angry. He said he would crush this David man and his business. I offered to take him to my house on the back of my bike. I said he could have a shower and borrow some of my husband's clothes. I would take him home afterwards.' Her voice had become shaky.

'Go on,' said Louisa, wondering seriously for the first time if Tererei could be the killer.

'He refused to go with me and demanded I had to go to his house in Betio and bring him some clothes and some money while he waited for me at the club. I said it was stupid for me to go all the way to Betio to get his clothes when he could come to my house. He called me rude names and said he wouldn't be seen dead on the back of my bike, not even in the dark....' Tererei drew herself up in the chair. 'My sister-in-law was a vain woman. She thought the way someone looked on the outside was more important than how they were on the inside. Joe was a strong, capable man but his mother had made him very weak when it came to the aspect of his appearance. I knew this but still I didn't mind meeting him in the dark because he didn't want to be seen with his fat, ugly auntie. Everyone is allowed to be a little vain. But I did not think he was also cruel or that he didn't care for me.' She paused to clear her throat again. 'The money in his bank account? My husband and I gave him that. Five thousand dollars at first to set up the business. A loan. He'd said. But when it came to paying me back, he'd needed more. And then more again. It was all our savings but still we helped.' Her cheeks sagged.

'Would you like a glass of water?' said Louisa.

She shook her head. 'He thought because I was kind, I was also stupid. I am not. I told him I would not drive all the way to Betio and back just because he was ashamed to be seen with me. I walked back towards my bike. When he saw I was really leaving he quickly apologised for being rude. He said his clothes being stolen had upset him. He wasn't thinking properly. He asked me to wait. I was angry. I couldn't look at him. I got on to my scooter. I couldn't leave though. I loved him. I was about to tell him I'd changed my mind, that I would go to Betio for him after all when he became angry all over again and shouted at me. He said he didn't understand why I was making such a fuss. Getting him his clothes was such a small thing to ask. He said if I'd loved him, I would help him and do it. I was so upset. He said this to me after all I had done for him? I drove away. I don't think he believed I would. He shouted more very ugly words. I didn't know it would be the last time I would see him.'

'I'm sorry, Tererei, but I have to ask, was he definitely alive when you left him and you definitely didn't go back?'

She nodded. The mountain of hair on top of her head slipped to the side. 'He was silly and vain and cruel but I loved him. As soon as I got home I wanted to go straight back and help him. At least give him some money for a taxi. My husband wouldn't let me—' She looked out the window. 'He said Joe didn't deserve my love. He was right but I didn't want to believe it. I promised myself the next day I would go straight to his house and apologise.'

'I'm sorry,' said Louisa, meaning it. 'This must be very difficult for you.'

'If I'd helped him, he'd still be alive. It's my fault he's dead.'

'The killer is the only person responsible for Joe's death.'

Tererei said nothing.

'You'll have to write out a statement. Constable Michael will help you with it, is that okay?'

Tererei blew her nose again, tucked her tissue back under the short sleeve of her blouse and nodded.

'Just one more thing. Did Joe say anything, anything at all at any time, about the death of one of his men called Tion?'

'You asked me this when we were outside the Royal Saloon. What has it to do with Joe's death?'

'Can you answer the question, please?'

Tererei puckered her lips, as if thinking. 'He called me on Thursday morning to arrange the meeting at the Ambo that evening. He said two cheeky men had taken his boat out the night before without his permission. He'd gone to the causeway bridge to catch them bringing it back in.' Tererei paused.

'And?' said Louisa.

'When he got to he causeway bridge, it was very late and dark. He couldn't see very clearly but his boat was in the channel not far from the bridge. Two people were fighting on it. Someone fell overboard. There was a lot of shouting and screaming followed by silence. After a while he heard the engine hum into life. The boat moved forwards. Joe waved it down. The man Nata was on board. He was distraught. He told Joe there had been a terrible accident and the other man, Tion, had fallen overboard. His body was on the floor of the boat. Joe said Tion was dead. But he had seen enough of what had happened to know it was no accident.'

Louisa felt a chill across her shoulders. 'He actually said that?'

Tererei nodded.

'Christ's sake, Tererei! Why didn't you tell me this before?' Was this, finally, something that could link the killings?

Tererei looked at her lap. 'Joe said he was going to deal with it. He said Tion's bad luck was his good luck.'

'Not a very nice thing to say. Did he explain?'

She shook her head. Her round eyes began to water. 'But it wasn't good luck, it was bad luck because the next day he was dead.'

57

Louisa sat on a leather swivel chair opposite Nakibae, conscious that her clothes were still both salty and sticky from her plunge in the lagoon when she helped Nicole. He'd been unimpressed when she'd knocked at his door and entered his office uninvited, but had agreed to listen to her when she insisted she had identified the true killer.

'The night before Joe was killed there was a fatal accident on his dive boat. An employee called Tion died.'

'You've come to disturb my day to tell me this?' he said, back poker straight, and his short-sleeved shirt perfectly pressed.

Louisa continued. 'I believe Tion's death was not accidental. A second man called Nata was involved. I believe he is responsible for Tion's death.'

'I asked you to write up a report on two killings and you

invent a third one. What? You were bored?' said Nakibae dryly.

'I further believe Joe witnessed the fight on the boat and blackmailed Nata to keep quiet about it, which is why Nata killed him.'

'We have arrested Paul Wilson for Joe's killing,' said Nakibae coldly.

She shook her head. 'I have hard evidence which proves Paul could not have killed Joe. There is only circumstantial evidence that Paul killed his wife. Nata has a history of violence. He recently killed a dog—'

Nakibae roared with laughter. 'We're investigating the death of dogs now?'

Louisa remained calm. 'Tion's death was sudden, yet there appears to have been no post mortem. I've checked but couldn't find a record of a death certificate, which means the cause of his death is not registered. This is illegal.'

Nakibae stopped laughing.

'I think Joe bribed someone to cover up the death.'

'Your proof?' said Nakibae.

'I haven't any. But the Kiribati Police Service are legally obliged to Tion's family to determine there were no suspicious circumstances associated with his death. If there is no death certificate—'

'What are you suggesting?' said Nakibae very deliberately.

'If we can show Tion's death was not an accident, we can link Nata to the killings.'

By the time Louisa left the Ministry of Justice building the exhumation was arranged to be carried out within the hour, before people could talk about it.

Ribbons of purple streaked a lilac-orange sky. Nightfall wasn't far off. Louisa had showered, at last, and changed into fresh clothes. Tion had been buried in his village within metres of his mother's house. Louisa didn't recognise the place without the funeral paraphernalia. A dozen villagers had gathered by his grave—the news was already out. Reteta was with them. She refused to look at Louisa. Michael asked everyone to move back.

In the early evening silence it didn't take long to set up a makeshift canvas barrier around the grave and throw up a strip light connected to a small generator. By the time the men had finished, Dr Andrus had arrived with Nakibae. Andrus gave Louisa an imperceptible nod. Nakibae ignored her.

While the men dug, the smoky-sweet smell of burning coconut husks and food cooked on an open fire started to fill the air. Dinner was on. No one at the exhumation spoke. Finally, Michael appeared from behind the canvas barrier-cum-screen. He was sweaty and covered in soil. With a nod he indicated they were done.

Tion's weeping body lay on a plastic sheet next to the graveside. It was covered in soil and still partially wrapped in the shroud he'd been buried in. At least, there was no coffin to have to break into. Louisa kept her mouth and nose covered with both her hands. It surprised her how incredibly human Tion still looked, despite his flesh being so misshapen. The gamey stench was overpowering even through her hands. Andrus, now dressed in a blue disposable plastic all-in-one, and wearing disposable gloves and a mask, knelt down and delicately picked at the corpse—Nakibae had demanded a preliminary 'eyeball' examination at the graveside. He would only allow the body to be brought to the mortuary for a full examination if Andrus said so.

After ten minutes of discreet prodding Dr Andrus stood upright. The sky was liquid black. He removed his mask. His face was ashen. 'There is clear evidence of a blunt force trauma to the back of head. His hair is so thick it is not apparent without looking closely. I cannot say for sure if it is post or pre mortem. However, I estimate it occurred pre mortem. At the very least it is very suspicious and warrants being investigated further.'

58

Nakibae gave Louisa a lift back to the station while the officers at the exhumation site helped Andrus with the body.

'I asked you to clear up one suspicious death and you find two more!'

Louisa said nothing.

'And the one person I am holding in jail appears to be innocent.'

Still Louisa said nothing.

'Three killings! A serial killer on Tarawa! If the international press get hold of this, they'll be calling Kiribati the new Papua New Guinea of the Pacific! You are absolutely certain Paul Wilson is innocent?'

Louisa placed her hands on her lap and stared out the windscreen into the night. The splattered bloody bodies of tiny insects smeared the glass. 'He's guilty of telling lies, yes, even of withholding evidence, but while he has motive and opportunity, we have no hard evidence that puts him at the house at the time of his wife's death, and he definitely did not kill Joe.'

'I am giving a paper next week in Brisbane at the Pacific Islands Chiefs of Police conference on Safe and Secure Communities and I have a serial killer stalking the country!' Nakibae slammed the steering wheel with the palm of his hand.

Louisa said nothing.

'What about David Trout, the I-Matang you had in for questioning today? You told me he had met Joe the night he died?'

Louisa shook her head. 'Joe was seen alive and well after David left him. I firmly believe Joe blackmailed Nata over Tion's death, which was why Nata killed him. Nata could have easily taken the dive boat and slipped up to the Ambo under cover of darkness. Perhaps Joe had arranged to meet him there—it seemed to be his favourite meeting place? It wouldn't have taken any time for Nata to hop off the boat, stab Joe, hop back on and disappear back to Betio. He could have reached Jill's house by the same means.'

'Enough!' Nakibae squealed the car to a halt outside Betio station. 'I don't care what it takes, you find this Nata man. And do it before anyone else dies and before the international Press get their teeth into the story!'

'The men are looking for him already.'

'I don't want to hear from you again until he's in custody, is that clear? And you'd better release Paul Wilson from jail. Now!'

'Yes, sir,' said Louisa. Nakibae stared straight ahead. It took Louisa a couple of seconds to realise he was waiting for her to get out of the car. She'd been dismissed.

Betio prison was remarkably quiet. No one milled about outside the hole in the fence and no inmates swept up or kicked a ball about the yard. One rickety street lamp threw a jumpy orange shadow over the entrance gate. A dog slept in front of it. Louisa walked around the dog, rang the bell and arranged with the warden for Paul to be released. Paul showed no emotion at being able to leave. All the way to Tom's, which was where he'd asked Louisa to drop him off, he said nothing. Louisa thought the shock of Jill's death was finally sinking in. He looked and smelled terrible.

'Did no one bring you fresh clothes, or toiletries or sleeping things?' said Louisa, pulling up outside Tom's house.

'Out of sight, out of mind, eh?'

'Not even Nicole or Christine?'

He laughed a dry bitter laugh. 'Especially not Nicole or Christine!'

'They seemed genuinely concerned.'

'They're good at that, looking the part!' he said. 'Bitches were never done making snide remarks about Jill.'

Louisa was shocked. 'Really?'

He mimicked Christine's slightly higher pitch, very proper, English accent, 'I'd invite her to mahjong, but she's not exactly the sharpest tool in the box.'

'She told me she liked Jill.'

'Sure, that's why they invited her nowhere. I had to plead with Nicole to take Jill out with them on one of their girly boat trips—' He mimicked Nicole's strident Aussie drawl, 'But, Paul, mate, she's so flaky, she wouldn't know her starboard from her engine.' Paul grew quiet. 'It was okay for Jill to help out at the nursery though.'

'Nicole seemed genuinely upset by Jill's death.'

Paul looked away.

Louisa pulled on the handbrake. 'I'm sorry, you probably won't want to answer any questions but can you tell me what you know about Nicole and a local man called Nata?'

'That's the name of her latest stud, isn't it? She likes her dark flesh. Her husband has affairs too, of course. As long as they keep them covert, it's okay. It's a weird relationship. Why are you asking about Nata?' His eyes flickered with life for a second. 'It wasn't him, was it? He didn't kill Jill?'

She was telling Paul nothing. 'Just following procedure and eliminating people from the inquiry. If Nicole's affairs are so covert, how do you know about them?'

'Nicole can't keep her mouth shut, that's how. What's the point of having it off with a stud if the world doesn't know about it? Jill said Nicole loved talking about her affairs when they were at the nursery school together. I think Jill was a little scandalised by the sheer number.'

'Did she ever say anything about Nata?' said Louisa.

He shook his head. 'Jill never went into detail and I didn't ask. Wasn't interested. I think she didn't want to betray Nicole's trust. Although she did once say that Nicole liked to go skinny dipping, late at night, you know, when it was dark.'

'That's a bit risky, isn't it?'

'The riskier the better. You've seen her boat, haven't you?' He didn't wait for Louisa to reply. 'It belonged to the Australian High Commissioner. It's a hybrid catamaran, he had it adapted to make it go faster. Some people say it's unstable. When his tour was up she paid way over the odds to get it. She's a good sailor, but that's not enough, she has to be the best. That boat gives her an edge in the yacht races. She's won at least three times since she got it.' He opened the car door and made to leave. 'Have Jill's parents been told?'

Louisa nodded. 'The British police passed on the news yesterday.'

'Did they say how she was killed?'

Louisa shook her head. 'All they know is that her death was suspicious.'

'I'll call them.' He got out of the car. 'They'll be devastated.' He shut the car door behind him. He turned to face Tom's empty house, paused then looked back. His eyes looked out of focus. His body drooped. 'What I don't understand is why? What did she do to make someone want to do that to her?'

'I don't know,' said Louisa feeling sorry for him, 'but I'm going to do my best to find out.'

59

One Stop was the expatriate supermarket. It was the only shop that stayed open late and stocked only imported food. Louisa took a frozen, microwavable cheese burger in a white polystyrene box from a shiny upright larder freezer. She waited in the queue to pay for it. There was always a queue at One Stop. It surprised Louisa how many locals as well as expatriates shopped there given the exorbitant prices of the mainly frozen foods. Today the queue was small. Was Nicole right? People were too scared to go outside? Louisa glanced around. The two women in front of her looked familiar. They avoided her gaze. Did they know who she was? What did they think? Was Louisa the woman who was solving the murders or causing them by letting the killer run around free?

Louisa slammed the burger in the microwave. She'd bought the machine from a departing expatriate family, that and a toaster, and never looked back. She whacked the burger on defrost and went to take her third shower of the day—the stench of Tion's rotting flesh seemed to have permeated her clothes through to her skin. She couldn't have too many showers. The cold water thundered on to her head and made her shiver. But she knew if she waited, she'd get used to it. Even like it. Just as she'd always, eventually, got used to the cold Scottish sea, despite the initial icy fright of it. Before he'd left them, her dad had used to take the family to Yellowcraigs, a beach half an hour's drive from Edinburgh. He'd said the cold water would put hairs on her chest. Why had he thought that was a good thing?

Louisa felt herself relax under the cold torrent of water. Nata had been spotted, heading for the island of Maiana, which was the first outer island south of Tarawa. It looked as if he'd panicked and made a run for it—the fact the police were looking for him had leaked to the press and was all over the radio. Maiana seemed a popular place, Tom was still there somewhere. Louisa didn't care about finding Tom any longer. Tererei had been the woman with Joe the night he'd died. She'd ordered Michael to contact the special constable on Maiana via the satellite phone. Nata was to be apprehended as soon as he arrived on the island and brought straight back to South Tarawa. If Louisa was lucky, Nata would be in Betio nick by lunchtime the next day and it'd all be over by the evening.

The shower was at last beginning to feel warm. Louisa thought about Nicole. Would Nicole really go skinny dipping—late at night or not, there always seemed to be someone on the beach somewhere. She'd have the nerve to do it, there was no denying that. If Christine was right and Nata had killed Nicole's dog, had it been a revenge attack because she'd ended their relationship, or was it, rather, a threat to keep her quiet? Did Nicole know something about Nata's involvement in Tion's death?

Louisa grabbed a towel she'd left hanging on a hook just outside the shower cubicle, dried herself and put on a fresh T-shirt and lava-lava. According to Paul, Nicole told Jill everything. Is that why Jill had to die? The thing was, Louisa had trouble believing Nicole was the kind of person to be intimidated by anyone, especially someone despicable enough to kill her dog.

Louisa went into the kitchen and checked her burger. It was thoroughly defrosted. She set the microwave on high. Could she believe Christine when she said if Nicole's lips were moving, she was lying? But, even if Nicole was a compulsive liar, would she lie about murder? Louisa laughed. What a silly question! No one on Tarawa seemed capable of telling the truth. Living here was nothing like she'd expected it to be.

The microwave pinged. The sizzling meat bundle reeked of plastic and sugar. The less like real food it smelled, the more appealing as far as Louisa was concerned. She grabbed a bottle of ketchup from the fridge, poured a dollop of it on to the melting cheese topping and sat down at the table in the living room to eat it. It was time to update her report. One thing was definite: the fight on the boat between Tion and Nata was linked to the other deaths and the sooner Nata was in custody the happier she'd be. By the time she'd finished writing out her report it was late. She set her alarm for six and went to bed, but not before checking outside first to see if TC was hanging around. He wasn't. No one was.

60

The port of Betio was small but busy. A creaking crane at the end of the only dock unloaded trunk-sized hessian bales from a cargo boat. Screeching black-headed gulls chased swoops of divebombing noddy terns. The hull of the boat next to the one being unloaded was packed with scuffed white cool boxes. The lid of one of the boxes was open. A deckhand took a bloodied shark fin from a smaller cool box, wrapped it in newspaper and placed the hacked fin beside similar newspaper wrapped bundles in the bigger box. The fishy smell was overwhelming. Louisa shivered.

Michael's call had wakened Louisa before it was light. Nata had escaped arrest on Maiana and had gone into hiding. The most the island constable did in a day's work was hand out the odd fine for an untidy garden or an escaped pig. Occasionally, he even locked up a drunk. Suspected murderers, who resisted arrest, were out of his league. He needed help. More crucially, the officer had no transport to bring Nata back to South Tarawa. Louisa wanted Nata and she wanted him that day. The police patrol boat was still docked in Betio harbour. It wasn't due to leave on a tour for another week. She told Michael to let the patrol boat sergeant know they'd need the boat for most of the day. It'd take less than two hours to get to Maiana on the patrol boat. She reckoned they could be there and back with Nata before tea time. She told Michael to meet her at the boat within the hour.

The patrol boat was a medium sized, all singing, all dancing, navy vessel with various antennae and twirling dishes attached to its central cabin. The harbour itself was a narrow stretch of water, protected from the open water by a tall L shaped sea wall on the one side and an island of giant boulders on the other. Apart from the shark fin boat and the hessian bale boat, three other working boats sat anchored in a line behind the patrol boat, including a three masted sailing boat, which looked as if it was old fashioned but on closer examination was decked with all modern fittings. Two frigate birds swooped out to sea. An enormous canning ship sat anchored on the horizon, way too big to come in any further, and the Korean fishing boat sat in the water just beyond the entrance to the harbour. The Australian supply ship that had arrived on Friday had already been and gone.

Michael and Tebano waited for Louisa by a wobbly gangway that went from the concrete harbour walkway to the deck of the patrol boat. Louisa sighed when she saw Tebano. If she wanted to bring Nata back in one piece, she'd have to keep an eye on him.

'Ready for a trip to Maiana?' she said.

The men looked away. Louisa should have known then that something was wrong, especially when Michael didn't say anything. She nipped in front of them and hurried along the gangway. 'Let's go.'

A heavy-set man in police uniform, with sergeant stripes on his short-sleeved shirt, obstructed Louisa's passage on to the deck.

She introduced herself. The stout man crossed his arms, shook his head and said. 'No woman on board.'

Louisa smiled, briefly. 'If this is some kind of joke, it's in bad taste.'

He didn't move.

She explained who she was for a second time and attempted to walk on to the deck. The man remained where he was. Louisa turned to Michael. 'I thought you talked to the patrol sergeant?' she said. 'It's supposed to be all arranged.'

Michael shrugged before looking away again. Louisa faced the burly man. She wandered if she could rugby tackle him but he was way too big for her. She tried arguing. Reasoning. Shouting. Swearing. And finally ordering. He absolutely refused to let her come on the boat.

Colonel Watts appeared at Betio station not long after Louisa had got back from the port. She'd left a furious message for him to call her at his earliest convenience. Watts was chief of four navy officers seconded to work on various marine aid projects on Tarawa on behalf of the Australian government. The patrol boat staff came under his control. He stayed on the navy staff compound with his wife and two children, in a gated area the size of a large Gilbertese village. The three other navy families lived there. Louisa knew all about the compound from the rumours in the office. Each family lived in a house the size of the president's house, cooled by seven giant air conditioners. When the machines were all on at the same time, which happened often, the power in Betio went out. The houses shared a swimming pool, courtesy of the Australian taxpayer. It sat on a raised platform, complete with pool room and veranda and pool chairs. It could be seen from every direction. It was the only swimming pool on Tarawa and in the country, although Louisa had heard a rumour that the New Zealand High

Commission now had a kiwi-shaped pool in its grounds. Only the chosen few got an invitation to dip in the Navy pool—Louisa imagined Christine and Nicole would have been to many pool parties, but not Jill. Louisa had certainly never had an invitation.

Colonel Watts was a tall, mean looking I-Matang with a weasel face. The buttons on his uniform gleamed. Louisa had barely reached her desk when he barged into the office without knocking. His visit was short but not sweet. Even though the police used the boat to patrol the Kiribati water, the boat, nevertheless, belonged to the Australian Navy, and so to him. With minimum words, he told Louisa that she, a mere sergeant, had made a grave error of judgment by thinking she could bypass him in arranging to take the patrol boat to Maiana to pick up a witness. She had no authority to use the patrol boat whatsoever. It was not a taxi. Given the seriousness of the circumstances, however, this time and this time only, he would allow his boat sergeant to take her men to Maiana and bring back the suspect. However, he had no intention of allowing his boat sergeant to suffer her on board. He had expressly ordered she not be let on board under any circumstances. Colonel Watts then left.

61

It hadn't occurred to Louisa that the police patrol boat couldn't be used for police business without asking Watt's permission. After the shock of his verbal attack subsided, and she'd reined in her fury at his attitude towards her, Louisa tried to contact Nakibae for help. He was in parliament and unavailable. There was no way Louisa was letting a shiny-buttoned arse of a colonel and his lump of a boat sergeant tell her what she could or could not do. Nor was she going to let Tebano and Michael pick up Nata without her. Especially not Tebano. Not after she'd seen the damage he could inflict on someone foolish enough to resist arrest—the drunk he'd left in the cell the other day was still in hospital. She needed to ask Nata questions and he needed to be in a fit state to answer them. She was going to Maiana with or without the patrol boat and Watts wouldn't stop her.

The village was quiet. The canvas barrier was still set up around Tion's grave. A cruel reminder of the exhumation that had taken place the evening before. Men and women, dogs, cats, children, chickens and pigs ambled around. The men in Reteta's family fished regularly and one of them had a boat. Louisa had come to ask if one of the fishermen would take her to Maiana. She was not going to let Tebano and Michael pick up Nata without her, that's all there was to it. A woman had her back to Louisa. She wore a long, loose flowing, brown skirt with a gold diamond pattern on it and a matching vest. She looked familiar. Louisa approached her. The woman in the brown skirt turned and smiled. Louisa started. It was TC.

'You're wearing women's clothes!' said Louisa unable to keep the shock out of her voice.

'So what?' hc said.

'But it's a skirt!' said Louisa, feeling nauseous, 'and that's a woman's top.'

TC arched his eyebrows. 'It's just for wandering about the village.'

She pulled him to one side. 'Do you like wearing dresses?'

TC laughed. 'This is what I dislike about I-Matangs, the importance you place on superficial things. All my clothes are being washed. Reteta let me use these ones because she's got far more clothes than me. She gets them from the secondhand market. There are always more clothes for women than for men. I just slipped them on to cover myself up while wandering about. What's the difference between this skirt and a lava-lava?'

'Nothing, I suppose.' Louisa couldn't think. 'It's just that you look so different.'

TC laughed. 'You think I'm a transvestite?'

'Are you?'

'No.' His smile vanished. 'But what if I was? It's simply a piece of cloth. What are you doing here?'

Louisa cursed under her breath. She'd pissed him off. It was the last thing she'd wanted. 'It's a long story but briefly I need a boat and a boatman to take me across to Maiana. Do you think one of the fishermen in the village would do that? I would pay, of course.'

He shook his head. 'Fishermen are notoriously superstitious. It's bad luck to have a woman on board.'

She hadn't expected there to be a problem. 'Couldn't you take me?'

'Sorry. I know I've been around the world as a seaman but navigating a small boat between these islands is another matter.'

'I only want to go to Maiana, it's not that far!' Why was he being so difficult? Was it because she'd questioned his clothes?

'Yes, Maiana is close,' he said coldly, 'and it is usually easy to cross the stretch of ocean between the two islands. But there's a wind here called the Long-armed Woman, Nei Bairara, and she's unpredictable. She can appear at any time, suddenly slamming the calm south-east trade wind to the north and creating a forty-mile an hour gale. You can be capsized before you know it. Only an experienced boat person should undertake the trip and that's not me.'

'The patrol boat's going to leave at any minute. They're going to pick up Nata—' She thrust her hands threw her hair. 'If Nata resists arrest that idiot sergeant of mine could batter him senseless.'

TC's eyes narrowed. 'Why are you arresting Nata?'

'I need to talk to him urgently. I think he's involved with the deaths.'

'Nata? A violent killer?' TC shook his head. 'I don't believe it.'

'Maybe not but I still have to ask him some questions.' The clean, freshly washed smell of TC's body standing so close to her made Louisa suddenly want him. Crossdresser or not. What was wrong with her?

'You may not have a choice,' said TC flatly.

She tried smiling. 'You're sure you don't know anyone who could help me?'

'Maybe one of your I-Matang friends has a boat?'

Was he being sarcastic? 'I don't have any I-Matang friends.' Wait a minute. She did know someone. 'There's a woman called Nicole. She's supposed to be a good sailor.'

'She knows about the currents and the winds?' said TC.

'I can always ask her,' said Louisa.

TC shrugged. 'If you do go, you make sure you talk to the old men, the unamani. They make up the island council. You can't do anything without their help, even if you are the police. It's the unamani who decide everything. And you'd better take them some tobacco.'

'I'm an officer of the law, I'm not giving bribes of cigarettes to anyone!' said Louisa indignantly.

He laughed. 'It's custom. Especially on the outer islands.' He caught her by the arm. 'And you be careful.'

'I have to go.' His touch had made her skin sizzle. How was it possible that she could feel so attracted to him, she was in the middle of a murder investigation—and he was wearing a skirt?

62

Nicole and Christine wore the usual baggy shirts, loose T-shirts and floppy hats. They crouched side by side and scrubbed the hull of Nicole's boat with small green scourers. Louisa wasn't sure about asking Nicole for a lift but there was no one else.

Christine saw Louisa first. She stopped scrubbing and pulled herself upright. 'We're keeping ourselves busy. Anything to take our minds off the murders. Any news?'

'We're getting closer.'

Nicole stood up. 'I talked to Paul last night, we're going to help him arrange a memorial service for Jill for the end of the week. He says he doesn't know when her body will be released but when it is, he'll be shipping her straight home.'

Louisa nodded. 'How are your girls? The death of their dog hasn't upset them too much?'

'I haven't told them yet,' said Nicole, throwing her scourer in the basin, 'They think he's living happily with another family somewhere.'

'Probably a good idea under the circumstances,' said Louisa. She hoped she'd not made a mistake in coming. 'Your boat?' she nodded to the catamaran behind the two women.

'What about it?' said Nicole, standing up.

'Have you ever taken it to Maiana?'

'A few times,' said Nicole, 'It's a straightforward enough trip.'

'The currents and the winds, you know about them?'

Nicole bristled slightly. 'How could I have got there and back otherwise?'

'What's happening in Maiana?' said Christine,

'I need to get there. It's to do with the case. I was going to go on the police patrol boat but the sergeant on board physically refused to let me onboard. He said women weren't allowed, something about it being unlucky.'

'What did you expect?' said Nicole. 'Don't you know yet that things are done differently here?'

'I expected to be allowed on board!' said Louisa, trying not to lose her temper.

'I agree. It's shocking!' said Christine. 'You should have asked Colonel Watts for help.'

'I did. He gave permission for the trip but because I'd inadvertently not asked his permission to use the boat, he told the boat sergeant not to let me on board under any circumstances.'

Nicole shook her head in disgust. 'Watty is a sexist dick!'

'They're about to leave and my sergeant has gone with them. If he gets to Nata before I do, there's no telling what he'll do to him—'

'Nata? What's he got to do with this?' said Nicole.

'He's on Maiana. That's why I want to go there, I need to talk to him urgently.'

Christine made a little gasp. 'Is Nata the killer?'

'I only want to ask him some questions.'

Nicole puckered her lips. 'You really want to go right now?'

She nodded. 'Everyone says you're the best sailor around.' Would blatant flattery work? 'And I don't know who else to ask.'

'We were getting the boat ready for a trip around the lagoon anyway. A few more miles won't make that much difference. We'll use the engine, there's no wind and it'll be quicker. We'll do the lagoon trip another time, eh, Christine?'

'Sure. Give me a few minutes. I'll let my house-girl know I'll be away for longer than I thought. I'll phone Ian too, tell him I won't be around. Be as quick as I can.'

Nicole pulled a scowl behind Christine's disappearing back. 'Invite yourself, why don't ya?' she said when Christine was out of earshot. 'She's as useless as a one-legged man in an arse kicking contest.'

'If it's going to be an issue, tell her.'

'It doesn't matter. She won't come. Ian will throw a wobbly when she calls him. He'll say there's no way he can feed the munchkins if she's not back by the time he clocks off. And you know why? Because when he finishes work he needs his down time sitting in his darkened bedroom playing Playstation games.'

Nicole was wrong. Christine was back within five minutes and ready to go. Between the three of them, they pushed Nicole's boat into the water. It was only then that Louisa realised just how inappropriate a blouse and three-quarter length trousers were for going on a boat journey. She should have gone home and brought a change of clothes. Nicole and Christine were already dressed in the usual baggy shorts, floppy hats and sunglasses. By the time they were all three safely on board and the anchor raised Louisa's clothes were wet through to her underwear. She hoped they would dry before she got to Maiana.

Nicole revved the engine. 'Hold tight!'

'Life jackets?' shouted Louisa, looking around for them.

'No need. It's not that far,' yelled Nicole. 'As soon as South Tarawa disappears, Maiana appears!'

'Accidents can happen at any time!' yelled Louisa.

'Sorry? Can't hear you because of the noise from the engine?' said Nicole, picking up speed and zooming away from the shore.

Louisa cursed Nicole under her breath, the woman was incorrigible. The boat zipped across the lagoon water and the wind whipped Louisa's hair into her face. As she swept it back, Christine leaned into her and said, 'You should have come to me before you talked to Colonel Watts. I play mahjong with his wife. I could have helped you with that.'

Louisa smiled coldly. 'I am sure you could have.'

'You think Nata's the killer, don't you?'

'I just need to talk to him,' said Louisa, gripping the rail of the boat as they flew forwards with a jerk and a splash.

'I told you he was violent.' She sat back. Her face was grim. 'Nicole's very lucky to be alive, very lucky.'

Louisa looked ahead. She wished Christine hadn't come with them. The way she seemed so sure Nata was guilty annoyed her somehow. The mast of the catamaran clattered, sea spray splashed over their faces, again and again.

After what seemed ages to Louisa, the last coconut tree on Tarawa disappeared behind them and a wisp of black appeared on the horizon ahead.

'The first tree of Maiana,' yelled Nicole over the noise of the throbbing engine. 'We'll soon be there!'

The trip would have been exhilarating had Louisa not been so inappropriately dressed and so anxious to get to Maiana before or at the same time as the patrol boat.

Nicole shouted and pointed to her left. Louisa and Christine looked. About five hundred metres from where they were, it was the all singing, all dancing patrol boat. It looked as if it was anchored in the middle of the sea.

'The lagoon is too shallow to get in close. There's a channel we can use but the patrol boat is way too big even for the channel. It's had to anchor out by the reef. It can't get in any closer.'

'How far away is the shore?' said Louisa.

'About three kilometres,' said Nicole, 'And look!'

She pointed ahead. At the water's edge four men got out of a small canoe. Even from that distance Louisa recognised Tebano's cabbage shaped body and Michael's gangly limbs. The other two men she assumed to be the patrol boat sergeant and one other.

'The canoe had to take them from the boat to the shore.

It's too deep for them to walk.' Nicole grinned. 'We've caught up with them.'

63

A dumpy man wearing the Kiribati Police Service regulation blue shirt and brown shorts waited for them by the water's edge. A few metres from the shore Nicole killed the engine and dropped the anchor. To Louisa's dismay her clothes were still wet. How had she imagined she'd dry off? It was not a good look.

'Think you may need these, matey!' said Nicole, chucking Louisa a dry lava-lava and T-shirt she'd got from a cool box strapped to the boat rail.

'Cheers!' said Louisa, relieved. She slipped the T-shirt over her wet top. Had she misjudged Nicole?

'We'll wait with the boat,' said Nicole. 'It's not safe to leave it unattended. It's not quite high tide, so we're okay being here a few hours but you won't be that long, will you? We'll not get out at low tide, not even using the channel, it'll be too shallow.'

'Don't worry, I want this over with as quickly as possible.' Louisa slipped off the boat into the thigh-high water. 'As soon as I find Nata, we'll be leaving.'

Holding the lava-lava, her sandals and her bag above her waist so they didn't get wet, well, any wetter, Louisa waded towards the shore. On dry land, she wrapped the lava-lava over her wet trousers and slipped her sandy feet into her sandals.

The officer on the shore introduced himself as the special constable for Maiana. He said Constable Michael and Sergeant Tebano were waiting for Louisa in the mwaneaba and he would take her to them.

Louisa followed the special constable along a dirt track that wound between coconut palms, straggly bushes and the occasional breadfruit tree. There was no proper road. Outer islands were like North Tarawa, underdeveloped to the point of not being developed at all. Louisa asked the officer about Nata, but he said Constable Michael would explain. After five minutes they came to a dusty clearing and a mwaneaba. It was very much like the Ambo Lagoon Club mwaneaba but bigger and shabbier. A scattering of scrawny chickens pecked at the neglected ground. Mange-riddled dogs hobbled between the chickens. The constable indicated to Louisa where she should enter the mwaneaba. She bent almost double and ducked under the side of the giant thatch roof, which reached down so low it was just over a metre off the ground. She saw the sandals immediately. Louisa didn't want to remove hers. The concrete floor in front of her looked so dirty. But she knew she would have to. This was a custom that had been drilled into her from when she was wee. She carefully stepped out of the sandals and placed them at the edge of the floor. The voices hadn't been around for a while. It would be fine.

Various groups of local people in shabby clothes sat on straw mats laid out along the edge of the rectangular concrete floor. Louisa also knew from when she'd lived on South Tarawa as a child that everyone had their place in the mwaneaba and each mat or set of mats belonged to a different family group. She sat down on the mat in front of her, presumably placed there for guests. Constable Michael and Sergeant Tebano sat on mats on either side of her.

'What are we doing here? Where's Nata?' whispered Louisa, conscious that the assembled people were staring at her.

'We have to wait,' said Michael.

'What do you mean, wait?' She nodded to Tebano, who ignored her. No change there then.

'The old men from the Island Council want to talk to us first.'

'Christ's sake! We're the police looking for a murder suspect. They do know that?'

'Oh, yes,' said Michael.

'Tell me that someone at least knows where Nata is?'

Michael shrugged.

'And why are all these people here?' she hissed.

'It's not every day the police from South Tarawa come to Maiana. It's an event.'

Louisa took a deep breath. All she wanted to do was nab Nata and go. She should have known it wouldn't be straightforward. 'Well, the old men had better come soon!'

More and more villagers arrived, nodding a quiet hello here and there before they sat down in their designated places. Children played chasing games in the middle of the hall. Louisa couldn't stop looking at their feet as they ran. They were black with grime. At last a hush descended. Four gnarled old men—the unamani, she presumed—hobbled into the mwaneaba.

The men wore washed out, knee length lava-lavas and no tops. One by one they sat down crossed-legged on the mats directly opposite Louisa. The first of the old men, all gums and bronze cheeks, started to talk. His accent was so strong Louisa couldn't understand his Gilbertese. She caught words like 'home' and 'family' and 'work'. When the man finally stopped, everyone in the hall turned to look at Louisa. Was she supposed to say something?

Michael leaned into her ear and whispered. 'You have to speak. They want to know where you are from, who your parents are, if you have any brothers or sisters. I'll translate for you.'

'We have a killer to catch,' hissed Louisa, 'Can you not just ask them where Nata is?'

'This comes first,' he said, while smiling at the old men.

'Wait,' whispered Louisa, 'You'd better give them this then.' She took a blue carton of Winfields from out of her bag. It had gone against all Louisa believed in to buy the cigarettes. Regardless of what TC said, she saw them as a bribe. But it looked as if she might need them. Miraculously, the carton was only slightly damp from the trip. She handed it to Michael, who looked vaguely surprised. He got up and shuffled across the hall, keeping his body bowed and placed the carton on the ground in front of the men. The men nodded their approval at the gift.

'You have to speak now,' whispered Michael, standing back beside her.

64

Louisa was very conscious her clothes were damp and her hair a mess but there was nothing she could do. She scrambled to her feet and told the assembled people about leaving South Tarawa when she was eight. About Edinburgh, the birthplace of the famous writer Robert Louis Stevenson, who had written about the Gilbert islands. She talked about her mother, her father and her brother and his family. When she stopped to catch her breath, Michael translated what she had said. Louisa struggled to understand him and it pained her to think her Gilbertese wasn't as good as she'd thought. Suddenly, everyone in the hall, including the old men, burst into laughter.

'I didn't say anything funny. What are you telling them?' she hissed.

'Nothing,' said Michael. 'May I ask you to please smile?'

Reluctantly, Louisa smiled.

A different old man began to speak. When he finished

Michael translated. 'He wants to know why you are not married?'

'Tell him to mind his own business! Can we just get on?'

Michael smiled at the men and began speaking, again, on Louisa's behalf. For a second time everyone burst out laughing.

'Will you stop doing that!' she said in a furious whisper.

The third old man now began talking. Michael translated. 'He wants to know what you want from them.'

'Tell him,' said Louisa wiping her hands down her side, 'I want them to help me find Nata so I can bring him back to Tarawa to help me with my inquiries into the investigation of two, possibly three, murders.'

Michael translated what she'd said. Everyone in the hall immediately became restless. Some began to make grumbling noises.

The fourth unamani spoke. Michael translated. 'When the police last came to the island, they told the old men there would be a tsunami and ordered them to make the necessary preparations to survive it. They did what they were told and went to a lot of trouble to prepare for the disaster but the tsunami didn't come. So now they don't trust the police and for that reason they don't want to help us.'

'If they don't help us, they'll be breaking the law of the land,' said Louisa firmly.

'It doesn't work like that,' said Michael, 'not on the outer islands—and, please, can I ask you to keep smiling?'

'They help me now or I'll have my fags back,' she said under her breath, before beaming at the men.

The first unamani spoke again and Michael translated again. 'If they help us, what we will you do to help them back?'

'Do?' said Louisa, trying to stop herself from losing her temper. She knew what she would like to do!

'Yes, what will they get in return for helping you?'

Louisa cleared her throat. If that is what it took, she would have to go along with it. She smiled at the unamani. 'What would they like us to do?'

The third unamani spoke. Michael said, 'None of the fishermen are allowed engines on their boats. The unamani say it makes fishing more equitable for all, but while there is a channel at this end of the island, there is no channel at the opposite end. They want the police to help dig a channel at the other side of the island. It will make the fishermen who live there less dependent on the tides and make fishing fairer for all.'

Was Michael serious? 'We can't do that!'

'If we don't help them, they will not help us.'

Louisa took a deep breath. 'Okay. Maybe we could try to do something under a community policing programme. Tell them I promise to look into it. Now ask about Nata.'

Michael talked. The old men talked. Then one by one various villagers stood up and talked. Eventually, when it seemed as if almost everyone in the mwaneaba had had a say, and Louisa thought she'd scream from frustration, Michael said, 'Nata is not from Maiana. It is believed he came here to visit a diver friend. The villagers don't feel it would be a big betrayal to help you. Nata is hiding out at the airport hangar. The special constable will take us there.'

65

The hangar was four kilometres away along a scrappy path. When Louisa asked about transport the special constable said there was none. The one council vehicle on the island had broken down more than six weeks ago and they were still waiting for a part to fix it.

By the time they got to the hangar the overhead sun was fierce. Louisa was seriously thirsty and insects were biting her ankles, and how. She refused to think about the tiny bugs hiding in the grass, too small to see. She made herself focus on Nata. The building was more a large shed than a hangar. It had a corrugated iron roof with a rusted metal sheet for a door. Louisa couldn't imagine a plane small enough to fit in it. The special constable said the field in front of the building was the runway. A biplane landed on the field once a month, delivering supplies. In between times it was used as a football pitch. There was no one playing football today.

'Has Nata got a knife on him, or a weapon of any kind?' asked Louisa.

'I don't know,' said the constable.

Louisa turned to Tebano and Michael. 'We must be careful not to panic him.'

'You go and stand outside the hangar door,' said Tebano, 'He will be surprised to see an I-Matang woman. He will come out to see what you want.'

Louisa laughed out loud. 'And what will you brave lads be doing while I'm fronting up to a potential killer?'

Tebano made a tutting sound. 'You will be safe. We will go around the back of the building and take him by surprise.'

Louisa didn't think much of Tebano's plan. But much as it pained her, she couldn't think of a better one.

'We avoid violence at all costs. I must be able to talk to Nata.'

She stopped a good six metres away from the hangar door. If Nata chose to attack her, he'd have to be fast, she was a good runner. 'Fear no one and respect everyone' had been her judo motto—and when not on the judo mat only fight if you absolutely have to. She had no intention of tackling a murderer. Hopefully, Michael and Tebano would be able to restrain him before anything happened. Louisa retied her lava-lava around her trousers and waited a couple of minutes, long enough for Tebano and Michael and Maiana's only constable to have reached the other side of the hangar. This was it.

'Nata? I am Detective Sergeant Townsend. I want to ask you some questions. Can you please come out?'

Nothing.

She called again. 'Nata, I know you're in there. Please come out. You have nothing to fear.'

Slowly, the rusty metal door creaked open and an emaciated, short, nervous thirty-something man blinked into the sunlight. He looked familiar.

'On the radio. It said I killed Joe. I did not kill him!' His eyes darted back and forwards.

'I just need to ask you a few questions. If you could please step forward where I can see you properly?' She was sure she knew him but she couldn't remember from where.

The man remained half hidden behind the door. 'A ghostly spirit killed Joe and then fed on his eyes. Everyone knows that! Why are they blaming me?'

'Where were you last Thursday evening?'

'The evil spirits are everywhere!'

'Thursday evening, where were you, please?'

He collapsed on to his knees in front of the door. 'My friend was also killed by evil spirits.'

Louisa started. She recognised him. 'You were at Tion's funeral on Sunday. You sat next to me.'

'We angered the ghostly ancestors. They took Tion. They want to take me. I came here to hide but you can't hide from the evil spirits.'

'There are no evil spirits, only evil people!' TC had said this man had not left Tion's side throughout the funeral-cum-wake. If that was true, Nata could not have killed Joe. 'I'll ask you again, where you were on Thursday night?'

'I should have died. Not Tion. It was my fault.'

'Thursday night!' she demanded, 'Where were you?

He looked up dazed. 'I was with Tion at the funeral.'

Louisa stepped towards him. 'What happened on the boat when Tion died?'

'Stop!' He was up on his feet. 'Don't come any closer!'

'You and Tion, you fought. Why?' If Nata didn't kill Joe, who did?

'Tion was my friend. I had no fight with him.' His eyes were bloodshot. His body trembled.

'Joe said he saw a fight on the boat.'

'It is true there was a fight but Tion did not fight with me.'

'What? There was someone else on the boat with you?' She took another step.

'Stay away!' He raised his hand. A machete. In his hand.

'I can't talk to you while you have a knife in your hand. Please put it on the ground.' She hoped she sounded calm. 'Who was with you on the boat?' A flash of movement. Tebano was behind Nata. His chunky arm was in the air. Thump! His giant fist thundered on to Nata's head. Louisa gasped. Nata fell.

66

The tide was almost completely out. Ahead of her, in thigh deep water, Nicole and Christine pushed the catamaran through the half-empty channel towards the outer reef. Were they leaving without her? Louisa kicked off her shoes, snatched them up and splashed through the shallow lagoon water after them. 'Oy! Wait!'

Nicole turned. 'Where the hell have you been?' Her

forehead was smeared with sweat. 'There's just enough water for us to push the boat out to where it gets deeper. If we'd waited any longer, we'd have been up shit creek! You said you'd be right back!'

'Nata's been hurt,' said Louisa, hurrying towards them. 'They're taking him to the hospital in the patrol boat and still the arse of a patrol boat sergeant won't let me on the boat! I'm investigating double, possibly triple, murders and I can't stay with a vital witness.'

'You beaut!' said Nicole, her voice acidic. 'We've been waiting for you for bloody hours in this bloody heat and you were going to go back on the patrol boat! When exactly were you going to tell me my services weren't needed?'

'You agreed to help in a murder investigation.' said Louisa, catching up with them, 'Not come on a picnic! Had I been able to stay on the patrol boat, I would have made sure you knew not to wait any longer.'

'Good on ya, mate!' said Nicole sarcastically. 'We can use the engine from here on in.' She hauled herself up on to the twin-hulled boat. 'You'd better get on if you're coming!' She yanked the starting cord of the outboard motor and the engine ripped into life. 'But if we scrape the bottom, I'm blaming you!'

Louisa sat on the narrow bench seat that ran around the edge of the boat. While she caught her breath Nicole guided the boat centimetre by centimetre through the channel. Louisa couldn't believe Nicole had tried to leave without her. Nicole was a bitch and pain in the neck, no doubt about that, but that was nothing compared to what she thought of the patrol boat sergeant. The man was an out and out fucking bastard!

At first Louisa had thought Tebano's battering thump had killed Nata—what bit of 'reasonable force' did the moron not understand? But Nata was still breathing, just. They needed to get him to the hospital on Tarawa and fast. The men had carried Nata to the shore in a makeshift stretcher. Louisa intended to stay by his side all the way to Tarawa. She wanted to be there when he woke up—if he woke up. There was no doubt in Louisa's mind that Tion had fought with Joe's killer the night he'd died. That person had most likely killed Jill. Nata knew who that person was. Under the circumstances Louisa had not expected the boat sergeant to bar her from boarding the patrol boat a second time. He did. Threats of disciplinary proceedings had made no difference. She'd ordered Michael and Tebano to arrest him. They'd refused. When she'd lost her temper Michael had taken her to one side and explained that apart from a woman on a boat being bad luck, and apart from the sergeant following Colonel Watts's orders, the sergeant was also the president's nephew. As far as 'old men' went, it didn't get much 'older' than the President. Rightly or wrongly, the authority of the President's nephew could not be questioned. If the boat sergeant said she wasn't allowed on his boat, there was nothing anyone could do. Louisa had left them carrying Nata across the lagoon towards the boat. She'd been beside herself with fury.

'She was going to leave without you. I only just persuaded her to stay,' hissed Christine, sitting opposite Louisa.

'At least two people have been murdered. Finding their killer takes priority over everything else,' said Louisa.

'I know that,' said Christine in a loud whisper.

'We've made it out of the channel.' Nicole shouted from the back of the boat. 'No thanks to you!' She threw Louisa a filthy look. 'Let's bloody shoot out of here!' She twisted the throttle. The engine throbbed then roared. The boat flew forwards.

'Earlier, why did you call Nata a witness and not a suspect?' yelled Christine, clinging to the boat rail behind her.

'He isn't a suspect, not any more!' shouted Louisa.

'I told you he wasn't violent!' yelled Nicole. 'Nata wouldn't hurt a gnat! Will he be okay?'

'He's unconscious. When they get to Tarawa they're

taking him straight to the hospital.' Louisa had momentarily forgotten about Nicole's relationship with Nata. It was difficult to imagine the anxious man at the hangar with the strident Nicole. But they said opposites attracted, didn't they? And he was good looking, in a fine sort of way.

'But why a witness?' shouted Christine. 'I don't understand, was Nata with Joe the night he died?'

Louisa shook her head. 'On Wednesday night, on Joe's dive boat, a man called Tion died. '

'That was an accident!' shouted Nicole.

'No. We exhumed Tion's body last night. There was a trauma to the back of his head. It wasn't obvious. We're treating his death as suspicious.'

'Bull!' said Nicole.

'I don't understand?' said Christine, flickering an anxious glance from Nicole to Louisa then back to Nicole. 'I thought you were looking for Nata in connection with Jill and Joe's death. What's this about Tion?'

'I believe there was a fight on Joe's dive boat on Wednesday night between Tion and someone else on the boat. As a result of the fight Tion died. Nata witnessed what happened, that's why I need to talk to him. I believe whoever caused Tion's death that night also murdered Jill and Joe. Nata knows who that is.'

'Let's hope he recovers then,' said Christine.

67

The boat swept across the water and into the open ocean. Louisa let the salty wind wash over her face and made herself calm down. She may have sounded confident when she talked to

Christine about Nata knowing the identity of the killer but she did not feel confident, anything but. Nata's mind was clearly disturbed, which made him an unreliable witness. But if there had been a third person on the dive boat, and assuming this person had fought with Tion, Louisa urgently needed to know who he was and where he was. She felt even Jill's death would make sense when she found out the identity of this third person—if he genuinely existed. Jill's death continued to puzzle Louisa. If Jill had known something, why had she not told Louisa? Had she not realised the importance of what she knew or was she protecting someone? Louisa looked around. The engine had died. The boat bobbed to a stop. Her guts flip-flopped. Had they broken down in the ocean?

'The wind's got up,' said Nicole, standing up. 'We're sailing back the rest of the way.'

'No, we're not!' said Louisa. 'I need to get back to Tarawa now!'

'This is a brilliant sailing wind, I'm going to take advantage of it. It's the right strength and the right direction and it'll be almost as quick as using the engine.'

'I'm investigating three suspicious deaths!' said Louisa furiously. 'What part of "I have to get back to Tarawa now" do you not understand?'

Nicole leaned over and thrust a thick rope into Louisa's hand. 'If you look back, you can still just about see the men carrying Nata across the shallow lagoon to the patrol boat. By the time they get to the boat we'll be halfway home. Take this, sit there and mind your head. If you don't like it, you can always swim. My boat. My rules.'

Louisa looked at the rope in her hand. She wanted to kill Nicole. With her bare hands.

Ropes, winches and rigging flew between them. The sails billowed. The boat bounced and they skipped across the waves. Nicole barked at Christine to pull on one of the two sails.

Louisa was to do the same. An unexpected swell drenched Louisa in a blanket of water. Christine and Nicole laughed. Louisa gritted her teeth. How had her glittering career in the force come to this?

'Hold on!' Nicole yelled, pulling on the rudder. 'Another swell on its way!'

Slap! Right in her face! Louisa shook the excess water from her hair. She refused to let the other two women see her angry. The waves grew bigger. Wilder. Sheets of water sloshed over them. The boat skipped across the waves. More water. In Louisa's face. Again. And again. Louisa gripped the rail with one hand and held on to the rope with the other. The rope pulled and heaved. More than once she nearly lost control of it. Its rough surface ripped the skin on her sore fingers. Ahead. A tumble of black clouds hurtled towards them. A giant ball of rage. Suddenly it was dark. As if someone had switched a light off.

'Christ!' yelled Nicole, 'it's a squall!'

'Take the sails down!' screamed Christine.

'Too late!' cried Nicole, heaving on the rudder.

The boat bucked. A loose rope whistled past Louisa's head. She ducked. 'Watch out!' The mast creaked. The sails flipped. Flapped. A scream. The boat bucked upwards. Louisa lost her grip on the rail. The rope she was holding flew from her hand. She was in the air. Another scream. Was it her?

Silence. Blackness. Louisa was cold. She'd been cold before. Where was she? Back home? In her bed? A hissing sound. Softness. Getting colder. She opened her eyes. Around her. Murky liquid. It was water. She was under the water! Kick! Her legs didn't move. Kick! Kick! Kick! Movement. Sluggish. But she was moving. Air. Her lungs. Bursting. She needed air! Kick! Kick! Kick! Blackness. A rush of grit in her face. Gasp! She could breathe! Ugh! Water. In her eyes. In her mouth. Up her nose. She coughed. She choked. She turned onto her back.

Better. She doggy paddled. Head up. She breathed. In through her nose. Out through her mouth. The waves tossed her up. Dropped her down. Down. Up and Down. She was a matchstick. Relax. She let the water carry her. Something solid. At the side of her eye. The upturned hull of the boat. Kick! Kick! Kick! One arm. Two arms. She grabbed the hull. She ignored the battering sea and the howling wind and pulled herself up.

68

Sheets of drizzle and waves of black-purple hammered the upturned catamaran. How long had Louisa been there flat out across the hull with her cheek squashed against the rough painted surface and her arms gripping the sides? One minute? Half an hour? The storm couldn't last for ever, could it? And as if by magic the wind subsided and the boat settled in the water. The afternoon sun stroked her back. The heat felt good. The boat became still. Very still. Someone called her name. Louisa prised her head off the base of the hull and looked around. Nicole sat on the other hull, her feet dangling in the water. She had an ugly cut across her forehead. Christine sat next to her, hugging her knees into her chest. Behind them the sky was a brilliant blue. It was difficult to believe there had ever been a storm. They looked dishevelled but unharmed.

'Are you all right?' said Nicole, her voice hoarse.

'I can't believe we're alive,' said Louisa, not moving. 'The weather changed so quickly.'

'That's what squalls are like,' said Nicole.

'Where are we?' said Louisa, closing her eyes.

'We're in the Tarawa lagoon,' said Nicole, nodding toward a tiny charcoal crinkle across the horizon. 'That's Betio.'

Her voice was thin and frail.

Louisa opened her eyes. 'Are you sure?'

Nicole nodded. 'Definitely.'

'Thank God!' sobbed Christine. I was worried we were still in the open ocean.'

Louisa breathed slowly and deliberately. 'The boat...' She tried to think. 'Can we upright it?'

'No chance,' said Nicole wearily.

Christine's pushed her wet hair out of her face. Her fingers trembled. 'We'll just have to sit tight and wait for someone to find us.'

'It'll be dark soon,' said Nicole, 'No one will look for us in the dark. It's not that far. I think we should make a go of swimming.'

Louisa shielded her eyes from the sun's fierce glare and looked towards Betio. 'It's so far away.'

'If you have an accident you should stay with the boat,' said Christine, her teeth beginning to chatter. 'That's what they always say, isn't it? Stay with the boat?'

'I think so,' said Louisa, racking her brain trying to remember what her dad had used to say. 'That's right. Never leave the boat.'

'Look.' Nicole pointed to a length of tangled anchor chain, caught around the hull she was on. 'The anchor's gone, we're drifting and the tide is going out. We may be in the Tarawa lagoon now but soon we'll be in the open ocean. Once there we could drift helpless on the currents for days, weeks even, before anyone finds us. If they ever find us.'

Louisa reluctantly prised herself up off the hull and into a sitting position. 'We should stay on the boat. Someone will find us before we drift too far.'

Nicole shook her head. 'There are thousands and thousands of square miles of ocean beyond this lagoon and no land anywhere to accidentally wash ashore at. We'll drift forever and never be found. Our only chance is to swim now.' She turned and lowered herself into the calm water.

'Are there no flares or life jackets?' said Louisa.

'We've capsized. What do you think?' Nicole clung to the hull. 'We head for the shore. It'll take a while but when it gets dark we'll have the street lights to guide us by.'

'That piece of sailcloth there,' Christine scrambled on to her knees and pointed to a piece of material floating on the water. 'I've been watching it. It's moving away with the tide but we're not.'

Nicole ignored Christine. 'Even if we survive the boredom and lack of food and water, we'll never survive the storms.'

'We're not moving!' yelled Christine, 'We're not moving!'

Louisa looked all around the boat. They did appear to be still. 'Could the mast be stuck on something?'

Nicole frowned. 'I'm going to have a look below.' She took a deep breath and ducked under the water.

'See if there are any life jackets!' shouted Louisa after her.

Christine stared at the dappled surface of the water left by Nicole as she disappeared. 'It'd be stupid to leave the boat if we're not drifting.'

Louisa nodded. 'The patrol boat will find us on its way back and even if it doesn't, they'll notice when we don't arrive and send a search party.'

'She shouldn't have put up the sails. Even a fool would know the increased wind meant bad weather was on its way. It's typical of Nicole.'

At that moment Nicole reappeared. 'The mast is caught on the reef! We're not drifting!'

It was dark. Louisa had no idea how many hours had passed

since the sun had set. An almost full moon stopped them being in total darkness. She was cold and thirsty and hungry. All that was nothing compared to the creeping sense of doom that was threatening to consume her. When the first blinking orange light appeared from out of the darkness, so tantalisingly close, all three of them had jumped to their feet and yelled and screamed for attention. The more they'd shouted, the closer the light had seemed to come. Was it the rescue boat? A fishing boat? They didn't care. It was life. They were not alone! Then, just like that, the light was gone. They'd not been able to believe it. The next light filled them with hope all over again. They were back on their feet in seconds, screaming to be saved until they were hoarse. But then it too disappeared and they were alone once again. Since that first light half a dozen more had flickered on and then off. It was as if someone was playing some cruel trick on them. They were now all three of them on edge and jittery. Louisa had been on enough courses, and in enough tricky situations in her job, to know people did all sorts of stupid things when they panicked. It was imperative that they didn't give into the fear. But it wasn't easy. Morbid thoughts crept into her mind when she least expected them.

The rough surface of the hull itched Louisa's legs and arms. She turned on to her back and closed her eyes. Nata would have reached the hospital hours ago. Had he regained consciousness? Did he know who the killer was? She shivered. At that precise moment the murderer could have been George W Bush for all she cared, she just wanted to see the morning sun come up over the horizon. A noise. In the distance. Like an echo. She peered across the horizon. Nothing. She shivered. Why had Reteta told her that story about the souls of the dead being carried to their ghostly home on the outgoing tide? Every swish of wind, every chimera of a wave and she imagined it was another ethereal being swooping homewards, to the land of the spiritual ancestors in Matang. And what of the evil ghosts and the lost souls, whining like crickets? Did they really feed on human heads and eyeballs? Were they flying around out there too, seething in the darkness, on the lookout for whatever human carrion they could scavenge? Corralling drunks outside the nightclubs in Lothian Road and arresting drug dealers in the high rises in Craigentinny, even looking for the sociopath father who'd axed his wife and children to death in Morningside, had never been as scary as this. She told herself to get a grip. To return home from Tarawa in a coffin would be the most spectacular of failures. She wasn't going to let it happen.

69

Moonlight glistened across the white hull beneath Louisa. She glanced around her. Something felt different. Nicole and Christine lay stretched out on their backs, toe to toe, on the hull opposite. She looked down. The lagoon water was about ten centimetres below the top of the hull. That was wrong. When they'd capsized and the water had calmed, there had been at least twenty centimetres between the top of the hull and the sea. She remembered that very clearly. It had reassured her. Louisa sat up. She ran her fingers along the side and top of the fibre glass hull. It was cracked and uneven. Could the cracks be letting the air out and water in? Was that possible? It didn't matter. One thing was sure. They were sinking. Why was she so calm about it? They were sinking!

'What are you doing?' said Nicole from where she lay. 'You look like you're inspecting the paint work.'

'Okay,' said Louisa, choosing her words carefully. 'We have a bit of a problem.'

Nicole pretended to laugh. 'You reckon?'

Louisa's throat felt raw. 'We mustn't panic.'

'What is it?' said Christine, hunching up into a sitting position.

'Well,' said Louisa, licking her lips. If only she had a drink. 'I don't know about your side, but somehow this hull I'm on is lower in the water than it was a few hours ago, which means we're sinking.'

'Can't be,' said Nicole adamantly, 'I've taken this catamaran out dozens of times. If the hulls were letting in water, I'd have noticed before.'

'All I know is the hull I am on is lower in the water now than it was before. The good thing,' said Louisa, trying to sound calm, 'is it's happening slowly.'

'She's right,' gasped Christine, 'our hull is lower too. We're sinking!'

'We have a few hours still,' said Louisa.

'No way!' said Nicole. 'No! No! No!'

'Don't panic. There'll be a solution.' Louisa hoped she sounded confident. 'Think! Think!'

Nicole wouldn't look at Louisa. Christine put her head between her knees. Her body shuddered—was she crying? From nowhere Louisa had a memory of her dad. Her small hand was inside his big one. They were in the hangar, looking at a gigantic aircraft engine. He used to take her there at least once a week, perched on handlebars of his bicycle. Her mother had disapproved of the trips. She complained that the hangar was no place for a child but Louisa had loved being there. Dad made her a mini tool apron. It had special pockets. She kept her very own small spanner and ratchet in them. The apron hung on a nail next to his. The hangar always smelled of a mixture of melting tar, warm grease, musky aftershave and cigarettes. The mechanics would make her sweet tea and give her biscuits and tell her stories. Dad usually talked about scientific stuff to do with hydraulics and physics, which she never understood. This time, for some reason, he talked about an old man who'd got this incredible idea in the middle of having his bath. In his rush to tell everyone about it, he'd run out into the street completely naked. His idea was to do with why some things floated while others didn't. It was years later she realised the man he'd been talking about had been Archimedes. Most of the talk had gone over her head but one thing stuck: an object will float if it weighs less than the water it displaces. They would stop sinking, if they could make the boat lighter. A glint of white caught Louisa's eye. At the back of the upside down boat the propeller of the upturned engine poked out the water.

'The engine,' said Louisa, 'if we can dump it, we'll stay afloat longer.'

'It cost me a fortune,' groaned Nicole.

'You're thinking of money at a time like this?' Christine sat with her knees gripped into her chest. 'Just do it!'

Nicole threw her a look but got on to her knees and crawled to the back of the hull. 'It's attached by a clip. I think I can release it. Give me a minute.'

Louisa and Christine watched in silence as Nicole fiddled around under the water by the engine. After a couple of minutes there was a thunk sound and the upside down propeller silently slid downwards and disappeared into the black water.

'It's made no difference,' said Christine, her voice cracking. 'None whatsoever!'

'There's only one thing left to do,' said Louisa. 'We'll have to get into the water ourselves.'

'Leave the boat?' gasped Christine.

'You're mad!' said Nicole.

Louisa ignored them. 'We tie ourselves to the hulls with those bits of rigging so we don't drift.' She nodded to the tangled rigging rope wrapped around the hulls. 'With us in the water, the boat will stay afloat longer.'

'But—' Christine was almost inaudible '—there are

tiger sharks in the lagoon.'

'There has to be another way!' said Nicole.

'Like what?' said Louisa, not knowing how she could sound so calm.

'Anything,' said Nicole.

'We are the heaviest things on the hulls.'

'I can't go in that water.' Christine's voice trembled. 'Not in the dark. We wouldn't be able to see the sharks coming. No, I can't. I can't.'

'If we'd only swam for it when I said so!' said Nicole, her voice tight and twisted, 'we wouldn't be in this bloody mess!'

'You stupid, stupid cow!' screeched Christine. 'Can't you shut your big fat mouth for once! If you'd not insisted on sailing, we wouldn't have capsized. This is your fault. Everything is always your fault!'

'Stop!' shouted Louisa. If they didn't stick together that could be the end for all of them. 'We need to stay calm!'

'My fault?' Nicole laughed. 'If you two drongos had done what I said and swum for it, we would have been in Betio by now!'

'Of course it's your fault. Everything is always your fault,' screeched Christine, 'Everything! Tion would still be alive if it wasn't for you!'

'You were the one who pushed him!'

'Tion?' Louisa began to tremble. 'What about Tion?'

Nicole looked away.

'Nothing,' said Christine. Her voice was so quiet it was a whisper.

'When were you were with Tion?' demanded Louisa

'It was an accident,' said Nicole finally.

Christine sobbed, 'I have regretted getting on that boat every single second of every single minute since it happened.'

Suddenly Louisa understood. 'You were with Tion on the boat the night he died? Both of you?' Louisa was overwhelmed by rage. The bitches! Sink, swim, live or die, she was going to get to the truth. 'No more lies! You tell me what happened now!'

'It started out as a bit of fun, that's all,' said Nicole, pinch-faced. 'We'd gone for a dip at the causeway. It was late. Tion and Nata were there with the boat. They had some stubbies with them. They asked us if we wanted one, we joined them.'

'You knew they'd be there,' said Christine, sobbing openly. 'You got me drunk and tricked me. I wouldn't have gone if I'd known they were going to be there. You tricked me.'

'What happened?' said Louisa.

'Tion got drunk. He came on to me,' said Christine quietly. 'I pushed him away, he stumbled and fell into the water. It was over in a second.'

'Nicole, is this what happened?'

'Of course it is.' In the moonlight Nicole's curly hair corkscrewed from her head like ghostly springs. Her mouth was a gash of grey. 'When he fell, it was no big deal. Tion was a good swimmer and we were only in the channel. We expected him to climb straight back on board.'

'I hoped the accidental dip would cool his ardour,' mumbled Christine, avoiding Louisa's glare.

'When he didn't reappear after a couple of minutes, we started shouting for him. Nothing. In the dark it was hard to see. We waited and shouted some more. After a while we decided he must have swam for the shore and buggered off home. Too embarrassed to face us. We were going to leave when his body appeared by the boat. Face down in the water. We hauled him back on board. It was too late. He was dead. He'd drowned.'

'It was a terrible, tragic accident,' said Christine, slowly recovering her composure, 'but we did nothing wrong. Nothing.'

'No,' said Louisa, so angry she could hardly get the words out. 'You did everything wrong. A man died because of your action!'

'It was a small push in self-defence!' yelled Christine. 'I

didn't think he'd drown!'

'You failed to report what happened and obstructed a murder investigation by withholding evidence—'

'We wanted to go to the police, but Nata wouldn't let us!' cried Christine. 'He went to pieces. He said it was bad to have women on board the boat and the spirits had killed Tion because we'd been there. We tried to explain it was an accident but he wouldn't listen, would he, Nicole?'

Nicole nodded wearily. 'He said if Tion's relatives found out we'd been on the boat with Tion, they'd accuse us of enraging the spirits and causing Tion's death. They'd seek revenge against us. We'd have to leave the country.'

'We wanted to go to the police but he made us promise to tell no one.'

'It was a horrible accident,' said Nicole flatly, 'but that's all it was, an accident.'

70

The water lapped close the top of the hull. How long had they been in the cold, wet, murky black water? An hour? Four hours? Ten minutes? Time made no sense. The rope looped around the hull and around Louisa's chest in a twisted figure of eight. The rough cord rubbed into her, shredding the skin under her arms. Had she dozed off for a few minutes? It hardly seemed credible in the circumstances. From the chest down she felt like a slab of cold jelly. Beneath her, every ripple, every soft swish of a wave, charged her with fear. She had to keep her imagination reined in—they all had to keep their imaginations reined in. Yes, there were tiger sharks in the lagoon but tiger sharks liked deep water. They wouldn't bother them by the reef, would they?

Louisa leaned slightly backwards and to the side, she could see the backs of Christine and Nicole's heads and shoulders. They were strapped side by side to the inside of the sister hull behind her. Their heads dipped towards each other. They looked as if they were sleeping. Behind them on the purple horizon the distant street lights of Betio taunted her. As long as someone started a search for them at first light, and as long as they stayed calm—any sudden movement sent the hulls shuddering—they should be okay. And she would stay calm because she was determined to lob Nicole and Christine in the cells as soon as they got to dry land and keep them there for as long as she could get away with. She turned away from them. All that time wasted thinking Nata was a killer when they'd known all along he was not. What else had they lied about?

In an attempt to relieve the rope cutting into her further, Louisa shifted slightly in the water. She glanced behind her. Nicole wasn't there.

'Christine, where's Nicole?'

'Oh, no!' Christine looked at Louisa. 'She must have slipped!'

Louisa struggled free from her rope and was across the metre of water that separated them in one stroke. She took a deep breath and dived under the water. Blackness. Hissing. Louisa pushed downwards into the murky blackness. She prodded and reached with her fingers. Desperate to feel something. Again and again. Something soft. It yielded to her touch. She grabbed. Pulled upwards. It was so heavy. She heaved. She couldn't breath. It was too much. Something beside her. Helping. Lifting. Helping. It was Christine. They were above the water with Nicole between them. Louisa gasped for breath. Christine said, 'I can't hold her much longer'.

Somehow, they managed to drag Nicole on to the shuddering hull. Louisa had scrambled up beside her and administered CPR followed by rescue breaths. She'd learned

CPR originally from her dad. He'd read that drowning was the leading cause of childhood deaths in the US and the third biggest cause of unintentional death in the world, excluding those drownings which occurred due to natural disasters. Being surrounded by water on Tarawa had made him anxious for his children's safety. By the time she was five she was a confident swimmer and knew how to carry out CPR and rescue breathing on her teddy. This was the first time she'd ever put the lessons into practice. Incredibly, they'd worked. Nicole's lungs started to move up and her listless body spluttered into life.

Christine lay flat out on the hull opposite Louisa, who stayed by Nicole, keeping an eye on her as she dozed. There was little point in going back in the water and tying themselves to the hulls again. Not with Nicole as she was. Louisa had saved her and she was glad. The weight of a dead person was way too much for anyone to carry on their conscience, even it was only for an hour, which was how much time Louisa reckoned they had left before the boat sank. In the ghostly silence she fought back tears and closed her eyes. Had Nicole been right? Should they have made a swim for it right at the beginning? Louisa didn't want to die here or anywhere. She didn't want her life to be over. It wasn't fair. Dying was for old people.

'Louisa.' It was Christine.

Her voice was so soft Louisa almost missed it. Louisa opened her eyes. Christine pointed to the sky. Pinks and yellows nibbled the edges of the bible black sky.

'It's dawn!' she said. 'It's dawn. We're going to be saved now, aren't we?'

'Yes!' said Louisa. They had to be.

71

The warm tingle of the morning sun on Louisa's body felt good. Someone would see them soon. She had to believe that.

'Why don't they come?' said Christine, her voice cracking with anxiety.

'They'll come,' said Louisa, 'We mustn't give in to doubt. They'll come.'

'The waiting is driving me crazy,' said Christine, 'it's making me think Betio is closer.'

Louisa glanced up. Betio did look closer. 'It must be an optical illusion.'

'No,' muttered Nicole from where she lay curled up on her side next to Louisa. 'The boat's moving.'

Louisa glanced around her. Cheeky little waves nudged the boat forwards. Were they really no longer stuck?

'It's the tide,' said Nicole, not moving. 'It's coming in. The increase in water in the lagoon must have lifted the mast off the reef and freed the boat. We're being carried into the lagoon.'

'That's good, isn't it?' said Christine.

'It's the best thing that could happen,' said Nicole.

Christine half laughed. 'Are you sure?'

Nicole heaved herself into a sitting position on the hull. The movement caused the hull to wobble but it settled quickly. 'If only we had a sail. Even half a sail. There's a perfect onshore wind. We'd be back in no time.'

'Shut up!' screamed Christine suddenly. 'Shut up! Shut up about your bloody sailing!'

Nicole looked shocked. Christine turned away.

'Are you serious?' said Louisa, ignoring Christine's outburst. 'Part of a sail could help?'

Nicole nodded.

'Wait.' Louisa slowly slipped her head under the water.

After a couple of seconds she'd seen enough to confirm the top half of the mast had been sheered off just as Nicole had predicted. She lifted her head out of the water. 'There's some cloth tangled around the stump of the broken mast. I can try and free it?'

'Do it,' said Nicole. Her voice sounded weak.

Louisa didn't know if she'd have the strength to dive under the water and drag a sail back up with her. But this could be their last chance.

'I'm not going in the water again,' said Christine sheepishly, 'but I'll do anything else.'

Louisa slowly lowered herself into the lagoon. After the delicious warmth of the sun the water made her shiver. She took a deep breath and ducked under. The first dive was a disaster. She was back to the surface in seconds. She gasped, 'I can't do it!'

'Take your time,' said Nicole, 'Don't pressurise yourself. You'll do it.'

'If you can get the cloth near the surface,' said Christine, 'I'll help you bring it on board.'

On the third try Louisa managed to pull the torn sail off the end of the broken mast. It took two further dives to heave it up to the surface where Christine took hold of it.

'Is it big enough?' panted Louisa, too exhausted to climb back on the hull immediately.

'I hope so,' said Nicole, panting for breath. 'You and Christine need to stand opposite each other and hold the material between you. The wind will catch the cloth and push us forwards.'

With effort Louisa hauled herself back on to the hull. It juddered dangerously. She got on to her knees. It felt as if she were trying to balance on a giant jelly. She waited for the hull to settle then slowly stood up. The thought of making it back pushed her to keep going. Licking her lips, she gripped her bit of the cloth in her hands and held it up. She could do this!

'Come on, Christine, you now,' said Nicole.

On the other hull Christine slowly pushed herself into a standing position. The hull wobbled. Christine froze. When it settled, she slowly lifted up her corner of the sail.

'Now pull it as tight as you can,' said Nicole.

Louisa tugged and Christine pulled. The heavy material remained limp, like a flabby tummy.

'It's not working!' cried Christine.

'Keep trying,' said Nicole.

'Okay. Okay.' Louisa struggled to swallow. Her fingers trembled. The rough sailcloth was difficult to keep hold of. She gripped the material tightly and heaved it towards her one last time. She felt Christine resist. The boat shuddered. Whoosh! A gust of wind washed over Louisa's face, the sailcloth flip-flapped then bulged and they glided forward.

'You beaut!' yelled Nicole. 'We're sailing!'

The material tugged to be free. Louisa refused to let it go. The boat continued to move towards Tarawa. Louisa could hardly believe it. She glanced over at Christine. Her body was rigid with tension. Tears ran down her cheeks. Louisa didn't know if Christine was laughing or crying.

72

At the hospital Nicole was rushed to A and E. She'd become delirious and in the daylight it was clear she had a nasty wound at the side of her head, sustained presumably when she'd slipped under the water. Although exhausted and a little dehydrated, Louisa and Christine were remarkably well under the circumstances. Dr Andrus had said they could go home. Ian had already taken Christine away. He'd offered Louisa a lift, but she'd declined. She wasn't leaving before checking on Nata. As far as she was concerned Christine and Nicole were liars. Their version of what happened on Wednesday night couldn't be believed. Exhausted or not, Louisa wanted to know the truth about what happened.

Nata was on a drip and unconscious behind a curtain in the last bed in the men's ward. The duty nurse couldn't tell Louisa if he'd regained consciousness at any time. There was no one else around for Louisa to ask. She listened to Nata's steady, sedative-induced breathing. His ashen face was almost the same wretched colour as his washed out bedsheet. A small, black Adidas holdall sat open on the locker by Nata's bed. The faux leather bag was scuffed and worn. Inside Louisa saw a faded but clean lava-lava and a bar of Lux soap. Someone had written one dollar on its glossy white wrapper in black felt pen. Had someone dropped the bag off for him? He'd certainly not had it with him on Maiana. It wasn't a lot: no deodorant, no aftershave, no underwear, no razor, no fresh T-shirt. She looked around the bed: no fruit, no get well cards, no flowers. The man was poor. His family were poor. She'd been an idiot! Joe could have stood to gain nothing by blackmailing Nata, because Nata had nothing to be blackmailed for. Only two other people had been on that boat: Nicole and Christine. Had Joe been blackmailing one of them? But even if that were true, they both had alibis for the time of Joe's death. Louisa's head began to throb. Her body seemed very heavy all of a sudden. She sat on a chair by Nata's bed. She'd wait till he woke up, even if it took all day.

When Dr Andrus found Louisa sitting by Nata's bed he'd given her a beaker of blackcurrant flavour dehydration fluid and insisted on taking her home. She'd eventually agreed: trying to question anyone in her exhausted state was probably madness. Louisa waited in the outer office of the mortuary for Andrus to finish what he was doing. The dehydration liquid tasted of plastic and salt. Louisa didn't like being in the sterile windowless office. Apart from a set of car keys on the desk and the chair she was sitting on, the room was bare. She shivered. The euphoria of being rescued was wearing off. Her head ached. Her limbs stung and her skin was crusty with sea salt and sunburn, this after only being in the early morning sun for a couple of hours—but, as her mother had never tired of telling her, the early morning sun was the strongest. At some point she'd have to tell her mum what had happened—if Reteta didn't write and tell her first. A pain in the chest. Stabbing. She couldn't breathe. Tightening. Dizzy. She had to get out of the little room.

Louisa stood for a moment outside the mortuary door, breathing slowly and deeply while letting the sun's rays soak her skin and warm her chilled insides. She smiled as she remembered the rescue. They'd managed to sail almost all the way back, only abandoning the catamaran when the broken mast got stuck in the shallows. Louisa and Christine had then half carried, half dragged Nicole between them, water up to their waists, towards the shore. She'd almost been disappointed at the sight of the rescue canoe—they'd come so far by themselves, she'd wanted to finish it by themselves. But, of course, she'd let the burly fishermen lift her, along with Nicole and Christine, on to the rescue boat.

A small crowd had cheered when the boat had brought them in. Louisa recognised Ian, Christine's husband, and Nicole's child minder and her family, and Nicole's two daughters. Assistant Police Commissioner Nakibae was there and Dr Andrus. She'd half hoped to see Reteta, or even TC, but they weren't in the crowd. Louisa had immediately wanted to talk to Nakibae but Dr Andrus refused to allow it. He'd said tomorrow was the soonest anyone could be interviewed and the three women were whisked away to the hospital.

'Everyone said you were dead.'

Louisa started.

It was Constable Michael. He looked genuinely pleased

to see Louisa by the mortuary door.

'Thanks, Michael!' said Louisa, laughing despite herself. 'As you can see I am not dead, although I feel like death. Have you come to talk to me?'

Michael shook his head. 'I am to be the guard outside Nata's room. He tried to run away from the hospital earlier but was caught.'

Louisa perked up. 'Did he say anything, anything at all?'

'He was very agitated. He talked about bad spirits chasing him. The doctor says his mind is disturbed. He is now sedated. When he is better Assistant Commissioner Nakibae is going to charge him with the three deaths. Dr Andrus has confirmed the blow to Tion's head happened before he died.'

Louisa dozed off almost immediately she got into Andrus's car and woke with a start to find him standing by the open passenger door. They were outside her house. She'd had the strangest dream. She'd been back on the boat and instead of helping Louisa rescue Nicole, Christine had been trying to stop her. Louisa gave herself a shake.

Andrus offered his hand to help her out of the car. 'As your doctor, which I am now, I suggest you rest. You have suffered a big ordeal and it will have taken a toll on your body.'

'Thank you,' she said, taking his hand and getting out of the big double-cabin vehicle. 'I am going to lie down straight away.' She paused. 'But I will need talk to Christine and Nicole as soon as possible.'

He looked surprised. 'Did spending the night together not provide enough time for discussions?'

She smiled. 'I mean in my professional capacity. It's urgent. Do you think they will be fit enough to talk to me later today?'

Andrus bowed slightly in her direction. 'Nicole, no, she

cannot be questioned for at least forty-eight hours. She suffered a severe blunt force trauma to the side of her head, which coupled with the ordeal of being in the water all night, has made her very ill. Everyone is not like you. You are a remarkably robust person.'

Robust? She'd never been called that before. If it was a compliment it didn't feel like it. Like her mother calling someone sturdy. 'And Christine?'

'It has surprised me how well she has coped with her ordeal. I was sure she would need to stay overnight in hospital and require much attention. But, no, she insisted on going home. This contradicts her behaviour of last Thursday when she was excessively agitated by a mere twisted ankle. I fear I have misjudged her.'

'I imagine waiting in outpatients for a couple of hours could make anyone agitated.'

Andrus raised his eyebrows in surprise. 'I invited her to stay in my little office. A man had sliced though his foot with a chainsaw. Half his village had come with him to the hospital. It was bedlam. There was blood everywhere. Most unfortunate. I did not want to distress Christine any more than was necessary.'

'She did say her ankle was very sore.'

Dr Andrus cleared his throat. 'It was little more than a mild sprain. That is what I mean. It is contradictory to be agitated about a mild sprain and yet be relatively calm after spending twenty-fours adrift at sea. Her husband seems to me to be very controlling, don't you think?'

'Sorry?' What did Ian have to do with anything?

Andrus gave a little cough. 'I have worked with someone like Ian Brown before. I imagine Ian's needs are paramount. I thought the sprained ankle by Christine was possibly a way of getting a little attention or sympathy, something she does not get at home. Hence the exaggerated pain she'd suffered. But I have changed my mind about her. She is robust. Just like you.

Please, now, you must rest for at least forty-eight hours and drink plenty of water.'

73

It was dark outside and Louisa's mouth was sticky and her head thumped. She licked her lips. They tasted of blackcurrant and sick. She checked the clock. It was seven. She must have slept for six hours at least. She wanted to phone Nakibae but couldn't think what it was she wanted to tell him. It was as if her brain was soaked in sludge. She got up. A searing pain fired up and down her legs and arms. It made walking difficult. She ignored it and looked outside to see if Reteta was around. Nope. The fire wasn't even lit. Louisa sighed. Much as she'd disliked the family hanging around, she missed them too. And if she was honest, she'd been disappointed no one from the family had been waiting for her at the edge of the lagoon when the rescue boat had brought them in. But it was her own fault, she knew that. She was just a tad too 'robust' with people. It was something she seemed unable to do anything about. She flicked the light switch in the living room. Nothing. Another power cut.

Louisa spread a smear of marmalade on a slice of white bread—could someone live off bread and marmalade and the occasional frozen burger? She'd have to ask Andrus. At least marmalade was made of oranges, one of her five a day—well, she liked to think so. She sat down in the lounge. She should have felt better: she was safely on dry land, and according to Dr Andrus she was well, but she didn't feel well and for some reason she didn't feel safe. Ideally she'd have liked a shower but no power meant no water pump. Unless she went outside, in the dark, and collected a bucket of water directly from the tank, she couldn't have a wash. Right now she didn't have the energy to do that.

She tried to focus her thoughts. Nata couldn't have killed Joe. Nor could Christine or Nicole. Then, like a smack in the face, the voices came back. A wave of screeching words. Volume on high, telling her over and over again: wash now or you'll die; wash now or your mother will die; if you don't wash away the germs on your body everyone will die. It was absurd! She was an intelligent person, she knew no one would die if she didn't wash immediately. She tried to ignore the voices. They grew louder. And louder. How could she still have this stupid, stupid problem at a time like this? What was wrong with her? She blinked back some tears, unlocked the back door and went to draw herself a bucket of water from the tank.

Louisa waited by the cold fire while the bucket slowly filled. The moment she'd turned the tank tap on the voices had subsided. She hated the voices. They made her feel so inadequate and weak. What was wrong with her? She took a deep breath and wiped her damp eyes. In the last thirty-six hours she'd had about six hours sleep. Her body was shot. Exhaustion was the reason the voices had returned. As soon as she was rested she'd be able to control them. She got up and checked the bucket under the tank tap. It wasn't even half full. She went to sit back down by the cold fire.

The crickets were out in force, whining and screeching so loudly they almost smothered the noise of the sea crashing against the shore. A faint moon created just enough light to see by. Daisy the dog snoozed next to the pig. At least Louisa wasn't entirely alone. She tried to focus on the case once more. She'd been so close to identifying the killer, it was maddening. What had she missed? Where had she gone wrong? Louisa went over what she knew. Tion had stolen Reteta's dagger. That dagger linked Tion's death with Joe and Jill's deaths. There were three people with Tion when he died that she knew of: Nata, Nicole and Christine. Joe told Tererei he saw a fight on the boat and that he was going to use that information to his advantage. In other words Joe blackmailed someone to keep him quiet about what he saw. Nata was at Tion's funeral on Thursday evening when Joe died. He could not have killed Joe. There were only two other people with Tion when he died: Christine and Nicole. Nicole couldn't have killed him, Louisa had twenty witnesses who saw her at the hash on Thursday evening. That left Christine. Louisa had an uneasy feeling. Time to check on her water.

The bucket was almost full. She turned off the tap and carried the water towards the house. It was heavy. The wire handle cut into her hand. After a couple of seconds she felt so tired she had to put the bucket down. The ordeal on the boat really had taken it out of her. No doubt Andrus would have told her off for not continuing to rest. She thought about his little sterile office at the mortuary. It was a sombre, unwelcoming place. Her tiny room at the station was small and decrepit but at least it had a window. She lifted the bucket again. For no apparent reason she thought about the bunch of keys on Andrus's desk. They were car keys. Louisa put the bucket back down. What if the keys had also been on his desk Thursday evening when Christine had been there, waiting for him to finish his surgery? Andrus had said it had been a chaotic night. Sewing the tendons in the foot of a man who'd had a chainsaw accident would have taken hours. Christine could have snatched the keys, taken Andrus's car, driven to the Ambo, killed Joe and returned without anyone noticing anything. No. It was way too risky. Besides, Nicole was the risk taker, not Christine. Louisa shook her head. Exhaustion was making her desperate. But what if Christine thought it a risk worth taking? Louisa suddenly wasn't tired. She really needed to talk to Christine. And now. The bucket wash would have to wait.

A noise. It came from the side of the house. Daisy growled. Low and long. Louisa held her breath. Scrape. Scrape.

There it was again.

'Who's there?' yelled Louisa, straining to see in the dark.

'It's me!' said Christine appearing round the side of the house.

Louisa tensed. 'What are you doing here?'

'I remembered something I wanted to tell you. About Nicole.'

'Really?'

'It may be nothing. Are you busy?'

Louisa shook her head. 'As it happens I was just coming to see you.'

74

Louisa couldn't move. She was on her side. A searing thudding came from the back of her head. She opened her eyes. The thudding intensified. It made her feel sick. It was dark. Was she out the back? There had been a power cut. She remembered that. Was there still a power cut? She tried to move her arm. It was heavy. Very heavy. She lifted it with effort and touched the back of her head where the pain came from. Her hair was matted. Wet. Was she bleeding?

'You're awake,' said a voice.

Louisa peered into the blackness to see where the voice had come from. It was Christine. Her body was shrouded in silver, shadowy blackness. She sat opposite Louisa. They were out the back by the cold fire. Louisa could see that now. She tried to speak but she couldn't make her mouth work.

'You shouldn't have turned away when you sat down,' said Christine. 'I hit you. With a stone. It was in my bag. I always have one in my bag to throw at the dogs. I hate dogs.' She picked up a rock the size of a fist. In the dark it looked black. 'This is it. A bit bigger than necessary but it makes me feel safe. And it did the trick on you. You weren't expecting it. Easy really.'

Louisa made herself slowly breathe in and out through her nose. She had to focus. How long had she been unconscious? She tried to move her head. Agh! She winced. Nauseating. Blinding. Pain. 'It was you,' she said, her voice barely audible. 'You killed Joe.'

Christine nodded. 'I knew you'd work it out.'

Louisa tried to speak again. Her body felt leaden and her lips were sticky with dried saliva. 'Why?'

'It's so ridiculous, you wouldn't believe it. Tion had developed a crush on me. It was crazy. I didn't even know him. He even came to the Ambo once while I was at the nursery and gave me a dagger wrapped in newspaper, like fish and chips. It had been very embarrassing. I tried to make him take it back. He wouldn't. When he left I didn't know what to do with it. I couldn't take it home. How would I explain it? I couldn't throw it away either. It was dangerous. I heard Jill arriving. I didn't want her to see it so I'd wedged it down the back of the bookshelf and then forgot all about it.'

'The ...' Louisa tried to speak. The words wouldn't come out of her mouth. Nothing.

'When I saw Tion on the boat that Wednesday night at the causeway channel I didn't want to get in. But Nicole said it'd be fun. That I should live a little. She said she could vouch for Tion—and Nata, of course.' Christine paused. 'It's very quiet here, isn't it? Don't you mind being all alone?'

'The police are coming...' said Louisa finally.

'I don't believe you. At first it was fun on the boat. We had a few drinks. Then a few more. At some point Nata and Nicole started snogging. I was furious. I was drunk but not that drunk. Tion must have thought if Nicole was up for it, I would be. He got that wrong. He tried to kiss me. I pushed him away. He resisted. I pushed him some more. He became angry. I yelled at him to leave me alone. I thought my shouting would attract Nicole and Nata but they were so far down each other's throats they were oblivious to everything. Tion thrust me on to the floor of the boat. He pushed his disgusting drunken mouth on to mine. There was a weight from a dive belt on the ground beside my hand. I picked it up and hit him on the head. He slumped to the side. I hit him again. Dazed, he staggered to his feet. I got up after him and pushed him. He fell overboard. Nicole saw me push him but Nata didn't. I hoped Tion would get swept out to sea and I'd never have to see him again.' Christine stood up and started to poke around Reteta's things under the veranda.

Louisa shifted slightly. Warm liquid trickled down her neck. Drip. Drip. Drip. Seeped into her blouse. 'I'm bleeding.'

Christine appeared not to hear her. 'I had no idea Joe had been watching us until the hash run on Thursday. He took me to one side and said I had until the next morning to persuade Ian to grant him a licence to export shark fins or he would tell everyone that he saw me push Tion overboard. I said no one would believe him and I was most certainly not going to ask Ian to grant him any licence and left.'

The pain in her head almost blinded Louisa now. 'I have to go to the hospital.'

Christine ignored her. 'I was so, so angry. I'd wiped that awful incident on the boat from my mind and now Joe was threatening to tell everyone who would listen about it. I needed time to think. I deliberately tripped myself up to get out of doing the run. My ankle didn't actually hurt much but when Paul offered to take me to the hospital and I said yes, anything to get away from the hash and not have to see Joe again. In the car I tried to tell myself I didn't care if Joe told everyone. I'd say I pushed Tion in self-defence. But I was worried no one would believe me. I could be tried for manslaughter, or worse. My children could be taken away from me. Ian could lose his job. No! No! No! I wasn't giving up my family and my lovely home in Britain, everything I'd worked for, abandoned my career for, because of a silly bit of fun that had gone wrong.

'At some point I happened to look out the car window and glimpsed Joe jogging between a row of coconut palms. Paul didn't see him. Joe looked as if he was heading for the Ambo. I knew I was going to have to talk to Joe again. The hospital was in chaos when we got there. A local man had had an accident with a chainsaw. There was blood everywhere. People wailed and shouted. Trying to get between everyone, my clothes got blood on them. Andrus found me and invited me to wait in his office until he could see me, which he said would be a few hours. The more I waited, the more anxious I became. I knew Ian would never grant Joe the export licence. Ian hated Joe and he was too honest a person to commit fraud. Joe needed to see there was nothing to be gained by telling everyone what had happened. Andrus's car keys were on his desk. Without thinking I picked them up, went to his car and drove to the Ambo.'

75

'Please... ' groaned Louisa. 'I need help.'

Christine continued to ignore her. 'The Club looked deserted when I got there. It seemed I'd been wrong about Joe heading there. I felt so stupid. I'd stolen a car, actually stolen a car! Then I noticed the school hut door was slightly open. Joe was inside. He wore a dirty lava-lava and nothing else. I felt sick at the sight of him. He didn't even look surprised to see me. I said I needed to talk to him. He laughed and said he knew I'd change my mind. I said I had not changed my mind, that I'd come to tell him Ian had too much integrity to compromise his principles and grant him his export licence, so Joe was wasting his time threatening me. Now Joe roared with laughter. He said I should talk to Nicole about Ian's integrity. I demanded to know what he meant. He said I must be the only person on Tarawa that didn't know Ian had been fucking Nicole—fucking is such a crude word, don't you think? I knew it was a lie. Nicole was my best friend on Tarawa and while I knew she slept with other men, she would never do something like that to me, not with Ian. And Ian would never do that to me either. I'd given up everything for Ian. I was going to tell Joe this when we heard voices. Joe pulled me into the hut and closed the door.

'The voices came from the path. It was dark inside the hut but we could still just about see each other. I didn't want to be in there with Joe but I didn't want anyone to see us together. The voices grew louder. Villagers. Men. They sounded as if they'd been drinking. Something thudded against the side of the hut. They were throwing things. I put my hand in my bag and took out my dog stone. The men started singing. We waited. Joe was so close so me I could feel his weasel breath on my neck. I wished he was dead. The men gradually left but we waited in the dark in case they came back. I told Joe I thought he was despicable to smear Ian and Nicole's names—'

'Christine, please call someone,' groaned Louisa. 'I'm bleeding.'

'He said their affair had been the talk of the Royal Saloon because Ian dumped Nicole for a younger girl and she'd made a scene.' Christine cleared her throat. 'I repeated that I didn't believe him, that Nicole was my best friend and Ian would never, ever betray me. I called Joe a cheat and a thief and a liar. I may have said some other things. Joe became angry. He said I was a greedy cow, so focused on maintaining the fancy lifestyle I'd bought into, I couldn't see it for the sham it was. I still had the dog stone in my hand. In the darkness I aimed for the side of Joe's head and struck him with it as hard as I could. Crunch! He dropped to his knees. I suddenly remembered the dagger Tion had given me was behind the shelf. Before Joe had got back to his feet, I found the dagger, and stabbed him in the head. He made a gurgling noise and fell back. Then he was silent...'

Louisa needed to do something about her wound. She reached out and dragged a pillow from Reteta's things on the veranda and shoved it against the side of her head. She hoped it would help stem the bleeding.

'He was dead. At first I did nothing. Just stood. In shock probably...' she paused and looked around.

Louisa pressed her head into the towel. She should have known Christine was involved. From the very start when Christine took Jill home before Louisa could interview her, she'd been interfering.

'Maybe I was waiting for him to say something. But he didn't say anything. I had killed him. It was wrong but I felt no guilt, only immense relief. He was a horrible, horrible man and the world was a better place without him. Then the enormity of what I had done hit me. I had to get out of there. No one saw me arrive, if I was lucky no one would see me leave. I was about to go when I remembered Tion had been Nata's best friend. Tion could have told Nata he'd given me the dagger. Nata would know I had killed Joe. I needed to take the dagger with me. I went to Joe's body. It was difficult to look at him. I took the handle of the dagger and pulled. It wouldn't budge. I tried again. It was stuck fast. I began to panic. Then I remembered a story Ian had told me about a local man who had killed his neighbour and then gouged out his eyes and eaten them. Ian said it was an ancient ritual the old warriors used to do. No one wanted to arrest the man because they feared he possessed the spirit of the dead man. I thought if I removed Joe's eyes it would look like a local crime. It would also frighten Nata. He was very superstitious and already running scared after Tion's death. I knew there was a palette knife on the painting shelf. I knelt down beside Joe's head. The floor was wet with his warm blood. I couldn't look at him but I had to. In the dim light the whites of his eyes looked even whiter.' She grimaced. 'I placed the palette knife at the corner of the first eye. My hand was trembling so much I had to hold it still with my other hand. I couldn't look. So I closed my eyes and dug into the eye socket. It was like scooping out a boiled egg. When I opened my eyes, his eyeball was hanging out of the socket. There was blood everywhere. I wanted to throw up. But I had to finish it. Someone could come any minute. I hacked the eyeball free. I can't remember what happened next. I must have gouged the second eye and left because the next thing I remember I was washing my hands and face in the lagoon. I already had blood on my clothes from the chainsaw mess, I didn't think anyone would notice a little more. I drove back to the hospital. It was as chaotic as when I'd left earlier. I parked the car and slipped back into Andrus's office. No one knew I'd been gone. I'd got away with it. It was as if divined.'

'Christine,' groaned Louisa, 'You're not well. Take me to the hospital and I'll do what I can to see you get support.'

'No, I don't think so.' Christine frowned. 'It goes without saying that I didn't want to let my children go to the nursery school the next morning but I knew I had to act normal. I expected Nicole to find Joe. I wanted her to. I didn't believe Joe's story about her and Ian but I was angry with her. If she'd not set up the meeting with Tion and Nata, none of the awful things would have happened.' Christine paused and began to walk up and down the veranda.

Louisa knew Christine was going to kill her. A rising sense of panic gripped her. She had to do something. In the darkness she saw two wide eyes peering at her through the bushes. It was Reteta. Louisa raised her eyebrows in a desperate silent plea for help. Reteta nodded and disappeared.

76

'Jill's death was her own fault,' said Christine, standing next to Louisa. 'I got back from the Otintaai party around eleven on Saturday night. Jill must have heard the car arrive. She wanted to talk to me urgently. We went to her house. She said she'd found a dagger in the school hut the week before when she'd been tidying up. She'd put it back where it was because she was worried we'd think she'd been snooping. But the more she'd thought about it, the more she thought it was very like the dagger that had been used to kill Joe. She believed it belonged to Nicole—it never occurred to her that it could belong to boring old me. She didn't know what to do. I said she'd done the right thing by telling me. Then, and I don't know why, but I asked her if she knew anything about Nicole sleeping with Ian. She'd blushed. I said I already knew about it and it was okay to tell me. She said, yes, Nicole had told her about the affair one morning at the nursery. I was stunned. It was true.

'Jill turned to get something. I had a new dog stone in my bag. When Jill turned back to face me I bashed her face with it. She fell to the ground. There was a big lump of coral on the floor. I picked it up and hit her with that too. Again and again. It was as if I was hitting Nicole and Ian. I couldn't stop. When it was over I left the house by the back door. Nicole's dog bounded up to me, barking and wagging its tail. He was so happy to see me. I told him to shush but he just kept on yapping and jumping up. I begged him to be quiet. It seemed to make him bark even louder. Someone was going to hear. I'd be seen. I was covered in blood. I picked him up and gripped him in my arms. I pleaded for him to shush. I liked that dog. He was like a naughty, overexcited child. He wouldn't stop barking.

'I walked into the lagoon. I knelt down and held him under the water. I felt his little body struggle in my arms. I held him more tightly. Gradually, he stopped struggling. I'd noticed a long piece of rusty wire on the beach. Still with the dog in my arms, I got the wire and waded back out to where Nicole kept the buoy for her mooring. I wrapped the wire around the poor soul's bedraggled body, attached the wire to the chain that held the buoy and let him go. His little body slowly sank out of sight. I unclipped the buoy and let it bob away. I knew Nicole would find him when she went to check what had happened to the buoy.' Christine paused to wipe her eyes.

Louisa was surprised. Christine was crying over killing a dog. 'I've told them all that Nata isn't a killer,' said Louisa, still unable to shift her body more than a centimetre at a time, it felt so heavy. Where was Reteta? Was she getting help?

'I was going to challenge Ian about the affair. Kick him out. But I didn't. He'd not go easily. It would be messy. He'd want control over my children. I wasn't going to have that. I realised I didn't care if he slept around. Sex with him had been awful for years anyway. His having affairs was a small price to pay to keep my home, my way of life and my family. As for Nicole? I thought I'd got her when we were on the boat but you saved her. I'll wait. It's divine intervention that I've not been found out. The gods really are on my side.'

'You have to give yourself up,' said Louisa, trying to push herself up on to her legs.

'Let me help.' Christine yanked Louisa on to her feet. 'We're going to take a little walk. You're going to drown. It'll look like an accident. I don't want anyone linking your death to the others, they might realise Nata isn't the murderer. You surprised me. I kept feeding you lies and you swallowed them. I think you let your dislike of Nicole cloud your judgment. But I knew it was only a matter of time before you guessed.'

'Stop this madness now,' said Louisa, her legs trembling.

'It's not madness. Move.'

Louisa refused. Christine's gripped her arms and pushed her. Louisa stumbled on to her knees.

'Get on your feet!' hissed Christine.

Louisa didn't know what to do. She was too weak to fight and Christine wanted to kill her. Drowned by a lunatic. What a pathetic way to die. A noise. Reteta was behind Christine. With one swift swipe of the arm Reteta pulled the string that held the mosquito net to the veranda ceiling. Whoosh! The netting unfurled in a wave of white. Reteta pounced on top of Christine. Within seconds Christine was wrapped in the netting and Reteta was on top of her.

77

It was ten days before Dr Jenny let Louisa out of the hospital—Dr Andrus was on annual leave. Back at the house Reteta had prepared a welcome home feast for her. It was dusk by the time Constable Michael dropped her off. Embarrassingly, she discovered the whole of the back garden was packed with people. Some she didn't know and some she did, including, even more embarrassingly, Assistant Police Commissioner Nakibae. On the plus side TC was there and Tererei.

Everyone sat on mats, placed around a central area laden with plates of rice covered in cling film and pink plastic basins covered with tea towels. They clapped when Louisa appeared and sat down in the place of honour, close to the fire and next to Assistant Commissioner Nakibae.

'Tikiraoi,' said Reteta, beaming, 'We eat first then we have the speeches after.'

Louisa smiled but inside she was groaning. Speeches?

Reteta barked an order at two giggling girls beside her and they at once began removing the tea towels from the round plastic washing up bowls.

Two big basins contained a green slimy vegetable that looked like spinach floating in a lumpy coconut gravy, and the remaining basins were full of various kinds of fish, including red snapper, yellowfin tuna and a thin long nosed glittery fish Louisa didn't recognise. Everything looked stone cold. Reteta asked Louisa to start. Cautiously, Louisa picked up a plastic spoon and put a little bit of rice on to her plate, then spooned up some of the green gravy and took one of each type of fish. She'd not think about germs, she'd just enjoy the food. She looked up. Everyone was looking at her.

'What's wrong?' said Louisa.

'You have such a small amount of food?'

'Isn't it enough?'

Reteta shrugged. The men started first. One of the young girls handed Louisa a mug of tea. It was sickly sweet and warm. Louisa sighed. The ocean battered the shore just out of sight and a warm breeze danced around her back—it made the warmth of the fire even more pleasurable. Someone threw some coconut husks onto the flames. They hissed and a sweet yeasty smell filled the air. Louisa watched as the flickering yellow faces of Reteta's family and friends concentrated on their food. TC looked up. She now knew that he and Reteta and the family had been out in boats looking for her, which was why they'd not been waiting for her at the lagoon edge with the others. TC smiled at her. She smiled back. Louisa felt good. It had been a long time coming, but she really felt at home on Tarawa with Reteta. She took some more fish. It tasted really good.

'E kangkang te amarake? You like the food?' said Reteta.

'It's delicious,' said Louisa. Of course, Louisa was now flavour of the month with everyone. At first, despite being caught trying to kill Louisa, Christine denied having anything to do with the murders. But Louisa was able to provide enough evidence to convict her and she'd finally confessed. A deal was done to have her serve her sentence in England and she'd already been taken away. The international Press heard of the case and hailed Kiribati as one of the safest Pacific countries to be. Nakibae was praised in Parliament and tipped to be the new Chief Police Commissioner. He'd sent a glowing review to the European Commission office in Suva, asking that Louisa spearhead the development of a new training programme to help the officers in Kiribati's Police Service improve detection into corrupt activities. Tom had reappeared, after spending a week on the outer island of Beru—not Maiana as had been reported—and then disappeared. It was rumoured he'd been sacked over a drinking binge. The British Aid Office was waiting for a replacement.

Reteta grinned. 'You really like the fish, eng?'

'Yes,' said Louisa, thinking how lucky she was to have met Reteta again. She was like the sister she never had.

'Have more,' insisted Reteta.

'Thanks. It really is tasty,' she said, digging in. 'Much nicer than a frozen burger.'

Reteta began to chuckle, so did a few of the others.

'What's so funny?' said Louisa, feeling slightly uncomfortable.

More giggles, from everyone now.

Louisa smiled awkwardly. 'Is there something I should know?'

'The fish you like so much, we call it "pooh" fish!' said Reteta bursting into laughter with everyone else. 'It makes you go to the toilet if you take too much and you have taken too much!'

'Oh, very funny,' said Louisa, blushing furiously.

'You must tell us if "pooh" fish makes I-Matangs go to the toilet just as often as it makes us I-Kiribati go, okay?'

Louisa feigned a smile and looked down at her plate of food. The flaky brown-white chunks of "pooh" fish no longer appealed. There was no way she was telling anyone about her bowel movements. As if? Louisa put her plate to one side and sighed. She looked back up at Reteta, who was laughing so hard she was crying. Louisa was always going to be an I-Matang to Reteta, and maybe that was just as well.